I0694535

The Somewhere Aching Series

A LOVER TO LIVE FOR

book two

Tanya Madsen

A Lover to Live For
© 2025 Tanya Madsen
All rights reserved.

No part of this publication may be reproduced, stored in a retrieval system, or transmitted in any form or by any means—electronic, mechanical, photocopying, recording, or otherwise—without the prior written permission of the publisher, except in the case of brief quotations used in critical articles or reviews.

This is a work of fiction. Names, characters, places, and incidents are either the product of the author's imagination or used fictitiously. Any resemblance to actual persons, living or dead, events, or locales is entirely coincidental.

Published by
Aching Hearts Press*
Stories that bruise beautifully™

Roy, Utah, United States
www.tanyamadsen.com

ISBN: 978-1-970593-02-0

Cover design by Tanya Madsen
Interior formatting by Tanya Madsen

Printed in the United States of America

To Patsy, who gave me the confidence.

Love looks not with the eyes, but with the mind, and therefore is winged
Cupid painted blind.

William Shakespeare,

A Midsummer Night's Dream

A Note from the Author

This story has themes that may be triggering for some readers. It explores issues such as attempted suicide, drug addiction, and sexual abuse. If you or someone you know is experiencing these issues, please seek help.

Suicide and Crisis Lifeline: **988**

SAMHSA National Hotline: **1-800-662-HELP**

National Sexual Assault Hotline RAINN: **800-565-HOPE**

Table of Contents

The First Year

Chapter 1

Judith

Judith stretched her long legs in front of Justin's garage. The air was pungent with the scent of wet grass. Red tulips adorned the main house in perfect rows. Cottonwood trees lined the pebbled drive out to the highway. Farmland stretched as far as the eye could see. She stared at her breath as it billowed into the dim, frosty air. The early morning twilight felt magical somehow. Transforming. And right now, she desperately needed transformation.

The April morning was chilly, and frost dotted the ground, but she was not dissuaded. Judith was an avid runner who loved competition, enjoyed pushing herself, and exceeding her own expectations. She planned to run a full six miles, three out and three back, as was her usual routine. After her warm-up, she gazed at the burgeoning sunrise, sighed, and then began to move.

A whole new world had swept her away just as she had always dreamed. She proved herself to be a daughter to die for by saving her mom, and now, in return, her hero, Justin, had saved her. She was committed to this dream come true and felt so honored that it was she who had saved her mom. But now, just a few weeks later, she felt terribly sad, which is why she decided to try to boost her serotonin levels with exercise.

Justin would be home from work by the time she returned, and she felt a wave of apprehension. Her hero cop had seemed perfect in every way. Why was he acting this way? Distant from her? He had tried so hard to win her over, begging her to move in with him. Begged! Wouldn't take no for an answer. Then he worked like a dog to furnish the apartment over his garage, catering to her every whim regarding the decor. Now, it felt like that man was nothing more than an illusion.

When they finally made love, it was heaven on earth. Judith discovered that Justin was the yin to her yang. So inexperienced, he was precious. It allowed her to be the aggressor, which she loved. His appetite rivaled hers, and his stamina incited her to arouse him beyond endurance. It was deeply satisfying to seduce her noble hero and turn him into a wild man.

Justin had introduced her to the night sky, birds of paradise and their mating rituals, the peaceful splendor of the countryside, and the aroma of oily car parts. She decided that she had made good on her promise to win the grand prize. Justin was every girl's dream. He was strong, hardworking, and hot as hell in bed. Then everything changed, all at once.

Judith sensed he was trying to keep her at arm's length, but she had no idea why. Moreover, she discovered that Justin had a perfect routine—one that didn't include her. Living in this apartment in the middle of nowhere was starting to feel like a prison.

He hadn't replied to the sext she sent him last night either, and she realized he was sending her a message to leave him alone. He liked her sexting when they first met. What happened? Judith understood he had a life outside of her. She didn't expect him to wait on her hand and foot, but this was too much. Yet, how could she say anything? He was her hero boyfriend. He had rescued her in the canyon after she escaped from Nicolas. He even forgave her for allowing Nicolas to seduce her, although initially he was furious. She had to feel grateful that he wanted to be with her at all.

As Judith thought of Nicolas and their encounter in the car, a thrill coursed down her spine. Since leaving that crazy fuckboy lying unconscious in the snow, she could think of nothing except his declaration that they were soulmates bound forever by the stars. The passion from their encounter consumed her. He brought her to the edge, and instead of allowing him to take her over, she rejected him, tried to kill him and ran away. Now, due to Justin's disappointing change of heart, it felt like the biggest mistake of her life.

What did she feel for Nicolas? Love? More like insatiable lust, but unrequited because he was forever out of her reach. How could Nicolas be her soulmate? He was a maniac! He had abducted and then nearly killed her mom! Then he had kidnapped her, seduced her, and begged her to run away with him! Plus, she had already made her choice. She had her hero.

At the halfway point, Judith stopped to rest. She gazed out at the rolling hills as the sun sparkled on the horizon. The countryside was beautiful, but she found it all rather dull. What was she supposed to do with all this time on her hands?

Justin worked the graveyard shift as a police officer, slept half the day, and then, as soon as he woke up, left for the gym to maintain his impressive physique. Afterward, he hung out with his mom and brothers before attending to some maintenance on his hot rod. In the evenings, they would have dinner together while Judith stared at him, already dressed in his cop uniform, thinking of a million things she wanted to do after dragging him to bed. Yet, he gazed at her so platonically that he seemed overtaken by aliens.

In the first few weeks, he was unbelievably passionate and wanted to go for hours. The sex was unforgettably hot. Now? He was as cold as ice. What was with this hot-and-cold mind game? Judith had no idea what she had done wrong. She obsessed over what he wanted and how to give it to him, crying herself to sleep when he was at work. Her heart was cracking, and she didn't know what to do.

As she jogged up the driveway, Justin rolled past her in his electric blue, restored 1979 Camaro Z28, a car that was nearly as sexy as he was. He waved as he got out and closed the door. God, that iceberg-melting smile.

"I didn't realize you were running in the mornings."

Justin walked up and kissed her lightly on the cheek, which felt like a huge letdown. Where was the passionate French kiss that was sure to prompt an immediate rush to the bedroom? She was so aroused after her run that she wanted to tear his clothes off right here, right now.

"I got out of the habit when I moved in with you, but I wanna get back to my routine."

"I get that. We can run together a few nights a week if you'd like."

"I would love that," she replied eagerly, "but not too late. I can't haul ass like you can after dark."

He frowned and folded his arms in that cop-like stance she found so irresistible.

"I warned you that the graveyard shift would be difficult to deal with."

"No, it's fine." Judith smiled reassuringly. "Wanna help me with my cooldown?" She stroked his chest adoringly and gave him a suggestive look.

"Ah, yeah. Maybe. Give me a minute. Gotta tell my mom something."

Justin headed toward the main house, and Judith checked out his muscled ass from behind. This man drove her crazy with lust. How was she going to survive him pushing her away like this day after day?

Slowly, she pulled her legs up the stairs and went inside to take a shower. The hot water rolled down her back, numbing her skin. She thought of Nicolas going down on her that night in the car and giving her the hottest orgasm ever, and wanted to lie on the tiled floor and masturbate. Judith knew she was a sex addict and had come to terms with this about herself long ago. She needed the constant emotional reassurance and stress release that sex provided. It was impossible to live with a man and not have sex with him every single day. That's what live-in relationships were for! Sex was her love language, and she was highly skilled in the art of pleasure. Loved nothing more than making a man come so hard he forgot his own name.

Then, thank God, Justin opened the bathroom door, naked. Her heart burst with joy.

Judith jumped out of the shower, soaking wet with shampoo still in her hair, and grabbed him by those impressive shoulders to pull him in with her.

"Whoa. What's up? I'm just brushing my teeth."

Justin shrugged her aside, and she stepped back in embarrassment. Water and soap suds flowed across the floor.

"I thought since you were naked." She felt humiliated. "It's been three days, Justin. Are you mad at me?" Tears welled in her eyes.

He shrugged and handed her a towel.

"You're making a mess," he said.

Left the bathroom, leaving the door open, he lay back on the bed, hands behind his head, sprawled out. Glanced over to see if she was watching him, then shut his eyes. Lust coursed through her as her eyes crawled up and down his gorgeous body. Justin was unbelievably hot, and he knew she was crazy about him. He was teasing her. Why?

Justin was playing mind games. Her exes had done this, jerked her around. Pretended to reject her until she was frothing at the mouth and tearing off their clothes like a trashy whore. They loved to rile her up because it gave them a huge ego boost to have a gorgeous beauty queen chase them down. She always grew ashamed of her behavior, which quickly ended the relationship. She was way too genuine and straightforward with her feelings, and hated putting up with that shit.

Judith returned to the shower and rinsed her hair, her body going nuts. She cried for five minutes, trying to come to terms with this. Justin was intentionally fucking with her and she didn't understand why. She was loath to leave the bathroom. Couldn't bring herself to face him, but she had no choice. She opened the door, and he was still lying on his back, flaunting a full-blown erection that mesmerized her like a honeybee to nectar. She wanted so badly to suck the life out of that delicious thing. Should she try? Would he let her? Desperately, she tried to conjure up a sex game that would leave him speechless and drooling. But her mind drew a blank. If he didn't want her, then it didn't matter what she did. Or did he? What was going on here? Everything had gone to shit so fast, and she had no idea how to fix it. Fix her. She couldn't handle this. Inching across the bed, she pleaded.

"Please tell me what I've done wrong. Whatever it is. I need you."

Lying next to him, Judith ran her hand slowly down. He stiffened, but didn't stop her. He writhed as she followed her fingers with her lips down his chest, but didn't stop her. Trembled as she tickled his belly, but didn't stop her. She continued her fervid descent down his happy trail. Almost there. Just a few more inches. And finally. She took him in her fist and began to stroke.

Judith had been delighted to discover on day two that Justin had never had a blow job before. His naivety was hot. Since she considered herself an apex seducer of men and an expert at fellatio, she happily went down on him and blew his mind. He came like a virgin and it was so damn sweet. Shy and self-conscious, he begged for a repeat performance, confessing that it was the best thing he had ever experienced. This was terrific news since she was a sex goddess and had every intention of making him her devoted sex slave.

Judith knew how to thaw a dangerously repressed man out between the sheets, and she had no qualms with getting aggressive. Now that she had the go-ahead, she crawled down between his legs and didn't give him a chance to reject her. Trapped his hands under his butt and held down his thighs, satisfied as he thrust like a jackhammer, groaning as she gorged on his sexy boy parts. She tried to slow his climax, but unfortunately, he was already so close that he came almost at once. Then rolled over and crashed out into a blissful sleep. She sighed with disappointment. There went her highly anticipated after-workout cooldown.

Lying next to him, Judith stared at her sleeping hero. He was so handsome and good. Did it matter if he played hot and cold? Once she warmed him up, he was so responsive to her that it was incredibly satisfying to please him. Why did he only want her in small doses?

Judith got up, got dressed, and went to make breakfast. As she opened her phone, she noticed she had received a message, causing her heart to race. She had accepted a Facebook friend request from an old schoolmate shortly after she was rescued, and now, two weeks later, he was reaching out to her. Ethan Fender? Who the hell was he?

But she had known immediately. She felt it in her gut. It was Nicolas. She accepted the request instinctively and felt her heart race as she watched him scroll back through the years, liking all of her old pictures of winning beauty pageants, kissing ex-boyfriends, and smiling for sexy selfies. He left a trail of googly eyes and fiery heart emojis as he Facebook stalked her. She had done the same thing to Justin! Flattered beyond belief, Judith basked in the adoration.

She shouldn't answer it. She should tell Justin! But he was so cold now, and she felt so lonely out here in the sticks, surrounded by the unfamiliar. Since Justin was pushing her away, she craved attention, and she knew that Nicolas was genuinely crazy about her. As a beauty queen, she had survived on accolades and compliments, flirtations and sexting for years. She needed this to survive!

And it's not like Nicolas could seduce her again if he had escaped to Mexico. Besides, even with Justin's mind games, she had already decided he was the man for her. Nicolas would simply be a diversion. Justin was her dream come true, and she was determined to make it work with him no matter the cost. In that moment, she managed to separate her needs from her wants and clicked on the message. And this is how Nicolas wormed his way in.

Chapter 2

Judith and Nicolas

Hey, what's up, Judith? It's Ethan. Remember me from chemistry?

Um, I'm not sure. I dropped chemistry.

Really? You look so familiar.

Who the hell is this? Is it you?

What do you mean?

Well, you've liked every one of my pics going back years. I'm getting stalker vibes. Nicolas?

Haha. Smarty-pants. You have some mad detective skills. I never asked. How did you figure out where my dad lived?

Dina told me that you said your dad was an off-the-grid building contractor. It wasn't hard to piece together.

What betrayal. That dumb bitch.

What do you want?

You're not happy to learn you failed in strangling me to death?

I already know you survived. Are you in Mexico?

I'll keep that to myself until you've earned some trust.

Why are you contacting me?

Haven't you guessed? I'm in love with you. Hopelessly, madly in love. I've never had a woman try to murder me before, and it's got me so worked up.

Sounds like you're a masochist.

With you I am. Then you abandon me before we can properly fuck. Dry humping doesn't count.

You went at me like a fiend. Sorta cute. Took me back to my teens. Horny teenage boys. Lol.

I'm embarrassed. Usually, I have moves like you wouldn't believe.

Oh, I believe.

We have unfinished business, you and me.

Sorry. I'm already in love, so you can go drop dead the way you were supposed to.

Cut the shit, Belladonna. You want me. My God, your lips on me. Those kisses were legendary. You've converted me, sex goddess. I'm your ardent acolyte. I'll never want another woman again.

What can I say? I'm a hot kisser.

I've never met a woman who could resist me and that includes you. I saw the hunger in your eyes when I opened the door that night.

Yeah, because I wanted to blow your head off. I wish I had, too.

Oh, come on, admit it. You were obsessed with me before we met. Otherwise, you would've waited for the cops. You wanted to take me on.

It's true. I have a death wish.

So do I. We both carry a trauma bond from our childhoods. Abused. In pain. Not something to be taken lightly.

Even if that's the case, what do you want?

Like I said, I'm in love with you. And I think you're secretly glad it's me and not Ethan.

I should wake up Justin right now so they can find out where you are.

But you won't.

Why?

I have your phone. You have a ton of nude pics and a dozen sex videos. Some of these go back to when you were still a minor. I'll start putting these online. You'll be the star you always wanted to be in a matter of days.

You wouldn't dare.

Na. I couldn't, but I need some leverage.

So what? You just wanna talk?

For starters.

Okay. Don't leak those. Please.

I love your collection. But I admit I'm possessive, especially of you. This is only the beginning.

The beginning of what?

You're a real ballbuster, nothing like Martha.

I can be a real bitch too.

But you are so gorgeous, you can do anything to any guy, and they'll forgive you, right?

I'm tired of this. I don't know what you think you will get from me, but I guarantee it will be nothing.

We'll see about that. If I hadn't abducted your mom, would you have gone out with me?

Nope.

Why the hell not?

I've met a ton of guys like you and hated them all.

What do you mean, guys like me?

Hot, vain, entitled, lazy, and will sleep with anybody.

You're right on three out of five, but I'm not entitled or lazy.

But you are a slut.

Yep. So are you. The sweetest, sexiest slut I've ever been crazy about. Been searching for you all my life.

And I've been searching for a real man all my life, and I finally found him.

That's hard to believe. Your cop is a complete hick. Has had like no pussy ever. Bet he's crazy about you, though. You're the hottest girl ever to give him a second glance.

I want him to be crazy about me. I must admit that I am a bit disappointed.

No surprise there. He's a cop. Jerks off to his own reflection.

He's not like that. It doesn't matter.

No. Tell me.

>He's here but not here, off and on again. And it's intentional. Did I do something wrong?

You mean playing mind games? It's not your fault. A guy like him has no idea how to please a woman.

>I'm confused. He begged me to move in with him. He is terrified of you coming after me and wants to protect me.

You mean, he wants to own you. What are you thinking? This guy is perfect on the outside with his hot body and cool car, but he's an insecure little boy on the inside. Wants to capture a gorgeous girl and claim her, then show her off like a gold star on his uniform. To do that, he needs to break you down first.

>I don't believe you. He's a genuine person. And I think he loves me.

He loves the idea of you. Not the same thing. Caging you out in the sticks will fuck you up. I promise. That's not the life for you.

>How are you so sure?

I know women. And I know you because you are my soulmate, and I can read your mind.

>That's creepy.

It is what it is.

>Okay. What am I thinking of right now?

You, my femme fatale, are thinking of this.

>A dick pic? You trashy boy. It's hard to forget that image.

And you couldn't stop staring. I remember.

>You are no twig. More like a mighty oak. Lol.

That's what I like to hear. Honesty.

>Usually, I hate dick pics, but I'll admit, yours makes me giddy with desire. I don't know why.

I know why. It's because I'm the man for you.

>How can that be? It's driving me crazy!

Me too. I've felt insane since I first laid eyes on you.

Will it ever stop?

Once we are together, we can consummate our love. So yes.

Since that can never happen, we're screwed.

I wish we had run away together. Trust me, I would have let you have your way with me. None of this hot-and-cold shit your cop puts you through.

Part of me feels the same. I can't resist saying—

What?

I wanna see this lovely thing in action.

Happily. So, am I right? Are you masturbating day and night like I am? Cause all I can think about is you and me in the car.

You've cursed me, you monster.

Am I the best you've ever had?

Thanks for nothing.

Music to my ears. I knew I got you off. Why did you lie to me?

That's for me to know and you to figure out.

I figured it out. You planned on escaping to get back to your worthless cop instead of following your heart and running away with your soulmate.

It wouldn't have worked. They would have tracked down your car. There were cops all over that canyon.

Maybe you're right. Do you know what I'm being charged with?

Well, you abducted me.

And your mom. Sorry.

I still can't believe you abducted her off the side of the road. You really are nuts, you know.

I am. But the compulsion was overwhelming. Like, I felt God telling me to do it, or something.

Huh. Well, maybe it was meant to be. My mom found true love. I don't think she told the police everything that happened between you either.

Seriously?

> But Justin says the detective doesn't believe
> her, and neither does he.

Of course that jealous fucker wants to take me
down. Does he know about you and me in the car?

> Sorta.

Awesome. I hope you told him everything!

> Hell no! But Justin is determined to find you.
> Says you are wanted on a felony charge for
> kidnapping, and you'll go to prison. It's a good
> thing all we did was dry hump because the
> rape kit turned up negative.

This sucks so bad. I fucked everything up.

> Yeah, you did.

By the way, your photo collection is helping me
survive our separation.

> You'd better promise never to leak those.

You'd better promise to send me more. I want to
see every square inch of you to create a 3D image.

> So, you're stalking me?

Yep. Don't deny it. You are delighted and flattered.

> A part of me, but not the part I will own up to.

You can run, but you can't hide. Contend with your
true self.

> Nope. I intend to become the good girl who
> deserves the good guy.

Please don't. You're perfect just the way you are.

> Justin doesn't think so. I thought he did, but he
> doesn't seem to want me anymore.

That's insane.

> Why am I telling you this?

Because I'm your soulmate, your soon-to-be best
friend, and hopefully even sooner, your fuck buddy.

> Well, he's blowing me off in bed.

You two aren't having sex?

> We fucked once before he crashed out. But he
> pushed me away first, and I had to beg him. I
> don't know what he's doing, but it's hell.

He's jerking you around, honey, using mind games. This guy is toxic. I can't imagine pushing you away for any amount of money.

You're so sweet. Finally, he let me, but since it's been three days, he came in, like, thirty seconds.

Oral?

Yeah.

He's using you! What a prick. Didn't even try to please you?

He doesn't care about that.

What a complete loser.

Am I being too demanding?

No, my darling girl. You aren't.

Once isn't enough for me. I guess I'm just a slut.

Na. Just a girl after my own heart. You think like me. The holy trinity, right? The first is a quickie to get the tidal wave of lust settled a bit. The second go is all about the tease, and the third time is all about the love.

That's straight out of the sex bible!

Yep. Written by the Sex God himself. Which is me, of course.

Now you have my attention. Why don't you give me a call?

Like right now?

I don't have shit to do.

Awesome. But beware. I'm gonna tell you all the sexy things I plan on doing to your body and give you plenty to fantasize about.

I can't resist. Call me now.

Tanya Madsen

Chapter 3

Justin

Judith lay in his lap while they watched a movie. Justin had a lot of chores to catch up on and couldn't concentrate. The gutters needed cleaning after winter, and his mom needed help prepping the garden for spring planting. He was a hard worker and didn't have time for movies. Hardly ever watched them. Staring blankly at the screen, he let his mind wander to the serious issue at hand.

After living with Judith for a month, Justin realized he had two problems. First, he couldn't handle this kind of lust. From the moment he met Judith, he felt crazy about her. Like crazy, crazy. She had awakened some dark inner persona he called his inner caveman, unleashing unholy cravings inside him. Now he was grappling with hardcore temptation every single day. Having been raised in a good Christian home, he was well aware of the struggle between good and evil. This was the first battle with sin he had ever faced, one that he felt certain to lose.

On day two, they barely made it into their apartment before his vixen had him down on the couch, fine-tuning his engine until he roared to life. He felt like a virgin as she gave him head, firing his pistons until he shot off fifty seconds later in delirious ecstasy, making him an instant fellatio addict for life. Dazed and crazed, they hit the sheets and drove each other for hours. But violent, erotic scenarios assailed him the entire time, and they took every ounce of his self-control to suppress. She had a dirty mind, a filthy mouth and the body of a porn star. How the fuck was he supposed to remain a good guy with this girl?

He had never cared all that much about getting laid. Girls up to this point had been blasé. No one had ever turned him on like Judith. But she kept him trapped in a state of perpetual arousal where all he thought of was sex and he couldn't concentrate on a Goddamn thing. Sitting in his patrol car through a long boring shift, all night long he envisioned her down between his legs, that coy smile on her pretty face, at the mercy of her hands and mouth as she sucked him off. He felt the constant urge to masturbate. Couldn't contain his erections and couldn't control his thoughts. She loved pushing him over the edge, even as he kept clawing his way back. His partner, Jones, recognized his dazed demeanor and, in good humor, gave him a hard time, although he totally understood because he, too, had met Judith.

Justin didn't think orgasms were meant to feel this way. Judith did things to his body and his imagination that were ungodly. Now, he struggled with going to work, getting to sleep, or doing his chores. He just wanted to fuck her nonstop. It was hell.

After two weeks of unrelenting sexual obsession, he was forced to make a choice. In an attempt to regain his sanity, he distanced himself from her. He absolutely had to return to the decent, controlled Christian guy he used to be.

Meeting Judith messed him up somehow. He had never felt this way about any girl before. She made him obsessed, possessive, and incredibly jealous, which led to the second problem. He resented her deeply for going up against Nicolas. She ruined their fairy-tale romance, defiled it, and wrecked it by insisting on confronting that criminal and then letting him seduce her. Jealousy ate him alive as he thought of another man's hands on her. Insecurity crushed his confidence as he imagined her comparing him to Nicolas.

Judith also wrecked their entire case. If the police had caught Nicolas at the house, they would have shot him dead, the way Justin hoped and the way he deserved. Now, Justin spent far too much time re-imagining getting there in time and landing a bullet in Nicolas's head. He felt trapped in a futile competition with an apex bird of paradise. That sexy Casanova had much better moves and Justin felt fucked.

Justin held Judith responsible for letting Nicolas escape. She ruined everything. Now she was perverting his sex drive, and he felt powerless. And the one thing Justin hated more than anything was feeling powerless. He loved control and holding down the law, and he judged mentally-ill fuckboys like Nicolas to the ends of the earth.

To survive his dysfunctional emotional state, Justin reverted to his pre-Judith life. He prioritized his needs, got back to babying his car, visiting his family, and wasting hours at the gym. He spent time with her, but also found plenty of excuses to stay away. He had her just where he wanted her—in his bed, in his house, all alone, growing more desperate for him by the day.

Justin also discovered that he couldn't stop playing his mind games. Wasn't sure why. Part of him wanted to punish her for fucking him up like this. And part of him enjoyed torturing her with coldness just to watch her chase him. He led her to believe he wasn't into her, even though he thought about her nonstop. Ghosted her at work when she sexted him, which made her sext him even harder. And of course, he spent half the night drooling over her nude pics and dirty innuendos, then drowning in his sex fantasies.

Judith hated rejection. It was a riot watching her grovel for his affection. Text after text, she'd send: Where was he? Was he mad at her? Was everything okay? He ignored them all, satisfied that she desperately wanted to please him and make him love her. This rocked because he needed constant validation. Truth was, Justin had no idea why Judith wanted him. He thought that getting this hot girl to move in with him would boost his confidence, but all it ended up doing was making him feel more inadequate.

And he punished her because he feared she still fantasized about Nicolas, fueling a jealous rage he couldn't control. His mind games gave him a sense of power, and it felt like a deserved punishment for what she had done to him.

Everything was Judith's fault. She seduced him, immediately cheated on him, then turned him into a despicable horny beast. Justin never considered for a second how he might be responsible for any of his behavior because he was a good guy, and if he changed into something else, it wouldn't be his fault. Caught in a vicious cycle of pushing her away while obsessing over her, there was no breaking free, not without some sort of divine intervention.

The movie rambled on, but he had lost all concentration as she burrowed deeper between his legs, pretending not to notice his massive hard-on. His unquenchable lust, combined with his jealousy, were warping him, and shit—the things he wanted to do to her were vile.

Justin had never been much for prayer but now he was forced to repent every fucking day. Was about ready to head back to church on Sundays. Felt like he needed God to save him and it really sucked. If he couldn't turn things around, he'd have to kick her out. He didn't like what she was turning him into one bit.

He endured, trembling with exertion, as he tried to maintain self-control. Throbbing with euphoric sensations in every part of his body. Finally, Judith decided to put him out of his misery. She tore open his jeans and smiled with satisfaction as his junk sprang to life. Gazed up at him with those magnetic green eyes, giggled as she tried to slow his frantic thrusting by stroking him tight and slow, moaning with pleasure as she licked and sucked so perfectly, just the right amount of speed and pressure, until he was groaning helplessly, melting inside his skin.

When he was just about there, she straddled his lap and said to choose how he wanted to finish as she pulled off her t-shirt. No bra. Mesmerized by her Barbie tits swinging inches from his face, her teasing taunted his inner caveman beyond endurance until he was growling, biting, and tearing off her clothes. Judith knew she had him entirely at her mercy and he hated her for it. The plan had been to wrap her around his finger, but that sure as hell wasn't happening.

Sexual fury kicked his ass into a frenzy. The movie was forgotten about as he pushed her over the side of the armrest until her head rested on the floor, and mounted her clumsily like a ravenous beast. She was crying for him to go in deep and fast, which made him want to fuck her so hard she'd beg for mercy. He nearly passed out when he climaxed. He felt bewitched, cursed by a she-devil, enslaved, and he wanted an endless amount of more. But on his terms, according to his fantasies. Not hers.

It didn't end there. Then she wanted to go at him for her own pleasure. Dragged him into their bed, and riled him up until he was sure he'd be stuck with a permanent erection, then rode him mercilessly through his orgasm until she had him hard once again.

Judith was live porn. A Jezebel. And he was starting to realize she had been sent into his life by the devil to test him. Since he met her, he fantasized about violent kink nonstop and craved fellatio every day, so he was failing this morality test miserably.

It was a sizable chunk of his precious day off before he returned to considering how to tackle his laundry list of chores. Even after two hours, she still looked hungry. What else did she want? What would it take to please this woman?

"Justin, might we, I don't know, plan a date night or something?"

Judith lay with her head on his chest, stroking his belly in a way she had quickly discovered gave him an immediate erection. Fuck. No. No more. Not right now.

"What do you have in mind?"

"Maybe head to Salt Lake City and go to a nice restaurant. Walk around the mall. Perhaps return to the aviary. It would give me a chance to dress up."

She looked at him sweetly, but he knew what she meant. A chance to wear something scandalous that would make him pant like a dog all night until he could get her home and strip her naked. The sexual attraction, which was instant and overwhelming, now seemed almost destructive in its incapacitating force.

"Sure. Whatever. Go ahead and set it up. You have my schedule. Listen, I'm sorry. I have so much work to catch up on."

"I understand. Can I help?"

"Not sure how helpful it would be to have you around distracting me."

Judith looked hurt.

"I mean, I'm not worthless."

"No, I appreciate the gesture. I have a lot of cleaning and helping my mom prep the garden."

"Let me help. I've helped with gardening before." Judith seemed eager.

Should he let her? Part of him wanted to. Yet, he had to keep her at arm's length, too.

"Maybe next time?"

Justin kissed her on the cheek, and he sensed disappointment.

"I don't understand why you don't include me in stuff. What do you expect me to do out here? You're gone all the time, and I'm all alone."

Why didn't he include her? His mom liked her, and Judith was sweet to his family. Justin didn't understand himself. But he had to get away from her. Judith was still naked, and he wanted to go again. Couldn't get anything done around her. He needed to force her to walk around in a sackcloth to cover up those gorgeous breasts.

"I'm so used to being alone and doing everything alone," he admitted.

"Then you aren't looking for a relationship," she snapped, "it's more than having a girl warm your bed. I'm not here just to have sex, Justin. I want to feel loved, included and understood. To have a friend and a confidant. I thought that you being a cop meant that you had your shit together. I'm starting to realize that you don't. I mean, we had sex for hours, and I don't feel any closer to you or that you love me. It's heartbreaking."

Judith looked close to tears, and Justin had no idea how to respond. When they first met, he was on the job, playing the good-guy cop role he had perfected over the past three years. But he wasn't that guy. He was selfish and preferred to spend time doing his own thing. Maybe he shouldn't have tried to hook up. He came off as the perfect dream guy. He was anything but, and he knew it.

"You aren't just a girl who warms my bed," Justin protested, "I want a relationship, too. I'm also under a lot of pressure. I don't have time to show you what needs doing, and I have only five hours left in the day."

"Well, sorry for wasting your time." She glared as she got up and went to the bathroom.

Judith returned, thankfully clothed, and Justin felt bad. She was like a dream come true in so many ways. He never imagined he would meet a girl like her, much less have a chance with her. When they first met, all he did was obsess over how to make her his. Judith was light-years out of his league. A girl from the city, a beauty queen who had tons of ex-boyfriends and tons of experience with sex. He was a country boy with a mundane life and limited experience with women. He had wanted her so badly. How had it all gone to shit?

In a sudden stroke of clarity, he understood the real motivation behind his hot-and-cold mind games. This was all about his jealousy of Nicolas. She still fantasized about that fucking Casanova, and he knew it. Justin decided to test her.

"I guess they had a potential sighting of Nicolas." Justin lied.

"Where?"

Was that a hint of excitement? Was it?

"I'm not sure. Nothing came of it, but he's out there. If he tries to contact you, please don't hide it. We hope to track this guy down. Despite what your mom told the police, which, from what I hear, was pretty much nothing, Nicolas is a dangerous predator who needs to be brought to justice."

"Yeah, of course."

Judith laughed nervously, yet he could see it in her eyes. She harbored a secret crush on Nicolas. How deep did her feelings go? He wanted to ask, but instead, he put his barriers back up around his heart and headed for the door.

Chapter 4

Judith and Nicolas

"Hey."

"Hey. Wow, your voice, Belladonna. I'm in heaven right now."

"From hearing my voice?"

"You sound beautiful. And sassy. I love it."

"I love your throaty voice. You could be a jazz singer."

"Maybe I will."

"So, tell me your life story, crazy boy."

"It's a horror story. Not sure you want to know."

"I do."

"I grew up in a house with two women who smothered me. My nanny molested me, and my mother made me sick with every sort of condition you could imagine. Between the two of them, I was a mess—a dysfunctional kid with no friends and always sick from my mom's meddling with my health. It turned Catrina's relationship with me into the silver lining, which is sick."

"Good lord. That's awful!"

"When I was thirteen, Catrina dumped me, and I was a wreck, which made my mom try even harder to fix me. At sixteen, I tried to drug her with the pills she gave me, was accused of second-degree murder when she fell into the pool and nearly drowned, and I tried to kill myself to avoid going to prison. You can't imagine how mean the cops were to me. I tried to tell them about the child abuse and my mom poisoning me for half my life, but they didn't care. It ended up putting me in a mental hospital."

"Did they help you in there?"

"Na. I got raped for the first time by a man, if you call that helping. The orderlies were a bunch of horny faggots, let me tell you."

"Jesus, Nicolas. I'm so sorry."

"I was in and out of the hospital, diagnosed with a mental illness, then put into a care home."

"My mom said you have borderline personality disorder?"

"She's right. Along with a few other issues."

"That's gotta be hard."

"When I turned eighteen, I figured out how to take the SATs, and because somehow, due to my dad's genetics, I'm a genius, I scored high and got into Berkeley. My dad stepped up and paid my tuition and living expenses, so I guess I'll give him that."

"I wish I were smart. The only thing I've ever done well at was winning beauty pageants—that, and firing a gun. Right before I tracked you down, I bought a gun. Justin showed me how to use it. He said I was a natural."

"So, it was intentional that you didn't blow my head off?"

"I guess I'm not a murderer. How was college?"

"Sucked big time. I never had any friends, so I had no idea how to make them. Got drunk off my ass and fucked a ton of girls and guys, though. I'm bisexual, by the way."

"Oh, sexy."

"You like that?"

"So, you're into both. Which is better?"

"I can't decide, but one thing I know for sure is that all I want is you."

"I'm flattered."

"You should be. I'm hot shit."

"Humility is not your thing, is it?"

"Nope. Anyhow, in college, I got a reputation as a slut, no surprise there, but all my hookups made me feel insecure, and I hated it. Ended up one night at a bar, and an older woman hit on me. She reminded me of Catrina, so I went home with her and began my quest to replace Catrina."

"Seducing all these Catrina wannabes lasted until you met my mom?"

"Yeah. After college, I started dating like crazy. Sharpened my seducing skills, but it wasn't very enjoyable. All of them were just looking for something on the side. I would never have been able to scratch my itch with that clientele. Thank God for Martha."

"Then you met me."

"Yep. And this is where I feel my life begins. With you. Like I told you the night you tracked me down, you are a game changer."

"What can I change for you?"

"All I ever wanted was to find a woman who would love me, who I could make happy, who would never leave me. Once I find her, I'm gonna slip the ring on her finger and never be a whore again. She's out there, and I believe that girl is you."

"It's so weird. You are this hot Casanova looking for your soulmate."

"I thought having these mad skills would bring her into my orbit. It's been very discouraging so far."

"Well, most people looking for a hook-up aren't looking to hook up."

"True. I just thought I could seduce her into staying with me forever."

"You're a sweet guy, Nicolas. A strange but sweet guy."

"I'll take that. Tell me about yourself."

"Well, you've seen everything about me online. I'm a boring, pretty girl who spent her entire life trying to win beauty pageant trophies for her dad. The same dad who dumped her ass when he divorced her mom and cut her off from ever making it as a model."

"Looks like you have plenty of talents—gymnastics, dance, performing, languages, karate. I couldn't believe your moves when you kicked my ass.

Thrust me into some Bruce Lee movie. That roundhouse kick. Shit. You almost murdered me like three times that night."

"You're making me blush. What are talents? Just a bunch of bullshit. I have nothing to offer this world. That's why I love Justin. He makes a difference. How can I ever do that?"

"Does he now? Driving around, trying to get people in trouble, and writing up police reports. Fucking people over financially and putting them in jail. Doesn't sound all that important to me."

"Well, he rescued me the night you abducted my mom."

"That's hardly a rescue. You romanticize him because he has a hot ass."

"You have me figured out."

"You're just a horny, lonely girl yearning for love. We are totally meant for each other. Even your mom said so."

"What did she say?"

"Well, I kept asking about you during the week she spent with me. She said she could see us together. That we were both insanely beautiful and desperate for love."

"I never believed in soulmates. But when we were fighting over the knife in your dad's basement, I felt the hands of fate pushing me into your arms. And I keep having these images of you and me run through my head. Things we've done and places we've been together, but none of it has ever happened."

"Same with me, too. Across time and space, right? Crazy shit. I guess we do live more than once. We've known each other forever, Belladonna. Do you realize that?"

"I guess. But I'm so confused. Something pulled me to Justin, too."

"Well, that was a fluke. I am your soulmate. Not him."

"Well, you'll have to convince me."

"I will, I promise. You are my new lease on life, Belladonna. I have big plans for us. Bye for now."

Chapter 5

Nicolas

Nicolas stared at his reflection, contemplating whether he liked his new look. His hair was now blonde. After noticing a couple of cops eyeing him on the street, he felt he needed a disguise. Still gorgeous, the light hair accentuated his dark eyes, making him appear more sinister than he liked. He preferred the sweet guy, not this rake.

Nicolas counted all the money in his bag. It wasn't as much as he expected—less than three thousand dollars—but it should last him until he found a job. He read and reread the first conversation between him and Belladonna, pleased for the most part. It was annoying that she was so fixated on her cop, but he knew that in time, he'd make her see sense.

It wasn't even about getting her for himself. That jerk was the last person to make her happy. Why was she so hung up on being a good girl? The abuse. Of course. Nicolas understood the need to reinvent oneself, although he tried, failed, and gave up almost immediately. Catrina had forged him into a slut, and that's all he would ever be. Thank God she also had the decency to teach him how to be a successful slut. There wasn't a person alive who could resist his charms.

Lying back, Nicolas reflected on Belladonna's admission that he was the best lover she'd ever had, overcome with happiness. All he ever wanted was to find a woman who would love him, who he could make happy, who would never leave him. Somehow, as impossible as it seemed, she was the one. He had to find a way to bring them together.

After living in Cabo San Lucas for a few weeks, Nicolas had been rejected for every job he applied for, perhaps because he wasn't bilingual. He had no idea what to do, as he lacked job experience beyond food service and had a seemingly useless degree in anthropology. Why anthropology?

Because he had to pick something and he loved ancient stuff. He found it fascinating how people and cultures evolved over time. Not much money to be made in that, though.

Nicolas stood on the boardwalk outside a bar, watching the moon drift over the ocean waves, hands in his back pockets, fantasizing about Belladonna, when a group of women walked by. They were older and enjoying a lively night out. One of them eyed him lustfully, and he couldn't help but respond with a flirtatious smile. She left her friends and sauntered over to him.

"How much?" She whispered in his ear.

Nicolas pondered her request. Did she think he was a prostitute? He decided to play along.

"How much would you be willing to pay?" He murmured, and she flushed with desire.

"To have you tune up my pussy, I'll pay top dollar, pretty boy."

"Then top dollar it is."

He had no idea how much that was, but money was money.

"Meet me at my hotel room in thirty minutes."

"Do you have cuffs?"

She grinned, revealing several rotten teeth. Well, it wasn't as if he intended to marry her.

"I'll make sure to have some."

"I need the cuffs if you want me to take you to Happy Town."

She smiled again. Nicolas realized she was closer to sixty than fifty, and he hoped he could get her off despite her age.

"See you soon."

She batted her eyes, and Nicolas felt pleased. Was it that easy? Considered what he would do for her. Were you paid by the orgasm or the hour? Should he Google it? He had never thought once about sex work. Why not? He was born into it, thanks to Catrina.

Nicolas walked to his small studio apartment and freshened up. He had bought some new clothes that made him look like a tourist, but with his great body, he looked hot in everything.

Part of him felt guilty. He wasn't cheating on Belladonna. This was transactional, and he wasn't going to get off. He might get hard being down between someone's legs, but that was it. Belladonna consumed him now. What they had was more than sexual. It was salvation.

Later that night, he counted out his cash. Almost six hundred dollars. As it turned out, she invited her friends. They lined up for orgasms. It was sweet. Of course, he exceeded their expectations, and they all promised to return for repeat business. It wasn't as nasty as he feared. What else was he gonna do? Locked away from his Belladonna, stuck in another country. He had to survive somehow. This was as good as anything else.

Heading home in the darkness, he closed his eyes as he walked, picturing Belladonna in perfect detail, the way she looked that night, cuffed inside the car, deliciously naked, entirely at his mercy, drowning in lust for him, trying to fake him out. Yeah right. Belladonna would die to have his mouth on her again. She would never feel as fulfilled with any other man. Now, he had to get her to run away with him, far away and for good.

Nicolas was afraid that his obsession was warping him. He wasn't sure he could continue living if he didn't win her heart. He devoured her text history and Facebook history, searching for every clue as to understand her. Belladonna had poor self-esteem and had never felt good at anything apart from being beautiful, which he understood so well.

His entire life revolved around being a beautiful fuckboy. It hurt his heart to know that this girl might understand him, but unlike him, she was in denial. She didn't grasp the root of her pain and wasn't self-aware. She needed to be with him to learn how to love and accept herself.

Nicolas realized he would have to tell her about his new job and was afraid of what she would say. It was stupid that the world was so dead set against sex work. What if it was the only thing you were good at? He decided to hold out for the time being.

When he got home, he lay in bed and categorized her nude pics by preference and watched the sex videos she made with a few of her exes. These guys sucked. She was faking her orgasms, and Nicolas wanted to laugh out loud. This poor, beautiful girl, and now she was giving it all to that fucking cop. Nicolas couldn't think about him. It made his blood rise with homicidal rage.

Shortly after two a.m., he stared at her Facebook profile. She still hadn't updated it with a picture of her and the cop, which was a relief. He saw that she was available. He wanted to talk. Instead, he opened her texts with Justin and reread them, feeling his insides churn with jealousy.

This guy had no idea how to awaken a woman's inner goddess. What did Belladonna see in him? It had to be his dick. Probably huge being a cop, asshole, fucker. He hated cops. They were the ones who tried to destroy him when his mom fell into the pool. They drove him to attempt suicide that first time.

Cops were all the same. Keepers of the peace really meant they kept the innocent from being heard. They didn't care about people like him. He added this to his growing list of reasons for loving Belladonna. He needed to save her from her cop before he completely broke her heart.

Chapter 6

Judith

Summer had arrived, and Judith was craving a pool. She had spent the entire previous summer lounging by the pool at their condo. How did people manage to survive living out in the sticks? There wasn't a single thing to do. At times, she felt as if she would lose her mind.

She couldn't borrow Justin's precious car. Her mom had offered to let her use her car when she moved in with Erik, but Lizzy had begged for it, and, as usual, she got her way. Now, Lizzy had wheels, and Judith was stranded in the middle of nowhere, waiting for Justin day and night. How could he not see she was going mad?

Things hadn't improved with Justin. She had no words to express the sadness and embarrassment she felt. Judith thought endlessly about their first night in bed, how she went at Justin with a vengeance, and he shoved her away. Why didn't she realize right then that they were incompatible? How could she love this man with her whole soul when he was so wrong for her?

Justin was in the garage right now, listening to music and rebuilding the engine in the car he was restoring. He claimed he was rebuilding it for her, but she didn't care about that. Judith just wanted him. Their apartment was stiflingly hot. It had a swamp cooler, which sucked compared to air conditioning. Country people lived in the Dark Ages. Preferred everything old and worn out, and were okay with it.

Her mom and Erik were off on another vacation, and Judith felt jealous. How did her mom manage to find the perfect guy? Between work, the garden, the car, the workout routine, the family and the endless chores, she rarely saw Justin anymore.

How was she supposed to survive? But he saved her. His hold on her made her feel desperate for his love and approval. Judith wanted to be his girl, even if he didn't want to be her man. What the hell was wrong with her?

The only thing keeping her afloat was Nicolas. He messaged her nonstop. He was like those annoying kids in high school who followed you everywhere, texted you constantly, and when you tried to ghost them, they didn't care—just kept bugging the shit out of you. Nothing could stop them. But despite his clingy, codependent nature, she found herself falling in love with him. And without him, she would have lost her mind. Their relationship had deepened over the last few months. He admitted that he was working as a prostitute, and it didn't bother her as much as she thought it might. He was so damn hot at sex that he might as well cash in on his mad skills.

But she was also jealous of everyone he provided services to, having thrown her chance with him away when she refused to crawl into the back seat of his car. And now, all she had was that perfect erotic memory of him going down on her. It was pure torture.

Judith reflected on her childhood and all the fantasies she had about her dream guy. He would have a decent job, be kind and passionate, and want to spend time with her, adoring her just as she would adore him. It drove her crazy because Justin seemed so close to perfect with his looks, his job, and his stability, but there was something about her that he didn't like.

She was willing to change anything about herself to win his heart. Nicolas didn't understand how deeply she yearned to be Justin's chosen girl. His rejection only fueled her obsession. His coldness made her so horny, it was unbelievable. The more he pushed her away, the more she wanted him, which was pathetic.

Judith heard the door open and then slam shut. Justin walked into the apartment and grabbed a soda from the fridge. His shirt was off, covered in sweat, and his jeans hung low, revealing his impressive abs and hinting at everything below. He turned to face her as if showing off his extremely hot body for her benefit. Consumed by lust, she stared like a fangirl until she forced her gaze away out of embarrassment.

"How's it going?" she managed.

"Fine. I'm running into town to buy some car parts. Need anything?"

Aside from spending an entire afternoon in bed with you, no.

Justin walked into the living room and plopped down on the couch. She stood by the window, trying not to look at him. She couldn't touch him. He wouldn't let her. Somehow, in less than three months, he had trained her and put her on a leash. This was hell.

Judith wanted to race outside, call an Uber, and take it all the way to Mexico. Find Nicolas and fall into his arms. Justin was an asshole, as horrible as that was to accept. He had to know she wanted him. This rejection broke her heart. Why was he doing this to her? Those first few days with him were precious, but now he forced her to endure this intentional cruelty, and it made her want to die.

"I guess I'm okay. How long are you gonna be?"

"Geez. I'm not sure. These projects never end. I still have a ton of stuff to do. I have no idea how people find time for everything."

Judith turned away, so overwhelmed with sorrow that she couldn't speak.

"Everything okay?"

Justin gazed at her with a mild expression of concern as he finished his soda, crushed the can, and flippantly threw it into the recycling bin.

She felt the vibes radiating off him. Vibes, she had come to realize, were generated by anger. Justin simmered with repressed rage, which fueled his libido, his workouts, and his zest for life. He was purposefully distant, concealing his true self from her, and she couldn't figure out why.

This vibration drew her to him and fueled her insatiable lust. She wanted to taunt him into action, tease the beast inside him, and feed his ravenous hunger with the hottest sex imaginable. But the more she tried, the harder he pushed her away. They were trapped in a power struggle, and had been so since the moment he first rejected her. Still, Justin mesmerized her as he had from the night they met, so she was fucked.

"Um, I don't know. Just emotional today, I guess."

Leaning over the counter with his hands together, he shrugged. Even her father, who abandoned them, had comforted her mom when she was down. What was wrong with this guy?

"You sure?"

He murmured distractedly, looking down at his phone.

"I'm fine." Judith wiped away her tears. "It's nothing."

"Okay. If you say so, I'll be back in a bit."

Heading into the bedroom, he rummaged through a drawer, returned to the living room while pulling on a clean t-shirt, and then left. Judith lay back on the couch and began to cry. She had no one to talk to. Her besties were busy with their lives, and she had no life of her own, so she had nothing to post about. Finally, she broke down. For the first time ever, she messaged Nicolas first and opened her heart.

Chapter 7

Judith and Nicolas

Talk to me. I'm going nuts here.

I'm so sorry.

What are you doing?

Sleeping in. Last night was busy.

Did you make a lot of money?

Got off three guys and five gals. 1000$$$$$.

Guess being a prostitute pays.

You should try it. You're so hot, you'd make serious bank.

Never.

Bet I make more dough than your cop.

Probably. His job is picking up people like you and throwing them in jail.

Why I hate that motherfucker.

He's one of the good ones.

Uh-huh.

You do know most girls don't wanna hook up with a prostitute, right?

This is just a side gig until we can be together. It's a job, nothing more.

What are you going to do with all your money?

I'm making plans for us.

I'm in hell here.

What's the shithead doing now?

Justin has chained me to a bed while everyone else gets to go on living. He hasn't touched me

in a week! Why is he doing this to me? I am
going to lose my mind.

Please leave him. Please.

How did I think he was the right guy for me? He
shoved me off him on our first date. I thought
his high ideals were sweet. But this isn't sweet.

His high ideals are bullshit. It's a mind game, honey.
He's teasing you, playing hot and cold, and
breaking you down, so you'll do anything, be
anything he wants. It's the shit that guys who have
never had a girl like you do so they can keep a girl
like you. He's a fucking loser.

Seriously? I thought he was such a good guy!

He's not.

I am hot in bed and make him feel amazing. It
should be enough to break his stupid games.

Of course. You're a femme fatale.

He doesn't want to feel amazing, so what do I
do?

This is not about sex. This guy is emotionally abusive.
He's withholding affection to either punish you or
break you, and it's only gonna get worse.

That's horrible. Can't bring myself to believe it.

Where is he?

Left. He was just here. He's been working on his
car all day. Comes in, shirt off, covered in
sweat. Suddenly, I'm lusting after him like a
fangirl. I'm so horny and lonely, and he doesn't
even care. I wanted to rape him! Isn't that
horrible?

Poor girl. Here. Get undressed and into bed. I'll do
the same. We can get each other off.

I'm so jealous of all your tricks. They get to have
you and I don't.

Don't say things like that to me. Can't handle it. I
want you so bad. It's like an infectious disease.

What does your fantasy girl include?

If you scream my name and beg for it, I'll get off so
fast.

Full name or nickname?

I've never thought about it. You're special, so you get my nickname. I love you, Belladonna. You think of everything. What do you want?

I'm ashamed to say.

Girl of my dreams, please don't be ashamed. You are perfect, and I wanna indulge every last one of your kinks.

Only have the one kink, to be honest, but I don't wanna admit it.

Nothing's too kinky for me.

I would never tell Justin that's for sure. He's way too straitlaced. He'd think I was a freak.

Now you have me panting with anticipation.

Wanna watch you touch yourself. See your hand in action.

You like watching guys give self-love?

I guess. I'm so embarrassed!

Don't be. Easiest request ever.

Feel bad about cheating on Justin.

Please don't mention him while I'm masturbating.

Do you want me just because you hate cops?

It is a huge plus. That night in the car, when you said that was your cop boyfriend on the phone, I was ecstatic. I LOVE stealing girls away from guys I HATE. But with you, it's so much more. You are my girl, and I will always see you as my girl, no matter who you are with.

Well, your girl is in her birthday suit, hotshot. Give me a call.

One hour later, both were lying in bed, gazing starry-eyed at each other on their video call.

"Ours is the first serious relationship I've ever been in."

"I don't think this counts as a relationship. You're a thousand miles away."

"Wrong. Every single minute I'm not paid to fuck someone, I'm thinking of how to bring us together. I think that constitutes a relationship."

"Well, it's impossible."

"I won't accept that. Today, you've proven you're perfect for me. A natural screamer."

"Why do you need to hear your name screamed? Why the begging? I guess you're a classic narcissist."

"I had to get Catrina screaming. If not, I was in trouble. Trouble was bad."

"God, Nicolas. I can't imagine."

"Wanna erase her screams and replace them with better ones. It gets me off so fast it almost counts as premature ejaculation."

"I scream like crazy with Justin."

"Does he like it?"

"I never asked. Maybe he doesn't. What if he doesn't?"

"I hate that guy so much. He doesn't deserve you."

"Maybe he wishes he could put a gag on me. Now I'm insecure. It could be why he blows me off now."

"That's why you belong with me."

"Seeing you stroke yourself was so hot. Send me a video."

"How did I get lucky enough to meet you?"

"I wouldn't call this luck. Our situation sucks."

"It does for now. But it's only temporary. I'm an optimist."

"Even if we could, how would I leave Justin?"

"Head out the front door. Adios, sucker."

"You don't understand how much I want him. It's hell."

"How can you love someone who treats you this way?"

"When he does want me, the sex is fantastic."

"Please don't stick up for that cocksucker. We're still in the afterglow, and I wanna stay here. Sorry. Any mention of him triggers me. Especially since he is treating you like shit, I wanna murder him."

"Why do you hate him so much?"

"Number one, he's a cop. So, I have to hate him. Number two, he's competition. The asshole shares your bed. Number three, I've pored over your texts back and forth. Practically have them memorized. You're so desperate for him like he's Jesus fucking Christ, and you wanna be saved. I don't understand. What is his power over you?"

"I told you. My whole life, I've been a stupid slut. I never imagined a good guy like Justin would even consider me."

"I'm sure your hero worship really gets him off. This guy is a true narcissist. I can't believe you're so easily fooled by this fucking cop."

"Justin loves me. I need to adjust to make him like me more."

"Stop trying to be someone you aren't cause you're perfect. He's the problem. Yeah, you are an intense, passionate girl who needs a ton of reassurance and sexual attention. Like an exotic hothouse flower when he was expecting some boring daisy that grows in a field. He'll never understand you. Sorry, things need to remain real between us. We are soulmates, remember?"

"You may be right. But please try to refrain from all the hate speech. It makes me feel like shit talking about him like that."

"Whatever. One more thing, watching me jerk off. Why was that your ask for video sex? And I saw the lust in your eyes when I jerked off in the car during our crazy getaway."

"It's embarrassing."

"No matter what you say, I'll understand."

"I think it arouses me because the man who molested me touched himself before, you know, and seeing him come in his hand mesmerized me and almost made me forget what was coming next. The expression of joy he got was like a message. This was okay cause look how happy he was, right? That's the real turn-on, the look of ecstasy. I want to give him that look instead of his hand, which is probably why I'm a sex addict. Like, he made me jealous of his hand. And it's made me so competitive to be every guy's sex fantasy. It's messed up, I know."

"Oh, Belladonna, I totally get it. My heart aches for that adorable little girl some fucker had to go and defile. There were so many things Catrina did that triggered me. Thank God for Martha. She dragged me out of those horrifying nine years of my life and took me through a boot camp for child abuse victims. She is my savior."

"I am so sorry you suffered through that."

"You are the first girl I have ever been able to talk about this stuff with."

"You are the first anyone I have ever confided in. Especially my nightmares."

"It is my honor, sweetheart. About the nightmares, do you let your cop know?"

"Never. I tried to tell him once. He couldn't care less."

"Well, I do. When you sleep with me, I'll soothe your nightmares and satisfy your kink."

"All you have to do is stroke yourself and I'm in heaven."

"You are so hot, Belladonna. I'm so glad I can satisfy you by doing what I do best."

"You definitely get my trauma."

"You've got me going. I'm gonna satisfy you again right now."

Chapter 8

Justin

Justin was so tired. He couldn't even blame it on Judith. She had left him alone lately because he had pushed her away day after day, so he was getting a full eight hours of sleep. Why the hell was he so tired? It seemed incomprehensible, but he was afraid he might be depressed.

He had no idea why that would be. He had a hot girlfriend, the perfect car, enjoyed his job, and had a lot of money saved. His mom relied on him for everything, and his co-workers treated him like a rock star.

Every night at work, he earned accolades for getting Judith. The guys wanted to know if he had any sexy pics of her. He did, of course, and was happy to share. They could look but not touch, and he now had an entourage of buddies. It felt like high school, except that he had a hot girlfriend and they didn't. Figured that Judith would be okay with it since she already had a ton of sexy pics online, and she loved getting attention.

He didn't share her nudes, though. Those were just for him and his hand. Although he didn't reply to her sexting anymore, it didn't stop him from lusting over the pics she had sent every chance he got.

Life was pretty good, but not good enough. Because they failed. Nicolas got away. He nearly raped Judith, and now she was all hung up on him, and the thought of it made him need to hit the punching bag at the gym and imagine Nicolas's face on it. Justin couldn't overcome his hatred for that guy. And it was the real reason he was cold now.

Sure, he liked playing his mind games, but the truth was, he was insecure. It didn't matter what he did to her in bed because nothing would ever be as hot as that fucking Casanova who got her off in one minute, and who knows what else they did.

She wasn't telling him the whole story, and it was her saving grace. His jealousy was so volatile that he'd most likely drive her out to the middle of nowhere and dump her ass on the side of the road to fend for herself.

Justin bought the car parts he needed and picked up a few things from the store. Thought about how Judith ogled him hungrily when he walked in. He could tell she was horny, and it thrilled him to know she wanted him while he refused to give in.

Why did he still tease her like this? Initially, it made sense to drive her headlong into his arms. Now it seemed cruel. And it drove him crazy, too. Why did he push her away when he wanted her like she wanted him? There was something wrong with him.

Then there was the other thing. Judith was crying when he left. Why did he freeze up? Was he like his dad? Should he discuss this with his mom? Everyone assumed they had a celebrity relationship, and he doubted anyone would understand why he played these stupid games.

When he returned to the house, he decided he needed to talk to his mom. Judith and he had been living together for almost three months now. Day after day, she looked miserable. He was sick of giving her the cold shoulder, but he couldn't stop himself. He was definitely screwing things up.

"Hey, Mom."

Justin walked into the house, and she put down the quilt she was working on.

"Hey, baby. You look like you're working too hard. Need a drink?"

"Yeah sure. Have a minute?"

"Always for you, sweet boy."

His mom handed him a root beer, and he sipped greedily. Summer was here, and it was already nearly ninety-five degrees every afternoon. He didn't have an AC unit in the garage and had meant to spring for one, but he was too cheap. Now, he was second-guessing that decision.

"It's about Judith. I think I'm messing everything up, and I'm unsure what to do about it."

"Have you prayed first? You know, God has all the answers. Not me."

"I've tried. But I think this issue is all my fault."

"She doesn't seem happy, let me tell you."

"Has she said anything?"

"No. But she walks around the yard glued to her phone most mornings, texting someone for hours. Sometimes, she talks on the phone. I think she's lonely, Justin."

Justin froze. Who was she talking to? Her mom? Friends from school? Or—

"She hasn't said anything."

"Some things are hard to say out loud. Bet she wants things to be different, but doesn't know how to make it happen. How's your sex life?"

Justin flushed. His mom. Always straight to the point.

"Um, why do you ask?"

"You are my son. And I hate to say it, you're a lot like your dad."

"So I'm doomed to be a fuck up," he muttered.

"You aren't giving Judith what she bargained for, son. You are going to lose that girl. Mark my words."

"I have too much shit to do. She wants to go at it day and night, and I don't have the energy. And part of me likes pushing her away, driving her crazy, and I don't know why."

"I warned you she would be needy. As for the second issue, it seems you like playing mind games. I can promise those never end well."

"I like sex as much as the next guy, but she—you can't imagine. She's like a thousand watts of passion all the time. I can't keep up, and I'm sure I can't make her happy."

"Has she said that, or is it just your low self-esteem talking?"

Justin paused. Did he have low self-esteem?

"She wants me. More than wants me. She looks like she wants to eat me every chance she gets."

"It's not the sex that scares you, Justin. It's the intimacy. That's why you push her away, and that's why you act cold. You don't wanna get too close. That's what broke things for me and your dad, and why he left. Your dad had plenty of opportunities to stay closer to home. He chose to remain active in the military because he wanted an escape from us."

"How did you hook up then?"

Justin had always wondered why his parents divorced. This was awful.

"Well, my boy, he was gorgeous. You are the spitting image of him. At first, he wanted me. Chased me like you wouldn't believe. I was pregnant by the time I realized he wasn't comfortable getting close."

"Geez." Justin felt sick. It sounded a lot like his situation.

"I couldn't take it anymore. I told him to find work here and commit to an emotional relationship with me, or we were done. Your dad chose to leave, and you know where that got him. That's why I was so heartbroken when he died. He had his chance, and he lost it."

His mom was crying, and Justin leaned over and hugged her.

"I'm sorry, Mom."

"It's okay. All in the past now."

"So, what do I do?"

"Some things you can change about yourself, but not everything. You two may just not be right for each other. But I'd say it's too early to give up."

"There's more, though. It's about that guy who abducted her. They had a fling that night. She won't tell me everything, but what I do know drives me insane."

"Oh dear. Justin, be careful. Jealousy can ruin even the best of relationships. If you have any doubts, discuss them with her. Don't let it fester, or you'll end up taking it all out on her."

"I'm afraid I already am. I'm punishing her for it, and I can't stop myself," he admitted.

"Here's what you do." She put a hand on his knee. "Put the stupid house chores aside. I have money. Let me pay a neighbor boy to clean the gutters and help with the garden. You take the time to develop your relationship. You've got to understand. Love doesn't grow on its own. It needs a lot of care and attention. Unless you want to let her go right now, you have gotta put in some effort."

Justin desperately wanted to tell her about his inner caveman, how it was taking over like a satanic possession, and he had no idea what to do about it. But he was too ashamed.

"But she makes me crazy. The things she does to my body are unreal. I can't handle it. She's turning me into something I don't want to be."

"You love her. But you fear intimacy. It's not the insane orgasms. It's the vulnerability. It can be terrifying to let someone get that close to you."

"Insane isn't the right word. More like out-of-body experiences."

"I'm happy to hear it. Sex, for most people, is humdrum. Justin, there's more to love than sex. You need to develop an emotional relationship."

"How? I've never been close with anyone."

"You are gorgeous, and I'm sure she wants you like nobody's business. However, if you don't make her fall in love with you, she won't stick around."

"Maybe I don't know what love is."

"You think love is what you have for your car: pride, possession and ownership. But it's so much more. You have to open yourself up to be close to her, and that starts with vulnerability."

"It's like you are asking me to stand in front of a moving truck."

"Until you force yourself past this hurdle, you will suffer and she will suffer. You should count yourself lucky. Most guys would give a lot to be in your shoes and have a passionate girl who wants them as much as she wants you. I'm sure you make your co-workers sick with jealousy. If you throw this away, I promise, you'll regret it for the rest of your life."

"I wanna be able to do to her what she does to me. Wrap her around my finger."

"Now you're talking mind games again, and like I said, those never end well."

"No matter what it means, I have to change. Can I change? Because it doesn't feel like something I even have control over."

"You have to want to change. At twenty-five, you're already stuck in your ways. You need to get unstuck."

"Okay. Well, you sure gave me some things to think about."

"You have a gorgeous, sweet girlfriend sitting above your garage, mooning away for you. You're an idiot if you don't drop all your chores, even your precious car rebuild project, and give her the royal treatment. Love is more important than all the bullshit life throws at us combined. And trust me, if you sit on your laurels, another guy will sweep in and steal her right out from under you, and there won't be a thing you can do about it. And honestly, you'll only have yourself to blame. Stop pushing her away. You're making life miserable for both of you when you don't need to."

Judith never left the house. She didn't have a car, had no friends, and he had her all to himself, just how he wanted it. How the hell was she gonna cheat on him? The thought made all the hairs on the back of his neck stand up.

"Now, go give your honey some loving before she makes you a part of history." She smiled, kissed him soundly on the cheek, and pushed him out the front door.

Chapter 9

Judith and Nicolas

Hey, beautiful.

I'm feeling beautiful this morning.

Why? Because your cop crawled down off his high horse and finally fucked you?

Something like that.

Well, good for you. You don't deserve rejection. I would never reject you.

Like I rejected you?

It's true. You rejected me that night. And I'm a sensitive guy.

Really? You?

I'm sensitive and sweet.

And psycho.

Maybe a bit, but you know why.

Excuses, excuses.

Okay, I'm crazy. Your mom understood, though. Remember how she said she wouldn't bring any charges against me? She would've run away with me, too.

I don't know. My mom looked pretty cozy with your dad.

Change of subject. Why won't you give me a chance?

I've already found the perfect guy.

Well, what makes him so perfect?

He's sweet, loyal, strong, hardworking, and cares for his family. So gorgeous, it's unbelievable, and he treats me like a princess, although I don't deserve it.

I could be a prince with a girl like you.

> You're too needy. I don't like needy. Justin has his shit together, and I love that about him.

I admit it. I am needy. Who wouldn't be after what I went through?

> I get it. It's not fair what happened to you, and I'm sorry you suffered so terribly.

Like I told you in the car, I've turned a corner. Your mom healed me. Took it all: the drowning kink, the need for older women. All of it. Then, life gave me you.

> I'm not yours.

Not yet.

> You are stubborn.

I'm not gonna give up. I can be persistent when I want something.

> Where you knock them out and make them do what you want.

I think about you constantly. I'm becoming consumed by you. Especially now that we've fucked. I'm crazy in love!

> Oh dear. Doesn't sound healthy.

What does it mean when someone says that? What is healthy? Is love not healthy?

> Consuming someone is not healthy.

I don't want to live without you. I know I fucked up. I was having a psychotic break that night and wasn't taking my pills, and Martha's cheating sent me over the edge. Of course, the cops won't care. They don't care about people like me.

> You broke the law. My sister and I went crazy the week my mom went missing.

Seriously, who did it hurt? Martha got to discover her sexuality, and then she met my dad. I saved her life.

> Maybe. But then you tried to kill her. Twice.

I was stupid. But I swear to God, she helped me work through my trauma, and I will never do it again.

> What about what you did to me?

Our crazy lovers' quarrel? See, I believe that was special. It revealed that we were soulmates.

And you pointing a gun at my head and shoving me down to rape me?

Don't remind me. Things got out of hand, I admit. I'm not an evil guy, but I was having a psychotic break. You called me out, beat me up, and got me so riled up. And the whole time I'm thinking, I want this girl so bad. I just couldn't express that. When I opened the door and saw you, my heart fell out of my chest. You are the woman I have always dreamed about. You're tough, sexy, vulnerable, volatile, and so beautiful, you're a goddess and I'm a god. We belong together.

Well, that's sweet. Okay, I'll admit it. When you opened the door, I saw the man I had been obsessively hunting for a week. I matched you to the gorgeous guy in the photo, and I wanted to shove you down to the floor at gunpoint and—

What?

Fuck the daylights out of you.

Now, finally, you're being real with me.

All my anger was fueled into one single point of origin. You.

When you said that my dick was the size of a twig. Traumatizing. A woman has NEVER said that to me before.

I had a real urge to fuck with you, and I'm not sure why.

I triggered your deviant nature from the moment we met. We're soulmates. We were brought together to murder each other, and we immediately fell in love.

No, this is different from what I feel for Justin.

You love him with your conscious self. He is the guy you CHOOSE. But you love me with your unconscious self. I am the guy you DESIRE. You need to decide who you want to be with.

I already made my choice.

Choice not acceptable. You stole my heart, and now you are my life support. I'm saying I can't live without you, and I won't.

That's codependency.

You shouldn't have strangled me. We were supposed to run away together. This is just a speed bump in the story of us.

I can't imagine that being true. I want to be a law-abiding citizen like Justin, and I believe people should pay for their crimes.

None of the stuff I did was my fault. And please don't tell me you're like him. I'll lose my lunch.

You won't take responsibility, but it is your fault.

You are such a hard ass. It makes me so horny. Our death match was the best foreplay EVER. Admit it.

It was hot. Don't think I've ever felt that horny.

I've never seen a woman so aroused. You are like every fantasy I've ever had rolled into one. By the way, the sex video you sent me is to DIE FOR. I'm saving it until I croak. And you better be lying next to me in your grave.

You are a hopeless romantic, aren't you?

Oh yeah. Especially since I found the love of my life.

Well, I knew you'd like it.

You played out my sex fantasy perfectly.

I have one more thing to admit.

I'm listening.

Pulling away from you when you were taking me to the back seat was impossibly hard to do. I wanted to fuck you to death, if that's even a thing. You warped me with that orgasm.

That is the hottest thing a girl has ever said to me.

Which means you are a serious freak.

Can you take a walk or something so that I can call you? I need to hear your voice.

Well, there isn't a goddamn thing to do out here but take a walk.

Poor Belladonna. You're bored out of your mind, aren't you?

Yeah, I am.

Did you think it would be different?

> I don't know what I thought. But now, I'm stuck. I can't move back home. My mom moved in with your dad, and they are like a couple of teenagers, fucking like rabbits and making out in public. It's embarrassing.

It's sweet. I got to know Martha, and what she went through with your dad was horrifying. That cold-hearted asshole never tried to satisfy her in twenty years, not once. She was nearly a 42-year-old virgin.

> It makes me so sad.

Don't worry. I gave her the royal treatment. I satisfied her like you wouldn't believe. My dad is gonna have some big shoes to fill, or else she's gonna be thinking of me between her legs for the rest of her life.

> You are so vain.

I bet Michelangelo was vain. When you're good at something, you earn the right to be vain.

> Well, you are definitely good at sex.

You can't stop thinking of me, can you?

> I'm trying hard not to. I feel—

Possessed?

> That's the word.

Me, too. You need to be honest with me about your feelings. Hiding them or denying them will only make things worse.

> I can't. I'm living with a guy. And he's a guy I desperately want.

I don't know how many times I will have to say this, but he's not the guy for you. I am.

> But I wanna be with him. I confess, you fill me with lust like I have never felt in my life. Your dark, dreamy eyes consume me, and I could stare at your pics forever. You are hypnotizing, like Dracula or something. But you don't make me feel like I can be a good girl.

You mean, I don't make you feel ashamed of who you are. You're like this because of your abuse.

Want someone to give you some value, but how
this guy is going about it will only break your heart.

I hope and pray you are wrong.

Trust me. I'm not.

Chapter 10

Nicolas

Nicolas was finally getting into the swing of his new profession. It was a little tricky. He had to broaden his horizons to include everything and everyone, but as long as he was between someone's legs, he had a vague feeling of satisfaction.

It also made him emotionally unstable and depressed, and triggered horrible memories of Catrina, but he needed to make money. His fellatio skills were to die for, and he was raking in the dough fast, which was a huge incentive.

Nicolas and Belladonna were now in a rhythm. He would make his rounds at the hotels and hook-up sites, do his business, and finish around eleven. Get home, brush his teeth, and wash his mouth for ten minutes to clean out all the juices. Have some dinner, then call Belladonna.

The video sex was nowhere near what it would be in person and was nearly torture, but it was better than nothing. He would stare into those blazing eyes and remember how he felt when he first saw her at the wedding reception and how he stared at her pics endlessly that first week. Even with the long distance, they were insanely adept at getting each other off. He never thought he could want a woman this much, be satisfied by a single person like this.

During the day, he would send her detailed fantasies of what he wanted to do with her, and she would return the favor. It was sexual salvation to have face time with her gorgeous, naked body. Belladonna was slipping into his arms, and he was ecstatic. Things were going so well that he was considering moving up their runaway date. Her loneliness was eating her alive. Thank God the cop turned out to be such a jackass. His stupidity was making this a whole lot easier.

Nicolas had a new customer tonight and hoped he would pay well. Some guy vacationing for the weekend. Nicolas dressed carefully and doused himself in cologne. Some guys were so difficult to please and picky as hell about their blowjob. It was a hundred times easier to get a woman off.

At the hotel, he had a few drinks in the lounge. He didn't mind going down on men, but being slightly drunk took the edge off. Presently, his body and soul were committed to his beautiful Belladonna anyway. Anyone else was simply money in the bank.

The customer was attractive and considerably younger than Nicolas had anticipated, which was unusual. He wanted to have drinks first, which was frustrating because Nicolas wanted to hurry back in time for his video call with Belladonna.

It turned out the guy had a kink. Shit. Nicolas debated. He didn't like cuffs. Having been tied up throughout his childhood, he hated it unless it was with someone he trusted, which, up to this point, was absolutely no one. But the money was good—five hundred for a single hour. In the end, Nicolas caved. It ended up being one of the biggest mistakes of his life.

Two hours later, he was at home in the tub, crying. That guy raped him three times in sixty minutes. It hurt like a bitch, and worse, he felt traumatized. Broken. He made an excuse to Belladonna and lay in the tub, drinking vodka straight from the bottle, feeling worse than he had in years.

Nicolas had been explicit about his limits. The guy wanted to blow him, so he relented but said oral only. No sex. This guy didn't care. First, he sucked him off viciously, then turned him onto his stomach and had his way. Nicolas screamed for him to stop. In reply, the asshole gagged him with a pair of dirty underwear and fucked him even harder.

When his hour was up, he released Nicolas, kissed him on the mouth, and thanked him for a great hook-up. Worse, the guy didn't use a condom. He might have HIV now, for all he knew. He'd have to get tested. Could never go through this again. He was a novice and an idiot. It was up to him to protect himself.

Should he limit his preferences to just women? If he did, he'd lose out on a lot of money. He just had to not be stupid. No cuffs. Ever again.

Belladonna was calling him. Nicolas debated and finally answered.

"Did you fall in love with one of your tricks and forget all about me?"

"Na." He rubbed his tears away and tried to calm his breathing. "Sorry, I had a rough night."

"What happened?" She sounded concerned, which made him feel loved, which, of course, was what he hoped for.

"I was raped." He let out a sob.

"Oh, Nicolas! I'm so sorry, baby. Go to the police!"

"I can't. First, I'm here illegally, so they'd put me in jail. Second, they don't give a shit about prostitutes."

"Fucking assholes. If I were there, I'd go vigilante on him. Can you buy yourself a gun? For protection?"

"That might not be a bad idea," he confessed.

"Are you hurting?" She sounded like she was crying.

"Yeah."

"Jesus. How? You're a strong guy, and I should know. How did he pin you down?"

"I was a dumbass and let him use cuffs. Don't know what I was thinking."

"He better have paid you a fuck ton of cash."

"He did."

"I wish I were there to hold you." She was definitely crying.

"It makes me so happy to know you care about me."

Now he was crying for this fact alone. All he ever wanted was a woman to love him.

"Of course. It breaks my heart to think of your delicious body being used like that. Do you have his last name? I will troll the fuck out of him online if you'd like."

"I don't."

How had he gotten so lucky to find her? She was as sweet as Martha, with a million other bonuses as well.

"I won't even ask for sex tonight, baby. You need to rest and let your heart repair itself."

"I got too greedy for the cash. I'm trying hard to save enough for us to run away."

"Maybe we can find another way."

"I can't think of any unless you plan to receive an inheritance soon."

"Your dad is loaded."

"He wouldn't give me a goddamn thing. Especially after what I did to Martha."

"It's worth a try. Of course, I never see those two. They're like on a permanent vacation."

"My dad is so lucky. His job takes him all over the world, and he's got the love of his life on his arm. Plus, he's rich. It's so unfair."

"Nicolas, I shouldn't say this. I don't know what it means or if it can ever mean anything. But I love you."

A thousand jolts of pure energy rushed through him.

"Belladonna. You have just healed me. Thank you."

"Take care and rest up. We have plenty more nights ahead to share. And don't be an idiot anymore, okay? And buy yourself a gun."

Nicolas hung up and lay back in the cooling water. She said she loved him. Was it real? It could all still change. That cop might pull his head out of his ass and try to make things work. He needed to use this until she was entirely his. But for now, only three months into his game plan, she was already saying the magic words. He'd take that. And he'd run with it.

Chapter 11
Judith

Judith didn't know what had happened the day Justin caught her crying. The same day she had had video sex with Nicolas for the first time, it was as if he knew. He came home, dropped the groceries on the kitchen counter, and then picked her up, taking her to bed.

They made love for hours, and it was so hot and steamy that she forgot all about Nicolas and climaxed again and again. Justin was everything she wanted. He was perfect. She felt guilty for cheating on him and decided to try to pull back from Nicolas. Maybe Justin was starting to realize what he was missing out on.

In the last month, Justin had tried hard. He worked out only four days instead of five, stopped doing chores for his mom, and gave up on the car rebuild because it was so hot in the garage. Now, they were lying under the fan in the bedroom, and she was kissing his chest when she noticed a look in his eye that concerned her.

"What?"

"I—It's nothing."

"No. Tell me."

"I've had a problem for a while and don't know what to do about it."

"What?" Judith stroked him softly across his lower belly in a way that drove him crazy.

"I can't let it go. What happened between you and him."

"Oh."

What the hell should she say?

"I know you aren't being honest with me, and I get it. But I'm so riddled with jealousy, Judith. It's ruining everything."

"We weren't in a relationship yet," she answered cautiously.

"That's why I feel like I can't talk to you about it. I don't have the right to ask."

Judith paused. Justin would never understand the curse or the obsession. How incredible Nicolas was at seducing. He was more than hot and sexy. Nicolas was a real-life incubus. But she had to say something. So, this was why he acted so coldly. Justin was insecure, and the thought tore at her heart. She needed to build him up and convince him that he was the best of the best.

"Justin, listen to me. Nicolas used every trick he had in his arsenal to seduce me and lure me away. He told me he was a class-A home wrecker who gets off on fucking over guys he hates by seducing their women and ruining their relationships. I fear half the reason he seduced me was because I made the mistake of telling him the cop on the phone was my boyfriend."

"I hate that guy so much. The thought of him roaming free makes me homicidal."

"I'll be honest. He got me off and it was dynamite. Imagine being in my shoes. Would it be your fault if a girl handcuffed you and sucked you off like I do?"

"It's not that. It's him. You haven't forgotten about him. I can tell. Means he has a hold on you, so he's between us now."

Justin was right, and God, he better never find out she was talking to Nicolas, or she was dead.

"But I lied to him and told him he failed, which broke his confidence so completely that he uncuffed me from the car. He nearly had sex with me. And yeah, part of me wanted to. He seduced me like the devil himself."

"I can't believe you strangled him."

"All I could think about was getting back to you. I didn't want to give up on my chance with you."

"What did he do to you at the house? It sounded pretty hot and heavy."

"Well, he had me half undressed, cuffed, and my hands above my head, and he went at my body like a fiend. No guy has ever devoured me like that. So, I kissed him because I knew it would make him crazy, and he would find my phone when he pulled my pants down."

"Nicolas tried to rape you. Why didn't you tell the police in your statement?"

"You read that?"

"Of course I did. You made it sound like you two had a fight followed by some crazy make-out session. You downplayed the abduction. At this point, that asshole may not even serve time, which is bullshit."

"My mom wants us to help Nicolas, and I thought maybe I led him on, got him riled up, and made him crazy for me. Guess I took responsibility."

"That's fucking stupid. He's a sex predator. Why do you women all want to cover for him?"

"He's sad, Justin. Heartbreaking, actually. Nicolas is just looking for one woman to love him."

"I can't believe it works. That's the cheesiest pickup line ever. He's only looking to fuck every girl he meets. Especially a hot girl like you. How can you fall for that shit?"

Was Justin right? Was Nicolas manipulative? Judith couldn't answer, so she didn't.

"The bottom line is, I could have taken off with him, but I didn't want to. He restrained me and seduced me, and I still resisted because I wanted you. I choose you."

Judith was so convinced as she said this, she feared how to proceed with Nicolas now. She was playing a dangerous game here. Justin was such a perfect guy, and she was crazy about him. And he was here. Nicolas wasn't and never would be. Of course she would try everything to keep her sweet hero!

Justin nodded and kissed her head.

"I'm just not like Nicolas. I've never played mind games to get laid. It's despicable. And I confess, I'm finding it difficult to be with a hot girl like you. You have no idea what you've done to me, and I never imagined I'd be such a jealous, possessive guy. It's embarrassing."

Judith wanted to tell him that his stupid hot-and-cold mind games were a ploy to make her crazy about him, but she didn't want to piss him off.

"Baby, you are incredible in bed. You are so hot. You make me so horny and get me off so perfectly. I don't want another. The guys I've been with all suck compared to you."

"Except for Nicolas. It's like he's the better bird," he sighed.

"Bird?"

"Remember? Birds of paradise? He's got the better moves. I'm fucked when it comes to him."

"You are crazy."

"Please tell me because I don't get it. What did you ever see in me? I'm a shy, stodgy, super-boring Christian guy from the sticks, and I'm sure no Casanova. I suck at being sexy, I am zero fun, and you could get a hundred times better."

"How can you believe that? Listen to me. Listen!" Judith took his face in her hands. "First, you are gorgeous with your soulful eyes and that iceberg-melting smile. You have a body to die for and so many great moves that I don't know where to start! You're noble, hardworking, reliable, mechanically talented, witty and intelligent. A dreamy gentleman and a natural heartthrob. A passionate and creative lover. Not to mention, lover boy, you are hung like a horse."

Judith fondled his crotch and pushed him over. Justin smiled as he grabbed her bottom, pulled her on top of him and kissed her.

"You're an alpha male, baby. Have I left anything out? And while I love everything about you and worship the ground you walk on, what drew me to you instantly was your integrity. Trying to be a good cop, trying to be a good guy. Don't you realize what you are? I told you that first night. When we met, I struck gold. You are gold, Justin. Solid gold."

"I don't know if I am a good guy. I used to be, but—I don't want to be a disappointment, is all."

"Justin, I am so crazy about you. You could become an ax murderer and I'd still want you."

"You know just what to say to make me feel amazing. It's like you are a mind reader."

"Nicolas doesn't have anything over you. Please don't push me away. If you do, I can't promise I'll stick around. I need love. I have a lot to give between the sheets, so you need to speak my language. Don't reject me. Okay?"

"I stopped replying to your sexting because I can't spend half the night at work thinking about having sex with you. Not because I don't totally love them."

"I'm sorry, Justin. I wasn't trying to make life hard for you. I had no idea. Of course, it hurt me when you didn't reply, but I understand. I'll be more respectful, I promise."

"You can still send them. Just keep it closer to the end of my shift, so I can still focus on my job."

"I had no idea I was that good at turning you on."

"Judith, you are unreal. You're like a Jezebel."

"Well, don't know who Jezebel is, but I'm thrilled to hear it."

Judith kissed him, and they went at it again. And when Nicolas called, she ghosted him. He had to understand. She couldn't give up on Justin. She loved Nicolas, but he was a criminal, and it was impossible to be with him. The video sex had to stop. She needed to commit.

Justin seemed to cheer up after their conversation and allowed her to initiate things when he got home from work. Judith was delighted to have her man back, and she did everything to please him. She even started learning to cook, which his mom was happy to teach her. Things were almost back to normal.

Except. She had led Nicolas on, telling him she loved him—and she did love him. There lay the rub.

She loved two men. Justin was her hot hero, with everything to offer except his heart. No matter how hard she tried, he felt distant and out of reach.

Nicolas was a bad guy, but with a heartbreaking backstory and a soul filled with love for her. She wanted Justin desperately but felt a deadly passion for Nicolas that she couldn't understand, and it scared her. Now, she feared there would be consequences for this travesty against his heart.

Chapter 12

Judith and Nicolas

Things have changed between us and I don't like it.

Not sure what you mean.

Yes, you do. You're fucking your cop again, aren't you?

Well, he is trying suddenly, so I have to try too.

No, you don't.

It's called making a relationship work.

What you two have isn't a relationship.

But I want it to be!

It's been months since I last saw you. This is a living hell. We need to meet.

That's impossible.

I have an idea.

Okay.

I'll call you tonight to talk about it.

We need to stop this. I can't have sex with you anymore. Not when he's trying with me. I'm not the sort of girl to be untrue.

You're tempting me to do something I don't wanna do.

What?

I have a friend. Name of Jo-Jo. He's always had a hard-on for killing a cop. Might send him up your way and give your boyfriend a visit. I don't like to threaten, but I can't have you cut me off like this.

I think you're a liar.

You'll never know for sure.

Don't you dare hurt him.

You're so loyal. When I replace him, you'd better be as loyal to me.

Why can't you find some nice hooker? We can never be together!

Nonsense. You know why. We are meant for each other.

I felt that way about Justin. I never wanted anything like I wanted him.

Why? I don't understand.

I want to be the kind of girl a guy like him would choose. It's like wanting to win a trophy, but a thousand times better. If he doesn't want me, I think I will kill myself.

Can't bear you talking about him like that. You need to feel that way about me. I've always wanted someone to be obsessed with me.

I'm not obsessed with Justin.

Well, I'm obsessed with you.

I do love you. You get me and Justin doesn't. But I feel like I have to be with him. He pulls me to him. He's so warm, and his body is so hot. I get goosebumps just thinking about him. I'm always cold, and he's the guy who can always warm me up.

What do you mean?

Justin says his body temperature runs high, and it totally does. He's like a furnace. He told me that if he could, he would move to Alaska. Says that's where he truly belongs. I guess he even inherited some land from his grandpa with a hunting cabin out in the backwoods, like near Anchorage. He's been hunting up there. Calls it paradise.

Alaska? Who can survive in that shithole?

Justin has a million talents. He can fix anything, cuts down trees, grows a garden every year, hunts and skins his own game, and crafts arrows for his bow. Is a crack shot. Can navigate by the stars and go camping in deep winter. It's incredible how talented he is. He's an Eagle Scout and says he could live off the land if he had to.

Wow, a real man's man.

Something like that.

Almost makes me feel jealous, except that I KNOW
he's not the guy for you. I am.

But I've never wanted any guy like I want him.
It's almost painful.

You want him because he doesn't want you, and
you love the challenge. Look at the way he treats
you.

He was cold, but he's trying now. So, I'm
happier.

It won't last. You screw up a tiny bit, and he will go
back to being the same asshole. I would never do
that to you. I would lay down my life for you and
give you everything you wanted.

You are a dark prince, Nicolas, some insanely
hot antihero. But I want to be with the real
hero.

You have to choose. You can't string me along.

I need time.

That's such bullshit. You're just weak and easily
manipulated.

That's not true.

From where I'm standing, it is.

What do you want from me? I'm stuck in his
house, living with his family. He's now really
trying. I think it's because he talked to his mom,
and his mom warned him he would lose me.
Now I feel even guiltier.

Fuck him. You need to live for you, not him.

Worse, he confronted me about what we did
in the car. He's jealous, which is why he has
been so cold. He's been punishing me, and I
can see that now.

Awesome. I hope you told him the truth. I gave you
the best orgasm ever and he's fucked.

I did tell him, but I also reminded him how I
incapacitated you to get back to him. I have
to reassure him right now. I have no choice. I
still can't decide between the two of you, and

I need you to understand. Please don't make
me block you. I can't decide and I'm in hell.

Fine. Fuck your cop for now. But I'm right. He won't
change. One bit of stress, and he's back to being a
coldhearted asshole. You need passion. You need
me. Not him. ME.

You're being too pushy.

I have to be. You'll never leave him otherwise.

But I don't want to leave him!

I feel like you are using me. Cause you're bored
and lonely. I feel used.

Maybe a bit? But I also do love you. But I also
love him!

He treats you like he does his car. You are prestige.
He's just another male with ego issues. His id is all
fucked up. You know, Freud?

Think so?

He objectifies you. You are the hot girl who wants
him, which gets him off, but he doesn't want to get
close to you. It's so obvious.

Then why does he seem so sad?

Because he's not making you happy, and that
means you'll leave him, and when you do, he'll go
back to being a lonely loser like he was before.

You are a terrifying study of human beings.

Maybe it's from knowing too many shrinks or having
to psychoanalyze my child-molesting nanny and my
abusive mother. I know your cop, and so I can
promise he won't change because he will never
see that he has a problem.

I'm depressed now.

I'm sorry. Please know that there is someone who
loves you for who you are. That person is me.

You are such a sweetheart.

He hates your power over him because he's used to
having all the power. Trust me, he'll find a way to
break you eventually and get you under his thumb.

You see what I've been going through.

But is it enough to make you open your eyes?

Maybe.

I want to be close to you now. Can we fuck?

I just said that we shouldn't, didn't I?

Please, please, please, please, PLEASE!

Oh my God. Fine, give me a few minutes.

And will you discuss my plan with me tonight?

Of course I will.

I can't wait to see you again.

It almost feels like you were a dream I once had. No longer real.

Oh, I'm real, alright. And counting the minutes until we can be together. You've made me completely obsessed. I'm warped and falling apart at the seams. I need you to survive.

Please don't make me the reason you fall apart.

I've thought of nothing else all day but our first night in the car. You broke my record. I've never gotten a woman off as fast as you. Was that even one minute? You were so ready for it. I'd like to think it's because of how you feel about me.

Don't take all the credit. I'm easily aroused. When Justin goes down on me, I have orgasms in my fingers and toes. They haven't created words to describe his mad skills.

I don't believe you. I think you love to torture me and make me jealous.

Okay. Justin has never gone down on me. I don't think he could hold out long enough.

I knew it. You picked the wrong guy.

You have it all over him, and I can't lie. You are phenomenal.

Hallelujah! I love being the best.

Don't remind me. That memory is pure torture.

I'm never gonna stop reminding you now. And that was only a taste. After a full ten minutes of exploring your lady garden, I will make you so crazy that you won't remember your name.

You are such a monster. My poor imagination can't handle this much fantasy. And my poor fingers hurt from masturbating.

You're so cute. Why were you trying to make me jealous?

Was I?

Yes, obviously.

Well, maybe a bit. It does get you crazy hot, right?

Yeah. But you have no idea what you're playing at. I'm gonna make you mine if it's the last thing I do.

Chapter 13

Justin

It was mid-July, and Justin was getting a plate of food for Judith at his annual summer church party, flushed with heat and dizzy with joy. Every guy here, married and single, was furtively checking Judith out, and she didn't even care. They were at the city park, baking in the sun, so naturally, Judith wore the shortest shorts and the skimpiest tank top imaginable, oblivious to the disapproving glares of the wives and girlfriends. She didn't flirt with anyone and kept her eyes on him, her arm around his waist. Justin felt like a million bucks.

His partner, Jones, who attended the same church, was talking to her, trying to keep his eyes somewhat respectfully off her plunging cleavage. Even the women were ogling her.

"So, Judith, what do you want to do with your life?"

"Um, well, I think it would be awesome to be a cop," she admitted.

"Does Justin know?"

"I've mentioned it. He says I'm an ace with a gun."

"Jones, she's a natural. I'm not lying. She also has kick-ass moves from years in Karate and Taekwondo. Got me on the ground. Swept my legs right out from under me on our first date."

"I would've loved to see it," Jones chucked, "being a cop isn't all it's cracked up to be. It can be a boring, repetitive job."

"Well, my first choice was to be a model. But my dad blew that for me by marrying a woman who spends all his money. So now, it's real life or nothing," she sighed.

Her phone buzzed. Judith glanced down at it and frowned.

"I'm gonna take a walk around. Be back in a few."

Judith got up and turned to get off the picnic bench, bent over to fix her sandal, displaying her shapely ass and long tan legs. Jones made the gesture of his eyes exploding, and Justin grinned approvingly. Judith walked away, oblivious.

"Holy shit. I have a full-blown boner. How are you keeping that hottie content out here in Timbuktu?"

"It's not easy. We've had our share of problems."

"Nothing a hot roll in the hay can't fix, though," Jones cautioned.

"It's hard to handle. She's needy, Jones."

"What do you mean, needy?"

"I'm letting a ton of chores slide to spend time with her and it's stressful."

"Trust me. A lady like Judith? It's all for the greater good."

"And she wants to have sex like every day."

"Of course she does. She's a passion diva who deserves the royal treatment. You aren't the man for her, let me tell you. You are too stuffy and insecure, my friend."

"I want to be," Justin protested.

"Well, you better acclimate fast, cause she'll be gone in a hot minute if you can't deliver. Sticks out like a sore thumb around here. Do you see the hate she's getting from the ladies?"

"Who cares? Judith doesn't seem to."

"Guess there's no point in bringing her to church. These gals will judge the fuck out of her and snub her like crazy."

"A bunch of jealous bitches."

Justin waved at a boring blonde girl he had dated last year, and she gave him a scathing look. Yeah, everyone hated Judith. He loved the attention he was getting as a result.

"I must say, the guys around the station have said you've been sharing her hot selfies. Is that cool? I mean, is she okay with it?"

Justin shrugged and Jones frowned.

"Salviati, you need to quit it. I am not cool with the disrespect of women. It makes us guys look bad."

"She's got hot pics online, too. I didn't think she would care."

"Well, I beg to differ. Judith's a sweetheart who, for some reason, is hung up on you. She doesn't deserve your disrespect. If I hear about it again, I will say something to HR."

Justin flushed. He didn't like feeling chastised, especially by his partner.

Jones tactfully changed the subject.

"Who's she talking to? Looks intense."

"Don't know." Justin studied Judith. She did look intense.

"Man, I would be all over that shit. Could be another guy."

"I am concerned. My mom says she texts someone all morning, and I am often away. When I'm home, I'm usually busy."

"You are a goddamn idiot if you let her slip through your fingers in order to fix one of those junkers in your garage."

"I never imagined being in a live-in relationship would be so time-intensive."

"Dude, you have a lot to learn. What did you expect? That she'd be like your mama? At your beck and call, but gone the moment you swish her away?"

"You treat me like an adolescent." Justin glared.

"Well, don't act like one. When you have a woman in your life, you put her first. Case closed. Or she will happily replace you. Trust me. I've fucked up enough relationships to know what it takes to make one work."

Justin watched Judith pace between trees, texting madly. Alarm set in. Who was she talking to?

After the picnic, they headed home. Judith lowered her chair, opened the window, and put her feet on the dashboard. She was breathtaking. Justin pulled out his phone and took her photo.

"What?" She squinted up at him.

"I want to remember this. The way you look right now."

Smiling sweetly at him, her eyes were sad, and he wondered why.

"Who were you talking to earlier?"

"Oh, no one in particular."

"You seemed bothered."

"I'm over it now. Your friends are all nice." She added.

"Well, they are all gonna be nice to you, that's for sure." He laughed.

"Why's that?" She frowned.

"You are the hottest girl most of these dorks will ever meet. It's practically the same as having a celestial encounter."

"Oh." Judith flushed, embarrassed. "I didn't think about that."

"Don't worry. You make me feel amazing around these eggheads."

"Anything for you, mister policeman." She gazed at him with an adoring smile that melted his heart.

Lately, Justin had gone all out and tried like hell to force himself to believe all the hot things she had said about his awesome moves. Realized his mom was right. He was low on self-esteem, which was probably why he worked out so hard to have a perfect body and overcompensated at his job. He had always been jealous of guys who had game with girls, so her encounter with Nicolas was his worst nightmare.

Judith had returned to sexting him occasionally. It was pleasing, and when he came home, she was waiting to crawl into bed with him. He worked hard on keeping his violent lust from lashing out. He couldn't bear for her to discover that he wasn't the hero she believed him to be. Let his twisted fantasies fuel his hard-ons. They were just fantasies, after all. He was starting to feel like he could restrain himself.

However, Judith loved to goad him. She'd wake him up with oral sex, get him ninety percent there, then take off to throw in a load of laundry, and act oblivious when she returned. Then ten minutes later surprise him in the shower, and suck him off until he collapsed to the floor.

Or even more perverse, come up behind him while he was bent over under the hood of his car, covered in grease up to his elbows, slip both hands down the front of his jeans, and masturbate him as he clung to the motor, shuddering and groaning. When he was about to climax, she'd walk away, gesturing with her finger for him to follow. He'd race to clean up and rush upstairs, so crazed with lust that by the time he'd find her in bed, naked, on all fours messing around on her phone, ass facing the door, he'd fuck her like a wild animal and finish in about twenty seconds.

If she only knew what she was doing by tempting him like this. Forcing him to his knees day and night to plead for strength to fight the devil. And his hunger was growing. He had started leaving for work early so he could park behind the dumpster, watch violent porn and get new ideas to fuel his fantasies as he felt the corruption spread.

When it grew dark, they jogged together, and then she stayed up late to help him organize his garage. She urged him to buy an AC unit, which turned out to be the best investment ever. Why was he such an idiot? He should have bought one years ago. They listened to music as he worked while she tried to get him to dance to a few tunes, which he refused, much to her disappointment. Then someone started messaging her. Again.

Justin saw her plop onto the couch, her face almost sad. It wasn't her mom, and it wasn't Lizzy. Her friends were busy with life and love, so it wasn't one of them. Suddenly, in the pit of his stomach, he knew, and he didn't even know how. It was Nicolas fucking Winters.

Desperately, he tried to control himself. Was there a way to unlock her phone? How could he find out for sure? This was so hard. He wanted to trust her but had no idea how. Should he ask? He would ask. He had to. Finally, she pocketed her phone and joined him.

"Same person you were talking to earlier?" He tried to sound nonchalant.

"Yeah." She waved her hand. "Just a friend from school."

"Which one?" He hoped he didn't sound too curious.

"A guy named Ethan. Bugs me occasionally."

"You were giving off intense vibes talking to him."

"He has a lot of drama."

Then she changed the subject and excused herself to go to the bathroom in the apartment.

Justin pulled out his phone and scrolled through her Facebook friends list until he found Ethan Fender. Justin clicked on his profile. He went to her high school. He had no pictures at all, not even a profile pic. Justin searched for him in conjunction with the high school's name. Nothing came up.

He didn't exist. Ethan didn't exist. Which meant Judith was lying to him. If she lied about this, what else was she lying about? He shot off a friend request to Nicolas fucking Winters. Hopefully, he'd take the hint that Justin was onto him. But knowing that psychopath, he wouldn't care.

Justin felt his heart sink into his intestines. Things had been fantastic the last month, but this was bullshit. If she was in contact with him, she was aiding and abetting a criminal. He couldn't have that. Justin raised the walls around his heart once again, and this time, they were going nowhere.

Chapter 14

Judith and Nicolas

How's my lovely Belladonna this morning?

Fucking miserable.

Why?

You were right. I must have done something wrong because he won't talk to me again. He's playing hot and cold, but it's like the dead of winter around here. What happened? What did I do?

My sweet girl, you did nothing. Please believe me. This guy is an asshole. I'm so glad he's showing his true colors. For a moment there, you had me worried.

So, like, for a few weeks he was all over me, but lately he's been sleeping in his garage. For instance, I can go two days without even seeing him. I try texting him. No reply. What should I do?

I've already told you. Leave.

This is so hard. From the moment I first met that heroic cop, I wanted him so bad. This is hell. And it's weird. Instead of sleeping with me, I think he hangs out in his garage and watches porn cause I heard sex screams the other night when I walked by the door. Sounded like rape kink which is impossible. Justin is way too clean-cut.

What a creepy fuck. If he's throwing you over for some online pussy he's a moron.

Usually, when a guy tries to dump me, I can seduce him back into my arms. But this time I can't. He's like in full protection mode. Even his mom is acting weird to me.

These people are a bunch of hicks. Get the fuck out of there and make plans to join me.

> I don't know. I don't want to give up on him yet. Maybe there's some way to talk to him, figure out what I've done wrong.

You're thinking about this too hard. He's a loser, honey. Kick him to the curb where he belongs. He'll never understand you like I do.

> He has gone completely cold—not hot and cold, just cold. And I'm afraid it's because I've been too pushy.

Tell me how you've been pushy. I want to imagine it all.

> I send him sexy pics, like very hot nudes.

Hotter than the ones you send me?

> God, no. I let you explore my lady garden, lover boy. Never done that before.

I feel so privileged.

> Justin is into soft core at most, and I respect that. But I do wanna be his sex fantasy. I mean, is that wrong? To want to drive a man wild and outdo all of his exes?

Hell no. You are so perfect for me. I love your sexy, competitive nature. And it's totally sweet and thoughtful. It shows how committed you are to your man.

> Not trying to bug him. Just rile him up a bit so when he gets home from a long, boring night at work, he's ready, and I'm ready, and it's so intense. We discussed it, and he asked me to send them at the end of his shift, which I did. But now he doesn't answer any of my texts, not even about groceries. Maybe he's blocked me.

Anyone with a dick wouldn't do that. You're beyond gorgeous. He's a fucking idiot.

> He's over me. I'm too hot for him. God, I knew this. From day one, I fucked up his perfectly organized life. Perhaps he thought he wanted me, but now he realizes he hates being with me. It makes me hate myself.

Your cop is pathetic.

He's married to his job and his routine. I'm in
the way a lot of the time. And if he's the
jealous type, which he told me he is, then I'm
royally fucked.

You said he's a goody church boy?

Totally.

Well, he's probably never had sex with a hot girl like
you, and he doesn't know how to handle it. He
can't love you and fuck you at the same time. He's
got to choose one or the other. There are a lot of
guys like this. They objectify women and treat them
like shit. And there's a place where they typically
end up. It's called prison. Justin is showing all the
signs of a misogynist.

How so?

He doesn't give you any freedom. He plays mind
games. He's possessive and controlling. I think he's
abusive. And clearly, he can't handle your feminine
wiles. You need to get the fuck away from him.
Seriously.

Well, that shouldn't be too hard. He won't even
notice if I'm gone.

You'll be doing him a favor. He might be down in
that garage jerking off to rape scenarios cause
that's what he wants to do to you. You have no
idea who this guy really is.

You're wrong. Justin is a good guy. He's
practically a virgin in bed. Can't handle
anything and isn't into the slightest bit of kink.
He comes in under three minutes every time. I
love to tease. It's fucking impossible to tease
this guy, because he comes so fast.

He is totally not the right guy for you. I can hold out
forever.

You couldn't hold out in the car.

Don't remind me. That was a one-time thing! You
told me that night you were aggressive in bed. I
fantasize about this all the time now about what
you will do to me when we're finally together. I've
never been seduced. I'm so excited.

Dear sweet Casanova, I will blow your mind as
well as your mighty oak. Trust me. You think you
have hot skills? You have met your match with
me.

I can't wait to see you again.

Don't know how that could ever happen.

When we do finally get to sleep together, it will be epic. I'm obsessed with my fantasies of you and me.

What is it you like about me? Is it just my tits? Or my face, or what?

I don't have enough time to list all of the things I LOVE about you. Your strong spirit and sassy, rebellious nature. Your brilliant eyes that shine with passion and love. Your coy smile and fun-loving personality. Your take-no-prisoners, no-bullshit approach to everything, except for that fucking loser you're living with. He's your kryptonite, my love.

You haven't even mentioned my body.

I'm getting there. Yeah, I'm so sexually attracted to you it's almost frightening. I have never felt this way about anyone. I didn't think it was possible to want one person this badly. And your body. Christ. I could go on and on. The bottom line is that you are perfect for me. There are a lot of hot girls in this world, but only one YOU. I can feel that our souls used to be a single entity, like the Greeks believed. We are soulmates, you and I, and we belong together.

No guy has ever said they like those things about me.

Because you've only been with assholes.

Yeah. This sucks.

Why?

I wish you weren't a criminal and a

prostitute.

Oh. I've told you already. It's only temporary.

But being a felon isn't.

Well, they will have to prove that in court.

True. I do love you, Nicolas. I think I love you more than Justin. But somehow his rejection makes me crazy for him. I wish I could just leave him and stop putting myself through this torture, but from the moment we met, he has felt like the center of gravity. I want his approval and love so bad. It's toxic, I know.

He seems that way because he's an alpha male with an ego the size of his dick. Sure, he demands all of the attention because he's a huge buff dude, and yeah, I'll give it to him. Justin is pretty hot, but that doesn't make him a good guy. His hero complex is a dead giveaway.

Of what?

He wants to be fucking worshiped. That's not a good guy.

You help to clear my head. Thank you so much.

Always. Ugh. I gotta run.

More tricks?

I can't wait until I'm done with this sex work gig. I never thought I'd say this, but I'm getting sick of going down on people. I swear to God, people have the worst hygiene. It's unreal how bad some of my tricks stink. Even the women!

You poor guy. Well, think of me when you're down between their legs.

Oh, trust me. You are ALL I think about. I LOVE LOVE LOVE YOU!

Chapter 15

Nicolas

It was a dark and stormy night when Nicolas discovered something he needed badly to help him cope with the growing stress of his job and his Belladonna obsession.

Heroin.

It started innocently enough. Plenty of prostitutes used, and dealers were all over that shit looking for new customers. He didn't find a gun, but he did find his way into a drug house, where he got high off illegal drugs for the first time in his life. For hours, he was able to forget everything. All his needs and wants, his horrifying childhood, and his endless quest for love were all consumed by a feeling of empty bliss. Nicolas was an instant addict.

Now, he watched his savings deplete faster than he would have liked. He wanted to escape with Belladonna, but he also desperately needed an escape from the triggering effects of being a sex worker right now.

Belladonna still gave him what he wanted, but her heart wasn't on offer. She was obsessed with her cop for the moment. He wondered if he should do the takeaway. Play hard to get. It seemed to work so well on his girl by the cop, which was sad. Then he realized that would fail. All he had was his ruthless ability to bug her day and night. He had to focus on what he had.

He shared his plan with her, suggesting she speak to Martha and Erik to convince them to go on a Christmas vacation in Cabo San Lucas. He asked her to ensure they thought it was all their idea. Belladonna figured it wouldn't work. Justin didn't even have a passport, yet Nicolas continued to push. He had to see his Belladonna soon, or he would go insane. Finally, she relented. Martha and Erik were game, so now a plan was in place. He would have to wait months, but the thought of seeing her again gave him something to hold on to.

Nicolas laughed heartily when Justin sent him a friend request, which he readily accepted. It was awesome that he figured it out. He tried to think of a way to use it to his advantage, but nothing came to mind—until the night Justin messaged him.

> I know who this is. I advise you to stay the fuck away from my girl.

What should he do? He didn't want Belladonna to suffer any consequences, so Nicolas decided to bluff him.

> I don't know what you're talking about. Justin, is it? So, you're her boyfriend? Judith and I are just old schoolmates.

> What year did you graduate?

Shit. He should have done some research. He racked his brain to recall how old Belladonna was and then fired off a random year.

> Nope. You're a liar. I checked for you in that graduating year. Nothing. How do you have the gall to contact her? After what you did to her?

> You've got the wrong guy.

> Nicolas fucking Winters. Listen closely. You need to stay away. Got it? She is not yours, and she never will be. She's mine. She chose me. So, fuck off back to the loony farm and leave her alone.

Wow. Justin was a real piece of shit. He acted as if he owned her. There was no point in bluffing now. Nicolas couldn't resist.

> She's not yours, and she can do as she damn well likes.

> I knew it was you. We will find you.

> I doubt you and your cop buddies can pull your heads out of your collective ass.

> I'll have you jailed for insulting a police officer.

> Cops. You gotta love them. They are such great comic relief.

> I want you to tell me now. What is the nature of your relationship?

> Do you really want to know? Be careful what you wish for.

Judith texts you day and night.

> Well, since you are doing such a shit job making her happy, it's only inevitable.

Has she said that?

> And a whole lot more. You need to give it up. You are not the right guy for this darling girl.

Are you in a relationship? Friends? What?

> Do you think a girl can handle just being friends with me? I am a seducer—the best. You might as well roll over and hand her to me because I will get her in the end.

I can't wait to find you and wring your neck.

> Good luck with that. Meanwhile, here's a little something. Imagine who's getting off on the other end of this.

Nicolas sent Justin the video of him jerking off with plenty of sexy hysterics and crying out her name, which Belladonna loved. Justin didn't reply for a long time. Nicolas texted maliciously.

> Maybe you are getting it on with my dick too. Belladonna sure did. Made her come so hard. Like it? There's plenty more where that came from.

You're a pervert and a degenerate. My girl would never fall for a criminal like you.

> Criminal? Ouch.

You belong behind bars. I won't stop until we remove you from decent society.

> You are so fucking self-righteous. I can't fathom what she ever saw in you. I've warned Belladonna that you will only break her heart, and from what I'm hearing, you are well on your way.

Her name is Judith.

> I gave her a special name, and she loves it—just as she loves everything I do for her.

I'll confront her. See if you are full of shit.

Do it. Please! I promise she will immediately walk out that door if you confront her.

I can't wait to tear you apart.

Of course you can't! Cop. You're just another bully in a world full of cocksucking bullies. I bet you boys go down on each other all night long. Does Belladonna know?

I'll make her confess.

Until then, be careful. When the fox is away, the mice do play.

Until I squash you beneath my boot.

You can't handle her vixen charms. Think you can control her with mind games, play hot and cold, and reject her? You are such a fucking loser. Let her go and be with someone who gets her, speaks her language, and doesn't need to break her spirit to feel like a man. And yes, she tells me everything, you misogynistic piece of shit, so I know how you treat her.

When I find you, and I will find you, I'm going to make you suffer like you can't imagine.

You're such a hard ass. If only your dick had that sort of constitution. I hear you can't hold out for more than three minutes. Poor Belladonna.

Man, you are so dead.

I get your obsession with her. I do. Belladonna could get a monk to forsake his vows. But you barely scratch the surface of satisfying that femme fatale. She needs a real lover, not some loser hick with no game. She needs me.

You are a perverted little shit who has to abduct a woman to get her to fuck you. I live for the day when I'll see you dragged away in chains.

Bring it on, you stupid cop. You can't touch me.

Judith will have hell to pay if what you say is true about the two of you.

Don't you dare hurt her.

I'll more than hurt her. I'll break her when I tear you out of her heart for good.

And replace me with you?

I'm the better man. She calls me her hero.

You are so fake. There's nothing genuine about
you, and you know it.

At least I'm not a criminal on the run. I can't wait to
find you and extradite your ass back to Utah. You
will pay for fucking things up for Judith and me and
for everything else you've done.

Maybe so. But know this. You will lose her.
Belladonna is my soulmate. We love each
other. You've already proven that you don't
deserve her and never will.

Soulmates? What a bunch of bullshit. Your—

Nicolas logged off. He couldn't handle the bastard anymore. Why had he done that? He was an idiot! Could they track him through his fake Facebook account? Hopefully not. Was this a pissing contest between two guys over the same girl? No. Not for him. He loved Belladonna with everything he had. The cop needed to go.

Then, Nicolas contemplated it further. This would make the cop grow colder. It was perfect. Now he was in between them in bed, the way he fantasized so often now. Justin would take his angst out on Belladonna, which would only serve to drive her further into his arms. Perfect.

Chapter 16

Judith

Martha and Erik loved the idea of a family vacation for Christmas. Judith passed the idea on to them, but she was terrified. She had been walking a fine line for the past six months. Nicolas was now dangerously obsessed and demanding, and she had a part-time job satisfying and talking to him. Justin had been working nonstop, and he withdrew into his shell during their limited time together. She stopped sexting him because he was so remote that there seemed to be no point. He cringed when she touched him. Passive-aggressive was an understatement.

Her mind was in constant turmoil. She loved Justin and yearned for him day and night, but he was so far away. She wished she could tell him about Nicolas and have him put an end to the stalking. A part of her did love Nicolas, but he was unstable. His obsession with her was too intense, even for her to handle.

How had she allowed this to happen? Judith felt completely at the mercy of forces beyond her control. If Justin had never pushed her away from the beginning, she would have told him about Nicolas immediately. But now it was too late.

Worse yet, depression consumed her, and she had no idea how to address it. Spending all this time alone, trapped in an empty apartment, Judith found her mind wandering far too often into the past, where darkness loomed. She became aware of deeper layers of pain.

Judith had always known she was molested at thirteen by the father of another contestant. However, she recently remembered other events from her past. A gymnastics coach when she was only eight. He couldn't keep his hands off her. Her heart couldn't handle it. The memories were horrifying and agonizing beyond all belief.

And then, remarkably, Nicolas redeemed himself from being a chaotic, obsessive presence in her life. He was the only person in the world she could confide in about her trauma. He listened for hours. Sweet and caring, she loved him so deeply. Nicolas encouraged her to talk to him, making her feel secure. Night after night, they burned the midnight oil, sharing their experiences of abuse.

Rehashing her horrid memories over the phone, Nicolas consoled her as she cried, like some dark knight in shining armor. And where was Justin? Sleeping, working and keeping busy. Nicolas was right. The moment Justin faced any stress, he shut himself off from everyone.

Why couldn't she take the best qualities of these two guys and merge them? She loved Justin's goodness. He was a hard worker who cared for the people in his life. However, he was cold and difficult to communicate with, and he didn't even like her, let alone love her. Nicolas was passionate and caring, emotionally and sexually aware, but he was also unstable and obsessive. The depth of his desire for her scared her, and she couldn't imagine a life with him. He would consume her.

Soon, all of this would come to a head. Nicolas wanted to meet, and once she had sex with his actual body, she didn't think she would be able to fake a life with Justin anymore. Their video sex was addictive. She hadn't had sex with Justin since July and had no idea how to touch him now. It was as if he had a force field around him. She almost wondered if he had found out about Nicolas. What else could inspire such a level of cruel coldness?

Judith heard Justin enter the apartment. He had spent the entire evening working on his mom's house. She got up and went to greet him, but he stared straight past her.

"You want to go grab some dinner? I'd love to take a ride in your hot rod." She smiled to warm him up.

"Uh, I'm exhausted." And he looked tired, too.

"Okay." She nodded, disappointed, wanting to come clean. Explain why she let this get so out of hand with Nicolas. Explain that she was lonely and struggling with emotional issues from her trauma. But she tried to tell him about it once, and he didn't seem to hear her.

"Justin," she started.

"Huh?"

He looked sullen, and she knew somehow that he suspected. God, she wanted to die. This was her fault. His anger and coldness were all on her.

"Please come back to me," she pleaded.

"I'm right here."

"No, you're not. You've been gone for months."

"I told you when we met. Working overtime kicks my ass."

"I'm not talking about that. I understand you're tired, and I try to do everything possible to make your life easier. I don't bother you or sext you. Keep quiet when you're asleep. Wanna rip your clothes off you, but I restrain myself." She hid a sad smile.

"Vacation season sucks, but soon I'll be going back to normal hours. So, you should start seeing more of me."

He spoke coldly. How could she possibly thaw him out? He stood in a cop stance, arms folded across his chest, trying to create distance. Why had she pursued this guy? From the beginning, he had pushed her away. What was wrong with her? She needed to gather her belongings and leave. What was stopping her? Should she try to explain herself to him? Was it even worth it?

"I've been going through a lot lately." Tears stung her eyes. "I have no one here. Especially not you." She was crying now.

Justin stared down at her, disbelieving and distrusting, and she wanted to die.

"I'm sure you have someone special who is willing to listen to your endless bullshit."

He said evenly, and she knew he had found out. It was over. Only a matter of time before he dumped her.

"The only one I want is you." She said through trembling lips.

"Really? It's kinda hard to believe that."

"Believe what you want. It's the truth."

Judith couldn't see through her blurry eyes as she headed for the front door. Where was she going? The sky was dark and stormy and she had no car. She no longer left the apartment, barely recognizing the person she had become—a shut-in.

"Where are you going? Need to message someone?" Justin inquired nastily as he tossed his keys onto the counter.

She had to leave him, or he might end up hitting her. Justin manifested this same rage the night she escaped from Nicolas when she realized he had anger issues. He hated her. Despised her. Then why didn't he kick her out?

"I need to get away from you," Judith cried and headed outside, down the steps, sobbing until her sides ached. An autumn gale whipped around her as she gazed up at their apartment, wondering what to do. There wasn't a single person who would understand.

All alone and trapped, Justin ensured that the only person she could rely on was Nicolas. If only he realized it was he who had pushed her to this. More hopeless than she had ever felt, Judith unlocked her phone and messaged her only friend in the world.

Chapter 17

Judith and Nicolas

I need you.

I'm here.

I can't take this anymore.

What's he doing now?

He knows. Somehow, he knows!

Yeah, he does.

Wait. How does he know?

Because you must have tipped him off. He friended Ethan a few months ago and called me out.

What?!!!!

I didn't want to stress you out. Let me tell you, I was freaked out. I tried to bluff him, but it didn't work.

WTF!? Why didn't you tell me!?

Sorry. I'm telling you now, aren't I?

What should I do?

I have an idea. Send him the sex video you made for me. You are so fucking hot, he'll drop dead from jerking off too hard. Then he'll no longer be a problem.

I would rather die. I wanna be his good girl!

Never gonna happen. You're too much of a slut like me.

This is hell. No wonder he won't come near me anymore. He acts like he wants to murder me. I can't touch him or talk to him. It's useless.

I find it hot that another guy would be trying to steal you from me.

Why? Wouldn't you be jealous?

Hell yeah. It's a common kink, one I've developed from all this torture. I never saw myself as the cuckold kind of guy, but life will surprise you. Do you think you could film you two having sex? I'd love to watch you fuck your cop. Maybe it's because I've never wanted a woman I couldn't have right this second. It drives me crazy. I'd also like to see my competition in action.

 Hell no.

What, afraid I might kill myself from boredom? Think I can survive watching all three minutes of your vanilla sex.

 Like I told you, he hasn't touched me since July. HE DOESN'T WANT ME ANYMORE. Now, I don't know if he ever did.

Even if he's pissed about us. What kind of guy rejects your luscious body? I think you are trying to make me feel better.

 I wish I were. No. He just hates my guts.

Seriously, leave him. Now.

 Maybe I should. Since the night he saved me in that canyon, I've gotten serious vibes from him like he represses a lot of anger. Rage.

That's concerning.

 Sometimes, I'm scared of what he will do to me. Like, I feel that he wants to hurt me. Especially right now.

I wouldn't get anything done if I lived with you. We'd hit the sheets like marathon runners.

 Sounds wonderful.

All the more determined to save you now. You don't deserve this.

 I'm so depressed. Now that he knows, should I leave him? He'll never forgive me.

You need to leave him. The sooner, the better.

 How?

Walk out the front door, my love, and Uber it back to Martha's. Call me from there, and we'll start making plans.

What if he follows me and begs me to come back?

Tell him to fuck off.

I can't think about this. So stressful. I've never cheated on a guy, never been with a guy who hates me but won't let me go. How do I deal with this situation? Arg!

All I can think about is our special reunion. I have it all planned out for how I'm gonna drown you in pleasure.

I have to say, it's all I have to live for right now. Don't want to go back inside the house knowing that he knows. But I'm cold and standing out here in my socks.

If I were him, I'd be so horny and doing everything in my power to win you back. This guy has no game. Somehow, he thought you would be an easy conquest. Play a few mind games, and you'll be panting for him by the end of the week. He doesn't realize that playing hard to get will backfire like it did here. A girl like you will have guys fighting for her all life long. He's not up to the challenge. I will be. When you're my girl, I am happy to beat my competition off with a stick. And if there's a piece of ass you particularly want, I'll let you have your moment AS LONG AS I CAN WATCH!

I don't think I'm that kind of girl, but I am seriously passionate. If he no longer wants me, I need to leave him.

Your cop is a wimp. He won't fight for you. Something's wrong with him.

He never talks about his feelings. Big time repressed. He doesn't notice I have feelings. What am I supposed to do? I worked so hard to win this guy. I even learned how to cook. Me! I suck at domestic shit and couldn't care less. But I wanted him to like me more.

Who cares if you can't cook? That's what restaurants are for. It's not the 18th century. Why are you trying this hard? I can't bear to hear you go through this.

He doesn't care that I cook now. We live in separate dimensions.

By the way, I'm an excellent cook, so you don't have to worry about that.

How much more perfect can you get?

A whole lot more, I promise.

I made a huge mistake by not running away with you.

I've been saying that for months.

Why do I want him? What is his hold on me?

He's manipulating you, trying to break you.

Why? I'll give him anything! He doesn't have to break me!

That's not what he wants. He's at your mercy when he wants you to be at his mercy.

He is not at my mercy. Trust me.

This is all about control.

I don't understand. He's already in control.

He's not in control. If he were, you and I wouldn't be talking. He knows about us. Now, there's only one way he's gonna keep you around. By making you desperate for him. He'll punish you until you grovel and beg his forgiveness, then he'll treat you like shit until he decides not to. It's the oldest set of mind games in the book for assholes.

I thought his high ideals were so sweet when we met. You were right. He was playing hard to get to make me crazy for him. I never had a guy shove me off him before, and he knew it. It drove me right into his arms.

And he's still playing the same fucked-up game. It's a loser's game played by dudes who don't have a chance with a girl like you.

He says you manipulate girls with your song and dance about trying to find your soulmate.

He can judge me. I don't care. I really am trying to find that one girl who will love me, who I can make happy, who will never leave me. He can't fathom a guy like me and never will.

I am so miserable. I feel racked with guilt. Nicolas, I love you, but you're fucking up my life.

I'm sorry! Trust me, the longer you're together, the more he's gonna figure you out. Eventually, you'll be so broken that you'll be all his, and he'll do whatever he wants with you. Please don't let it reach that point.

> I find this so hard to believe. He's a good guy. He's a cop. He's my hero!

You have built him up in your head. He's not a good guy.

> My heart feels like it's gonna burst.

Let me call you. I'll make you feel better.

> He'll be back soon.

Where is he?

> Walked right past me a minute ago to go hang out with mommy or clean his beautiful car. But he'll be back to get ready for work in a bit.

You're jealous of his car?

> Well, he loves it a ton more than he loves me.

What a fake asshole. That's heartbreaking.

> I'm under some illusion that I can't break out of. I see him—tall and handsome, noble and good, sexy as hell with his iceberg-melting smile—and I immediately feel unworthy. That awful feeling makes me love him more. What is wrong with me? Am I a masochist?

You're a survivor of abuse, and that makes you easy to manipulate.

> Is he doing it on purpose?

He's trying to. Clearly, he hasn't figured you out yet. Thank God.

> Well, thanks for caring and listening to me. I'm so desperate to get him back. I'll do almost anything.

Please don't. I need you more than he does. I'm so lonely here. I can't survive this life without you. You fulfill me completely. Please, let's talk.

> Call me when he leaves for work.

I'm busy tonight. I need to see you now.

> Okay. But just for a few minutes.

We have to make plans. We can't go on like this.

We can never be together!

I promise I will find a way. Are you ready?

He'll be back any time. I'm serious. Actually, I think he's in the kitchen. We've gotta be silent.

We'll make it a quickie. I wanna get you off so bad and give you that warm-fuzzy feeling.

Me too. I'm in the dumps.

We're fucking while he's right outside the door. SEXY! If he walks in on us, disconnect. I'll understand.

I'm in bed now.

With your spicy eggplant?

As you wish.

Perfect. Answer my call.

.

Chapter 18

Justin

Justin had fallen into a state of mute despair over the past two months since discovering that Judith was in contact with Nicolas. He tried to keep his jealousy in check, but it consumed him. All night, he raged at work, imagining what they were doing, and when he finally went to sleep in the morning, he knew she was getting up to chat with that bastard. She was sad all the time now. Nicolas was right. He didn't do it for her. He wanted to turn things around, figure her out, and find a way to make her his perfect girl. Now, that seemed like a lost cause.

Justin wondered if she now sexted with that criminal the way she used to with him. She hadn't sexted him in months because he started ghosting her again. She was quiet now, subdued. Didn't talk at all during dinner or on his days off. She was pulling away as he pushed her away, and he didn't know what to do about it.

They lay in bed. They hadn't had sex in a while because he couldn't bring himself to touch her. He punished her and enjoyed seeing her miserable, even though it made him just as miserable. But tonight, she forced her way into his arms, and for some reason, he was unable to push her away. It felt good to hold her, even if it went against his principles.

"Ready for work to calm down?" she whispered.

"Yeah," he confessed.

Did she really tell Nicolas he couldn't hold out for more than three minutes? Was it true? Was he that bad of a lover? Justin couldn't stop thinking about that bastard. It was going to kill him.

"Do you love me?"

Judith asked abruptly, staring up at him with glistening eyes.

"Why do you ask?"

"I want to ensure I'm giving my heart to the right guy."

That fucker. Nicolas was in her head. Planting doubts day and night. Justin felt like someone had tied him to a post, blindfolded him, was beating the shit out of him, and he couldn't do a thing about it. Nicolas called the shots. Justin felt a profound sense of dread. He was going to lose her. He had driven her into that animal's arms with his mind games and absence. What could he say to keep her? Although he wasn't sure he wanted her if she was cheating on him.

It made sense to him now why he always dated the same kind of girls—easy to get, easy to dump, never a threat, and definitely not a challenge. He didn't even shed a tear when his long-term girlfriend ended their two-year relationship. But from the beginning, Judith made him feel crazy in every possible way. He couldn't handle what she did to his body or his soul.

Now that they weren't having sex, his porn addiction had gone into overdrive. He looked for girls who resembled Judith in rape scenarios and his imagination did the rest. When he wasn't looking at porn he was ogling Judith's sexts and thought nonstop of her giving him oral sex. He was becoming a sex addict. It was kicking his ass, trying to fight these urges. God didn't seem to give a fuck. So much for him caring about his children.

"Justin?"

"Hmm?"

"What happened?"

"What do you mean?"

"To us."

"Um, I guess things haven't been easy for us."

"I still think you are the better man."

"Compared to what?"

Was she ready to confess? She paused for a long time.

"I just wish you wanted me," she replied cryptically.

But he knew what she meant. She meant that he was the good guy, not the criminal. And while she wanted to fuck the criminal's brains out, she wanted to nest with the good guy.

"Well, you make me want to be a better man." He lied. "And I do want you."

"You do?"

She looked so surprised that Justin felt sick to his stomach. She didn't believe he wanted her anymore. Why would she? He couldn't touch her now. That snake had poisoned him and turned him against her.

"You drive me crazy, Judith. What more proof do you need?"

"You haven't let me drive you crazy in months. It's hard to believe."

"Well, it's the truth."

"You've never said I drove you crazy."

And there it was, staring him in the face. He was terrible at expressing himself. Nicolas had a witty, gilded tongue, that viper. Judith was constantly on her phone, which meant Nicolas had plenty to say. A real chatterbox. He probably shared his feelings all day and sexted her all night.

"I think about you all the time. Things were great for a while there."

Justin touched her face, feeling uncomfortable telling her this.

"Baby, I think about what I want to do to you day and night. But you have a force field around you so tight it's impossible to get through. I watch for the signs, hoping every second that you'll let me in. And regardless of what you think, I choose you."

It didn't matter if she ultimately chose him. If she was in contact with Nicolas, it canceled out everything.

"I'm fucked up. Don't know why or how to fix it."

"Justin, there's so much I want to share with you. I'm not sure how this mountain got between us, but I will do anything to move it out of the way."

The mountain was Nicolas fucking Winters. But he couldn't do a damn thing about removing it until she chose to be honest with him.

Justin stared into her eyes and noticed she had dark circles. She wasn't getting enough sleep. She looked miserable. Whatever was happening in her life wasn't bringing her joy. Was it all his fault, or did at least some of the blame lie at Nicolas's feet? His whole body vibrated with desire. But he pushed her away so often that she wasn't going to initiate anything, and he did have his principles.

He wanted her desperately. It had been almost two months since the night Nicolas had responded, and he was dying for her. Who cared if that fucker was getting some action? It would be video only—pure torture to see her luscious body and not be able to touch it. Justin caved in, his vulnerability filling him with shame. He pulled off his t-shirt, and she slid on top of him eagerly.

"I'm gonna come fast since it's been so long, so apologies in advance."

"That's okay. We'll follow the holy trinity."

"What's that?"

"The first time is all about the lust, the second is all about the tease, and the third time is all about the love."

Sounded like something that asshole said to her. Always had the right thing to say. He couldn't compete. Nicolas would win eventually. Should he surrender now or keep fighting for her? But for the moment—

Judith pinned his hands above his head and kissed him until he was panting with anticipation. Nicolas was right. He had no staying power. Couldn't handle her teasing. Wanted to cut to the chase and get instant release. Should've stuck with the perks of being a bachelor. He understood his own pace. This foreplay was torture.

Finally, she slid down his chest. Her hands, mouth and tongue were everywhere as she undid his jeans. By the time she had him out of his boxers between her hands and pressed against her lips, poised to explode, that's precisely what he did. Less than thirty seconds and his orgasm lasted for fucking ever. One out of three. God almighty, how could he ever give this woman up? She crawled back up his chest, stripped naked on top of him, and took him straight to heaven for the next three hours.

Chapter 19

Nicolas

Two months into his new life as a heroin addict, Nicolas was robbed. He had made serious bank off a group of tourists and was heading to score some dope when they knocked him down and rummaged through his pockets until they cleaned him out. Afterwards, he lay in the street, dizzy and nauseous, trying to comprehend how his life had gone to shambles.

Was it all his dad's fault? That's what he had told himself for years. But now, looking back, he realized that his dad had no power over anything. He wasn't even his legal guardian. Maybe it was time to bury the hatchet and forgive his dad. He was worried that circumstances like getting mugged were a result of bad karma. He needed to generate good karma so that he could end up with his soulmate.

Just as he had hoped, Justin took out all his angst on Belladonna. She was miserable now, and it was possible she would move out on her own. If so, the whole process of getting her to run away with him just got ten times easier. They were having video sex every night, and she had opened up to him about all her trauma. Nicolas felt electrified by the intimacy and was honored that she had chosen him to share her innermost feelings.

He called her. It rang and rang. Finally, thank God, she answered.

"How are you tonight, my sweet incubus?"

"Some thieves mugged me. I feel sick. Might have a concussion."

"Nicolas! You stress the shit out of me! I thought you went to high-end hotels to do your business. Where were you mugged?"

That's right. He hadn't told her about the drugs. For some reason, he felt ashamed that he was using and made something up.

"Right outside the hotel. They worked fast. Usually, my clients Venmo, but these folks paid in cash. It's as if the thieves somehow knew."

"Are you on your way home?"

"Yeah."

"Miss you."

"Miss you too. Your cop still cold?"

"He let me touch him after two months, but the next day, he was even meaner. As if angry at himself for breaking down."

"Call Martha. Tell her to come pick you up, and we'll start planning our lives together. I can't bear to see you treated like this. Even if you are having an affair, he's the one who pushed you straight into my arms with his stupid mind games—that, and of course, my supreme seduction skills."

"Why is it so hard for me to give up on him? He has given up on me!"

"He's a fantasy. What you hope to achieve from his love is a fantasy."

"Should I confess that we are in contact and see what he does?"

"Don't. He seems like the kind of guy to rage on testosterone."

"What I have done is horrible. I deserve it."

"The only wrong thing you have done is not follow your heart. You and I belong together. Leave this asshole and let him suffer the loss. He never deserved you for a second."

How could he make her see this?

"Belladonna."

"Huh?"

"You are so much more than a sex object. I see your amazing soul. You're smart as hell, and yes, you have a ton of talents to make this world a better place. On top of that, you are compassionate, sincere, and loyal to those who love you. I can see you starting your own business and earning a college degree. Rocking it in any career you choose. Being a wonderful mother someday, or flying to the moon. Or both! You have no idea who you are, my sweet. You have so much more to offer than just your body. I want to give you the freedom and confidence to find yourself. I have loved you for centuries. I can feel it. I have known different iterations of you down through time, and always, always you have blown me away."

She was crying.

"Really? You mean what you just said?"

"Hell yeah."

"But how can you give me this freedom? You're a prostitute."

"I swear, it's only temporary. Don't judge me as you see me right now. Give me a chance."

"We'll see. Please go home and be more careful!"

"I promise. Will you dream of me?"

"Oh, don't you worry. You know I will."

Nicolas got home and considered. Should he grab more cash and go get high? Yeah. It was all he had right now. His fantasies were the only thing he had to hold on to. When he and Belladonna were finally together, he'd give it all up—the drugs and the prostitution. But for now, he had to survive as best he could. Drowning himself in his dream world was the only way to make that happen.

Chapter 20

Judith

Judith felt like she was losing her mind. Justin had gone off the rails, acting cold, mean, and outright hostile, itching for a fight, which made her afraid for her life. If only she could explain it to him. Nicolas was her only friend. She couldn't talk to Justin! He barely said two words to her anymore. She tried to keep quiet all morning while he slept. When she texted Nicolas, she went outside and only called him late at night. Nicolas was terribly demanding, but he was also incredibly sweet and loving. She missed him and wanted him, and she felt horrible about nearly killing him that night. She sacrificed everything to choose Justin, and all for what?

She wondered if she should try to move back to her mom's, but with Lizzy there, she felt she no longer belonged. Everyone seemed glad to be rid of her. So, she watched Justin sleep each morning, overcome with a desire to touch him. In the afternoon, she saw him rise and go about his life as if she didn't exist. It felt like a nightmare.

Finally, Judith was done. One brisk October morning, she decided that she needed to move out. Searching the house for boxes, she found none. Justin was sleeping, so she went to the main house and knocked on the door.

Nora answered.

"Judith! How are you?"

Judith shrugged and spoke.

"Not too good. I wondered if you have a couple of boxes I could use?"

"I'm sure Justin can help you with that."

"Na. Truth is, I'm moving out." Tears sprang to her eyes.

"Oh, honey. Have you told him?"

Judith shook her head.

Nora opened the screen door and pulled her into a hug.

"Come on, sweetheart. Let's talk."

"There's nothing to talk about. Justin hates me and I can't change a thing. He doesn't even look at me anymore. I'm done. I can't take this abuse. I thought he was my hero. This gorgeous cop with a heart of gold. What the fuck happened?"

"Honey, he thinks you're cheating on him."

"I—"

"Are you?"

"I have a friend. It's nothing like what I feel for Justin, but they are my only friend. I have no one. You don't understand. I know he's your son, but something's wrong with him. From day one, he's played mind games with me like you wouldn't believe. The night we met, I thought he was a dream come true. I can't take this rejection. I've done everything possible to make this work, but it's been miserable."

"I'm so sorry, honey."

Then, I had a friend who listened to me and helped me deal with my pain. If Justin had been there for me, nothing would have ever developed. I've tried to shut it down. But now, it's impossible. And what's the point? Justin doesn't want me. I gave up everything to move in with him. I have no job, no friends here, nothing but him. Why does he torture me like this? I'm sorry, but could you find me some boxes? I'm gonna suck it up and call my mom. I'm done with this."

Nora looked aghast.

"Just a friend? This friend. Are they local?"

"No, they're a thousand miles away. It's nothing serious and I'll never see them again. Someone to talk to online. To help me survive this life of loneliness. I'm always alone, Nora. You have no idea."

"Honey. You need to tell Justin. Explain this to him. He thinks it's something serious. Don't leave him. Please. When his dad left, it was hell on that boy. I'll be the first to admit that Justin has intimacy issues, and he's not adept at getting close to people. I know he comes off cold and even heartless, like his dad. He has had very few friends and almost no girlfriends. But if you leave him, he's going to fall apart."

"Justin doesn't even recognize I'm here anymore." Judith laughed as she wiped her tears.

"Not true. He's talked to me about how he's failing you and is clueless about fixing it."

"When? He's always gone. I never imagined my life could be this miserable. Besides, he'll judge me for clinging to someone else, but he made me desperate when he stuck me in this lonely prison!"

Nora took her hand and held it in both of hers.

"Judith, I saw this from the first. Your passion attracts him and his stability attracts you. Together, you share the possibility of real love. But you must learn how to communicate your needs. Please, honey. Will you try? Here. Let me mediate and see if we can't resolve this."

Judith knew mediation was pointless. She had hoped to head out before he woke up and didn't want to face him. What should she do? Her phone buzzed. Nicolas. Fuck. She pulled out her phone automatically. She texted, not right now, then put her phone away.

Nora hadn't waited for her reply. She was already on the phone talking to Justin. Judith felt as if her insides might burst. Nora was going to tell him about her online friend. It would all come out. Fuck. Fuck! She ended the call.

"He'll be here in a few. Let me make some coffee, okay?"

Beaten and outnumbered, Judith sat down. Ten minutes later, the front door scraped open. Justin walked into the room, haggard, making her feel terrible for waking him. However, it was his day off, so he could catch up on sleep later. He stared right through her as his mom came over and took his hand.

"Son, Judith is about to walk out the door. What are you gonna do about it?"

"I don't fucking care," he muttered.

"Why? Do you want to go back to being alone?"

"I'm already alone. She's not, though." He pointed accusingly, then folded his arms, hate broiling off him.

Judith finished her coffee and stood.

"I'm not putting up with this, Justin. You've pushed me away from the beginning!"

"Why do you think that is, huh? Because you've had something on the side the whole fucking time!"

Judith faced him, her eyes glazed with guilt and pain.

"Ethan? I friended your schoolmate, and he responded. Nicolas fucking Winters. I know Judith. Everything."

Her insides swirled and churned—time to face the music.

"Okay. I admit it. Nicolas contacted me. I have no friends. Because of you, he's all I have!"

"And this guy is a friend? Huh? He's a criminal, and he tried to rape you at gunpoint! He abducted you! Beat the shit out of you!"

"Well, actually I beat the shit out of him."

Judith giggled, remembering that night when she had beaten Nicolas to a bloody pulp. Justin glared so hard it was as if her hero had developed laser eyes that could cut her in half.

"Whatever. How can you bring yourself to talk to him?"

"Justin, I have a hard time saying no to guys. And Nicolas isn't like most guys. His powers of persuasion are unreal. I tried to tell you how I was molested as a kid, and it's why I'm this way. You already made it clear that you don't understand or care. Let me go, okay? You can't love me. You don't understand me. I thought you were my hero, like the knights of old. I never thought I would have a chance with a guy like you. But you are the coldest, cruelest guy I've ever met, and I can't take anymore!"

Nora was crying as she wrapped her arms around Judith.

"Sweet girl. I'm so sorry for what you've endured. Honey, come here."

"Listen." Judith opened her phone. "See this? Ethan's profile. I'll unfriend him. Right now! I get it. It seems like I'm having an affair, and yeah, he's obsessed with me. He's sent me like a million dick pics, and coerced me into having video sex. Which would have never happened if you had treated me like your girlfriend!"

Justin was embarrassed and mute. He looked furious and humiliated.

Nora pulled her back into a seat beside her. Judith couldn't control her tears. She was sacrificing Nicolas, but she had to. Justin was right. Nicolas was a mess. He stalked her, coerced her and even blackmailed her. Although he was her soulmate, she had to let him go or risk losing Justin for good.

Judith glanced up at Justin. His eyes were cold and his body language was frigid. Suddenly, she saw Justin as he truly was—an angry, lonely, jealous, insecure guy desperate to feel better about himself, to find some value within himself. This realization made her love her imperfect man with the perfect facade one thousand times more. She believed she could transform him into the hero she envisioned. If only he would let her!

"Why the fuck didn't you trust me?"

"Why would I? You didn't want me after, like, two weeks. At least Nicolas wants me. I've never felt rejected and undesired by any guy like I've been with you. I can't handle the loneliness. I need to feel wanted. You don't care anyway, so let me go."

"Judith, I do care, but I admit. I am possessive and jealous and don't want to share you."

"I would rather not share me, either."

Judith lay against Nora's chest, racked with sobs. This hurt so much. She had driven him to hate her. Now, she had to sacrifice Nicolas, and Justin might not take her back even then. Judith felt torn apart.

"Can I intervene?" Nora said. "Judith, this online friend, you need to cut him off. His hold on you is destructive, and he's clearly using you. Justin, you have made Judith vulnerable because of your intimacy issues. You need to own this and fix it. Judith doesn't deserve your coldness and cruelty. She has suffered enough. You, of all people, should know how victims of abuse are easily revictimized. How can you be so concerned for those in your line of work yet have no sympathy for this beautiful girl to whom you once pledged your love?"

"She should've come to me and she didn't."

"Justin! She couldn't come to you! You're as hard as ice! Look in the mirror, son. You're a chip off the old block. It's heartbreaking."

That hit him. He slumped into a chair at the table.

"Shit. I've been raging with fury for months. Ever since Nicolas replied to me in July. And I've hated you ever since. I didn't even consider that you were at his mercy. I mean, I knew it, but I didn't really accept it. Somehow, I've just blamed it all on you."

"Justin, that night. You have no idea what I went through. Nicolas seduced me and made me his. I can't break away from him. His power over me is real, and he's in my head now. I care for him. I feel bad for him. He's a prostitute now, and he's been raped and mugged, and I feel responsible for him. His current situation is my fault and I owe him. I need to love him and I do. Save him and I want to. Can't you please try to understand?"

"I don't understand. Nothing he did is your fault."

"But he has convinced me otherwise. I never wanted this to happen. I'm sorry, I'm too much for you. Too intense. Too needy. I should've seen that you would hate life with me. You pushed me away repeatedly, and I took it as a challenge when I should have taken it as a sign. I have to leave you. Let you get back to your life. Relinquish my fantasy of my hero. You're not my hero. You're just a guy who can't handle a girl like me. Give me some fucking boxes and I'll leave."

Judith pulled away from Nora's arms and stalked to the door.

"Judith?" Justin stared, pleading, his hand outstretched.

"What?"

Eyes flashing, she turned around. He would never understand, and he would never change. She wanted out of this toxic relationship. Now.

"Please." He gestured for her to come to him. "Not like this."

Judith didn't want to come. Her instincts urged her to run away and text Nicolas to assure him that her hero was history. But Justin emanated such sadness and loneliness. He felt like the center of gravity, and she couldn't resist him now or ever. Against her will, she took three steps, and he threw his arms around her waist and clung to her.

"I'm so sorry. I should've tried to talk to you about it. I've just pushed you away."

I should have told you what was happening. It's on me, too. I let him in. I gave him everything he wanted. I'm ashamed and I'm sorry. I wanted to confess to you so many times. But he said he would leak all my nude selfies online if I told you."

"This guy sounds like a monster, Judith," Nora declared.

"Nicolas can't help it. He experienced terrible abuse as a kid, so he understands me. We share trauma, and it binds us together. I want him to be happy. I do love him. All he ever wanted was to be loved. You can't imagine how that gets to me."

"It's just a fucking game, Judith. There's nothing genuine about that piece of shit."

That wasn't true, but Judith decided she couldn't continue defending Nicolas and still win Justin back.

"I wanna see you unfriend him and block him right now," Justin said, holding out his hand expectantly. She opened her Messenger app and let him scroll through. Tons and tons of messages.

"Wait a minute. I thought this was, like, a two-way relationship."

His mom asked, "What do you mean, honey?"

Justin gazed up at her in shock.

"He's been stalking you, do you realize that? This is illegal."

"I know," she whispered.

"Judith, this is straight-up harassment. Blackmail? Coercion? He hasn't left you alone for a minute in all these months."

"I know," she repeated, tears springing once again.

He scrolled and read, scrolled and read.

"He was calling you every fucking night. These calls lasted hours. No wonder you've been dead tired. Good God. You should've said something."

"I didn't know how. Nicolas is obsessed with me, and he's all alone. I got hooked, like my mom, trying to help him. And I'm sorry, but I do love him. I'm trapped."

"Nicolas blames you for everything," Justin muttered.

"It is my fault. He would never have had to run away if I hadn't gone into his house."

"He threatened to send a hitman after me?" Justin continued to read. "This guy is a psychopath."

Judith cried uncontrollably. She hurt so bad. She loved Nicolas, and now she would lose him forever.

"Justin, he hates you with a deadly passion because you're a cop. When he said he'd have you killed, I believed him. He wants to take your place and has nothing left to lose."

That was a blatant lie. Nicolas didn't know any hitmen. However, if she wanted to win Justin back, she had to make Nicolas the villain in order to make Justin the hero. That was what he desperately wanted.

Justin stood. His face was grim.

"This bullshit is gonna end today."

Judith slumped to the table, and Nora took her in her arms again.

"Justin, do you think he will send someone after you?" His mom asked.

"I doubt it. Nicolas is a piece of shit who preys on women and hates authority. Judith, you're not going anywhere. Stay here. I'll be back soon. I'm taking your phone, but I'll return it, okay?"

"Okay," she whispered.

Nora rocked her back and forth, and Judith felt her love for Nicolas slide off her shoulders onto the floor. She felt so guilty. What would he do? Would he try to kill himself? Oh, God. What had she done?

Judith could feel Nicolas from a thousand miles away—how devastated he would be when he realized she had blocked him. Justin tore out of the driveway, and she began to shake, her whole body reacting to the situation. Nora held her and comforted her. Judith let her. She had no idea how to cope with this, but it was now beyond her control. She had surrendered her power to Justin, and that was probably for the best.

Chapter 21

Justin

Justin parked outside the police station in his hangout at the back of the parking lot behind the dumpster, and opened Judith's phone. He had wanted to do this for months, scheming to unlock her phone and discover what she was hiding from him. Now, he was dying to read every single thing they shared. He couldn't believe his mom. Getting Judith to confess was astronomical. He was still pissed as hell, but he felt a flutter of hope too. She had finally given him up. Things were moving in the right direction.

This wasn't even about Judith anymore. Nicolas had called him out, humiliated him and talked shit about his manhood. This was about that asshole encroaching on his territory and trying to steal what was his. He scrolled up to the very top and started at the beginning. The first text Nicolas sent her, pretending to be an old friend from school, was sent less than two weeks after he disappeared. What a ballsy little asshole.

> Why are you contacting me?

> Haven't you guessed? I'm in love with you, hopelessly, madly in love. I've never had a woman try to murder me before, and it's got me so worked up.

> Sounds like you're a masochist.

> With you, I am. Then you abandon me before we can properly fuck. Dry humping doesn't count.

Justin gritted his teeth. He dry humped her? That was almost the same as fucking. Judith said he went down on her for one minute. She lied.

> I've never met a woman who could resist me and that includes you. And I saw the hunger in your eyes when I opened the door that night.

This vain jerk. How was he so incredibly confident? Justin was seething with envy, and it had only been thirty seconds.

> If I hadn't abducted your mom, would you have
> gone out with me?

Ha! He knew it. Knew Nicolas had abducted her!

> And I've been searching for a real man all my
> life, and I finally found him.

> That's hard to believe. Your cop is a complete hick.
> Has had like no pussy ever. Bet he's crazy about
> you, though. You're the hottest girl ever to give him
> a second glance.

> I want him to be crazy about me. I must admit
> that I am a bit disappointed.

> No surprise there. He's a cop. Jerks off to his own
> reflection.

His heart raced as it had the night they tried to track Nicolas down. Justin had never experienced homicidal rage like this until now.

> I know women. And I know you because you are
> my soulmate, and I can read your mind.

> That's creepy.

> It is what it is.

> Okay. What am I thinking of right now?

> You, my femme fatale, are thinking of this.

A dick pic. Something that Justin was far too self-conscious to do. Nicolas had plenty of lovers and knew he was hot stuff. Wonderful, Judith thought he was hot, too. Compared him to a mighty oak? It made her giddy with desire? Wanted to see it in action? Her trashiness was so sexy, though. He paused, imagining having the guts to send her a dick pic, then visualized all the dirty innuendos she would sext him with. This is what he wanted: to replace that Casanova in her heart.

In the weeks that followed, Nicolas demanded Judith's constant attention. Night and day, he harassed her endlessly. The texts were constant and often the same. How much he loved her, how gorgeous she was, how he had never known a girl so beautiful. She was his soulmate. Begged her to share everything about herself and lauded her for every accomplishment. No wonder she didn't say a thing. He treated her like a goddess.

Then he worked on her sympathy by sharing details of his tragic life. To Justin's shock, Judith reassured and sympathized with him, trying to help Nicolas feel better about himself. Every word felt like a betrayal, fueling his jealous rage.

> We're soulmates. We were brought together to murder each other, and we immediately fell in love.

> No, this is different from what I feel for Justin.

> You love him with your conscious self. He is the guy you CHOOSE. But you love me with your unconscious self. I am the guy you DESIRE. You need to decide who you want to be with.

> I already made my choice.

> Choice not acceptable. You stole my heart and now you are my life support. I'm saying I can't live without you, and I won't.

Nicolas was terribly persuasive. Judith didn't stand a chance against him. When she told him he was like the devil, he didn't understand, but she was right. He was, without a doubt, the serpent in the garden.

> Your cop doesn't get you off?

> We fucked once before he crashed out. But he pushed me away first, and I had to beg him. I don't know what he's doing, but it's hell.

> He's jerking you around, honey, using mind games. This guy is toxic. I can't imagine pushing you away for any amount of money.

> You're so sweet. Finally, he let me, but since it's been a week, he came in, like, thirty seconds.

> Oral?

> Yeah.

> He's using you! What a prick. Didn't even try to please you?

> He doesn't care about that.

> What a complete asshole.

Sweet. Nicolas was sweet. Fuck him. Justin knew he wasn't satisfying her, but hearing her confess it to Nicolas was humiliating. He might as well be canceled all across the internet.

> Last night was busy.

> Did you make a lot of money?

> I fucked three guys and five gals and made 1000$$$$$.

> Guess being a prostitute pays off.

Wow. A prostitute. Guys and girls? Icky. He was religious and conservative. And shocked that Judith was okay with it.

> I'm in hell here. Justin has chained me to a bed while everyone else gets to go on living. He hasn't touched me in a week! Why is he doing this to me? I am going to lose my mind. How did I think he was the right guy for me? He shoved me off him on our first date. I thought his high ideals were sweet. But this isn't sweet.

> His high ideals are bullshit. It's a mind game, honey. He's teasing you, playing hot and cold, and breaking you down, so you'll do anything, be anything he wants. It's the shit that guys who have never had a girl like you do so they can keep a girl like you. He's a fucking loser.

How did this jerk know him? Nicolas called him out for the insecure, foolish guy he was, making him sound like a thirteen-year-old idiot who had never been with a woman.

> Where is he?

> Left. He was just in here. He's been working on his car all day. Comes in, shirt off, covered in sweat. Suddenly, I'm lusting after him like a fangirl. I'm so horny and lonely, and he doesn't even care. I wanted to rape him! Isn't that horrible?

> Poor girl. Here. Get undressed and into bed. I'll do the same. We can get each other off.

Nicolas was in her panties from a thousand miles away. He was an idiot to have pushed her away for all those months, and he felt more like a loser than he ever had in his life. Nicolas was exploiting and taking advantage of her, but he had made it all too easy.

What does your fantasy girl include?

If you scream my name and beg for it, I'll get off so fast.

Full name or nickname?

I've never thought about it. You're special, so you get my nickname. I love you, Belladonna. You think of everything. What do you want?

I'm ashamed to say.

Girl of my dreams, please don't be ashamed. You are perfect, and I wanna indulge every last one of your kinks.

Only have the one kink, to be honest, but I don't wanna admit it.

Nothing's too kinky for me.

I would never tell Justin that's for sure. He's way too straitlaced. He'd think I was a freak.

Justin let go of the phone and stared ahead. Did he come off like the guy who wouldn't understand? Some judgmental creep? Who cared if she liked watching guys jerk off? He was happy to do it for her, although it probably wouldn't be very satisfying since he usually came in under a minute. He thought of the masturbation video Nicolas sent him, so cocky, claiming that Judith loved it. At the time, he didn't believe him. Now, he shuddered with feelings of hate and envy as he imagined Judith drooling over this guy's dick.

Do you want me just because you hate cops?

It is a huge plus. That night in the car, when you said that was your cop boyfriend on the phone, I was ecstatic. I LOVE stealing girls away from guys I HATE. But with you, it's so much more. You are my girl, and I will always see you as my girl, no matter who you are with.

If he ever saw Nicolas again, he would murder him. This went beyond rage. It was personal and visceral. Justin wanted to hang his head on the wall like a trophy and eradicate him from the earth.

Judith confided so much in Nicolas that he seemed more like a gal pal. Justin didn't think girls talked to guys about these things. She went on and on about her feelings, dreams, sorrows, regrets, and even her menstrual cycle. Nicolas listened, consoled her, boosted her confidence, and shared all his feelings in return.

He seemed to care, which hurt like a stab to the gut. She had never discussed anything like this with him before. Justin was starting to see a picture form—one illustrating how he was the true villain here. He didn't spend time with her. No wonder she caved in. Justin had made it easy for Nicolas to manipulate her.

By summer, it had evolved into long video calls throughout the night while he was at work. He could only imagine what those entailed. Nicolas texted his sex fantasies in splendid detail and demanded that Judith text hers. And yeah, once she stopped sexting him, she sexted the hell out of that criminal instead.

Jealousy ate its way out of his heart as he ogled her pics, forwarding each to himself. These were all meant for him! Justin thought the nudes she sent him were explicit. That was nothing. Their sexting lasted for hours each day, filled with flirty innuendos and dirty jokes. They had fun together. Fun. Justin had no idea how to have fun.

Nicolas was specific in his kinky demands, and Judith eagerly gave in to his every whim. Didn't need to be asked twice. And worse, she had kinky demands for him, too. He thought he knew this girl. He thought he had saved this girl, and then she turns around and goes along with this?

Justin opened a video Judith had sent to Nicolas. Somehow, she managed to film herself overhead. Did she hang her phone from the ceiling fan? On her back, naked, legs spread. Holy fuck. She owned a vibrator? As he watched Judith masturbate, he frantically pulled out his dick.

She was crying out *Nic!* over and over. Disgusted, he turned down the volume, his eyes glued to her bouncing breasts as she writhed, hips gyrating as she pleasured herself. He jerked off so fast that he came before she did. Heart pounding, his inner caveman screaming for release, his lust devouring him as she climaxed theatrically, then smiled coyly and blew a kiss at the camera.

Eyes closed, he spent the next twenty minutes tormenting himself with thoughts so erotic that he was forced to stop intermittently and mutter a futile prayer to God, repenting of his wickedness, and then defeated the purpose by forwarding her sex video to himself to watch again and again.

Justin sat there in agony, hands behind his head, staring down at his swollen penis, inflicting punishment. Trying to control these urges inside his head was pure torture. Judith had seduced him and warped him. He wanted to make her suffer, since she deserved to reap the consequences. Throbbing with exquisite pressure, his mind at war with his soul, he tried to force away the erection, but the vicious fantasy played on relentlessly.

Judith, trembling with fear as he drags her naked down to his garage, bends her over a sawhorse and ties her hands and feet to the legs. Judith, moaning in ecstasy as he whips her until his dick is rock hard. Judith, begging for him to fuck her, then writhing and screaming in pain as he does.

He pictured her luscious ass, tilted at just the right angle for maximum penetration, decorated with red streaks from her beating, her elastic pussy, tight and wet. Start front and center and finish in the rear. This was gonna hurt so good. Son of a bitch. Fuck this.

Furiously, he gave himself the undeserving release, spasming so hard he hit the goddamn horn. Sat up, terrified that someone was watching. He lay back and sighed. Remembering a few months back when he had scoured the apartment and garage looking for the perfect apparatus for this fantasy. Since he was tall, the sawhorse was the ideal height. He set it up, bought some nylon rope that wouldn't leave marks on her delicate skin, and a whip off a sex paraphernalia website.

He acted out the sex game, which he coined Sex on the Sawhorse, whipping the air, imagining her porno-hot body bound and bent in half, torturing him with lust. Imagined what it would feel like to fuck her up the ass. Wondered how much pain he could inflict and how much she could endure. He knew he was sick, but he couldn't control it. Finally, he lay on the saggy couch in the darkness and forced himself to edge his cock until he was engorged. Then he masturbated until every last detail of this obscene scenario was burned into his mind forever.

How did Nicolas have the balls to make demands on her like that? Could he do the same thing? Could he leverage her infidelity to indulge the kink she cursed him with?

He hated her. He loved her. He wanted her. Silently begging that she somehow sense what he so desperately craved and give it to him willingly. He was obsessed with her and the evil she aroused in him. Whores were willing to do anything, right? Judith was already starving for any sign of affection. And obviously, she was good with any kink. But no. Wait. He didn't want to be a sick pervert. He wanted to be the good guy!

Turning his mind back to her affair, Justin wished that she had trusted him. Didn't she realize this was coercion? She should have ratted that bastard out. But the truth was that Nicolas made her feel loved, while he didn't try to validate her feelings. That asshole understood her, and they shared trauma, making Justin the outsider. Nicolas filled her with pleasure and joy. They were fuck buddies, soulmates, and best friends. Sure, he stalked her and texted her constantly, plagued her for kinky video sex, obsessed with making her his, but clearly, she loved every bit of it.

It had been happening all those months. Where was he? Living right next to her! But never with her. He had constructed walls around his heart almost as soon as she moved in. He had failed his girl from the very beginning. Judith was too fragile to go up against a desperate, tortured guy like Nicolas. He really did eat her for breakfast.

Justin headed into the station and spoke with the tech department. They couldn't trace Nicolas's whereabouts with his fake Facebook account. They suggested he do what he had already figured—unfriend and block him. He asked them to print out all the texts, and they handed him a thick stack of paper before sending him on his way. Discouraged by the anti-climactic solution, Justin headed home with no idea what to do. Judith cheated on him, but it was also his fault. Enraged, miserable, and completely at a loss, he didn't want to lose her. But in a way, he never had her to begin with.

Chapter 22

Judith

Late in the afternoon, Justin returned. He strode across the room to the table where she sat drinking tea with his mom and placed her phone beside her. He was the epitome of the cop she had met that first night, confident and filled with righteous indignation. Judith opened it. The texts and videos were all deleted, and Nicolas was no longer listed as one of her friends. Her heart wept silently. Nicolas was gone for good. She had to let him go. Justin stared down at her, radiating judgment, anger and sadness. Then she gazed up at him, ashamed and ready to grovel.

"How can you ever forgive me? I let this go on and on. I couldn't stop it, and I couldn't tell you, and I felt married to him. We met in a dark place, and he understood my trauma. He listened to me and said he loved me."

"I know," he sighed, "I can't pretend it doesn't rip me apart. I'm trying. I can see you were stalked, blackmailed, exploited, threatened and coerced repeatedly, but you could've come to me, and you never did."

"You were never here, and you've pushed me away for months! When was I supposed to tell you? And if I did, you would have just dumped me!"

"I—" He rubbed his face and shrugged helplessly. "I don't know what's wrong with me."

"I know what's wrong. I'm too much for you. You only want me in small doses. You should never have hooked up with me!"

She screamed in his face.

Nora stepped up to Judith and took her arms, pulling her back down into a chair.

"Let's calm down, honey. He's trying to work things out."

"Yeah, let's not go there now," Justin agreed, "focus on the main issue. This fucking affair, which has been going on for months."

She withered beneath his gaze. He was never going to let this go, and she knew it.

"Of course, let's not deal with the root of the problem," she snapped, "it's true. The night I met Nicolas, I had a death wish. I saw his hunger and responded to his need. Tried to fight it and lost."

"You didn't have the skills to take him on. You were like a deer trying to attack a wolf."

"Nicolas loves me, though. He really does! I've betrayed him by cutting him off like this. He's going to lose his shit."

"His love is sick and destructive. I doubt he could ever make you happy."

"We got so deep. I'm not sure why."

"I read the texts. He is beyond obsessed with you and wants you more than he wants to live. His emotions crash into you like unforgettable storms, and I understand why you caved. He is persuasive, and he's one hell of a lover boy. He let you vent your trauma when you didn't feel safe with me. But his intentions are all selfish, and he wants you for himself, no matter the cost."

"I'm so embarrassed you read all that."

"And hours upon hours of sexting back and forth. Not to mention the videos. Shit."

Judith glanced over at Nora and flushed deep red.

"I'm not the sort of girl to cheat. All I can say is, I'm a sex addict and I can't say no to sex. Especially if I'm stuck in a sexless fucking relationship," she snapped, then sighed, "but still, I'm deeply ashamed. I should have gotten help for my abuse as a kid. It's all connected to that and now I'm screwed."

"I should have listened when you told me about that. No wonder you never felt like you could share anything with me."

"That and you've ignored me except for the occasional fuck."

"Judith. Enough of that."

Nora chastised her in the same way Justin did.

Justin's face went beet red, like that first night she kissed him. She was too hot to handle. Her fire turned his icy nature into a world full of blinding, confusing steam.

"I have issues. I love you, but you're too much. You choose him anyway, so what am I even doing?"

"He got in my head! Then he was there for me! I didn't mean for this to happen. I tried so hard to push him away."

"You pushed him away? Really? By making out like crazy lovers and dry humping during your hot getaway less than an hour after you met? I mean, I guess technically you didn't lie. He didn't fuck you that night, right? I feel like a complete jackass for trusting you."

Judith sobbed quietly. Her mom was the only person in the world who understood how persuasive Nicolas was.

"He forced me into the car. Handcuffed me to the seat. I was at his mercy! He could do whatever he wanted to me. And all he wanted was to make me fall in love with him. It was manipulative and selfish, I know that. But it also sorta worked! You can never understand."

Justin's eyes melted on her. He had a tiny bit of compassion, although not enough.

"I'm trying not to be a jealous asshole, but I can't help it."

"The passion was unreal. He seduces like the devil! I'm sorry, Justin. Nicolas is like an incubus. He can get any woman he wants!"

"I hate that guy so much," Justin muttered through his teeth.

"I didn't ask for this. I only wanted you! All these months. I kept waiting for you to want me, but you didn't and he did. It's so hard to explain, but ultimately, I choose you!"

"Why? Clearly, he satisfies you completely, including your kink. You can talk about anything with him. He shares his trauma with you, and swears that you're soulmates."

"Justin, I fell instantly in love with you the first night we met. You must be a fantasy because I have never been as unhappy as I have been with you. I want you so bad, but you don't want me. I thought you were going to save me from a miserable life, but this is unbearable."

He folded his arms and gazed at her critically, like he was about to give her a lecture on how to not be a slut.

"I saved you, huh? Who did I even save you from? The guy with whom you started having video sex a month later?"

"My God. You get off on rejecting me, don't you? Is it your kink? Watching your girl pine away for you? Make her feel unworthy of your love? Drool over you as you push her away? This is why you chose me. I'm the hot girl who wants to tear your clothes off, and you just love to torture me, don't you? Well, fuck you! I have never had a guy shove me away day after day like you do."

"It's hard to wanna fuck a girl you know is putting out for criminals and perverts," he said darkly.

"Even before you knew we were texting, you were like this."

"Well, I guess when you turned me into a horny beast, I no longer saw you as the sweet damsel in distress I saved. You changed me."

"It's not my fault you're a horny beast! You do that to yourself! If you stopped pushing me away, we'd find our rhythm, and you'd get comfortable with me. You have no idea how much this hurts my feelings!"

"It's hard to give a shit about your feelings when I have my own to deal with. Most of them fucked up by you."

"Justin," his mom reprimanded, "you need to stop. Right now. Judith has suffered enough. I can see now what you have put her through. Son, I love you, but you can be incredibly cruel when crossed and have no idea how to manage your emotions. You must decide right now whether you will forgive Judith or let her go. This treatment of her is barbaric. You aren't married and she doesn't owe you a thing. And if you aren't making her happy, she is within her rights to find happiness elsewhere."

"Wow, Mom. Thanks for being on my side," he glowered.

"Even if you lose Judith, you will never find a woman willing to put up with this shit. No one likes feeling rejected. I can't believe she's stayed as long as she has! I'm not condoning this online affair, but you pushed her into it. You need to face that fact. Then learn to rein in your jealousy and show some love."

Judith couldn't say a thing. She had never cheated on any guy before, and this was tearing her up. Justin sighed deeply.

"God, I don't wanna go back to being alone."

"What are you willing to do about it?" his mom demanded.

Finally, Justin said, "If he tries to contact you again, you need to swear to God to tell me."

Justin's expression was grim and exhausted, but he opened his arms and Nora pushed her forward.

"Of course," Judith promised.

"As I read the texts, I realized how much you shared with him. I've never felt so jealous. You've never once tried to share your feelings with me."

"I honestly didn't think you cared. You have your perfect routine and there's no room for me."

"Well, you never even tried."

He still wanted to blame everything on her. Judith caved in and nodded in agreement.

"Justin." Nora patted him on the shoulder. "You are the one who needs to try. Your dad never did. But I believe you have it in you to be different."

Judith felt his strong arms around her and melted into his warmth. This was all she wanted. She could give up Nicolas if it meant having Justin for the rest of her life.

"Thanks, Mom."

Justin led Judith outside and up the stairs into their apartment. He didn't miss a beat. Eyes locked with hers, intensely driven, as if nearing the finish line. Judith was ecstatic. It had been months. The makeup sex was going to be nuclear.

Justin slammed the front door, then tore off her clothes in the entryway. Judith felt his size and strength as he picked her up and held her against the wall.

"You're mine, Judith. I can't share you and I won't."

She frantically pawed at his groin, itching to find the zipper. He carried her with ease through the apartment and dropped her on the bed. On her back, her body tingled with desire as she watched him strip off his t-shirt. Expose the rippling muscles down his arms and across his sculpted chest. Her hot hero was perfect. This is why she went so crazy after that gorgeous cop. She wanted this.

"Are you really sorry?" he demanded.

"Yes," she whispered.

"I wanna hear you say it."

"I'm sorry, Justin. Please forgive me."

"Say it again. I wanna hear you say it again and again."

"Please forgive me."

"You don't deserve forgiveness, you know. You're a cheating whore."

He declared boldly as he pulled down his jeans and boxers. Her eyes teared up at the cruel insult, but she blinked them away as she ogled his erection. Her heart was pounding as if she had been sprinting for miles.

"I know I'm unworthy of you. But I can make it up to you, I promise."

"How?"

"I'll do whatever you want."

"Okay, then. Sit up."

She moved to the edge of the bed, grabbing his hips, excited by where this was going. She'd be back in his good graces in less than a minute.

"You need to learn your place. It's with me, your eyes on *me*, your mouth between *my* legs."

"Gladly."

Never had she met a guy who preferred oral sex like Justin did. Came so hard every time. It was so sweet. He could barely handle the stimulation, but he loved it. Thirty seconds later, he was groaning and his knees were shaking. He surprised her by shoving her down and crawling on top of her. She looked up at him coyly.

"You don't want me to suck that orgasm out of you?"

"I can't fucking handle it. It's too intense."

"I wanna swallow on you so bad, though. Maybe I need to tie you up first."

"Shut the fuck up, Judith. I can't contain this much longer."

"What?"

"My inner caveman."

He mumbled as he thrust aimlessly, so aroused he couldn't coordinate his movements.

"Oh, sexy. I wanna meet him. Tell him, I'll let you get in there so deep, we'll need a winch to pull you out."

Flushed and delirious, he bit her face and neck, gnawing like a dog with its bone.

"You drive me insane."

"I wanna be your ultimate sex fantasy."

"You fucking are and you know it."

"You have no idea how much I want you."

"Even after Nicolas's symphony of dick pics?"

"There's only one dick I want. The biggest one of all."

"You always say the right thing to push me over the edge."

He penetrated clumsily, the weight of his lust throwing him off balance, and came prematurely.

"God, I'm sorry," he apologized.

"No worries, baby. There's plenty more where that came from."

"After freeing you again from that asshole, I can go for days."

They went for hours. Finally, when they were starving, Justin did something he was usually too cheap to do and ordered pizza delivery.

"How are you feeling?"

He asked as he finished off the entire pizza on his own. Judith watched in satisfaction as her big boy ate with gusto. It was all back on between them, and all it took was ripping Nicolas out of her heart and throwing him away.

"Sad, but a bit relieved. Nicolas said he loved me, and I'm afraid I've broken his heart."

"It's not love. With a guy like that, it can never be love."

"I hope you didn't watch my sex video."

He flushed deeply. Fuck, he had.

"I didn't know you owned a vibrator."

He sounded very disapproving.

Why did she feel like Justin judged her for every goddamn thing? He saw her as a trashy whore, just because she liked sex? It was getting irritating. She replied defensively,

"well, you haven't touched me in months. I was going crazy. I'm used to having lots of sex."

"And Nicolas asked you to get one for your video sex. I know. I read it in the texts."

"That's straight-up pervy, Justin. I can't believe you read all of those."

"Maybe I wanted to torture myself. I forwarded all your pics to myself too, since you should've been sending those to me, not him."

Judith felt so guilty. She had legit cheated on Justin with Nicolas. She justified it because he was pushing her away. But now she could see that she really was a slut.

"The truth is, I can't handle the thought of sharing you with anyone. It makes me feel insane. I want you all to myself. Guys can look, but they can't touch. The first week we met, I discovered how jealous and possessive you make me. I want to build you a home where I can keep you forever and ever. I like having nice things, and you are every man's dream. You are way out of my league, the hottest girl I will ever meet. But you're mine now, and I'll never give you up or let you go."

Judith thought about this, feeling slightly alarmed. Why did he want to own her yet remain so distant? Was Nicolas right? Was she merely his property?

"Justin, please don't push me away anymore. I need you every day. I'm needy, and I'm sorry. But your body is like a drug, and I can't live without it."

"I feel the same about you. Just unlike you, I'm not comfortable with that. I feel so—"

"Vulnerable?"

"Yeah," he admitted, "you have me at your mercy. You're an insatiable cock tease. With your dirty mouth, your sexting, and your insanely hot body. I love it, I do. I mean, I think I'm obsessed with you, actually. But also, I don't know. It pushes me too far, I guess."

Judith felt hurt. She wasn't a tease. She had never been a tease. When she wanted a guy, she happily spread her legs for him. She had never strung any man along. But she did like being a sex goddess. Was that so wrong? To want to be a man's fantasy girl? Hotter than his porn collection, hotter than all of his previous girlfriends? She wanted to blow them all away! Satisfy every single kink until he couldn't live without her. She was a seducer like Nicolas, Judith realized with chagrin.

It hurt to think that maybe Justin despised her for this. He saw her as a whore. But she wasn't! She wanted so badly to be his good girl, and now she realized that he would never see her that way. She would never be a good girl. Judith collapsed onto the couch, desperate to bury this pain somewhere deep inside her. Eager to see Justin as her hero, not her worst enemy.

Justin plopped down beside her, and she shook his arm.

"You have me at *your* mercy! I'm so desperate for you, I can't see straight. But you have to stop pushing me away. It makes me crazy."

"Well, it makes me crazy, too. I'm sick of jerking off to your sexts when I'd rather be fucking you."

"If you don't, we won't make it."

"You're right." He laid his head against her belly. "Nicolas told me you said I couldn't last more than three minutes. Did you say that?"

Shit. She had told Nicolas that because it was true. Oops.

"God, no." She lied. "I did the exact opposite. Nicolas has a kink. He's obsessed with you and me having sex. Begged me to film us secretly. It gets him off so hard to hear how hot you are. It's an odd kink for a Casanova like him."

"What a freak. Am I? Hotter than him?"

"How can you ask me?"

"I'm nothing like Nicolas."

"You are precious. I love you the way you are. Everything about you is perfect, except for the part where you reject me."

Judith leaned down and kissed him.

"No more. I promise. I don't wanna lose you. Especially not to him."

"Then let's make sure nothing ever comes between us again."

Chapter 23

Nicolas

Belladonna was gone. The cop discovered their secret, and now it was all over. Nicolas couldn't handle it. He sat on the bench in the park and cried until he could cry no more. How could she choose him? Justin was horrible to her, and he would never understand her.

Nicolas knew guys like Justin never changed and often got worse. Now that he was Facebook friends with Justin, he stalked him too. This guy was as fake and pretentious as could be. All he cared about was his workout routine and his fucking car. Uber masculine bullshit for men who didn't understand women. He was vapid, shallow and incapable of giving Belladonna the life she deserved. He studied the photos of the land around Justin's country home and tried to imagine his diva stuck in that shithole. It was awful. She had to be crawling the walls with boredom, miserable day in and day out. He had one last chance. Two months from now. He already had their travel itinerary. He'd track Belladonna down and seduce her like the devil himself. Would make her so crazy for him that she'd never want another man as long as she lived.

Nicolas rolled a joint and smoked it as he stared into the night sky. It would be so hard not to have their daily chats and video sex. He wasn't sure how he'd survive, but somehow, he would. He survived being locked up in a mental hospital and a whole childhood of lonely misery. He'd survive this.

Nicolas realized he was too much to handle. He wasn't stupid. Belladonna was probably glad to be rid of him on some level. But he had also been her confidant. And he wasn't faking it, either. He was ecstatic that she trusted him. This was all he ever wanted—a close relationship with a girl he loved. But he was afraid he'd screw it all up from either the drugs or his mental illness. Maybe Martha was right and he needed professional help.

He regretted that whole night. Hurting Martha, hurting Judith, and running away because of his psychotic break. Couldn't take it back now, though. It was too late. All he could do was suffer through the next few months and hope his mad seduction skills guaranteed that she'd commit to running away with him. Where together, they would share the life he had always dreamed of.

His dealer sat on the park bench next to him five minutes later, and Nicolas emptied his pockets of all tonight's earnings because he needed the dope. Planned to float through the next sixty days until he had Belladonna in his arms. Settling into a high, he gazed at the sky for hours, blissfully zoned out. His only thought was his beautiful girl.

Imagined what they were doing right now. Her cop would be all over her day and night, marking his territory, which got him seriously aroused for some reason. He imagined them fucking in all sorts of places and positions. Compared Justin's skills to his, knowing that no matter how much hotter Justin was than he, Nicolas was still the better lover. Belladonna had admitted that Justin loved oral sex, so he fantasized about watching Belladonna suck him off. It got him so horny, thinking of his soulmate having sex with another man. What the hell was wrong with him? Belladonna would be happy that Justin was finally giving her some love and attention. But it would never last. A guy like Justin was too set in his ways.

Nicolas pulled out his phone and went back through their messaging, reading every line of text, feeling like they were more of her legendary kisses. Belladonna had shared everything with him. He had never gotten so close to another human. And he shared everything with her. It was painful that their secrets weren't shared eye-to-eye across from each other on a mattress with plenty of breaks for fantastic sex, but soon they would be. It had to be. Just as he had decided when he arrived in Mexico, Belladonna was his new lease on life.

Nicolas thought of all the romances he had read throughout his life. He loved the classics, even the tragedies, where horrible obstacles stood in the way of true love. That cop was the obstacle. But once exposed for the selfish bastard that he was, Nicolas was convinced he would finally win the hand of his perfect dream girl.

Chapter 24

Judith

Six weeks after Judith last spoke with Nicolas, she felt so empty, lost in the void where he once belonged. Justin drove their relationship forward with urgent passion and no longer pushed her away, which was a dream come true. But she had developed a lasting, deep connection with Nicolas, and she didn't know how she would learn to live without him.

She fantasized about him constantly. Remembered all the things he promised to do to her body. It was hell. She wanted to be happy with Justin, so what was this? Why couldn't she break free of this obsession? The truth was, they got too emotionally close and codependent. Nicolas helped her survive for months, and she couldn't cope with the withdrawal of him. Justin was such a good guy. So hardworking and gorgeous. She loved everything about him but found it impossible to share anything with him. Couldn't shake the feeling that he didn't really care and would much rather be doing something else.

Justin was a restless guy. He liked to stay busy and didn't care to waste time chitchatting when he had chores to do or could be busy maintaining his hot physique. She hated to be a burden, so she hid her feelings from him, and the repression grew as she longed for Nicolas and the connection she had now lost.

A dichotomy had formed in her mind. Justin was her hot cop, and Nicolas was her sweet soulmate. She wanted both but had to make a choice. How could she possibly choose? If she were honest with herself, she would admit to wanting Nicolas with as much lust as she felt for Justin, plus the soulmate connection. But he was crazy in love with her, obsessed beyond all reasoning, and a prostitute besides. She wanted to be the good girl who hooked up with the good guy! Plus, Nicolas was on the run in another country and had a warrant out for his arrest. It was impossible to ever be with him. She had to make it work with Justin. And now that he wasn't pushing her away, life was good. So why was it not enough?

Judith mashed potatoes while Nora basted the turkey. Judith didn't understand his holiday. She had never celebrated a traditional Thanksgiving. Why were celebrations all about food? Butter doused everything, allowing only a single bite of each dish or risk gaining five pounds.

The trip to Cabo San Lucas was in a month. What if Nicolas remembered? What if he followed through and sought her out? How would she react? Her heart ached for him. She wanted to sob for hours at the thought of how she had betrayed him. She had to. Had to! Justin was done with her and hated her. She had to throw Nicolas to the wolves! Still, it made her feel like shit.

Video sex with Nicolas was cathartic and liberating and he loved her slutty nature! Loved to hear her scream his name and beg for him, and she loved doing it. Watching him jerk off was so hot, and she didn't feel like a pervert with him. Felt like she could share any kink or fantasy, and he would embrace them all. Their roleplay was so satisfying. It pulled her right into the moment, even though he was a thousand miles away.

Justin was all undisguised lust and got down to business. He couldn't handle foreplay, and she now realized that although he liked to tease her with mind games, he wasn't into being teased himself. It frustrated him, and he couldn't hold out long enough. What he did for her was satisfying. He went at her with a focus and intensity that took her breath away. It wasn't quite the level of ecstasy she had experienced the night in the car with Nicolas, but it made her crazy for his body, and she longed for him to pound at her every chance they got.

But she wanted to go deeper. Get dirtier. And Justin refused. She sensed his repression, and it drove her crazy. She fantasized about tying him down to the bed and doing all the things he wouldn't let her do. Teasing him endlessly, then riding him through one orgasm right onto the next. But he always kicked her off him when she tried anything even remotely kinky. Vanilla sex and doggie-style quickies were his forte. Justin was such a prude! He couldn't handle the intensity, and she hated it.

She was accustomed to the fun and excitement of guys letting her do as she pleased with them. Judith loved pleasuring a man until he was speechless and drooling. Not Justin. He wanted complete control. Still, someday she would succeed at pushing his buttons and get him to show his true colors. She imagined him to be like the Incredible Hulk—sexy and powerful beneath that placid, noble exterior.

Judith wondered what Nicolas was doing right now. Was he being safe? What if he had been hurt or killed? She felt so protective of him, so concerned for his feelings, and so terrified that she broke his heart. Nicolas brought out her latent nurturing tendencies. She had felt nothing like this for Justin, who didn't seem to need anything from her other than sex.

The feast was almost ready, so she walked outside to call Justin in from the garage. A few inches of snow lined the path, and she studied her steps as she made her way. The country landscape stretched out in every direction, desolate, the way her heart felt now. She needed Justin's warm arms around her to pull her back to his reality. In time, she would get over Nicolas and control her overwhelming heartbreak when she thought of him. Learn to live without the spoils of their shared trauma and deep connection. She could be the happy girl with the good guy and the perfect life, even if it was fake and didn't accommodate her entire soul. It would require cutting some pieces off her to fit, but she had to do it because, like Justin said, he would never let her go.

Chapter 25

Justin

Justin was obsessed with Judith and Nicolas's relationship, even though he brought it to a successful end. He read through the printout of their text history every night before work. It seemed the only way to get to know Judith, and she spilled her guts to this guy. Nicolas had done the same with her. It was agonizing to realize they truly loved each other, and that was wrong. That criminal didn't deserve a girl like Judith, and Justin felt righteous indignation at being the one to end their illicit affair.

And yeah, Judith was right. He was a complete pervert. He read and reread their sexting like a preacher with his bible. It was fun, perverse, and both of them were experts. How did you become that way? He had never sent a single sext. He felt like the shy, stuffy farm boy he was, ashamed and self-conscious.

Imagined being like that with Judith. Replacing Nicolas in every sense. He pulled up Nicolas's masturbation video and compared dicks. Nicolas was big. He was bigger, but still, Nicolas had a big enough dick to feel threatening. Justin felt one thousand percent threatened by this Casanova, and he hated it.

They used affectionate euphemisms when referring to each other's genitalia. Honey pot, love muscle, lady garden. Used sexy emojis in every message, many of which he had to look up the meaning of. Justin had never used an emoji once in his life. He hated Nicolas with a passion.

Judith shared tons about herself and some of her memories of abuse. He carefully read how Nicolas responded. This guy knew exactly what to say. Every time. Justin could never find the perfect words, and it made him angry. He realized more and more that Judith wasn't at fault and felt like shit for punishing her all those months.

She was a sad and lonely girl searching for someone to make her happy and understand her. Nicolas swooped in and did just that. Their sexual relationship was foisted on her mainly by Nicolas.

Justin took notes on her feelings, likes and interests. She loved her mom and secretly wanted to be more like her. Wished she was bright like Lizzy. Missed her dad like crazy and believed Justin had somehow filled the void in her life that her dad had left. She loved the beach, any beach, the sound of the ocean waves, and the cold, bracing sea air.

One of her fantasies was camping under the stars and going at it with her honey in a sleeping bag. Why? Because the thought of being cold and having to share another body for warmth was so sexy. Justin felt intensely aroused by this thought and knew with absolute certainty that he was the right guy for her. His body temperature ran high, and she loved this about him.

Her favorite color was green, like her eyes—any hue of green. She enjoyed spending time in the great outdoors. Her dreams included driving fast on the highway along the ocean with the windows down. He was more than happy to make that dream come true in his hot rod and fantasized about taking her to California, cruising down the highway at breakneck speed. She hoped to try parasailing. Planned to hike up to Machu Picchu someday.

She loved animals, especially dogs. Considered herself a spiritual person, which surprised Justin, and she liked the idea of old religions. Justin was pissed to read how Nicolas, with a degree in anthropology, encouraged this passion and was a wealth of knowledge on the subject. She treated him like he was a genius, and that sucked. Judith made this guy feel amazing the way she did him, and that sucked too.

It went on and on. Justin's obsession grew the more he read. He didn't give a shit about Nicolas. Was tempted to black out any content about his life or personality. But he loved getting to know Judith and pored over every word where she talked about her cop, declared her love for him, defended him, or praised his skills as a man. Judith did love him. Nicolas tried so hard to tear him out of her heart but was unsuccessful. Thank God.

Life with Judith since she ended the affair had been a dream. She was right. When he stopped pushing her away and playing the stupid mind games, he no longer felt like a horny beast. She relaxed him in a way he had never felt relaxed before. She was like a drug that treated anxiety, low self-esteem and depression, and eliminated his sexual frustration. He knew he could never live without her. This meant he needed to become everything Nicolas had been to her, plus everything he already was, and he was up for the challenge.

But still, he caught a hint of sadness in her eyes. She still held a torch for Nicolas. Justin had no idea how to eradicate Nicolas from her mind for good, but he was determined to figure out Nicolas's weaknesses and exploit them. Make Judith realize how unworthy he was to share a space in her heart, even as a brief memory. Justin wanted him gone entirely.

Justin was taking a plane for the first time in his life in a few weeks, and he felt terrified. He had never left his home state. Everyone at work was proud of him and jealous that he was vacationing in Mexico, so he went along with it. He had no idea why Martha and Erik had invited them on this trip. Initially, he refused to go, but Judith insisted. Said it would make her mom happy.

It was Thanksgiving afternoon, and Judith was in the house with his mom, helping with the meal. Justin was out in his garage when Judith came in and wrapped her arms around him.

"We have enough food to feed an army in there. You better be hungry."

"I am hungry. Especially for you." He pulled her down onto the saggy old couch.

"Remember our first date? How you rejected me in this same spot?"

"I do. We have to create some new memories, don't we?"

"I am more than happy to."

"You excited about our trip?" he asked.

"I'm apprehensive about it, to be honest."

"Lizzy's coming. You haven't hung out with her in a while."

"True, but we have nothing in common anymore."

"Well, family is still family."

"You're right." A shadow crept across her eyes. She looked afraid.

"If it means seeing the ocean for the first time and chasing you around in a bikini, I'm all in."

"I can't believe you've never seen the ocean."

"Nicolas was right. I am a hick," he admitted.

"Let's not talk about him."

They made out until his mom showed up at the door, interrupting them with a happy smile.

"Time for a feast, lovebirds."

"One sec, Mom."

Justin knelt in front of the saggy couch and pulled a small diamond ring from his pocket. He knew this was sudden, but he felt it was the only way to make her forget about that criminal and claim her as his woman.

"Judith, will you do me the honor of becoming my wife?"

She looked astonished, then her eyes glazed with tears, and she threw her arms around his neck. He slipped the ring on her finger and kissed her.

"Yes, oh yes, I will!"

Justin shared the good news over dinner, then ate until he was stuffed. That night, he held Judith in his arms and thought about all the things he had learned about her from her conversations with Nicolas. Wished he had been the one she shared those things with. Even now, after they made up, they didn't talk. Spent most of their time having sex, which was great but made him sad. Was it his fault? Hers? Why couldn't they communicate? Maybe his mom was right, and he was stuck in his ways. He was determined to change. The thought that Nicolas connected with Judith in a way he was incapable of was unacceptable to him. Justin vowed to figure out how to make her open up to him the way she had with that criminal. And he would do anything to make that happen.

Chapter 26

Nicolas

Nicolas watched with unbearable envy as his Belladonna rode Justin's back into the ocean waves. They were laughing hysterically and looked to be having a great time. Since Belladonna had cut him off, she had mended her relationship with that cop, which was a huge disappointment. Still, he couldn't fail. As soon as they made love, everything would be back on track. He was going to inject her with passion, then watch her squirm with pleasure as he made her an addict for life. Justin had nothing on him.

Nicolas accepted the fact that he was a masochist who got off on the pain from seeing those two together. He was a voyeur to this vixen and her fucking cop. He jerked off so hard at the thought of them fucking and imagined himself cuffed to their bed, watching, tormented beyond endurance. Why this got him off, he didn't understand. But his lust was fueled by this kink now, and it sucked big time. Along with his addiction to drugs, he drank himself stupid over the last few months. Miserably alone and morbidly obsessed, holding out for this moment when he could finally consummate their love.

Still, nine months after that fateful first night, they were here in Cabo San Lucas, as he had so meticulously planned. Where he told Belladonna he would take her, and it would be him on the beach, stroking her beautiful skin. Not Justin. Him. He had to walk away before he attempted murder. Watching her flounce around in her bikini, Justin's hands all over her, his jealousy rode him like a fiend. Belladonna belonged with him and always would.

Martha was tucked under his father's arm, walking along the seashore. Erik whispered something in her ear, and she shone like the sun. She looked radiant. Nicolas sighed with contentment. Because of him, Martha and Erik had found each other, and now, he was strangely at peace with it. The perfect couple. Exquisitely happy. For one second, Nicolas struggled against a tidal wave of agony as it swept through him. And he remembered the way he felt until he tried to kill Martha—how he wanted to run away with her and keep her forever. Now he understood. Martha was Catrina number two. He fixated on her because of that alone. All he wanted was to get his nanny back. But you can't go back. You just can't. He understood that now.

He glanced at Lizzy, who sat on a beach towel and wasn't even trying to hide her drool, as Justin carried Judith back to their towels. So, the little sister wanted a piece of him? Perfect. Maybe she would fuck it all up for the happy couple. Not a chance. She was so-so-looking but couldn't hold a candle to Belladonna's beauty. Nicolas almost felt sorry for her. It had to suck to have a sibling who outdid you in every way possible.

Poised with anticipation, Nicolas watched the boy he paid as he handed Martha his letter. She opened it, recognized the handwriting, and read. Martha's hand went to her mouth in shock, and her head swerved around the crowded beach looking for him, hope gleaming in her eyes. His savior. The mother he never had.

The letter passed from hand to hand. Each in turn read his message to them. He held his breath for Belladonna's response. She placed her hands on her hips, her pretty head whirling around the beach, and the hatred rolled off her. He beamed with satisfaction. God yes. They still had their insane connection. She wanted to kill him still, and it filled him with heat and desire. She twisted her fists and screamed.

"Nicolas! You asshole!"

Her violence was so erotic. He was satisfied forever, knowing he had brought about this boiling burst of emotion. He drove her wild in a way that her cop never could.

Justin pulled on his shoes, called someone on his cell, and ran into the street. Nicolas sorely wished he might rush out in front of a car. Adios. His hatred for that cop knew no bounds. Erik held Martha in a death grip, reassuring her as she searched for a glimpse of him. Caught in the throes, all because of him. He thought of what he wrote.

Dear Family,

I know these words won't change anything. I screwed it all up and that's that. But I want you to know, Martha, you freed me. I no longer have the death kink or the nightmares. You are an angel and the mother I never had. Sorry that I abducted you and tried to seduce you. It was fucked up. I'm so happy you survived my psychotic break.

Belladonna, you tore off my mask, revealing a raging monster, and then nearly killed me. You are my soulmate and I will have you. You should have run away with me and you know it. I am in your head. I am between your legs. You will never be rid of me.

Dad, you tried to save me at the end there, and that almost makes up for my shitty childhood. I see now. Catrina wasn't your fault. It wasn't my fault, either. It was a war that nobody started, and I was the sole casualty. I forgive you, and I want you to know that.

Justin, believe me when I tell you I fuck her, and she loves it. She's not yours. She's mine. I bet you wish every day that you got there in time to fill my head with lead. Sorry to disappoint. A 'good guy' like you can never truly comprehend Judith. Best of luck trying.

Anyhow, I'd like to rewrite at least some of the past, but I know that's impossible. I lost my shit and hurt you all in different ways. Take care, and know that, in my eyes, you will always be my family.

Justin hurried away to contact local law enforcement. Belladonna donned her shift and ran off without saying where she was going. Martha, Erik and Lizzy gathered around, rereading his note. Nicolas crashed their party and sent Justin off on a wild goose chase, just as he intended.

Nicolas followed from a distance, contemplating when to grab her. His carefully crafted plans were finally paying off. He recited in his mind what he had fantasized about for months—how he would please her, make her scream with delight and then solidify their plans for the future. He was still the best. He could steal any woman, no matter how happy or fulfilled she seemed. Even if she was with fucking Captain America.

Belladonna would never break free of him now.

Tanya Madsen

Chapter 27

Judith

Judith scrambled down a street twinkling with Christmas lights. She was terrified. Nicolas was here. He had sent that letter and now he was looking for her. What should she do? Should she tell Justin? But Justin had hurried off to notify the authorities. It was time to return to her hotel, lock the door, and not come out until Justin was back.

Heart pounding, she felt like a hunted animal. Nicolas was following her, his dark eyes fixed on her somewhere in the crowd. If he found her, it was over. She couldn't say no to Nicolas. He cast his love spell on her and stole her heart. Nothing she could do would ever get it back.

Judith rounded a corner, pushing through a crowd of tourists. She spotted her hotel up ahead. Almost to safety. Almost. And then he appeared before her. Tall, slim, pale, blonde, and tragically beautiful, as always. Their eyes linked, and together they spiraled into that space between lifetimes where they belonged. Nicolas rushed towards her, picked her up, and held her against the side of a building, kissing her so passionately that all of her stomach butterflies burst free. Sandwiched tightly, she kissed him back ferociously, Justin immediately obliterated from her mind. It was a hopeless cause, trying to reject this man.

Wordlessly, Nicolas took her hand and pulled her through the crowd, along foreign streets to an apartment complex, where he raced up the steps, dragging her behind him. A storm brewed and the wind whipped at her hair, tickling her bare skin. Lightning flashed in the sky as he unlocked the door and pulled her inside. Thunder cracked as he drew her to his chest and kissed her so hard that she had to push him away to catch her breath. The rain rattled against the roof as he tore off her shift, lifted her as effortlessly as Justin ever had, and carried her to the bed. Her slim Casanova was deceptively strong.

"Nine whole months, Belladonna. We have a lot of fucking to make up for."

Brandishing her wrists with joy, Nicolas cuffed her, then cuffed her to another set of cuffs that were secured to the headboard. This was it—the culmination of a thousand daydreams. Down into the abyss she went, as he dragged her straight to the depths of his fantasy. Nicolas took her face in his hands.

"I love you. I love you. I love you."

He whispered his mantra as he kissed her. Nibbling her ears, he then turned her head aside, making sensual wet love bites along her neck, sending chills through every nerve. He knew exactly where to stimulate, as if he were a surgeon with insight into all of her most sensitive spots.

"I love you more!" she cried as she spread her legs in eager anticipation.

He stared down at her like she was a hit of heroin, then attacked her in a frenzy. He tore off her string bikini with his teeth and devoured her skin.

Every time his lips touched her, she cried for release. Nipples, hard against his tongue, he rolled them back and forth, biting softly. Wet, throbbing, so aroused she could hardly bear it, as he explored between her legs, circling her clitoris with his fingernail, then probing her vagina until she was shaking. Then he sat back and beamed.

"Belladonna, you're so nubile. I can't wait to get in there."

"Nicolas, you're driving me insane."

"Good."

Judith shuddered so violently that she was soon covered in sweat, and he licked it off her. This was too much. She had never been seduced like this, had never felt anything like this. His open, wet mouth nibbled its way down her breasts, belly, inner thighs. Pinning her legs apart, he swept her into slow motion with his agile tongue. Spread her labia. Inflamed her. Teased her. Slowly. Building. So good. So damn good. Moaning, grinding against his lips. Climax peaking. And oh God. Oh God. He held her down and sucked as she spasmed, melting her into mindless ecstasy. She squealed in delight as the orgasm raged through her body, like it had the night they met. But now, she wasn't pretending. She had given herself tons of orgasms but had never come this hard. Nicolas was a fucking sex god.

"Wow. You came as fast as you did in the car. In less than a minute."

"More. Give me more."

"That's the plan, my sweet. I've been starving for your pussy for months. I'm gonna eat you out until I'm stuffed."

"It's too sensitive still. Wait," she cried breathlessly.

"That's why I need the cuffs, so you can't stop me. Belladonna, I'm making you my addict for life."

He went down on her again and tenderly induced a second, even more mind-blowing orgasm.

This was beyond mere pleasure. Beyond her wildest dreams. This was the seventh heaven. A thousand times more satisfying than the video sex they engaged in for months. This was where she belonged.

"Twice, Nicolas? No guy has EVER done this to me before."

"I know. I'm gonna make you come at least six times. You won't forget today for as long as you live."

Judith groaned and spread her legs in submission, urging him to go again. And he did.

At some point, Nicolas dragged her out of her delirium and back to earth, sat her up, and propped her up with a few pillows so she could see him. She stared at his perfect naked body, lust burning through her. She loved every single thing about him on both a primal and a spiritual level. He smirked as he straddled her, tilting his pelvis and stroking his erection.

"I love how you ogle my penis. Makes me feel like Zeus or something."

"I could eat you alive. How can you hold out like this?"

"Belladonna, I'm the best of the best, remember?"

"You're an incubus, Nicolas. Or maybe even a god."

"Oh yeah. I joined the Greek pantheon years ago. I've waited months and months for this moment. I can hold out a bit longer. But first, I gotta indulge your kink."

Her eyes went wide and her mouth watered. She felt the saliva pooling, and she stuck out her tongue, hungrily licking into the air. Nicolas dramatically thrust his long hard dick through his hand, squeezing as he cried out her name, acting out the sex video he had sent her. To her amazement, he didn't ejaculate. Just stroked himself until she was vibrating with desire. Then he moved forward and hovered in front of her mouth and slid the wet tip along her lips. She tried to grab it, to suck that delicious thing in. Caught the head, moaning as it pulsated against her tongue. He quickly pulled away.

"Please, please, please, Nicolas. This is torture!"

Flushed and shaking, he laughed.

"Okay. No more of that. Or I won't hold out much longer."

"What are you doing to me?"

"I'm seducing the fuck out of you, my sweet. Trust me, I'm just getting started. Now, I'm gonna get you off by sucking on your tits."

"Impossible!" she cried.

"Watch me."

Nicolas laid her back down and feasted on her breasts, tormenting her nipples, taking turns on each side. Just the right speed and pressure like he had done in the car that night, mercilessly driving her lust on a rampage. Until she was once again groaning and fuck. He got her off again. Licking his lips, he smiled with satisfaction and kissed her, then whispered.

"Told you so. Okay. Time to get kinky, my beautiful girl."

Nicolas turned her over onto her stomach. Holding down her ankles, he began to tickle her.

"Tickling?"

"Catrina used to tie me up and tickle torture me until I peed my pants. Then she'd suck me off. It was pretty fucking intense. Just let the sensation build, Belladonna."

Judith had no idea that tickling could be this sexy. It was unreal. Her pelvis tingled as she giggled and squirmed. He tormented the backs of her knees. She kicked viciously, pleading with him to stop.

"Does it turn you on?" he murmured as he licked inside her ear, while tickling her hips until she was convulsing. Stopped to probe her vagina. "Oh yeah. I've got you so juicy. I'm in heaven right now. Never done this to a woman. Only dreamed about it."

She shuddered as his fingers caressed her thighs, slowly making their way up encircling her butt. It felt so good, she moaned and moaned, the anticipation driving her insane as he grazed along her back and sides in soft, exquisite circles until she was intoxicated by his touch.

"Have I died and gone to heaven?" she cried breathlessly.

"Not yet. But soon," he promised.

He pulled her to her knees, arms taut, straining against the cuffs, head down. Hovering, he tickled her breasts and belly as he rubbed his erection against her. It was sensation overload. She quivered and groaned.

"Please fuck me now. Please."

"We're almost there. Okay, tighten up, my angel. It's time to head into your love tunnel and drive you wild."

She constricted as he tried to wriggle two fingers up inside her. He pried her legs farther apart and tried again. She tightened even harder.

"You're so perfect, Belladonna. You like it?"

She wiggled her butt in reply and he smacked it playfully.

"Then you're gonna love this."

Nicolas probed his way past her stiff defenses, and the pointer and middle fingers went up and in. Plunging, grinding, she moved against his fingers, moaning.

Then he leaned over and began licking her derrière. Back and forth, up and down. The long, wet strokes of his warm tongue as he masturbated her were so erotic, she was never gonna be satisfied with any other man again. All-consumed, soul-abandoned, and heart-wrenched, she wanted Nicolas for all time and eternity.

He groaned as he massaged her G-spot expertly, his ravenous tongue revealing he was finally at his breaking point. Momentum building, her fifth orgasm peaking. He eased his dick in, grinding hard, two fingers polishing her clitoris like a precious gem, she felt the orgasm detonate everywhere all at once.

"Oh, my God, Nic. You are fucking huuuge. Pulease! Now. Oh yeah. So perfect. Nic. So hard. Come on. Go faster! Now! Yes. Yes!"

As she spiraled through the afterglow, Nicolas lost his shit. Breasts cupped in his hands, he took off at lightning speed. She braced herself, clinging onto the headboard, as if standing in the ocean, indignant against the waves as he swept her away. Euphoria exploded inside her as he bore down hard, filling her with seven point two inches of ungodly pleasure. She felt him from the tips of her fingers down to her toes. Prostrating herself, she tilted to get him in there deeper. He clenched her hips, lifting her off the bed with each thrust.

"Harder. Faster. Nic, oh Nic!"

"My Belladonna. You. Are. A. Fucking. Goddess!"

He cried in bursts as he slammed his way to the finish line. By the time he climaxed, they were both screaming.

Nicolas shoved every sexual encounter she had ever experienced into a ditch, even the lustful bed-thumping sex she shared with Justin. After an hour of the most erotic rapture she had ever experienced in her life, Nicolas turned her onto her back and lay his head on one breast. Gasping for air as he listened to her racing heart, staring at her other breast while tracing her areola with his finger. He plucked at her nipple, sending sparks through her, making her brilliant eyes plead for more. He was the hottest lover in existence, and he only wanted her.

Chapter 28

Nicolas

Raising his head, Nicolas captured her eyes, inquiring. Desperately hoping it was everything she had fantasized about for months.

"My God, Nicolas. What was that? Are you even human?"

Smiling happily, he uncuffed her and pulled her to his chest.

"So, it was good?"

"Good? Not a chance. There isn't a word in the English language to describe what you just did to me."

"I'm so happy you love the cuffs. My dream girl, a million times over. And I've had that planned down to the last detail for months—especially the grand finale, licking your luscious ass while masturbating you. I've jerked off like a fiend to that fantasy. You came so hard. That was sexy as hell. We should've filmed it."

"I love the cuffs as long as you wear them too." She smiled coyly as she took his wrists. "Kiss me, lover boy. Then it's my turn. I'm gonna tease you even harder than you teased me."

"We'll see about that." He grinned. "I'll wear them for you and only you."

"You are everything you promised, you sexy beast. I forgot how gorgeous you are in person. I feel like I'm fucking one of the fallen angels," she whispered as she secured him to the headboard and leaned forward onto his chest.

"Did you like my diversion down at the beach?"

"It certainly worked."

"I caught Lizzy on the beach today, drooling over your cop. Beware. She wants to rip his clothes off."

"Wonderful. One more thing to stress about."

"Was it hard to convince them to take a family vacation here? They didn't suspect anything? I figured your asshole boyfriend would."

"Justin, yeah. He's never even left Utah. Getting his passport was traumatic."

"What a hick. Like I told you, you've made the wrong choice. You need to choose me. I can't believe that bastard blocked me. It was him, right?"

"Of course. We had an awful fight. I almost didn't make it out alive. He confiscated my phone, took off for hours, and read through all of our messages like a pervert, then deleted them. Pretty much hated my guts and said so many cruel things to me that I should be traumatized for life."

"Why didn't you leave him right then and there?"

"Justin convinced me to stay."

"How?"

"He looked so sad. As if the cruel things he said to me hurt him, too. I felt bad. I'm sorry I threw you to the wolves. I don't know what's wrong with me."

"Why are you here? You could have told them to cancel the trip."

"Because all those months made me obsessed with you. I can never get you out of my head. And now, after today, I'm royally fucked."

"Belladonna, you've broken me. If I can't be with you, I'll have to kill myself."

Belladonna stroked his chest. Nicolas knew he wasn't as muscular as Justin, and definitely not as manly. Justin was a true-blue alpha male. But his sinewy muscles were well-defined, and his fair skin was delightfully tender. She looked like she wanted to kiss every square inch of him.

Right now, Nicolas was high as a kite. He had popped Ecstasy and a Viagra before chasing her down, but the heroin was also in his system. This hookup felt surreal, like an out-of-body experience. He just hoped to God she wouldn't notice he was strung out. He couldn't bear Belladonna to know he was a junkie, since he planned to get clean, starting tomorrow.

"Whatever this is between us is more addictive than the most addictive drug. After I choked you nearly to death that night, all I could think about was ripping your pants down and riding you until you woke up."

"I fucking wish you had. Then we wouldn't be in this predicament. Tell me. I must know. Now that you've experienced the real thing, am I bigger than him?"

"You have a perfect dick, Nicolas. But I hate to break it to you, Justin's is bigger. Still, you really are some evil sex god. And to be honest, I like yours better. You fit me like a glove."

"I don't believe you. I think you just want to torture me with jealousy."

"There's nothing I want more than to torture you."

"What are you gonna do to me?"

"I'm gonna give you the hottest fuck you can possibly imagine."

"Wait. Wait. See my phone? I need you to film this. This is momentous. Being full-out seduced by a girl my age."

She quickly set up his phone on the dresser alongside the bed, ensured the camera screen captured everything, and then pressed the record button.

Nicolas trembled with anticipation. This had evolved into a competition between two apex seducers—an epic Tyrannosaurus Rex versus Velociraptor showdown in bed.

"So, my Casanova, since you like tickling so much. Let's start there."

She sat on his ankles and tickled up and down his legs, kneecaps and thighs. Oh God. It felt so good, just as he remembered it as a child—erotic sensory overload, provoking an immediate erection.

"Wow. That didn't take long."

"I haven't been tickled in twelve years. It brings back so many horrifying but super-hot memories. It's sexually confusing, let me tell you. I'm so happy to have met a girl I can share all my kinks with."

"I hope you know, I'm gonna edge the fuck out of you, my dear, sweet Casanova."

"I've never been seduced before or been with a woman who calls the shots. I mean, not since Catrina. I've been too afraid. But now, I'm so excited."

"So am I."

Belladonna bent over, pushed his legs apart, and licked along his inner thighs, then nibbled her way up, avoiding his prominent genitals. Back and forth over his belly and chest, as if searching for all his sensitive spots. Sucked on his nipples. Then his earlobes. Tickled his armpits. French kissed him. Nibbled at his neck. Jiggled her breasts inches from his face. Tried everything to seduce him. He loved it all. Then she scooted down and rubbed his dick along her lips then between her breasts, eyes locked with his.

He stared, his starry eyes absorbing every detail, for when he had to survive off these memories until they were finally united for good.

"My God, you are so erotic."

She played with him until he was dangerously close to an orgasm, which she sensed. So she sat up and waited for him to calm down a bit. He watched her gaze around the room until she found a couple of his t-shirts.

"Nicolas, I'm gonna reveal to you my dark side. This is one of my hottest sex fantasies. I like to get aggressive, and that scares some guys. I hope you enjoy it."

She hooked his feet through one armhole, twisted tightly, spread his legs apart, and hooked the other armhole around the posts on the footboard. Now they were talking. Full restraints. Hot. Belladonna was his soulmate in every sense of the word.

"What are you gonna do to me?"

"I'm gonna make you come so hard, and I don't want you kicking me away like Justin does. He can't handle anything."

"I knew sex with him was totally vanilla."

"Well, he grew up a good church boy."

"Sounds disgusting."

She giggled, then crawled down between his legs. Held his penis upright and licked all of his sexy boy parts until he was gasping. Then, so very softly, she rolled each testicle around her tongue.

"Shit!"

His legs were spasming within seconds.

"What is it you like about fucking guys?"

She asked coyly as she stroked and licked him.

"Um—"

Distracted by her hands and mouth, he shuddered and moaned.

"Is it this?"

She felt her way down with her finger, found his anus and shoved her pointer finger in. Curled it forward and scratched an itch he didn't know he had. Holy Shit. Belladonna was making him feel like a novice. He was speechless, incoherent. Every nerve in his body vibrated with pleasure. It was like the psychotic break equivalent of sex. Yeah, it was the drugs heightening the experience to the nth degree. But it was also this sex goddess who somehow knew exactly what his body craved.

She returned to lightly sucking his balls and slowly pumping his dick, while rubbing up inside him until he was whimpering and groaning.

"Shit, Belladonna. You are as good in bed as I am."

"It is so satisfying to watch you go rabid."

She sucked the tip and he strained to get in there deeper but she pulled away and smiled.

"Not yet. I love teasing you too much. You're so fun, Nicolas."

"This is a full-body immersive fuck. More, I want more!"

She gave him more. Took him to the edge and yanked him back again and again. Played with his genitals and then let him hang there while she tormented his inner thighs, which she had quickly discovered was one of his most sensitive spots, back and forth between unbearable ecstasy and mere teasing.

"You have that delirious look in your eyes that men always get when I play with them too hard."

"You can't imagine how good this feels. Like I'm climaxing every ten seconds."

"Seeing you tied up like this is the sexiest thing ever. And your sexy boy parts. Yum-yum."

She went down on him again, rubbing the perineum on the outside and massaging it on the inside while sucking his throbbing appendage until he was convulsing and crying for release.

"You've driven me beyond endurance, Belladonna. Please."

Quickly, she moved up and straddled him.

"Okay. I guess. But you know, I could torment you for hours if I wanted."

"If I'm an incubus, then you are definitely a succubus."

"I guess I am. Now, I know you're gonna come fast."

"You bet I am. I used to be able to last forever. But with you? It takes everything I've got to hold out five minutes. Now I feel bad for making fun of Justin about it. I had no idea you were this good in bed."

"I have one more surprise for you," she whispered in his ear as she mounted him, sliding in and out. His eyes rolled backward with euphoria. He could barely move. She had all the power, complete control, just like Catrina used to.

"Justin is the man for me. He has the bigger dick, the better job, a hot body, and a hot rod. Imagine me on top of him right now. Close your eyes and see it. Me, riding his big dick. Him groaning. Me screaming. Oh. Oh. Justin. Oh God. Harder. Justin. Oh. Oh. Harder! Justin. Pulease!"

"Fuck!!!"

Nicolas climaxed violently and moaned helplessly as she rode him hard and fast. It felt like three explosive orgasms in a row.

"Oh God, I'm coming again. Oh shit!" she cried.

Nicolas watched her writhe and shudder on top of him until she collapsed. It was the sexiest thing he had ever experienced.

"Justin never lets me torment him like this. I LOVE that chain reaction, where I get an orgasm from your orgasm."

He felt so dizzy with euphoria that he could hardly see straight.

"What the fuck did you just do to me?"

"I love you, Nicolas. Just trying to satisfy your jealousy kink."

"Do it again," he mumbled incoherently, "like, act out a whole scenario with Justin. Torture me."

"Oh, you poor horny boy," she crooned.

"You have no idea how much I've masturbated thinking about you and Justin having sex. This kink has seriously fucked me up."

"Well, I do love foreplay."

Nicolas watched Belladonna lie on her back between his legs, spread wide open in front of him, and touch herself as she acted out sex with Justin down to the finest detail. Engorging his imagination with the dirtiest talk imaginable. She faked an orgasm since, she claimed, there was no way she could give herself one after having him go down on her. And when she finally sat up and peered at him, she giggled.

He probably looked like a chained animal as he imagined it all. Taunted and teased, unable to touch himself as he pictured Belladonna in restraints, Justin on top of her, driving *his* soulmate into a state of permanent delirium. The envy and the lust combined into something beyond the scope of his comprehension. One thousand lifetimes of yearning for this woman all channeled into this single erection. He feared he wouldn't survive the orgasm. It would melt him from the inside out. Never, never in his life had he felt this way. Completely unhinged by a woman.

"Look at you. Am I driving you insane?"

His wrists were raw from writhing against the cuffs, eyes glazed with drug-induced euphoria. Belladonna smiled with sadistic glee.

She grabbed his glistening dick and began to stroke it, cleaning it with the sheet. What was she gonna do to him? She stared with complete satisfaction as he gyrated wildly.

"I can't believe how fast you get me there with this kink. Put me out of my misery."

Belladonna lay forward, holding him at the base like an ice cream cone, then licked dramatically as she kicked her legs playfully behind her, looking up at him wide-eyed.

"Tell me how you like your blowjob, you sexy beast, and I'll remember it forever."

Seriously? Nicolas had given a hundred blowjobs up to this point in his life, but hadn't had a woman go down on him since he was a kid. He had fantasized about it a ton, though. Never thought he could ever trust any woman to touch him, bind him, arouse him like this. Thought that Catrina reigned supreme, and so far, he hadn't been able to dethrone her. It was liberating to realize that, finally, she might be replaced. Belladonna had no idea how much of an honor he bestowed upon her in his heart by surrendering to her like this.

"I love you so much, Belladonna. Okay, this is what I fantasize about, but I've never had a girl actually do it to me before. So here we go. I'm restrained, which is perfect. I love the feeling of you having complete control. Now, cradle my ass with one hand. To prod me when I lose my mind and forget how to thrust. Then stroke my dick with the other, tight and slow. The insane pressure will drive me bonkers, but don't speed up. That's what Catrina used to do. I'm sick, I know."

"Oh, baby. I understand."

"I'm good with it now. Anyhow, do whatever you want to me, but stay away from the tip so I can hold out."

"That's gonna be hard. It's the best part."

"Okay, go for it. Anything for you."

Nicolas watched as Belladonna slid her hands under his butt then lifted him off the bed like an offering. Rolled his throbbing head around and around her tongue, joyously sending a flurry of delicious currents up his legs and into his groin. No. Not yet.

"Fuck, oh fuck. Hold off. Stop!"

"So sexy. I love how responsive you are."

"I'm gonna spontaneously combust here. Shit. So when you see me start to ooze, like right now, slide me in. Take it slow. Make it last. Make me beg. I wanna feel that tickle as you gag just a bit. Then blow me until I'm blubbering. Take all the time you want. I fucking love the buildup. When I start to cuss, you'll know I'm at my limit. That's when you'll take me down, down, down, pump me tight and fast. When I start to shoot off, suck hard. Ride me with your tongue until I'm delirious. No matter how badly I squirm, don't stop until I'm limp."

"Won't it be too painful?"

"Hell yeah. Catrina tortured the fuck out of me and ruined me for life."

"Can I swallow?"

"If that's okay. Catrina always did, even when I begged her not to."

"Whatever it takes for you to achieve nirvana."

"I hope you take me all the way to Shangri-La, my sweet."

"Oh, I plan to."

"Finally! I can replace that bitch in my memories."

"Are we recreating the past right now?"

"No. We are rewriting the past."

"Nicolas, you are the fantasy man of my hottest dreams."

"I know."

Belladonna exceeded his wildest expectations. Strung him along, made it last and last. And when she finally let him explode in the back of her throat, it was half ecstasy-half agony, as she sucked him through a full minute of post-orgasm torture. Just like Catrina used to do, but better. Because she was his soulmate, sent by the universe to liberate him from his past. Now, he would no longer feel like a freak for having his hottest sex fantasies be the disturbing result of his child abuse. Sex with Belladonna was the deepest form of catharsis. He wouldn't survive this life if he couldn't share it with her.

Now, he needed to convey his well-thought-out plan to her. Get her to buy it, get her to commit. Get her to promise to run away with him, where they could finally be as one. Free to satisfy and heal each other for the rest of their lives.

Chapter 29

Judith

All afternoon, they took turns making each other speechless with ecstasy, fulfilling every fantasy they had shared all those months. Now, she was experiencing it in real time, and it was phenomenal. His body proved so easy to arouse, and he couldn't get enough of her. She didn't think a guy could get it up again and again so quickly. Was it due to her, or was it because Nicolas was a sex addict? He climaxed repeatedly, and he didn't push her away, no matter how hard she teased him. He held nothing back. She instinctively knew exactly what drove him crazy. In return, his first thought was for her satisfaction. He satisfied her over and over. Never in all her years had she been with a man like him. He was more than a Casanova. Nicolas was her Casanova.

Later, post coitus, bound up in a lover's embrace, Judith said,

"I can't believe you're a prostitute when you should be an actor. Why don't you try out for one of those Mexican soap operas? You can play the hot American."

"Because I already have a job, obsessing over how to make you mine. I won't give up until I make that happen. How are you managing to survive being stuck out in the sticks? That's the life you want, shacked up with some hick cop?"

Oh God. Justin. The memory of her fiancé came flooding back to her. Like a meteor shower, it crashed into her, pinning her with a thousand pounds of guilt. How would she hide this from Justin? He was her hero. He had even forgiven her online affair with Nicolas. She was a horrible person!

Justin is the best man in the world. I don't deserve him."

"Belladonna, you need to choose. Me. Not him. ME. You have my dick in bondage. I can't consider anyone else. You've wrecked me. Drowned me in obsession."

"You deserve to be drowned after what you did to my mom." She reminded him with a kiss.

"We exchanged hearts the moment you walked into my dad's house. You may have had the gun pointed at my head, but I knew instantly that you belonged with me, body and soul. And forget about what happened to your mom. Martha is alive and well. They look happy together."

"They are."

"I have to admit, you are the worst actress I have ever seen. Your fake orgasms are atrocious."

She smacked his arm playfully.

"You're so mean!"

"It's cute. I mean, I love it about you."

"Why?"

"Because you'll never be able to deceive me."

"I can sure convince Justin."

"He's a fucking loser, is why."

"He doesn't care if I have an orgasm, so maybe you're right."

"What should we try next?"

He was ready to go again.

"I only have thirty more minutes. Justin will wonder where I've gone."

"I don't care about that piece of shit. I'm tempted to lock you up and keep you with me until we can get the hell out of the country. If I had the means, if there were any way I could, I would."

"I wouldn't be the wanton temptress if you locked me in a cage. I'd be a sad girl. You don't want that."

"I'd take a sad girl if it meant I could have you all to myself. And trust me, you wouldn't be sad for long. I know how to make you happy. How do you expect me to survive without you?"

"There is no easy answer."

After another thirty minutes of tearing at each other like wildcats, Judith put on her bikini and shift, then slipped into her sandals. He gripped her hands, and his eyes looked glassy. For a moment, she wondered if he was on drugs. He was so pale. With his blonde hair and dark eyes, he looked like a gorgeous Anne Rice vampire.

"They didn't need to catch me and throw me in prison. I'm already in hell down here, a thousand miles from you."

"Please, don't ruin my life by telling Justin about today. It pissed me off what you wrote in your letter."

"Your outburst was priceless. I have to watch the two of you ride off into the sunset day after day, since Justin loves to torture me by posting pictures of you together on Facebook. It's a little hard to deal with. You've both driven me mad."

She grabbed his lovely locks, which were growing shaggy and made him look like some boy-band heartthrob, and tackled him onto the bed, watching his eyes light on fire at her fury. Stroked his naked body and kissed him fiendishly. If only she could beat him at his own seductive game, but it was impossible. She had met her match. After having Nicolas in the flesh, she now knew her love for him would survive the apocalypse.

Nicolas grabbed his phone and turned on some music—a heartbreaking song with a good beat—and took her in his arms. He grabbed her waist, clasped hands, swung her under his arm, twirling her around, then pulled her close. She moved her feet, remembering how much she loved to dance. And he was a sweet dancer, too. She felt like she was growing wings.

Tucked into his chest, she lay against him and imagined a whole life like this, having this gorgeous, sweet guy by her side day and night. It hurt to know it could never be. And it hurt worse because her hero was such a terrible disappointment. Justin had never done anything like this, and he never would.

They danced in silence, song after song. Time seemed to slow as they kissed and kissed again. Nicolas whispered.

"What are you thinking?"

"I wish—" Her throat burned with tears.

"This could last forever?"

"Uh-huh."

"It will."

"How? I only met Justin because of you, and he'll never let me go."

"He is a roadblock. You were meant to find me, just as I was meant to find you. We have fate to contend with. We are meant for each other. Walk away from this pretentious bullshit life with him."

"He'll never let me go," she repeated.

Nicolas stood back and took her face in his hands.

"He'll have to. Belladonna, we belong together. You know it. The sooner you accept this and embrace a life with me, the happier you will be."

"Nicolas, you're right. But Justin has a hold on me. He is so good that I feel unworthy of him. Somehow, that gets me super-hot and makes me want him more, and when he makes me say I'm unworthy, he gets so aroused it's unreal. It's like a kink, but I don't understand it."

"I do. He's an emotionally abusive asshole. Making you feel unworthy gets him off."

"Ugh. When you say it that way, it sounds sick."

"It is sick. Belladonna, I have lived through what you are dealing with. I wanted Catrina's love so badly that I nearly wrecked your mom's life trying to recreate it. Some people can get in our heads and melt us into their minions. Justin is doing that to you."

"Really?"

"All the signs are present. You are obsessed but unhappy, constantly trying to convince yourself that he's the one. It's all a lie, honey. He isn't the guy you think he is."

"He wants to be, though."

"I'm sure he does. He's scheming on how to become a clone of me as we speak. But it's never gonna happen. He hasn't been tested. Life has been too easy for him, and he will never understand people like you and me."

All Judith could feel was guilt throbbing through her. She was a cheater. She had never been a cheater! She thought of Justin calling her a whore last fall and felt the truth burn a hole through her heart. He was right. Loving Nicolas had turned her into a whore.

"I gotta go. He's going to send the cops to look for me if I don't. Take care of yourself, my sweet soulmate."

"No." He grabbed her arms and pushed her back on the bed, crawling on top of her again, his dick dragging across her belly, his eyes boring into her like lasers. "You need to commit to a date when you'll leave him."

"There's no way," she said finally, "I love you, Nicolas, but I don't want to be the girl who hooks up with a criminal prostitute. I wanna be with the good guy."

"You're breaking my heart. I don't like being this guy, either. But with you, I see who I can be. My whole life has been a nightmare. I spent the last twelve years pining for the fantasy of getting Catrina back. Martha healed me, and then I found you. I know I'm a criminal, and I'm fucking nuts, obsessed and too needy, but I can't stop. I need you, Belladonna. Please, choose me. Let Justin go."

"Justin is like a gold star for getting all A's. I want to be the girl he saved."

"Is he saving you, though? You're still lonely and depressed after he made this miraculous change. He's only trying to compete with me."

"I can't think of leaving him. I can't make those sorts of plans."

"You don't have to make plans. I already made the plans. All you need to do is promise to run away with me."

"I'm engaged to him, though." Judith displayed her ring, and he looked shocked.

"When did this happen?"

"Thanksgiving."

He paused, then took her finger in his mouth, tore the ring off with his teeth, and spat it on the floor.

"That's what I think of that bullshit. It's all so fake. Justin, pretending he's your hot superhero boyfriend. You, pretending he saved you when here you are, crazy in love with me."

"I love you so much it hurts," she confessed, "when Justin deleted all our texts and videos, I thought I would die."

"My poor Belladonna. It only hurts because we're not together. It won't hurt forever."

It had been four hours. Justin would be wondering what the hell had happened to her. What would she say? That she was a complete slut who couldn't say no to Nicolas Winters? He would murder her, then bury her in the desert. Being a cop, he would get away with it, too.

"This was the best day of my life, Nicolas. But I do have to go."

"I wish I could force you into a blood pact with me. I need your word that you'll follow through and join me. I don't think I can let you leave this room without it."

"What do you need from me?" She lay back in his arms, and he played with her hair as he laid out his plan.

"First, give me your phone. We are back in touch, whether you like it or not." She handed him her phone, and he entered his number into her contacts under the name Martha. "I'll explain how it's all gonna play out, and you need to promise to follow my plan to the letter, got it?"

Judith nodded in agreement, and Nicolas explained his plan to her. She would leave Justin and her family without saying a word. Take a flight to Cabo San Lucas. Together, they would move to a country with no extradition treaty with the United States. Presently, he was thinking of

Indonesia. Liked the idea of Bali. She would have to ask his dad for money in cash, so she would need to make up an excuse to obtain it. She would return in six weeks, and they'd escape together. Nicolas had it all worked out. Helplessly, she agreed. Like he said, the moment she walked through that door with a gun to his head, ironically, it was she who surrendered herself to him.

"Can I have my ring back? He'll freak."

"Sorry. I'm going to sell it and buy our plane tickets. You don't need it now anyway." He took her face in his hands, his black eyes mesmerizing. "Please don't bail on me. I won't survive it. We are meant for each other. I can't live without you. Repeat after me. I am the one who makes you happy."

Judith stared at the mess she had made of her life and ran to the door before she broke down into a flood of tears. This fateful, traumatic, and insane connection with Nicolas was a tidal wave that washed her away from the first moment they met. Justin would never understand. No one could understand because she barely understood. They kissed forever under the threshold. Nicolas was loath to let her go.

"This is hard, Belladonna. Only six weeks. Then it's just you and me for the rest of our lives."

Judith turned away from him, let go of his hand, and ran down the steps. Darting through the streets, the rain pelting her bare skin, she wanted to melt away. Cease to exist. Soon, very soon, she would have to choose which man she wanted to be with. It would kill her to decide.

Nicolas was the right man for her. She knew it! So, why the hell couldn't she follow her heart? Because Justin was standing in the way. His powerful body, his demanding persona, the force of his sexual desire sucked her to him. He felt like the center of gravity and always would.

Outside the entrance, Judith recited her fabricated excuse as to where she had been for hours. She had to fake Justin out. She entered their hotel room, and Justin rushed to her as she walked through the door.

"You were gone forever. Are you alright?"

"Yeah, just needed some time alone. I took a long-ass walk and got lost. That letter. Geez."

Justin gathered her in his arms, so muscular and strong. She wanted to jump off the balcony before he kissed her. Her betrayal was suffocating.

"Don't worry. I informed the local police that they have an illegal with an outstanding felony warrant in their midst. I doubt Nicolas has a visa. Another criminal offense. They said they'll keep an eye out and will happily arrest the bastard. Wanna grab dinner?"

"Sure, let me get changed."

"I know I said I'm not much for travel, but maybe we can make this an annual trip. The beach is spectacular. And getting to see you walk around in that sexy bikini for days on end is worth every penny," he said lightly, and she smiled in agreement.

Judith wept in the shower for twenty minutes, as she tried to erase Nicolas from her mind and off her body. She wanted to be Justin's girl and only his, but she had opened Pandora's box by sleeping with Nicolas, and this was her punishment. Bound to two men. Her noble but distant superhero and his antithesis, an obsessive, broken sex maniac. Both satisfied something in her, and she had no idea how ever to resolve this.

"What happened to your ring?" Justin asked over dinner.

"I'm so sorry. I think I lost it on the beach."

"I have it insured. No worries."

Justin kissed her, but her body was still drowning in Nicolas's bed beneath his touch. She had to pretend to be happy now, but Justin only cared about the surface of things. As long as she faked him out, they were fine. If he cared, then he would notice, and she would spill her guts. But if she did, he would dump her ass in three seconds. It was hopeless.

And in the darkness, she felt Nicolas—stalking, consuming, madly in love. Judith worshiped Justin and wanted to be a part of his future, but Nicolas needed her, and his depths somehow completed her. This love triangle was her reward for saving her mother, and it would ultimately tear her apart. Hopelessly, Judith downed another margarita and ordered a third.

Chapter 30

Lizzy

Tonight was the best night of Lizzy's life. After nine straight months of fantasizing about Justin, Lizzy finally had a chance to be with him all to herself. Judith was off having a drama queen moment, which allowed Lizzy to get him alone. Justin sat on the lounger by the pool, and she envisioned him as he had looked on the beach earlier: shirtless and in his swimming trunks, so hot that he took her breath away. Lizzy knew without a doubt that she and Justin were meant to be. Judith was the obstacle, and somehow, there had to be a way to eliminate her.

Justin asked about her degree in environmental science, and they spent over an hour discussing Utah geography. Justin was smart, funny, and so attractive that there weren't words in the English language to describe him. She tried not to gawk but it was impossible.

Since Judith moved out and she and her mom moved in with Erik, life proved to be miserable. Lizzy always struggled to make friends, and her family, as imperfect as they were, filled the void in her life. This last year was horrendous. Living out in Bluffdale sucked, and she was struggling in school for the first time ever. Not with grades. She was brilliant, and academics came easily to her. It was the social stuff. She either didn't get along with people or just hated them. She didn't have many friends, and guys didn't seem to like her. Not like they went whoring after Judith.

It made no sense. Lizzy wasn't bad-looking, and she was tons skinnier than Judith, but something about her sister made men pant like dogs. It was hopeless. She felt invisible, and when she wasn't invisible, she felt homely and unimportant. That's why she loved Justin. He came off like a man people listened to. He owned the room when he entered, his tall and muscular stature commanding attention. She knew that if she were on his arm, life would be a lot different.

"So, you like living with Martha and Erik?"

Justin kept checking his phone, hoping that Judith would reply. Of course, her selfish sister was up in her room, trying to gain sympathy for her headache. Everything was always about Judith. Throughout her life, everything revolved around her beauty pageants and numerous extracurricular activities. Why her parents even had a second child was a mystery to her. It was clear they didn't want her.

"It's fine. They are gone most of the time, so I have the whole house to myself."

"I lived with my mom until just this past March, when Judith moved in."

"That's so sweet."

He smiled, and Lizzy felt her insides quiver. He had a gorgeous smile.

"I like being around my family, you know? I hope Judith is okay with it. I'm sure living out in the country isn't everything she hoped for."

"I can't imagine how she can be happy," Lizzy stated bluntly, "Judith goes crazy when she has nothing to do."

Justin looked sad, and she felt terrible for planting doubts, even though that was precisely what she wanted to do.

"I'm sure you make up for any loneliness or boredom she feels."

"I hope. Are you having fun so far on this vacation?

"It's been a nice change of scenery. What do you think of that note we received today?"

"I don't know. If it is Nicolas who sent it, I sure hope they find the bastard."

"I still can't believe my mom lied to the police about everything. We went crazy that week when she was gone. There's no way she abandoned us on purpose."

There's something about that guy—women all want to save him. It drives me crazy."

"Well, he's cute, but there's more to it. He's the kind of guy who wraps women around his finger. He's like a male version of Judith."

"What do you mean by that?" He sounded defensive.

"I'm not sure exactly. I just know the type. These hot people can seduce anyone. They make me sick."

"Me too," he admitted.

Justin looked about ready to get up. She quickly asked,

"Wanna go walk down by the beach with me?" She gazed at him eagerly, and she could tell he wanted to say no, but for some reason, he relented.

"For a few minutes. Then I wanna check up on Judith."

Lizzy grabbed his arm before he could change his mind and let him lead her through the gate down to the beach. They walked in silence, and Lizzy thought about the last nine months. Most days, she spent at least an hour fantasizing about Justin. She was hopelessly obsessed, and now he was providing her with new mental footage for her obsession. This was wonderful.

"I heard you and Judith have had a rough time this year. My mom told me."

"Oh. We're doing fine now," he assured.

"If you ever need to talk to someone, I'm here. I know Judith better than most, so I can interpret her weird behavior."

Justin was silent. She clung to him closer and sensed that he wanted to pull away. Why didn't he? Because Justin, unlike most guys, was a gentleman. God, she wanted this man so much.

After their walk along the beach, she followed him to the bar. She wasn't old enough to drink in the States, but she was in Mexico. She ordered a beer, while he had a beer and a shot of dry whiskey. She sipped her drink and stared. He wasn't looking at her. What would it take for Justin to notice her? Was it even possible? Probably not.

Still, she was a girl who had spent most of her life inside her head, pretending to be a different girl from a different family. Just being this close to him tonight gave her plenty of new content to fantasize about. Justin was her dream man, and she dedicated every single fantasy to him. If only he knew that she was the one for him. Finally, he said,

"Well, it's been fun, Lizzy, but I'm gonna head up now."

Impulsively, she stood up from her stool and gave him a full-body hug.

"Thanks, cowboy," she whispered and kissed him on the cheek. He reddened slightly, then walked away. She watched him all the way out the door, already caught up in the throes of her newest fantasy.

Chapter 31

Justin

Lizzy was a sweet girl, but he could tell she had a crush on him, which was flattering yet made him feel slightly uncomfortable. Justin had never given her much thought, but tonight, they talked about everything from agriculture to Utah history. She was smart and witty, just a bit shy. He thought it must have been hard growing up in Judith's shadow as he headed back to his hotel room. After dinner, Judith complained of a headache, so Justin sat by the pool with Lizzy for a few hours. Now, he hoped Judith hadn't fallen asleep yet. He had his hands all over her at the beach and felt so horny that he hoped to get some release.

Judith was out on the balcony, staring at the moon.

"Have fun hanging out with my sister?" She sounded distinctly jealous.

"Uh, sure. We were just chatting."

"Yeah, she's good for conversation about some boring shit or another."

"Hey." He grabbed her. "Are you okay? You've been off all evening."

"Sure. I just wanna go home. This vacation is not at all what I expected."

"We leave tomorrow."

"Thank God it's only five days. I couldn't handle a week of hanging out with those lovebirds and clingy Lizzy."

"Your mom deserves to be happy." Justin frowned.

What had gotten into her? She was itching for a fight. Maybe he should leave her alone.

"Wanna come to bed?"

"Uh." She stared up at the moon, tears welling up in her eyes. "I'm tired and sore from walking for hours."

"Judith." He pulled her to him. "What is going on? Please talk to me."

"I can't." A sob escaped her.

"Why?"

"You won't understand."

She threw her arms around him and he stabilized her. What the fuck was happening here? Something right outside his peripheral vision was moving, but he was too distracted to make sense of what it was. This was their first Christmas together. And they were engaged, so it was a special occasion! Why was she acting like this? So unstable? So out of it?

"Come on. Let me hold you. We don't have to do anything. It will be like our first week together. Remember?"

Judith lay against his chest and sobbed for ten minutes straight. Listening and musing hard, he stroked her hair as a horrid feeling rose in his gut. It was too horrible even to consider. Too awful to think about. But he knew, absolutely knew, that Nicolas was here. Judith saw him, and he staked his claim. Tonight. He fucked his girl, and that is what Nicolas meant in his note. *I fuck her and she loves it.* Chills rolled up and down his spine as he thought frantically about what to do.

"Judith, I swear to God, you can tell me anything. I won't judge you. I won't hate you. I want to help you, honey. Please, let me help you."

"You can't help with this," she said hoarsely.

Nicolas was a malicious, manipulative psychopath, and Judith didn't stand a chance against his mind games. He probably tried to convince her to stay with him. Coerced the shit out of her. Justin had to get aggressive. Come out guns blazing. It was the only way to keep her.

"It has been a battle from day one for us, hasn't it?"

He nuzzled her neck and petted her until she was moaning.

"Justin. What is this?"

"What? You don't like it?"

"I do. Why do you want me, though? I'm so much trouble."

"You aren't trouble. I'm sorry, I don't have the right words like some guys. I can't find the words to describe the way you make me feel. It's like every happy day I've ever had rolled into one moment. That's what I feel when I look at you."

"I don't deserve you." She wept.

"I don't care whether you do or not. I don't care what you did. All I care about is keeping you next to me until I die."

"There are things between us now. I can't make them go away."

Of course, she meant the asshole-criminal maniac who would never leave her alone.

"I will make them go away for you. Trust me, baby. Why won't you trust me?"

"Because I don't understand why you put up with me. I have tried and tried to connect with you. Even with all the great sex, it's mostly been met with failure."

"At least we have our insane attraction for each other."

Swallowing all his inhibitions and wishing he had downed at least three more shots at the bar, he grabbed her gently, backed her up to the bed, and ripped off his shirt. Justin pulled her tiny little sundress up over her head, pushed her over onto the bed, looked down at her gorgeous body—no bra, just a pair of lace panties—and let the lust build. Let the image of that other man inside her fuel his desire and channel the hatred he felt for Nicolas into pure sexual energy. He was going to fight for her. Go up against that Casanova and give his girl the ride of her life. Fuck that evil little shit. He might know a woman's pussy like the back of his hand, as he so claimed, but Justin had the upper hand because he wasn't a villain. He was a good guy. And the good guy always got the girl.

Judith looked up at him, fragile and broken. Nicolas had broken her. Justin stripped, knelt at the edge of the bed, and pulled down her panties.

Shoved his insatiable craving for violent sex deep down inside him and prayed to God that it would stay there.

"You are everything to me. Let me show you how much I want you."

Pushing her legs apart, she melted against him. Justin was afraid of this. He had never tried to go down on her and knew he didn't have the skills, nor did he know how to acquire them apart from practice. And foreplay like this was extremely hard for him to handle. Didn't have the willpower. But he pushed past his insecurities, convinced himself to endure the pressure, and went at her, giving her everything he had.

Judith was easily aroused, and he felt ecstatic when he got her off within a minute. She held his head against her and cried out his name until, all too soon, he was past his limit. Then he took her up against the wall, something he was sure that skinny-ass little prick didn't have the physical strength to do, and held nothing back. Judith loved every bit of it.

Maybe he could go up against Nicolas after all. One thing he knew for sure—it wasn't over yet. Judith was still his. He saved her from that criminal. Justin was the law and the voice of reason. Judith needed him to keep her safe. This may be war, but wars could be won. And he still had plenty of fight left in him.

The Second Year

Chapter 32

Nicolas

Belladonna was ghosting him. Nicolas stared at his phone, stoned out of his mind. He was mixing pills with booze and heroin, and he didn't care. How had it gone wrong? She loved every minute in his bed, everything he did to her. She even promised to follow through. Was he doomed to a repeat of Martha? Would he ever win the heart of a woman? Nicolas hated his life now. He was sick of sex work. Sick of being alive. If he couldn't have his Belladonna, what was the point of anything?

Nicolas had been texting her nonstop for a week now, but had heard nothing back. He called repeatedly, and still nothing. Had the cop figured it out? Made a grandstand? What did he have over him?

Vicious and desperate, he racked his brain for ways to unravel this situation. Nicolas browsed through all the texts he had sent recently, most of which she hadn't replied to, and realized he was horribly clingy. She had said she didn't like clingy. Was it possible not to be clingy? No. He was this way and knew no other way to be. He scrolled through Justin's Facebook, finding it ridiculous that the two of them were still friends, and studied the pics Justin had posted from their trip. They were all for his benefit. They were all for his benefit. Justin—kissing Belladonna over dinner. Justin—carrying her around the beach. Justin—his arm around her, staring out at the planes at the airport. He wanted to rub it in.

Somehow, Justin figured out that they had hooked up. Nicolas shouldn't have written that note. He was too obvious. Shit. So that's what was happening. He had called Justin out, like two men in an 18th-century duel, and Justin had his pistols ready. This was war. Nicolas felt such rage that he had no idea what to do about it. He drank half the bottle of vodka and lay back, letting the high take him away.

Tears filled his eyes. If Belladonna didn't run away with him, could he bring himself to get on that plane himself? He already had their tickets. He had researched where they might live when they got to Indonesia. He wanted to visit Bali first. Belladonna had scored twenty grand from his old man, which was phenomenal. He was really excited. He loved adventure and thoroughly enjoyed traveling. But if she bailed, what would he do? Nicolas took a selfie. He looked miserable and stoned shitless. He sent it with a message.

Baby, don't ghost me. I'm dying without you.

And hit send.

Two hours later, finally. Finally. She called.

"Are you okay?"

"Yes. Yes! Where have you been?"

"I've been sick. I always catch something nasty at this time of year."

"Why didn't you drop a line? I've been worried out of my mind."

"Sorry. It's been a lot lately."

"Please tell me we are still on."

She paused, which was terrifying beyond belief.

"I bought my plane ticket to Cabo. It's a red-eye flight. I'll call an Uber to take me to the airport after Justin leaves for work."

Finally. Thank God!

"I am so relieved. And you got the money too. You are so amazing."

"Thanks." She paused. "I don't know, Nicolas. I'm scared. I'm not sure if I can follow through. I don't know if I can bring myself to leave him. You have no idea the hold Justin has on me."

"Don't say that. If you say that, you are sentencing me to death."

"What do you mean?"

"I will throw myself off a bridge if you abandon me. I'm serious. You said we have a death wish. I will make mine come true if you choose him."

"I can't handle this pressure."

Nicolas felt bad. She was crying and it was his fault. But he had to get her away from that cop. He knew Justin was bad for her, and once she escaped him, she'd see it for herself.

"Listen, it will be hard at first. Getting to the airport will be the hardest. But once you board the plane, I promise, it will get easier."

"Maybe. He's really trying now."

Of course he was, the fucking cop. This was full-out war, and Justin was armed to the teeth. Nicolas burned with a hatred so profound for Justin that he wished he believed in witchcraft—to curse the bastard with boils, a deadly disease, or turn him into a frog.

"What do you want from me? Want me to back off and give you time to decide?"

"I doubt you could do that." She laughed weakly.

"For you, yes. Belladonna, I have told you he won't change. He is stuck, and while he might put in a little effort when he sees you drifting away, the moment you are back, he will return to his same asshole behavior. And I know things will only get worse. I don't think you've even scratched the surface of who Justin really is."

"I'm so tired. Something about the trip. It triggered like a fuck ton of repressed memories of so many events I had as a kid. I think it was the plane ride. It's depressing. I wonder if that instructor did this to any other girls on my gymnastics team."

"Let's go online and call him out. Hell, I would support you even if you wanted to go at him with a lawsuit."

"It's just the depression. I should talk to my mom. I've never felt this depressed before. Plus, it's the dead of winter. I always get depressed at this time of year."

"I am here for you. Don't let things spin out of control. If you feel like you're losing your shit, reach out to me, okay? I've been depressed enough to kill myself before, and it's no fun. But I promise, once we are together, I will make your pain go away. My love will heal you."

"Nicolas?"

"Huh?"

"I do love you. Please, no matter what happens, know that I love you, my sweet incubus. I'm a broken girl right now. I feel so empty. I have nothing left to give. Justin, I think he knows we hooked up in Cabo. He's been passionate day and night which makes me feel like shit. I don't know what the fuck to think."

Nicolas knew what to think. Justin was all about the game. Getting the girl, not keeping the girl. He had no idea what a relationship meant. Besides, this was war now. Justin versus Nicolas. He was an egotist who would never let a guy like Nicolas beat him at anything.

"The truth is, if I leave with you, he will hate me to the end of time. He will see me as trash, the way he sees you. I will be a criminal in his eyes. How can I live with that?"

"You can live with that by moving to the other side of the world with me, where he won't be able to touch us."

"You are right. I wanted to be with Justin because I hated myself. I wanted him to change me. And I feel like you liberate me, but it's terrifying. I have spent years hating myself and wishing to be someone different. Then you come along and love me for who I am."

Nicolas had no idea how to win her over. How could he make her see how perfect she was? She didn't need to change for this guy. She just needed to choose the right guy. Him.

"Listen, as hard as it is, I am going to give you some time. I'll back off. I'll let you recuperate. Promise me, if the thoughts become too evil, call me. I couldn't bear the thought of anything happening to you."

"Okay. Thanks. Love you. Bye."

Nicolas stared at his phone and thought about how he tried to talk Catrina into staying. Used every defense and every ploy to keep her, and none of them worked. In the end, he had to watch her abandon him. But it was heartbreaking, and he was terrified. He wasn't lying. If he lost Belladonna, he really wouldn't know how to go on living.

He walked down to the ocean and lay in the sand. He gazed up at the stars and thought of his childhood. He was so lonely as a kid that he would have conversations with the stars. He learned enough about them to identify which was which. It wasn't quite praying, but it was close. He felt close to something when he looked at the night sky. Wasn't sure what, though.

In his mind, he formed a plea to help him survive this. He was going to lose her, and he didn't know how to cope with it. Belladonna was going to choose the man who could never make her happy because, if you compared them on paper, he was a loser and everything else in between.

How could he live without her now that they had made love? He was in torment. He smelled her, knew her heartbeat, tasted her sweet juices, and felt her nubile body against his. Why was this happening to him? Hadn't he suffered enough? He burrowed in the sand and cried himself to sleep.

Nicolas awoke in the dead of night. A horrible premonition came over him. He rushed home, counted his money, checked their tickets, texted her, and called her.

Belladonna?

Please, honey, don't do this to me.

Where are you?

Why won't you message me?

Have you made your decision?

You aren't coming, are you?

Don't ghost me. Even if you decide not to leave, just don't abandon me!

I miss you so much. I need you, baby. I NEED YOU.

I don't know how you can choose him over me. I get you. He doesn't.

Remember our first night when I said we had unfinished business, lots of it—a lifetime of it? This is what I mean. Don't do this.

Where are you? I'm gonna bleed myself dry unless you choose me. I CAN'T LIVE WITHOUT YOU.

And nothing.

Chapter 33

Justin

After the trip to Cabo San Lucas, everything changed. Judith no longer touched him. She lost all interest in sex overnight, which only made him fuck her like crazy in an attempt to bring her back to him and make her want him again. He knew what was happening, and he wasn't about to let her go. Judith stopped eating, grew quiet, and her bubbly personality turned off, leaving them both in darkness. Justin didn't know what the hell to do.

At first, he tried talking to Judith. She was defensive and said nothing was wrong. That she was just tired. He asked his mom for advice on what to do. She suggested Judith might be pregnant, which thrilled Justin, so he bought her a pregnancy test. It was, of course, negative. When Judith took the test, she went into her room crying, "Thank God, thank God." So, she didn't want to have kids with him?

Two weeks after the trip, she stopped hugging him or kissing him goodbye when he left for work. She slept in as late as he did, as if she had been up all night long. Justin repeatedly asked what was wrong. Was it something he did or said? She shook her head, got all teary-eyed, and left the room. Justin grew more alarmed by the day. He knew what had happened in Cabo but didn't understand how it was affecting her this badly. She wasn't on her phone at all, so he doubted Nicolas was back in contact. What should he do?

By four weeks, her clothes were hanging off her. His voluptuous vixen was becoming increasingly thin and now shied away from his lightest touches. He caught her crying at odd moments. Once, he found her lying against the dryer, weeping into a pile of towels, and when he tried to hug her, she pushed him away.

By six weeks, Justin was losing his mind. He had tried everything he could think of. His mom was as perplexed and worried as he was. Finally, he got in his car and drove out to Bluffdale. Martha would know what to do.

"Justin! This is a lovely surprise! Where's Judith?"

"Ah, she's at home. I was hoping to talk to you alone."

"Of course. Come on in."

"Where's Erik?"

"He's at work. Here, let me make some coffee, and we can go and sit on the porch. Enjoy the last of the winter." Coffee in hand, they sat, gazing out at a beautifully manicured yard.

"So, what's up?"

"I'm concerned about Judith."

"Oh. Why is that?"

"Well, ever since we got back from our trip to Mexico, she's been acting differently. I don't know what I did."

"Okay. Tell me how."

So, Justin did. He told Martha everything.

"It sounds like she's suffering from depression."

"Why so sudden?"

"Well, you know she asked Erik for a huge loan, right? For modeling school?"

"What?"

He looked at Martha in shock.

"She didn't tell you? Yes, I guess she's all signed up to attend this modeling boot camp in California. She's getting a portfolio put together and everything. It's costing a ton of money. I can't believe she didn't tell you."

"No. She didn't."

Why hadn't Judith said anything?

"Maybe she's trying to slim down for the shoot. Girls can feel a lot of pressure about their bodies when modeling. It is odd, though. Erik offered to pay for everything online, but she insisted that she needed the cash. Weird, huh?"

"What the hell is going on, Martha? Judith doesn't want to be a model. She gave that up a while ago. Something's not adding up."

Martha shook her head, set her coffee down, and went inside. When she returned, she was holding a piece of paper.

"Remember this?"

Justin peered at it.

"It's the note we believe was written by Nicolas and delivered to us while we were on the beach, right?"

"Justin, I spent a week with Nicolas. He is horrifyingly persuasive."

"Yeah." Justin nodded in agreement.

"I have a fear that when Nicolas lost me to Erik, then took Judith, a transference occurred."

Justin downed the rest of his coffee. He never got much out of his psychology classes in college, and this sounded like mumbo jumbo to him.

"Tell me plainly."

"Nicolas is a sex-love addict, and I think he transferred his obsession for me onto Judith. I think there's a lot we don't know."

"What?"

Justin had raised his voice. Terrified, she was going to confirm what he already knew.

"I wondered why Judith begged us to set up that vacation."

"Wait a minute. It was her idea?"

"Of course. I thought she told you. Judith even suggested that specific resort. And I feared from the first moment that it was because—it sounds crazy. Why would he take the risk, right? I think he lured her there."

Justin sat back, overcome with the realization that the whole thing had been planned. All that time, he thought they had mended their relationship, and she was biding her time until she could see Nicolas!

"Did she ever take off alone?"

Justin stalled, too embarrassed to admit the truth.

"She took a long walk after we got the note. Said she needed to clear her head."

Martha shook her head.

"It concerns me that those two might have hooked up."

"If she did, then what? How can I win her back?"

Martha took his hand in hers.

"I think we have all been a bit naive about what went on between them in the car that night."

"He fucked around with her a bit, but that's it. Nicolas is an asshole, and he tried to kill you. I'd like to think that if she knew where he was, she'd give him away in a heartbeat."

But Justin knew it wasn't true. They loved each other. That was the problem.

"I just have this feeling. Listen to these words: *I am in your head, I am between your legs and you will never be rid of me.* He's not using the past tense. This is now. I am in your head. I am between your legs. Just consider. What if he's made plans for them to run away together?"

"They were in contact for months, but once I found out about it, I blocked that fucker. Judith hasn't talked to him since."

"Nicolas is insatiable when he wants something, and he won't give up until he has her. I saw the passion in his eyes when he kissed Judith that night. If I'm right, then he sees her now as his."

"Even if that were the case, he's a thousand miles away."

"The distance would mean nothing to him. He is a survivor of abuse, used to having to work a hundred times harder for anything he wants."

"Should I ask her straight out? Things have been good between us ever since I blocked that bastard, and then this trip ruined everything."

"Give it a few days. Confront her about the modeling camp first. See how she responds. Erik has already prepared the money. In fact, I can give it to you to bring to her."

Justin felt devastated. If Judith moved to California, their relationship would be over.

"Sure. This is too horrible for words. I was afraid Nicolas would make a comeback. I had hoped I could end this thing between them. Having you back up my fears is too much."

Martha retrieved the suitcase of money and handed it to him.

"Kiss her for me and tell her I love her. Erik and I are taking a trip to Colorado for a few days. We'll drop by when we return and see if she's improved."

Justin sped home. He found Judith on the couch. He dressed quietly for work, and when he went to kiss her goodbye, she pretended to be asleep. Judith had never withheld a single thing from him—not her opinions, her heart or her body—this was driving him insane. He held her hand and whispered,

"Please come back to me."

"Why?" She was crying.

"We are getting married, remember? Judith, I can't live without you. Please don't choose him. I couldn't bear it if you did. You are my girl. MINE. He wheedled his way back in. I know he did. Please don't do this to me. Don't put me through this. I can't be held responsible for what I'll do if you put me through this again."

"What do I do?"

"I don't know what he is asking of you, but I'll lock you up and chain you to the bed if that's what it takes to keep you safe. That guy is sick and dangerous, and I won't let him near you."

"Do you even love me? Because I don't feel that you do."

"Listen, I'm your hero. I'm the good guy. The one who saved you from him. Let that be enough."

"It isn't enough, Justin. I need to feel loved."

Trying to rein in his fury, he clawed her by the scruff of the neck and whispered in her ear as she whimpered.

"You have fucked me over from day one because of that guy. You owe me, okay? I'm never gonna let you go. I'll never let him have you. No matter where you run, I will find you and take you back. Trust me, I have the resources and insane detective skills. I have access to every database on the planet. You use your passport anywhere and I'll know. I won't let him win. He's a criminal, and he doesn't deserve you. I do."

Judith writhed out of his grasp and backed to the other end of the couch.

"I made a mistake, Justin. We aren't right for each other."

"I'm the good guy. I thought you wanted to be my good girl."

"I do."

"Well, without me, you're just a cock-teasing whore. You need me."

"Maybe I don't want to need you."

She said defiantly as she cringed as far from him as possible. Couldn't look him in the eye. And Justin knew absolutely that she was still hung up on that motherfucking criminal. Nothing he did was enough for her. He wanted to hit her. Smack her down to the floor then fuck her in a vicious rage.

"Judith, fuck you. *You* hit on *me*. *You* kissed *me*. *You* seduced *me*. You. Don't. Get. To. Abandon. Me. Now!"

He punched the floor with each word, trembling with fury. Feeling the same way the day his dad walked out, never to be seen or heard from again. A long silence fell between them. Finally, he stood.

She nodded, terrified and sad.

"Did my mom give you the money?"

"Yeah. It's on the counter. I wish you had told me. I had no idea. I would have been happy to help and support you."

Justin tried to control his breathing and calm the fuck down.

"I don't believe that."

He shrugged. It was a complete lie. He would never let her work as a model or work anywhere, for that matter. Judith was his, and if he let her out of the house, she was bound to leave him. Like Jones and his mom warned him, some other guy would come along and steal her. And he enjoyed their power struggle. Loved the fact that he had ruined her affair with that criminal. The harder she tried to get away, the more he wanted her.

I have to get to work or I'm gonna be late. We'll discuss this further in the morning. Please try to get some sleep."

She turned her face away from him and began to sob. At a complete loss for words, Justin finally blew her a goodbye kiss and left.

Chapter 34

Judith

Judith was down to the wire, and she had no idea what to do. In two days, she had to board a plane and leave her whole life behind. She had already bought her ticket. Nicolas had left her alone, but it didn't help. It almost made it worse. Without his constant demands, she had to make the decision all on her own.

Justin had tried to win her back since Cabo San Lucas, but seeing Nicolas had broken her. His body was like a drug, and she was now an addict. She wanted him so badly that it felt like she would die if they couldn't be together, but she couldn't do this. She just couldn't leave Justin. He was all over her now. Every morning, he came home from work, marking her with his scent, marring her skin with passionate hickies, and rubbing her raw on the inside from desperate sex. She felt his desperation but not his love. He didn't love her, regardless of what she did. The realization made her want to kill herself.

Justin suspected what had happened in Cabo. That was the only answer. Which meant this was a ploy to win her back. And still, she couldn't leave him. She loved both men, but Nicolas understood her and loved her down to the core, and she had shared every single hope, dream, desire and obsession she had so far in her twenty years. Nicolas was her best friend and her fantasy man. That was love, wasn't it? But he was a prostitute and a criminal. He didn't have his shit together. He was too emotional. How could she choose him over the good guy with a stable job, the land along with blueprints for a house?

This depression wasn't even entirely about the hard choice she had to make. It was about those goddamn memories. They hurt physically and emotionally. How could she make Justin understand her trauma? And why would she when she already had Nicolas to confide in?

She wanted to text Nicolas. Tell him her troubles. Her head was pounding with agony. She had to choose and watch one of the men she loved turn into a miserable wreck.

She finally decided to message her mom. She needed to tell someone.

Mom, I need to get something off my chest before I go. I was molested at eight years old by my gymnastics coach. It went on for months. Then I was raped repeatedly all through my thirteenth year by Janet Green's dad until they moved away. I never told you or Dad because I thought it would somehow affect my chances of winning the trophies. It messed me up. I'm a sex addict, and I have anger issues as well as emotional problems. I can't talk to Justin about them. The only person I can trust in the world is Nicolas.

Please don't hate me. I love him. I've loved him since that first night. He's a criminal, but he's also my soulmate. He wants me to run away with him. I can't choose, but he's forcing me to. I would rather die than choose. Justin wants me, but he doesn't understand me like Nicolas does. And he doesn't love me like Nicolas does, either.

What should I do? Please help me. Please help me. Don't tell Justin. Don't tell Erik. I'm so depressed, and I keep having these memories come back to me. I can't handle it anymore. I'm haunted. I'm in hell. I need your help now more than ever.

I'm sorry. For so many years, I blamed you and treated you like shit because of it. You were always so nice to Janet's parents and my instructor, and I assumed that meant you were complicit. Somehow, I convinced myself that you and dad didn't give a shit whether someone was hurting me, as long as I always won the grand prize.

I don't know how much more of this life I can take. I think I'm done. No matter which guy I choose, someone will suffer. So, I'm not gonna choose. Why did this happen to me? How can I love two men?

She deliberated. Should she send it? What if her mom told Justin? He'd probably have her committed to a mental hospital to prevent her from leaving him. She thought about how vicious he was with her before he left for work. His rage was frightening but she understood it. Of course, he was angry. She had seduced him. Introduced him to a world of hedonistic pleasure, and she sensed that she had awakened some sort of darkness inside him. It was both thrilling and terrifying.

Judith thought back through her whole life. How much she wanted to win her dad's love. She excelled at everything if it meant winning a beauty pageant. But then he abandoned her, and there were no more pageants and no more rewards. Somehow, when she met Justin, she thought he was the kind of guy who would never leave her. It turned out there was more than one way to abandon someone.

Why didn't she feel loved by him? It drove her crazy trying to figure this out. He was passionate, and he no longer pushed her away. He filled her with his desire, but there was nothing vulnerable about Justin, and she wasn't sure why. He was closed and distant, no matter what she did. Should she give up on Nicolas and take her chances with Justin? Or should she bet on the sweet, crazy guy who was all heart and passion, and no sanity or brevity?

She considered calling Nicolas again. But he would say the same thing. Running away with him would fix everything. But he didn't understand. First, Justin would find her and take her back. Like he warned her, he would never let her go. He wasn't codependent. It was something else. He needed to save her. That's what heroes did.

Maybe Nicolas was right, and Justin viewed her as his property, like his car. Whatever it was, it was deadly serious. Thus, the getaway plan would fail spectacularly, even if they managed to reach Indonesia. And also, she just couldn't leave Justin. It felt as if she were on stage at a competition, and leaving him would be like walking off in the middle of the awards ceremony, letting someone else take home the gold.

Somehow, she had convinced herself that Justin was the better choice. Nicolas was her soulmate and understood her perfectly, but he was a wreck on the outside, and no one would think he was the better option.

Goddammit. She didn't want to deal with this anymore. Two days left, headed for the guillotine.

Suddenly, overwhelmed by a heavy feeling of loss, she collapsed. She was breaking down. Having her own psychotic break. So many nights spent alone in this house, waiting to be loved by her hero. Praying to become a good girl. Dreaming of escape. Wanting to run away. Board that plane and follow her heart. But if she did, she would be calling out Justin as a hollow disappointment, and he would never tolerate that.

It was time to end this. She could never be with Nicolas. Even if she managed it, she feared that he'd be a whacked-out mess, and life would prove unbearable.

Judith wandered into the bathroom, sobbing uncontrollably. This depression felt like being on her period, but a thousand times more intense. Her emotions were dragging her to hell, and she was fine with it. That's probably where she belonged after cheating on Justin.

Rifling through the cupboard, she found a bottle of sleeping pills. Scribbled a quick note and placed it on the floor, swallowed half the pills, returned the container to the cupboard, and lay down against the wall. This was it. The only solution. She couldn't have the man she wanted because she couldn't leave the man she needed.

It was game over for her.

Chapter 35

Justin

Around 11 p.m., Justin looked at his phone. He had missed nine calls from Martha, and she was calling for the tenth time. He answered.

"Martha?"

"Go home. Now."

"I'm at work. What's going on?"

"I know it's breaking confidence, but Judith sent this to me tonight."

A forwarded text from Judith came through. The only part he read was where Nicolas asked her to run away with him, and those words, "before I go."

"Oh my God."

"Yeah."

"Let me get out of here. Are you on your way?"

"We're about twenty minutes from your place."

"Oh, Martha, you were right. That fucking asshole."

"She couldn't give Nicolas up. He probably convinced her he would kill himself if she told anyone about their plans."

"I'm leaving now. See you soon."

When he tore into his driveway, his mom was standing outside. Only Justin had the key to the deadbolt. He often locked the door when he went to work, to keep Judith safe and to keep her home. He rushed up the stairs and unlocked the door. The apartment was dark. Martha was right behind him as they walked from room to room. The bathroom door was ajar, with

Judith lying on the floor. He rushed to her side. She was unconscious, lying next to a single sheet of paper. He felt for a pulse.

"Anything?" Martha asked.

"It's faint. She's not breathing."

"Work your magic, Justin. I'll call 911."

"I've gotta stay calm. I've trained for this."

Martha called 911 as Justin performed CPR. And together, they mourned the beautiful girl who finally surrendered to her death wish.

In the hospital emergency room, Justin clenched Judith's phone and had a flashback to four months ago when he discovered all those texts. Once Nicolas disappeared from their lives, things were great.

Justin couldn't believe she had done this to him. He was afraid his brutal warning before he left for work had triggered this. He came on strong, but he was trying to make her understand that he couldn't live without her. He wasn't trying to push her to do this!

Justin unlocked her phone, grateful that she hadn't changed her password. In his other hand, he reread her suicide note.

> Justin,
>
> I'm sorry. I'm not the girl you think I am. I'm a
> broken, sad girl who doesn't know what she wants.
> Let me go and find someone worthy of your love.
> Judith

He found a new contact under the name *Martha* and discovered the whole itinerary. He read through the recent texts. Yeah. They fucked in Cabo. And Nicolas was so high on the affair that Justin wanted to crush the phone between his fingers.

Judith repeatedly tried to tell Nicolas she couldn't run away with him. He read how pushy and relentless Nicolas was, and how she ghosted him continually. She didn't want this. She wanted Justin. She chose him. Nicolas was a predator who wouldn't stop gnawing on her soul.

Justin read through Nicolas's plan for when and where they would meet, how she would leave everyone and everything behind. And with a backpack full of cash, they would run away. This was the catalyst. The reason she tried to kill herself. That bastard pushed her to it. Judith was a warrior, but even she could only take so much.

A few hours later, the doctor arrived and delivered the verdict. Judith survived the drug overdose barely, but was on suicide watch for the next twenty-four hours. At that time, she would either be moved to a mental health facility or be released, depending on how emotionally stable she was, and he wasn't allowed to see her.

Justin felt like he needed heart surgery for what he was going through. He tried praying but didn't feel a shred of comfort. Yet, he knew what he needed to do next. Have the cops catch Nicolas at this rendezvous in two days, and bring that piece of shit down.

Judith convinced herself that she was in love with two men. But this thing with Nicolas wasn't love. It was just the response to the assault. The night Nicolas abducted and dragged her through the canyon and then seduced her, he made her his victim. There was nothing equal or healthy about their relationship.

Finally, Justin contacted Detective Finley and told him everything. Finley reached out to the local authorities in Cabo San Lucas, and they collaborated on a plan to arrest Nicolas. He had a warrant out for his arrest on a felony charge in Utah and was living and working in Mexico illegally. Once apprehended, they would allow the state prosecutor to work in conjunction with the Office of International Affairs on extradition. At least being in jail would prevent him from contacting Judith.

That night, Nicolas messaged to confirm their escape plan. Justin had to pretend to be Judith, a moment in his life he never wanted to relive. Having to converse with that asshole and convince him the plan was still on was traumatizing. Then, Justin did something he never imagined he could do. He went online and bought a last-minute plane ticket. He didn't know how and had to Google it. But he needed to meet Nicolas face-to-face and let him know that it was he who put him behind bars.

The night before their rendezvous, Justin lay in bed in his hotel room. Martha messaged that Judith had been moved to the Huntsmen Mental Institute for a few days for further evaluation. Justin was drifting off when a call from Nicolas came through. Shit. He let it ring. It rang again. And again. Then the texts.

Where are you? Why aren't you answering?

Justin had no choice. He couldn't respond, and he hoped to God that it wouldn't spook him.

The following day, he met up with law enforcement and then headed to the coffee shop where Nicolas and Judith were to meet. He sat across the street with his Americano, watching it all unfold. The arrest was anti-climactic. Nicolas dropped his bag and slowly lay on the ground. He looked deflated and scared, and Justin, seeing him in the flesh for the first time, saw nothing more than a manipulative sex offender who belonged behind bars.

After Nicolas was admitted to jail, Justin scheduled a visit. The look Nicolas gave him was priceless. His eyes screamed bloody murder as he sat and took hold of the phone.

Justin gloated inside because he towered over this guy by three inches and had at least sixty pounds on him. Skinny-ass bitch. Nicolas was experiencing withdrawals, he could tell. A junkie and a prostitute. No surprise there. The thought of this piece of trash fucking Judith made him feel homicidal. But calmly, he sat, faced his opponent, grabbed the phone, and stared balefully at the man who had tried to ruin his life.

They sat across from each other, two men who loved the same woman.

"I guess you were the one who fucked up our happy ending?" Nicolas hissed.

Grim and self-righteous, Justin glowered with indignation.

"So, on top of fucking guys for money, you use. What, smack? Wow. How did you ever think you could score a girl like Judith? You are a junkie-whore. The literal scum of the earth."

Nicolas grimaced and looked away, ashamed. "You don't know anything about me."

"I do know that because of you, Judith tried to commit suicide and is now receiving treatment in a mental health facility. I believe it's the same one where you spent some of your earlier years. I came because I wanted to look you in the eye and tell you myself. You lost. I got to her in time. I saved her once again. She'll live, and she'll do so without you."

Nicolas reacted like he had been shot in the stomach. Tears sprang into his eyes.

"I love her. I would never do that."

"You did do that. You drove her over the edge. I read your texts. I know a predator when I see one, and that is all you are. You targeted her, stalked her, and wore her down until you got what you wanted. I hope you go down for all your crimes. And if you ever try to contact *my* fiancée again, I will have even more charges brought against you."

"She loves me. Me. Not you. She doesn't belong to you."

"And she definitely doesn't belong to you."

"I understand her in ways you can't dream of. I am her soulmate. You are nothing."

"You may be her soulmate, but you are the last person she needs in her life. Just stay the fuck away, Nicolas. I hope you rot in a cell for a very long time."

"You had to go and ruin our chances because you're jealous. Of what we have and what you'll never have."

"You're just a sad, twisted guy who had to break a girl to get anywhere with her. The only thing you had in common was pain, mostly the pain you caused her."

"We fucked online for months behind your back, and she was so happy. I satisfied her from a thousand miles away. And when we met in Cabo, it was unforgettably hot. I made all her dreams come true. She shared nothing with you."

"You share trauma. That's not love. Just a bunch of awful experiences you had in common. You used it to trigger her and break her down. You're a misogynist who took a girl who lived on rainbows and made her want to die. Who the fuck does that? Oh, yeah. A monster. That's the result of your love."

"Rainbows?" Nicolas scoffed, "you have no idea who she is, do you? You think her thrill-seeking and sex addiction are part of her personality? Did you even notice when she was deeply depressed? Slept all day? Na. You were too busy. That dear girl is haunted by her trauma. She's been going through hell for months, and I was the only one she could turn to. She's a wreck, and no one ever noticed because she's too fucking beautiful for anyone to care."

Justin stared at him, shaken to the core. This was the one thing Nicolas had over him, his understanding of Judith's emotional condition.

"And I'm not the misogynist. You are. You control her as if it were the 18th century. When she hooked up with you, she went to prison. No fucking car. Stuck in the sticks. No friends. No job. Waiting night and day for you, but you're always too busy with your family and hobbies, and she's just the girl who warms your bed. You don't love her, and you don't know her. You need her to be the girl you saved so you can feel like a hero. I hate cops."

Now Justin was red-faced and pissed. He wanted to kick his ass. So bad.

"Of course, you hate cops. Criminals usually do."

"When my mom had her accident, you came in all full of yourselves and tried to throw the book at me. You didn't listen to a thing I said. Didn't even investigate the abuse."

"I've read the police report. The evidence of you nearly drowning your mom was compelling, but still, when you got institutionalized, they realized you were a messed-up kid and dropped the charges, so you got off big time. Man, you need to own your pain like the rest of us do, instead of making it someone else's problem."

"You wanna know why she did this?" Nicolas asked softly.

"Because you pushed her to it."

"It wasn't me who pushed her. IT WAS YOU." Nicolas pointed at him through the glass. "You, Justin. *You* are the criminal here. She couldn't face your disappointment. She wanted you to love her, but all you wanted was the sexy, crazy girl ready to go down on you when you were in the mood. She knew you'd judge her to the ends of the earth for choosing me, and she couldn't bear that. She was consumed by guilt. You make me sick. The so-called good guy, but you know nothing about making a woman happy. Always making her feel unworthy and getting your rocks off on it. You don't love her. You don't know how to love her, and you never will."

"I wish to God every day I had gotten to the house that night and put a bullet in your brain," Justin growled.

"I bet you do. I warned Belladonna. I told her you didn't give a shit about who she really was. Saw the amazing tits and wanted that piece of ass all to yourself. All these months, you didn't notice a goddamn thing. She was so lonely and sad. Heartbroken when you stopped replying to her sexy texts. You worthless piece of shit. You broke her fucking heart! Why do you think I begged her to leave you and run away with me? I couldn't bear to hear what was happening to her. You supposedly saved her, then cast her aside like something you didn't have the time for. By the way, we weren't sneaky. We were obvious. Fucking while you were sitting just outside the room." Nicolas laughed. "You're such a loser. You should have noticed, but you're so full of yourself. You think you're so special. Such a *hero*. You self-deluded asshole."

Justin felt his insides pounding, his face flushing deep red with shame and humiliation. He had to clench his fists against his hips to stop from punching the glass partition.

"Well, maybe I fucked up, but at least I ruined this. You'll never have her, and she'll never have you. I'm gonna throw a party the day they sentence you to prison."

"Wait," Nicolas pleaded, and Justin felt his misery hit him like a hurricane. "I can't live without her. I'll kill myself without her."

"There is that option, but I doubt you will. You'll find someone new to suck the life out of. I think you'll be just fine. And by the way, since we're still Facebook friends, look forward to seeing a fuck ton of photos of her and me preparing for our big, beautiful wedding. Cause I am going home to make her mine for good. I'm gonna make you suffer for the rest of your life, you junkie whore."

"She will never marry you." Nicolas met his eyes and wouldn't look away. They stared each other down.

"I am the man she wants. I am the one she chooses. Watch and weep in misery, fuckboy."

"Tell Belladonna I love her, and I'm truly sorry. I wish to God I had been there."

"Tell her yourself. Oh. That's right. You can't."

Justin gave him a satisfied smile, hung up the phone, and walked out of the jail. He had done it. Faced off with that unbeatable bird of paradise and clipped his fucking wings. Justin felt on fire.

It was over. Nicolas was caught and contained. Now, a year too late, they could start to pick up the pieces and repair. But repair what? What was left? Justin wasn't sure which charges would stick since Martha didn't tell the cops what truly happened, so abduction, rape, and attempted murder charges were never filed. Still, he would hopefully go down for Judith's abduction, and at least some justice would be served.

Chapter 36

Lizzy

Lizzy was a sick person, and she could admit that. When her mom burst into her bedroom, telling her how Judith was in the ER for a suicide attempt, Lizzy felt nothing but joy. Maybe she would drop dead. It was something she had longed for since she was nine years old. Instead, she feigned sadness and followed her mom out into the living room, where they talked about nothing but Judith for the next three hours.

Her mom shared the text, and Lizzy wanted to roll her eyes. Who cared if Judith was molested? She was probably asking for it. Okay, the gymnastics coach at eight—that was sick and wrong, but she didn't feel bad for Judith. Her sister had ruined her ability to be loved by her little sister back in elementary school. Lizzy had hated her for as long as she could remember.

"What are we going to do?"

"Well, that's why I asked you in here. I thought you might offer to stay with Judith for a few weeks. She's going to need constant supervision, and Justin works a graveyard shift. I am scared to have Judith by herself all night long, and I don't think I can take the time off to stay with her."

Meaning she didn't want to leave Erik to do her job as a mother.

"Yeah, that's fine."

"Thanks, honey. You're a lifesaver." Her mom hugged her, then went to text Justin.

Oh, my God. This was her chance. The universe was being kind to her! Finally giving her a chance at winning Justin's heart.

"She really met up with Nicolas and was planning to run away with him?" Lizzy asked, incredulous. It was shocking, even for Judith.

"I guess so. Please don't judge her too harshly. You have no idea what Nicolas is like. That boy can charm the birds right out of the trees. I believe he transferred his obsession with me to her that night. Judith didn't stand a chance against him, knowing her history."

Here they went again. More Judith drama. Her whole life had revolved around Judith everything, and she was sick of it. If only her mom knew how much it hurt to be endlessly pushed to the side so that Judith could stand in the limelight. All that mattered now was that she had a chance to steal Justin. If Judith had just cheated on him, then she would have broken his heart. Perfect.

She looked through her clothes and realized her stuff was all junk. If she was going to be hanging around Justin, she wanted cute stuff—at least one sexy nightie and plenty of tank tops she could wear without a bra. She didn't have boobs like Judith, so she had to emphasize everything she did have. She took after her tall, lanky dad. But being tall and slender counted for some guys. Not many, though. Especially not this tall. Another reason she liked Justin was that he towered over her five-eleven stature. She felt demure next to him.

Her mom gave her a credit card, and she excitedly took off to buy all new clothes, including sexy panties and shorty shorts. She thought of everything Justin might find attractive for the next few hours and came home with four bags stuffed with new clothes. She needed to make every second count. She went online and researched the area where Justin lived to discuss the local agricultural and environmental concerns affecting the farmland in his town. She loved to impress guys with her smarts, and she had a sexy, crooked smile. She'd make sure to smile as much as possible.

Still, Judith was possessive. If she even sensed a hint of what Lizzy intended, she would shut it down. She'd have to be sneaky and conniving. Judith told her about his garage, where he spent a lot of time. So, she made sure to get overalls to wear. She would offer to clean the floors with her tongue if it meant hanging out with him. It did suck that she had to commute to school a few days a week, but there were only two months left in the semester. Of course, her mom said they would only need her help for a few weeks, but she would make sure to milk it for all it was worth. Hopefully, she would still be there come summer.

It was a long stretch. She wasn't sure she could pull it off. Justin was starry-eyed from the moment he laid eyes on Judith. It was unlikely that he would allow himself to be led astray, but she had to take her chance. Lizzy knew from the night they met that Justin was the perfect guy for her, and all the fantasies she had indulged in since had only solidified this belief.

Lizzy had only had sex a handful of times. She didn't possess the same seduction skills as Judith. She had no idea how to please a man in bed. But she sensed that Justin was, like her, practically a virgin. They were a perfect match. Why he chased after the whore was no surprise. At least in all the romances she had ever read, the noble hero might fuck the whore, but he married the good girl. She was a good girl, and he was her good guy. And that meant they were a match made in heaven.

Chapter 37

Judith

Four days later, Judith was released. Justin, Martha and Lizzy picked her up from the hospital. Judith couldn't meet Justin's gaze. She was overwhelmed with shame. Her hair appeared dull and frizzy. Dark circles surrounded her emerald eyes. Her bra hung loosely on her, and she could see her rib cage for the first time in her life.

Martha gathered Judith in her arms and told her she knew everything, and Judith wept. Their shared relationship with Nicolas would bond them for life, but now Martha understood the root of her daughter's issues and vowed to help her become whole again.

"Oh, my dear girl. I'm so sorry. I wasn't there for you." Her mom held her close, and Judith felt her tears on her forehead. "I am going to find you the best therapist and pay for everything. I promise we will get you the help you need. Judith, I wish you had told me, honey."

"I know," she whispered, "I wanted to. But I was so afraid of losing the competitions."

Let's consider taking legal action. At least with the gymnastics coach."

"I can't handle that right now. Maybe at some point."

"For now, we'll focus on getting you better. I'm here, no matter what you need. Lizzy has offered to stay with you for a few weeks. She'll drive you to therapy and help around the house. Is that okay?"

Judith looked at the back of her sister's head in the front seat, her hand resting on Justin's shoulder. To her shame, Judith didn't realize what that meant. Did she want Lizzy around?

"I guess. For a few weeks," she relented.

"Right now, you need to focus on your mental health. Everything else comes second."

"Okay."

Judith lay back and thought about Nicolas. She didn't have her phone, so she couldn't check if he tried calling. He was probably so disappointed. Now that she had failed at killing herself, she realized she had made a colossal mistake. She should have gotten on the plane. When Justin tucked her silent, skinny frame into the back seat, he didn't look at her. She could sense he was angry. There would be a price to pay for her stupidity.

Across the windswept desert farmyard, the sun nearly setting, Martha guided her to the front porch. Left her to confront Justin, then sat with Justin's mom in matching rocking chairs to discuss the horrible situation.

Judith finally raised her eyes to him, her lips trembling. Justin enveloped her in his warm arms and squeezed her tightly.

"In Cabo, you should've trusted me."

She heard the chastise in his tone like the first week they met, when he was constantly pissed at her for stalking potential suspects.

"You wouldn't have understood."

Judith pulled away and sat on the front step, feeling the wetness as a layer of ice soaked through to her bottom. The evening was brutally cold.

"I hold a degree in criminology, and I'm a cop. I know how predators groom victims and manipulate them. Nicolas knew you were abused because he was one of your abusers. He stalked you and had this all planned out. Why didn't you tell me what he was planning?"

"I couldn't go through with it. If I had run away with him, then you would know who I really was. I couldn't face that. I wanted to be your girl, even though I have never felt like you were mine."

She glanced up and watched Justin nod his head slowly.

"Have you ever loved me? Has this all been a lie? I gave you everything. I made us a home and saved you from that monster again and again, and still, it wasn't enough."

"How can you ask me? As hard as it was, I gave him up for you. I tried to kill myself out of love for you!"

"Even after I shut your online affair down, you still gave yourself to him in Cabo. I can't believe I'm going through this."

"You are going through this?" Judith was aghast, standing now, tucking her hands into her armpits for warmth. "I'm the one who nearly died!"

"That was your choice, one that he drove you to. I can't believe how weak-minded you are." He glowered when he said it.

"You need to let me go, Justin. You will never love me. Please, just let me go." She started walking toward their apartment, but he grabbed her arm, turned her around, and pulled her into his arms again.

"I can't do that, and you know it. You need to give him up in your heart. For good."

"I'll never be free of him. Nicolas will always find a way to get in touch with me. This connection we share will haunt me to the end of time."

Judith rained tears on his chest and wiped her nose with her hand. She felt gross, ugly, and so dead inside. The drugs should have worked. Why didn't they work?

"Judith, you're wrong. You are free of Nicolas Winters forever. Local officials in Cabo arrested Nicolas the morning you were supposed to meet with him. I was there when it happened. I made it happen! He currently sits in a jail cell awaiting extradition, where he will be remanded to the State of Utah and face felony charges. We're talking prison time."

Judith stared at him in amazement.

"Are you serious?"

Justin nodded with relief.

"You got him arrested? How is that possible?"

"He messed with the wrong girl."

"I care about him, Justin. He is such a mess. He won't survive prison."

"He is. But he's not your problem. He needs to pay for his crimes. And after stalking you and trying to steal you from me, he deserves to be put in front of a firing squad."

Her heart pounded with the delayed effects of her suicide attempt as she pulled away and folded her arms, looking out over the desolate landscape once more. She had done this, brought about this terrible fate for Nicolas. It was so difficult to abandon him and not follow through with their plans. She loved him dearly, but even worse, felt psychically connected to him. Some of the pain she experienced right now was his. And now he was in jail because of her. Why hadn't she considered that this might happen? Of course, Justin would ensure he got caught! In her newfound lease on life, she was now sentenced to hell.

"Well, you will never forgive me now, so we're already doomed."

She threw her hands up in the air and stalked toward the apartment. He followed.

"Judith, I want to move past this, but it's going to be hard. You cheated on me for real this time. I thought seeing him cuffed and in jail would free me from this jealousy, but I can see that you still love him."

"This is why I tried to kill myself. So I wouldn't have to face this."

Judith couldn't stop crying. She was gonna lose him, and Justin had made damn sure she lost Nicolas.

Finally, Justin sighed and reached for her hand once again.

"Well, Nicolas is gone now. I say, let's get on with our lives."

The weight of his words crushed her heart into dust. Nicolas was gone. NICOLAS WAS GONE. She should have gotten on that goddamn plane.

"Let's go and try to make up, okay? See if we can put this behind us."

"You're never gonna forgive me, and I'll never feel worthy of you now."

"I don't need you to. I already know you're unworthy."

She looked up at Justin. Was he joking? His strong jaw was square and firm. His eyes shone, self-righteous, so sure of his judgment. He saw her as trash and loved her because she was trash. It was sick and wrong but she had no power over the way he made her feel. Unworthy.

"I don't want to feel unworthy," she said with defiance.

"In time, you won't. I know you'll make it up to me. You're gonna marry me and have my children, and it will all be fine one day. Trust me. Right now, I wanna go make up like we did last October when I ended your affair. Hot as fuck. Then I want to start planning our wedding. I have one goal now. To make you mine. Come on. Let's go get wild, baby."

Justin seemed excited, and she couldn't understand why. Was he just relieved that she survived?

"No, I'm exhausted," she admitted.

"I think I can wake you up, baby." He rubbed her hand over his hard groin. "See? Even though you fucked him, I want you as much as ever."

"You're so happy. Why's that?"

"Well, I beat that little shit at his own game, which rocks. You can't imagine how miserable he was in jail. Practically gave me an orgasm seeing him break down in tears when I told him what you did."

"You told him?" she asked, her voice cracking.

"Oh yeah. It was awesome. Nicolas threatened to kill himself. I hope to God he does—one less thing to worry about. Now, nothing stands between us, so I can finally have my girl all to myself. What's not to celebrate?"

Justin guided her through the snow up the stairs. The apartment was warm as he carried her to bed in the first step towards erasing Nicolas from her body and soul. He was as passionate as ever as he tried to win her back. But that afternoon in Cabo, Nicolas wrecked her when he claimed her as his soulmate for life. And now that he was lost to her for good, it felt like half her soul was missing. How could she make Justin understand this? She was depressed, but he thought she didn't want him. He looked consumed by jealousy, and nothing she could do would make him trust her again.

"Justin, please, give me time."

"You're still thinking of him, aren't you?"

"I'm just depressed. The hospital was horrible. They treated me like a criminal. There was no sympathy."

"Well, suicide is against the law. Of course, they'd treat you that way."

Always the good guy, always the cop.

"We're trying to fix things too fast."

Judith protested as she rolled away into a ball. He pried her open, shoved her onto her back, and then crawled on top of her.

"I saved you from him. You owe me."

"We went for months last year when you didn't touch me. Why are you so demanding all of a sudden?"

"Because, like I said, he's gone. And I wanna erase him from your mind forever. I never wanna feel like you're thinking of him again."

"Justin, I'm not in the mood. I really am depressed."

"We'll make this quick." He promised, trembling with desire.

Should she give in? He had ruined Nicolas's life. He only wanted sex, and he didn't love her. She had to make a stand!

"No," Judith said firmly, shoving him off.

He fell back on the bed in shock. A darkness crawled into his eyes.

"Are you rejecting me? After I just said I would forgive you?"

Was she? Did she still want him? She wasn't sure. Had no idea how she was feeling. She needed time!

"Give me a couple of days, Justin."

"Fuck that. I want you. Now."

"Well, you're not gonna have me. I need to heal."

She turned to her side and wiped the tears as they fell heedlessly. Nicolas was gone. Gone. Gone. Gone. Gone. The pain would never end.

"Fine. It's your funeral," he muttered angrily, pulled on his clothes, and left the room, slamming the door behind him.

Chapter 38

Justin

Justin was lying in his mom's arms, crying like he did when he found out his dad died in Afghanistan.

"Mom, what do I do?"

"Have you prayed for comfort?"

"I tried. But I'm so mixed up, I can't feel anything but rage. God can't help me right now."

"Only He can give you an answer. But I'd say, right now, you need to process your grief."

"The worst part is that it's my fault. By the time I pulled my head out of my ass, it was too late. Nicolas had already made the plans for them to meet."

"Son, she chose to cheat on you. She could've told you. Canceled the trip."

"I feel like things were already screwed up, like I deserve this."

"You are a prince. You don't deserve this. But remember, you aren't married. You can kick this girl out and move on. You don't have to forgive her. Please know that sometimes the best choice is letting someone go."

"I don't want to lose her. She's made me into more than some shy, loser country boy. I don't wanna lose that feeling."

"Don't let your insecurities guide you here. You have your whole life ahead of you. Just throw yourself back into your routine and let things settle down a bit."

"I am so angry with her. I hate her."

"Of course you do. How could she do this to you? I can't understand. You're the perfect guy. And you even forgave her after finding out about their online affair. Then for her to do this?"

"I wanna keep her around to make her suffer, isn't that horrible?"

"It is, but it's also totally understandable. Honey, you need some sleep. Don't let this woman wreck your entire life. Where are you sleeping?"

"On the couch."

"That's bullshit."

"It's fine."

"Send her back to her mom's. She's not your responsibility."

"Maybe I will. I'll think about it. Thanks, Mom."

"Justin?"

"Yeah?"

"Whatever you decide, please decide quickly. Judith was a fool to cheat on you, true, but I still think she's crazy about you. Her issues that led to this affair have nothing to do with you. In my heart, I hope you two can move past this. If you can, that is. Otherwise, let her go. Soon. Don't torment her. Okay? The poor girl has already suffered enough."

Justin nodded sadly, kissed her, got up, and left. In the front yard, Lizzy was standing by the garage.

"We need some groceries. Want me to go shopping?"

"Sure, if you don't mind."

Lizzy wrapped her arms around him, pressing her body to his.

"Hang in there, cowboy. She'll pull through."

Lizzy wouldn't let go of him, and he stood awkwardly until finally, he pulled away and gave her a wan smile. She replied with a peck on the cheek, and then he walked up into the apartment.

Justin was so tired. He needed sleep. He hadn't slept well at all since he started sleeping on the couch. The thought of her lying in bed thinking of Nicolas burned holes through his mind.

Justin had no idea what was wrong with him. Initially, he was positive that he could forgive her. But somehow, that had changed. He felt the same hatred and angst he had all last summer after discovering they were in contact online. He didn't think he could forgive her, but he hated accepting that because he wanted to be a good guy, and a good guy would understand and forgive.

It was because he had met Nicolas face-to-face. That is what warped his feelings for Judith. That prick accused him of being the problem, and Justin feared he was right. But to have a fucking criminal judge him was too much. Judith had slept with that psycho! How could he ever forgive her? Nicolas had won for a moment there, and it was a truth that was too hard to accept.

His body ached for her, and she had begged him to come back to bed countless times, sobbing for him. Was he punishing her? He was doing so at his own expense. But after that first night, when she rejected him, something twisted inside him and he felt malicious. If she were going to reject him, then he would pay it back threefold. She wouldn't get a goddamn hint of comfort from him if that's how she wanted to play it.

Justin stared at the couch. He needed his bed, but no Judith. She no longer left the bedroom, so he would have to suffer through sleeping next to her. If she had a problem with it, she could leave. He opened the door to their bedroom and saw her lying awake in her bra and panties on top of the bed sheets, motionless and staring out the window. He stripped, closed the blackout curtains, and crawled into bed. Just being this close to her got him aroused, and he wished she would send him off into a blissful sleep like she used to. But she couldn't. Because she betrayed him, lied to him, and chose that criminal over him and—

Her hand was on his belly. Stroking him the way she knew drove him wild. He groaned and shuddered.

"Please let me," she whispered, "don't reject me. You will end us. Do you want that? To end us for good?"

"This is your fault."

He gritted his teeth.

"I know. Please forgive me. I'm unworthy, but I can't live without love."

How was he supposed to endure this? He had to push her away. She needed to recognize how much she had hurt him! But God, oh God, her saying those words, begging his forgiveness, he needed release right this instant.

"No sex. I can't look at you," he muttered.

"I promise. You don't have to see my face."

Her words made him want to break down and weep. He loved her face. He wanted to drown himself in her eyes, kiss her mouth for hours, and trace the contours of her jaw, nose and eyebrows. She was so beautiful and divine. He wasn't capable of being this cruel. How could he be this cruel?

Judith crawled on top of him and made her way down, her hair tickling his chest. He wanted to tear her bra off, take her in his mouth, take her back, and make her love him and only him. But he couldn't stop thinking of her doing this to Nicolas, and that made him want to choke her to death. It was awful. He felt pure evil. His jealousy had warped him completely.

"Did you do this to him? Suck him off like you do me?"

She didn't answer as she licked his belly button and down his happy trail, which meant that yes, she had.

"You're so hard. Huge. It's been weeks. You need this, Justin. Come on. Give in to me like he did. Let me take you all the way."

What could he say to that? If Nicolas received her royal treatment, then it was only right that he be given it too.

His inner caveman stared out at her through his eyes. He saw her hanging from that hook on the ceiling like a punching bag, gagged, entirely at his mercy. Pictured himself smacking her, fucking her. and immediately said a prayer. This was hell. He couldn't pray for God's mercy *while* fantasizing about this shit *while* getting a blowjob!

He succumbed to the temptation. Shoved her head down on his groin in reply and let his imagination run wild. This time, she didn't get him off fast. Hell no. Turned around so her gorgeous ass was staring him in the face. Fondled him softly as she stroked and squeezed. He wanted to shove her away like he usually did. But if Nicolas could handle it—

She took him to the brink, then eased him back until he was delirious. He had never let her do this before. It was fucking amazing. She crawled back down between his legs. Took his junk one mouthful at a time, sucking him into insanity, fueling his violent fantasies and propelling them into overdrive. Never in his life had he felt this close to an orgasm for this long.

When she had tormented every last inch of him, at least ten minutes of pure, unfiltered ecstasy, she stroked him fast and tight.

"I've teased you long enough," she giggled, "you are deliciously engorged."

"I'm gonna fucking explode."

"This time, I'm gonna make sure you hit your target when you do."

Judith held down his thighs with her knees, lifted his ass in her hands, and rode him with her mouth. Faster and tighter. Son of a bitch. Why hadn't he let her do this before? This was fucking paradise. He clenched his buttocks, gripped the mattress, and endured as the rush of semen surged and he erupted in the back of her throat. She moaned as she sucked as if his cum were the most delicious thing, which he found unbelievably erotic. He squirmed and groaned helplessly, but for the first time ever, he let her swallow until he was spinning, strung out on what felt like a deluge of orgasms.

"That's what a blowjob should feel like," she declared, licking his dick as he rode the dark waves rushing though his filthy mind.

Justin realized he had been cheating himself this whole time. That was the difference between him and Nicolas. Nicolas took whatever he wanted and indulged his carnal appetite without a shred of guilt. In contrast, Justin deprived himself. Being a good Christian, it's how he had been taught.

He wanted to forgive her right then and there then incite a three-hour-long fuckfest. However, she had admitted to doing this to Nicolas. So he had to make her suffer first. He was a cop. He believed in corporal punishment and that every crime had a consequence. This was a matter of principle. But eventually, he would forgive her because there would never be anyone like her.

Of course, Nicolas went insane to get his hands on Judith because she was a goddess, and a blessing from her made all your dreams come true. Judith crawled up beside him, tried to drape her arm over his chest, but he kicked and shoved her away. He had to make his point. She owed him a hundred blow jobs. He didn't owe her a goddamn thing.

Judith curled up into a ball, her muffled sobs echoing through the quiet, as his heart withered away, as he fell asleep.

Chapter 39

Nicolas

Nicolas's mind had broken. He needed a fix so bad. He couldn't believe that Belladonna had betrayed him like this, allowing that cop to access her phone and discover their getaway plans. This was hell. He thought of all the charges the police had against him. He was fucked. There was no escaping it. He was going to prison for years.

Why had she done this? He begged her to call if she was depressed. He wished with all his heart that he were with her right now. He felt thrust into some horrible tragedy about to be sacrificed to an ancient god.

Jail sucked. No privacy. No drugs. They served dinner. He couldn't eat. He couldn't sleep. Just wanted to die and join his Belladonna. Or had she pulled through? The cop made it sound like she had. But she would never break free of that self-righteous bastard now. Bitter tears rolled down his cheeks. He didn't speak much Spanish, so he didn't understand anything anyone said to him in here. It was hot and crowded, and he had no privacy. He had to score some dope. He'd lose his mind if he didn't get stoned.

Nicolas watched a guy leaning against the wall. He looked like a guard, and he was seriously checking him out. Perfect. He sauntered over to him and smiled his prostitute smile. The guard ogled him hungrily, displaying a set of grotesque teeth.

"Hablo engles?"

"Un poco."

"Quando?"

Nicolas made a sign like he was smoking pot.

"Posible."

The guard smiled, eyeing Nicolas up and down. Nicolas knew what that meant. This was gonna cost him, but he nodded eagerly.

"Sí, sí."

"Dame diez minutos."

Ten minutes later, the guard opened the cell and ushered him down a hallway, glanced around, and shoved him into a small room. He pulled a baggie of what looked like meth from his pocket as he unzipped his uniform pants. He smiled at Nicolas, who had done this so many times that it was automatic.

Nicolas got down on his knees in front of him and gave this guard the royal treatment. Slow and sloppy. The guard was moaning so loudly that Nicolas was afraid they'd get caught. When Nicolas finished him off, he gazed at Nicolas with starry eyes. Nicolas controlled his gag reflex and kissed the guard on the mouth, who then shoved Nicolas up against the wall and practically sucked his face off. Nicolas let him. He was going to be a repeat customer, and Nicolas needed this more than he had ever needed anything in his life.

Lying back in his jail cell, stoned, he stared up at the ceiling and tried to remember her naked body beneath his. It had only been two months, but it felt like years. Could he have done something differently? His poor, sweet Belladonna, pushed too far. It wasn't him. He knew it was the cop's fault. But still, maybe she felt coerced by his incessant pleas to run away with him. Tears sprang to his eyes once again. So, the drugs weren't too helpful. He needed heroin to wipe away this much pain.

Nicolas drifted off. When he awoke, an angry guy was standing over him and said,

"Mira al hombre gay."

And punched him in the face.

Finally, ten minutes later, when Nicolas could no longer cry out in pain, the guards dragged him out and took him to the infirmary, where he was tended to by a nurse who treated him like the devil. So, someone had seen him leave with the guard and ratted him out.

Great. He was gonna die in here. He would never see the States again, much less the inside of a courtroom. He knew how long extradition could take. He might be stuck here for months, even years. Should he try to end it? If he couldn't talk to Belladonna again, what was the point?

Finally, in such pain and so exhausted, he rolled over and crashed into oblivion. The cops won and he lost, just like when he was sixteen. Life dealt no mercy to people like him. He might as well die because there wasn't a person alive who cared about him anyway.

Chapter 40

Judith

Weeks passed. Judith couldn't stop the tears. She was unable to contain her misery. Justin was slipping away from her, regardless of what she did. He had returned to his perfect routine, which meant he hardly had time for her and was never home. Heartbroken and wrecked by his callousness, she lay in bed, staring at the wall. He started sleeping on the couch and refused to touch her. Ignored her. No longer loved her or trusted her. She begged him to come back to her and try again. He looked tired, sad, lost and emotionally closed off.

Everyone had somehow forgotten that she had nearly killed herself. All anyone talked about was her affair, mainly Lizzy. Judith wanted her gone, but she didn't know how to get rid of her. The affair wasn't the real issue. Her pain was. But nobody cared about her pain. Judith didn't understand why Justin couldn't forgive her. He knew he pushed her into Nicolas's arms. That he was cold and cruel, possessive yet lacking in love. But somehow, she deserved this punishment.

Judith needed to leave him because he had come to hate her now. It was inhuman, and even her mom thought his behavior was unforgivable. Yet still, no one intervened. No one cared. And now that Nicolas was gone, no one would ever care about her again.

She couldn't eat and didn't care about bathing. Lizzy had made herself a permanent fixture in the guest bedroom and offered to stay long-term to help without being asked, which was awkward. Drove Judith to therapy appointments and reminded her to take her meds. Judith wished a hundred times over that she had succeeded in killing herself.

The therapy helped a bit, and the drugs lowered the pitch of the screaming in her head, but not enough. She lay in bed thinking of Nicolas languishing down in Mexico, and wanted to kill herself over and over. She had done that to him. He was imprisoned because of her. Was he alive? Was he surviving? Why the fuck hadn't she gotten on that plane? How did she think Justin was worth it? He was beyond cruel and clearly never loved her.

Judith was so confused. Did she love Justin at all? She could only think of Nicolas. If she had loved him, then it would have been easy to run away with him. What was wrong with her heart? She lay in bed, listening to the silence. Justin was sleeping on the couch. She spent all morning trying to learn everything about extradition. She begged her mom to have Erik hire a lawyer to represent Nicolas, desperate to unravel her mistakes. Messaged Nicolas repeatedly, hoping that somehow he had gained access to his phone, but received no reply.

Enough of this shit. She had to get up, take care of her body and eat something. She couldn't wallow in her misery forever. It would be impossible to leave Justin at the rate she was going. Judith pulled herself out of bed and went into the bathroom. She turned on the hot water and took a luxurious shower. Pampered herself with the routine she had maintained throughout her teenage years. After the shower, she pawed through her drawers for clean panties and a bra when the door behind her opened. It was Justin. Bent over, ass pointed at him, she pretended not to hear him as he shut the door. This was his chance. She was clean, awake, and ready to make up if he would only take his chance.

"Are you standing there like that on purpose?" he growled. She stood and turned. Regarded her sleepy hero and his dick prominent beneath his boxers. He was an idiot.

"Justin, why don't you kick me out? You don't want me. You'll never forgive me. Are you planning on keeping me around just to torture me for the rest of my life?"

"I don't know what I want yet."

She should get dressed, but remained naked and defiant. Couldn't help but notice how aroused he was. That meant nothing. Justin wasn't lying when they first met, and he told her he had the willpower of a bull. He could maintain a hard-on all day long and do nothing about it. Well, maybe she'd get lucky and his dick would explode. He deserved it.

"You might wanna come to a decision soon because I am sick of being jerked around," she shouted.

"I don't think your opinion matters all that much."

"What do you want from me?" she screamed and threw a hairbrush at him.

"I want you to take back what you did!" he shouted.

"It's impossible, Justin. I did it, okay? And you know what? I would do it again! I should have gotten on that fucking plane."

"Think he's worth it, huh? You're saying that criminal is worth more than me?"

"I'm saying you are an asshole, and you weren't worth dying for! I sacrificed my life because I couldn't leave you, and you don't care. Fuck this. What am I waiting for? For you to come home one morning and shoot me? Cause that's the kind of hatred I feel from you."

Judith ripped open the closet and grabbed her suitcase. Justin wrecked her life, and he wrecked Nicolas's too. She gave it all to her hero cop, and he turned out to be the biggest disappointment in human history.

"Judith. Stop." He grabbed her suitcase and threw it across the room. "I said, stop."

"Why? Are you gonna strangle me if I don't? Chain me up and starve me? What the fuck do you want from me? Haven't I suffered enough?"

She screamed and went at him in a flurry of fists, clawing at his arms and chest. He took her by the shoulders, and she kneed him in the groin. Enraged, he lashed out and backhanded her across the face. Judith lurched to one side, then retaliated, fist aimed at his jaw. Heard the crunch and the groan as she made contact. He grabbed her wrist and twisted, and she twisted along with it. In a dance, she twirled, flung her head back, slamming it into his chin.

"Fuck!" he screamed as he flipped her around. "Judith, for God's sake. Stop this."

She pounded away at his chest, and he smacked her again. Then again. Her face glowed with red welts, and she screamed in fury as he slapped her so hard she collapsed onto the bed. He climbed on top of her. She felt his dick and his trembling arms. His eyes were black and luminous, and he wanted her. He wanted her!

"Do it. Justin, fucking do it."

Breathing heavily, trying to rein in his anger, she rubbed up against him, but he pinned her hips with his knees, held her arms above her head, and waited for her to calm down. Finally, she was tired of her anger, sick of carrying around this massive weight of furious rage. He released her arms and she pulled him on top of her, sobbing.

"Why do you love him?" he pleaded, "why can't you love me?"

"I do love you, Justin. What do you need from me to prove it?" She wiped her nose on her wrist, then smeared it next to her on the bedspread.

"But you love him too."

She sighed and nodded in defeat. He let her up, and she crawled over to the pillow, tucking it between her legs. If Justin wasn't putting his dick there she needed some sort of comfort. Her face burned from his hand. Why had he slapped her like that? Something was developing between them. Something dark and toxic. And she wanted more and more—anything to feed this misery inside her.

"The only way I can describe it is that I love you like the sun. You fill up my life with warmth, hope, and happiness. Or so I thought you would when we first met. But Nicolas is like the moon. I love him for understanding my darkness and filling me with light when I've been so unhappy."

"Can't I be both to you?" He sounded in such pain that Judith felt tears in her eyes once again.

"Justin, most of the pain Nicolas was helping me to deal with was the pain you caused me." She sat up against the headboard and stared at him.

"I can't accept that," he whispered, "I'm a good guy. I haven't done anything to hurt you, not intentionally."

"So, all those months last year you rejected me were an accident? You should have let me go last October. I am not the right girl for you. I don't know why you want to keep me around. What? Do you think I'm going to transform into an entirely different person?"

"I can't give you up because I want you so bad that it hurts. But that same feeling is soul-crushing. I can't live with it. It makes me insane with jealousy and possessiveness. So, I guess my love for you is all fucked up."

"You have never known how to love me." She smiled at him sadly. "I should never have chased you. I should've let Lizzy have her chance. You know she's crazy about you, right?"

"I don't fucking want Lizzy, Judith. I only want you."

"Then why don't you act like it? So what if I fucked Nicolas? He is every girl's dream, Justin. I hate to tell you, but the guy is like the devil himself. There has never been a woman who could resist him. I'm sorry. I was weak. But I couldn't say no to Nicolas. It was almost impossible not to get on that plane. The only reason I didn't is because of you. You have me wrapped around your finger somehow, and it's hell. But now, I don't know what the fuck I was thinking."

"Hearing you talk about him like that makes me wanna murder you both."

"You're not hearing the important part, you idiot."

"You still chose to fuck him, so what does it matter? I thought you were mine. All mine."

"Justin, you need to see me as a person, not just a possession like your car. Please let me go. You don't want me as I truly am."

"I do want you," he protested.

"Do you?" Judith shoved him off the bed. Then she got up in his face. "Huh? Then show me, Mr. Good Guy. Prove it. Or I'm done and I'll be gone by morning."

This was it—an ultimatum. Judith was tired of being strung along and not knowing what would happen next.

"I haven't had sex with you because I want to release this rage. And I'm afraid I'll take it out on you," he confessed in a low voice, "I don't want to hurt you, but actually, I sort of do."

"So, you wanna fuck me super hard, is that it? Think I can't take it? I'd rather be fucked by a maniac than not be touched. What you are doing to me by pushing me away is murder."

"You awakened something I call my inner caveman. I can't let it out."

Finally, some honestly. They were getting somewhere.

"Hello, caveman. Tell Justin that I get off on thrills because they make me feel the terror of my childhood abuse. I'm one fucked-up girl. Tell him, I can take rough sex. Don't be ashamed. Give me violence. Give me pain. Give me something, or I'm done."

"I thought you liked the good guy. I'm not the guy I thought I was. Not after meeting you. You've changed me."

He looked at her like a starving man, and Judith now understood his repression, his distance. Justin had never allowed himself to experience his emotions. He had no idea how. She would feed his furious lust, and by doing so, maybe he would come back to her.

"What do you want? Cuff me to the bed? Smother my face with a pillow? Want me to deep-throat you until I choke? Tell me. I'll do anything for you." She stepped closer and cupped his groin. He was so ready. She would give him everything if he just let himself surrender.

"I can't," he muttered and shoved her away, "I can't give in."

He left her standing there, went into the bathroom, and slammed the door. Judith stared down at her naked boobs. How was he able to reject her? She was willing to do anything. Justin was an idiot. She pulled on a bra and panties, put her suitcase away, and lay back on the bed. Her desire to eat had vanished, as did her desire to escape. He would give in eventually. Cave into his violent proclivities, and when he finally did, she'd be waiting to let him heal his soul by taking out all that well-deserved rage on her.

Chapter 41

Justin

In the shower, Justin leaned up against the wall and jerked off viciously. Judith would've let him do what he wanted to her. Why didn't he give in? When he slapped her again and again, it was so satisfying that he nearly ejaculated. Hoped to God she didn't notice how aroused he was. And she liked the abuse. No. She fucking loved it. The violence got her off like it did him. So why couldn't he just give in?

It's not like he wanted to try to kill her or anything. He just wanted to hear her scream as he fucked her. He fantasized that she loved the pain and imagined her begging him for more and more. Torturing her with the cold shoulder until she groveled for sex, then tackling her down with a vengeance. Hear her plead with him to stop, while loving every second. Eyes bright with excitement as he penetrated her from every angle.

Justin had seen Judith as the ultimate fuck toy from the moment they met. This hot girl he wanted to bend into a pretzel, then break her. He wanted to break her so bad. Make her addicted to him instead of Nicolas. He knew that she loved roleplay from her sexting with Nicolas and that she embraced all sorts of kinky shit. He knew he could play out all his fantasies in a steamy, sexy way. Satisfy them both better than any drug and hotter than any porno.

Dressed for work, he dawdled in front of the mirror, hoping she would be gone when he left the bathroom. Judith was lying on the bed, staring out the dark window. His dick had settled somewhat, but seeing her gorgeous body in a thong and bra made him want to call into work sick and give her everything and take everything at the same time.

Judith was ignoring him. He debated what to do. Finally, he sat on the edge of the bed and took her hand in his.

"Give me some time, Judith."

"It's been two months."

She said into her pillow, muffling the despair.

"I know. I don't know what I need."

"You need to get laid is what you need. So do I." She said without looking at him. "Or maybe we need therapy. Try couples counseling."

"Perhaps we should get away for a weekend and try to get back to a place where we once were."

"We can't go back."

"I'm afraid that if I touch you, it will only make you think of him. Even if you tell me that you aren't, I won't believe you."

"Justin, you and Nicolas might as well be from different planets. You are complete opposites. Having sex with you is nothing like having sex with him. I miss your body. You are so intense. You get insanely hard and pound away at me, and it's so sexy that I don't have the words to express it. And I feel something roiling under the surface with you. Something violent and fucking addictive and it drives me crazy. Makes me want to push you over the edge. Why can't you believe me when I tell you I want you?"

"I guess it's my ego. I never wanted to share you, and now I've been forced to, and I can't deal with it."

Judith sat up and looked at him, taking his face in her hands.

"I won't last like this. You, starving me of love. You will lose me, okay? You will lose me, and I will lose you."

"I'm all dressed for work, but I don't know. Take off your panties, and I'll go down on you."

He wanted to. It would give him something non-violent to fantasize about. Had only tried it once in Cabo, but getting her off made him feel like a Casanova, a title he wished to God he could steal from Nicolas. He hated that she thought Nicolas was a Casanova, and he wasn't. No. Justin was just a regular guy, while Nicolas was blessed by the gods. Fuck him.

Judith froze.

"What?" he asked warily.

"Um, not that. Anything but that."

She looked out the window, her eyes glistening with tears.

"Why not?"

"Because," she paused then admitted, "that is what Nicolas did to me."

"What? I can't compete?"

"No." She took his hand to reassure him. "I don't want a reminder of our hookup in Cabo right now. I can't handle it."

Justin felt the walls rise up around his heart, like an anti-aircraft system with the world's most powerful force fields.

"Wow. One minute you say you want me, then I open my heart, and you tell me I'm nothing next to that criminal."

"It's not that. I can't bear to be reminded of him," she protested.

"And my mouth on your pussy will always make you think of him? Well, I'm fucked then."

"You never go down on me. It's not your thing! I know this. I mean, you don't give a shit if I have an orgasm and you never have. Nicolas, all he cares about is my pleasure. So no, I don't want your mouth on me, reminding me of what he gave me and what I will never have again!"

Acute embarrassment flushed his cheeks until he felt burning hot. Because she was right, he had never once even considered what Judith liked. She was there to service his dick and that was it.

"I don't, I don't have those skills—"

He felt so ashamed he couldn't look her in the eye. She took his hand.

"I know that, and it's fine. We have a different sort of relationship. Let's have our kind of sex. The kind where you go at me with everything you've got, and I'm happy to take the beating."

He thought of all his violent fantasies. Could she have an orgasm with him hurting her like that? Probably not. He closed his eyes in misery. So inexperienced, he never learned what a woman needed. Never even tried to find out. He was a loser, and he would never be able to satisfy her like Nicolas did.

"What about in Cabo? Did I get it right then?"

She looked away. Now, the shame had erupted into mortification. Finally, she shook her head.

"You were lying to me. That's all you know how to do, isn't it?"

"So what if I faked an orgasm? Everyone does it! I got you so riled up that you took me up against the wall! No guy has ever done that to me before. It was so hot. Please believe me!"

He had two choices here. Either believe her and forgive her right now, or wallow in his self-loathing. But he wasn't strong enough to love himself and he never would be.

"How did I get it wrong?"

"You don't understand my body. You are way too rough and impatient. If you don't climax in less than three minutes, you act like you're gonna die. Women require a gentle approach and targeted stimulation in specific areas of the body. They need the build-up, the slower the better. Because Nicolas was abused by a woman, he knows how to pleasure one."

"And you prefer that devilish seducer. I am nothing to him."

"Since you're so fucking competitive with him, why don't you try learning a thing or two? Have you ever even thought about a woman's orgasm, or what it takes to get her there? Do you even know what the G-spot is? No, you don't. You only care about yourself. Don't you dare judge me for loving every second of my affair with that Casanova!"

He stood, disgusted and pissed, more humiliated then he had ever felt in his entire life.

Fuck you, Judith. I am done. Leave if you'd like. I can't handle this."

"Your jealousy is going to ruin us, you jackass!" she yelled as he left the room and slammed the door.

All of his insecurities united and buried him in a claustrophobic pile of misery. His rage boiled, and he wanted to punch holes in the wall all the way out the door.

This is how he felt when his dad left. Betrayed. It's why Judith made him so angry now, and he wanted to punish her because she had betrayed him, just as his dad had done. This rage was deadly, and he had no idea what to do with it. There was no hope for him. He was going to lose her. Because if he didn't, she would probably end up dead by his hand. Justin pulled out of the driveway in a flurry of dust, trying not to think of the woman he had sworn his undying love to and the pain she had caused him by crushing his heart.

Chapter 42

Lizzy

Lizzy listened to them fight and felt her insides roar with joy. Things were almost over between them. Thank God. The last two months had been like waiting in line for a movie that was supposed to be the best ever. She was waiting in line for Justin, and now, finally, he was within her grasp.

Late into the night, she planned it all out, how she would make him hers. First, she needed to get rid of Judith. Why her sister hadn't left yet was a mystery. He treated her like shit and hadn't slept with her since she got out of the hospital. Justin wanted to be free of her. She was convinced of that. He just didn't have the strength to kick her out.

The next morning, she listened as Justin came in from work. Threw his keys down and kicked off his shoes. Anger rose from these muffled sounds. Lizzy waited for him to eat and settle down. Then she walked into the living room, completely naked, and lay on top of him.

He opened his eyes, looked at her in shock, and shoved her away.

"What? You aren't fucking her. Don't tell me you aren't desperate for it. Please, Justin. Give me a chance."

He stared at her so long she wondered if he heard her.

"Lizzy, how did you ever come up with the idea that you and I could be together? Because it's never gonna happen."

Now she felt humiliated. Sitting next to him on the couch, she wished she hadn't jumped the gun like this.

"Justin, things are over between you two. It's so obvious. You don't want her. You may not want me now, but I think you will eventually."

Justin eyed her up and down. Lizzy sensed his judgment, and her face flooded with shame. He was comparing her to Judith, and of course, she would fail miserably.

"Lizzy, it's not my intention to hurt your feelings. But I don't want you in that way. I may not be sleeping with Judith, but that doesn't mean I'm over her. I don't know if I'll ever get over her, if we can't work things out, and I don't need you interfering. Please, if you're going to stick around, try to show some respect."

This was mortifying. Somehow, she thought that his interest in her opinions and how he listened to her go on about school and life meant he liked her. Now, it was clear that he didn't. How could she change this? Failure was unthinkable. He was so close to her grasp for the first time since she first laid eyes on him. She couldn't back down.

"I'll try. But I love you, Justin. I loved you from the moment we met. I haven't been able to love anyone else since. Please understand that I won't give up. I want you, and I am convinced that we belong together."

He stared at her as if she were crazy, shaking his head in amazement.

"I can hardly believe this situation. It's as if I'm caught up in some soap opera. I'm glad you were honest with me. And this gives me the chance to be honest with you. I won't change my mind. I have never wanted a woman like I want Judith, and I never will."

"How can you treat her the way you do? You are so cruel."

He flushed deeply, his face so sad that she wanted to throw her arms around him.

"I don't know what's wrong with me. I keep thinking that somehow it will get easier. I don't know what I'm waiting for. It's hell, though. I miss her so much. I'm in hell."

"Then you deserve to be. You reject her and me. You don't want to be loved, do you? Justin, you want to suffer. It's sick."

He lay back on the couch, eyes closed. His bare chest was so gorgeous that she wanted to devour him.

"I need some sleep. Please leave me be. Get dressed and don't forget what I said. I don't wanna have to tell you again."

She got up and tried to sway her naked butt as she walked away. She peered back to see if he was looking, but he had already turned on his side and had the blanket over his head.

Back in her bedroom, she slowly pulled on her clothes. He outright rejected her. This was the most humiliating experience of her life. How had she convinced herself she had a chance? Because he was a gentleman, and he drew her to him with his loneliness and pain. Pain that she understood. She had never been loved by any man, just as he had never felt loved by Judith. They were soulmates.

Lizzy needed more than just their relationship problems and her body to make him hers. She would require an act of God. But it had to happen. She wanted him more than anything in the world. Justin would help her become the girl she had always dreamed of being. Having him by her side would legitimize her and make her feel beautiful, sexy and desired. Having a cop as her boyfriend was the perfect solution for being a middle-class, spoiled brat with no real-life experience. She needed Justin a hundred times more than Judith did.

Dressed, she grabbed her bag and headed out for school, as it was finals week. She was a straight-A student, and college was a breeze, but school no longer brought her any satisfaction. There was something she wanted far more than a bachelor's degree. She wanted the man of her dreams.

Chapter 43

Nicolas

Somehow, Nicolas had been given a copy of "The Count of Monte Cristo," and he was reading it for the third time. He felt like Edmond Dantès, wholly fucked over by another man. Of course, Justin wasn't his longtime best friend, but the theme still applied to his situation. Justin had gotten him imprisoned and stolen away his beautiful Belladonna, and now he was fucked.

Life was bearable when kept in solitary confinement, where he could lie back and masturbate to his hot memories of Belladonna seducing him during their rendezvous in Cabo. But when placed back in the general population, it was hell. Word had gotten around that he was a fag, and this bit of gossip seemed to get passed down to every new cellmate. Nicolas had never had his nose punched until he went to jail. Now, it was a near-daily occurrence. Worse, he was forced to give blowjobs to cellmates on occasion, and it was either that or get shanked.

Nicolas promised himself if he ever got free, he would get his shit together. Give up the drugs, forgive his dad for real this time, and make peace with Belladonna. He needed self-talk. He needed The Secret. Those two efforts brought Belladonna into his life. He needed help from the universe. Now.

Belladonna still burned in his mind. He could never forget her lovely face or blazing eyes, but his memory of her perfect curves was eroding. Too many cocks in his face were obscuring his fantasies. What would he do if he were to forget her for good?

Nicolas was stoned off his ass when he got word that his lawyer wanted to see him. He was ushered into the visiting area and sat down, flashbacks of Justin's visit erupting in his mind. He looked at the attorney, who seemed bored and annoyed to be here.

"Good afternoon, Mr. Winters. Are they treating you okay in here?"

What sort of question was that? Of course not. Nicolas shrugged.

"So, your father has hired an attorney in the States, who in turn hired me to visit you today and let you know they are looking into the extradition. Normally, you could waive it and return home of your own volition. I guess they are working things out. Hang tight. From what I hear, it should be another few months."

Nicolas nodded. None of this was news, except for his dad hiring a lawyer. That was surprising. The lawyer, a guy with a dirty suit coat and scuffed cowboy boots, leaned closer.

"You know, since you are here illegally, they would be gratified if you disappeared. I've also heard that some of the guards may be susceptible to bribes. You got any money?"

"I do. But it's in the bag they confiscated when they arrested me."

"I'd say to reach out to a guard and offer him some dough to get you out. If you get free yourself, the whole process will go ten times faster if you return to the States on your own."

"When I return, though, what will happen?"

"Well, there's a warrant out for your arrest, so you have to contend with that first."

"Where do you suggest I go if I do get out?"

"Tijuana. Contact your dad and have him arrange for you to leave the country. I hear he's rich."

"I only have about five thousand dollars, and that's if no one has already stolen it."

"Should be enough. They really don't like having to take care of people like you. I can tell from your face. How many times have you been beaten up?"

"Enough," Nicolas replied shortly.

"Tell a guard you'll pay him." The lawyer glanced around. "See that guy?" He pointed at Nicolas's lover boy. "He's an easy target. Once you convince him to get you out, then run like hell. I'm only telling you this because I know how long these cases can take. Even with them trying to speed things up, you might not be alive by then."

"Well, thanks,"

"But, as I said, then you need to leave Mexico. Without a visa, you are in deep shit if they catch you again." He stood and nodded, then left.

Nicolas sauntered over to his guard buddy, who smiled and put up his fingers. Three. Or was that thirty? Nicolas hung around until he finally opened the gate and led him out down the hall to their special spot.

Once the guard shut the door, Nicolas said,

"I have money. Dinero. Get me out, and it's yours."

The guard nodded and smiled in excitement.

"Cuando?"

"In my black bag." Nicolas made the shape of a bag and imitated carrying it. "Can you find my bag?"

The guard nodded, shrugged.

"A lo mejor."

The following morning, the guard was standing outside the cell, holding his black bag. He opened it up and showed Nicolas. His money was gone.

"Fuck," he cursed softly, "lo siento." He said, shaking his head.

The guard smiled sadly, handing him his cell phone.

"Aquí."

"Gracias." It wouldn't help him escape, but it was a kind gesture. "Esta muerto." Nicolas held out his phone and asked for him to charge it. "¿Puedes cargarlo?"

The guard nodded and took the phone. "Te lo cobraré."

"Eres el mejor." Nicolas blew him a kiss.

"Vamos." The guard nodded eagerly, opened the gate, and took him back to their special spot, where Nicolas rewarded him generously down between the legs.

The next day, the guard returned his cell phone to him, now charged, and Nicolas was suddenly back in heaven. Thank goodness, he had paid for a year of cell service when he had the cash.

Nicolas scrolled through his unread texts. He had about thirty from Belladonna. She apologized again and again. He wanted to reply and say he understood, but the problem was that he didn't. She chose that fucking cop over him, and in so doing, threw him to the wolves. How could he let go of that? His soulmate, the woman he loved more than any other woman, did this to him. He wanted to reach out, but what was there to say? I'm in jail. Thanks for nothing. Plus, she was still living with that fucker. He wanted to forget her. Erase her from his mind and let go of the pain she caused him. But he couldn't. He would never stop loving her.

Instead, he read through their message threads, stared at her nude pics, and remembered how much he wanted her from the first moment they met. He was screwed now. No money for a bribe, stuck here until they sent him back to the States, at the mercy of the judicial system. If Martha confessed the whole truth he was looking at two counts of abduction, countless counts of rape, two counts of attempted murder, and aggravated assault when he lost his shit and demanded Belladonna get undressed at gunpoint. He was so fucked. Thank God, the guard had more pills on him. Nicolas let the high take him away as he hid his phone. At least Belladonna thought about him after she tried to off herself. He was tucked away in her thoughts, and he had to hold on to that for now because there wasn't much else.

Chapter 44

Lizzy

Lizzy closed the toilet seat and plopped down on it, staring at the pregnancy test. Positive. She was having a baby. She felt numb. Patrick was a hookup. Nothing more. What the hell was she going to do? It was a rash back-seat fuck with a guy from her study group, committed out of desperate sadness because Justin didn't want her. And now she was pregnant? God. What about school? What would she tell her mom? She laid her head against the sink counter and cried.

If only her sister hadn't been such a bitch and stolen Justin that first night. Didn't Judith see how much more compatible she was with Justin? Since moving in, she and Justin had had a few more conversations, like they had at the pool in Cabo, and it was heaven. He was the first guy who seemed to think it was cool that she cared about environmental issues in their home state. Her intelligence didn't intimidate him, and although he didn't flirt with her, he was at ease with her. Judith hated living out in the country, and apart from the sex, she had no idea what Justin and Judith ever had in common. Now, it was clear that their relationship was over. No wonder Lizzy was taking it as a sign. Although Justin rejected her sexual advances, there had to be a way to get him.

How could Judith cheat on a guy like Justin? He was perfect. Gorgeous, successful, and a perfect gentleman. And to cheat on him with that criminal who stole their mother! Judith was a stupid slut, though, so it didn't surprise her.

There had to be a way to fix this. What if?

Could she? Would Justin give her a chance? If she cajoled him to have sex with her just once, that's all it would take to convince him the baby was his. She balled up the pregnancy test in toilet paper and threw it out. She had to muster her seductive skills now. It was clear that Justin was nearly done with Judith. He wasn't sleeping with her anymore. Slept on the couch, although Judith begged him to come to bed with her.

Lizzy had to work with this. She'd follow him everywhere and find an opportunity. All it would take was a hint that they were having an affair, and Judith would move out. She was easily jealous and hated losing at anything. Just the suggestion that she was losing Justin, and she would be done with him. Lizzy smiled. This would work. It had to. She belonged with Justin. Not Judith. Her.

Back in her bedroom, Lizzy lay down and fantasized about the whole thing. How Justin would act when he discovered they had a baby together. Him getting down on one knee and asking for her hand in marriage. She touched her breasts, and her heart went cold. She didn't have tits like Judith. In fact, she had no curves at all. She wasn't naturally pretty or sexy. She'd have to push past her insecurities. The fact was, Justin wasn't getting any sex, so he'd be desperate.

In the kitchen, Justin was bumbling around, trying to make some dinner.

"Here, let me do that. You go take a break, cowboy."

"Really?" He looked relieved.

"You haven't been to the gym in over a week. Take some time for yourself. I got this."

He smiled at her, sadly. It ripped her up to think he was still mooning over her stupid slut sister when he deserved to be loved and worshiped. It was such bullshit.

"I'd love to hit the gym. Can you make sure Judith eats something? I'm getting concerned. She's losing weight again."

"She needs to get off her ass and start to live again," Lizzy said acidly.

He shrugged, but the weight on his shoulders was apparent. He was miserable and deeply ashamed.

"Why don't you kick her out? It seems to me you two are finished."

"Um, I don't know what's going on, Lizzy. I really don't."

"I do. You're done with her, but you feel guilty as hell because she tried to kill herself, which makes you feel obligated toward her. But you're not, you know. Judith brought this on herself."

"Brought what on myself?"

Judith stood in the doorway of the bedroom. Her hair was a mess, and she was wearing yesterday's pajamas.

"Well, your situation."

"Thanks for giving a shit, Lizzy. Why the fuck are you still here? I thought you were supposed to head home like a month ago."

"You need a ride to your appointments, and Justin needs his sleep."

She smiled at her cowboy as he stared down at his phone.

Avoiding Judith, he walked past her into the bedroom and returned with his gym bag.

"If you don't mind making dinner, Lizzy, that would be great. And, as I said, make sure she eats something."

Wow. He didn't even address Judith directly as he headed out the door, letting it slam behind him.

Judith turned and returned to her room, slamming the door behind her in reply.

Lizzy flicked her eyes side-to-side. This was perfect. Justin would be hers in a matter of weeks. All it would take was a single kiss, where Judith was guaranteed to catch them. And as soon as her stupid sister was gone, she'd move on to claiming the prize and winning the heart of the cop that should have been hers from that very first night.

Chapter 45

Judith

Two more months dragged by like a prison sentence. Justin hadn't even tried to talk to her since. He avoided her now and talked through Lizzy if he needed to say anything at all. It was over. She had to accept that. Although she didn't know how. How could she let go? She had attempted suicide because she couldn't leave him, and that meant nothing to him. Obsessively, she thought of Nicolas and her betrayal. No work had been done on the extradition process while Nicolas languished in a jail cell.

Judith wished she had never told the police he had abducted her. It was the only charge against him, she had since learned. Her mom hadn't told the police anything. If she had kept her mouth shut, he would have been free to come home. But, of course, Justin would never have allowed that. He found her naked in the canyon. It was impossible to hide that Nicolas had abducted her and stripped her naked. And she couldn't claim she had gone by choice when there were three witnesses on the phone call who had heard otherwise.

She thought of that night, cuffed to his car, and how Nicolas had poured his heart out to her, telling her they were soulmates. He was the guy for her. Justin wasn't. She had thrown it all away for her hero, and it turned out that was all a mirage. If Justin was nothing more than smoke and mirrors, then why couldn't she let him go, move out and get on with her life?

She watched Lizzy hang all over Justin, wait on him hand and foot, make dinner, clean his laundry, and try to give him back rubs. She knew Lizzy wanted him, but it was shocking how desperately she threw herself at his feet. He didn't seem to care. Didn't notice Lizzy or her. Maybe he wanted to be rid of them both.

The night came four months after her release. Lizzy had asked her to meet her outside once Justin left for work. She had no idea what her sister wanted to talk about, but around eleven, she headed down the stairs of their apartment. A set of lawn chairs sat in front of the garage, and she saw two figures seated in them. Justin was talking softly. Judith eavesdropped as he confided in her sister.

"Judith was never mine. From the very beginning, he was always there. She never chose me."

Lizzy had his hand in hers, and the other hand was resting on his shoulder.

"I know Justin. It's not your fault. You did everything right. It's her. It's just the way she is. Judith has fucked over every guy she's ever been with."

"Why didn't I see it?"

"You were dazzled like guys always are by the beauty queen."

"I thought she loved me."

"She loves guys, as in plural. She can't be true to anyone."

He sighed and sat back, and Lizzie leaned over, lifted Justin's face to hers, and kissed him. Justin didn't kiss her back, but he didn't pull away either. Judith watched in stunned silence as daggers tore through her heart. She lost her hero. She turned to run away and leave her evil sister to have him. But no. It wasn't going to end like this. She stalked over and shoved Lizzy's chair over, disrupting the kiss and sending Lizzy flying into the dirt.

"You are a fucking liar, Lizzy. You snake. Come into my home, pretending to care about me when you just want to steal my boyfriend."

Judith turned to Justin, who wouldn't look at her.

"Justin, look at me." Automatically, he did, but his eyes were blank and empty. He didn't want her anymore. That was the cold, hard truth. "Lizzy has hated me since we were kids. Now, I realize I've broken your heart, and that is on me. But I'm not a whore, Justin. You don't understand this situation, and that bitch lying there on the ground really doesn't. I have loved you with every part of me, and you are the biggest fucking idiot to let me go. Once I'm gone, you'll have lost your chance for good."

Lizzy hopped to her feet, shoved her chair upright, and yelled,

"Judith, you're a liar. Remember Quincy? You totally cheated on him. He told everyone!"

"Quincy was an asshole who tried to rape me. I was never his girlfriend. He was fucking delusional and thought we were together when we weren't. You don't know anything about me, Lizzy. You've been hateful and jealous for years, and have never seen me as I truly am."

"I know you've fucked every guy you've ever met. And you're a whore."

"Just because every guy I've met wanted to fuck me and told everyone they did fuck me doesn't mean they did. Guys have always lied about me. I don't sleep around. When I give my heart, I give it with every ounce of my soul. And none of my high school hookups or relationships even matter. That was all kid bullshit. What matters is that right now, you are living in my house and pouring poison into Justin's ears, right after I experienced one of the worst things ever. You are all focused on what I did back in Cabo, but you forget what was done to me. As a child. An innocent child. You are straight-up evil, Lizzy. And a horrible sister."

"Well, if I'm a horrible sister, I learned from the best. Because you have made my life hell since I was born."

Judith's eyes filled with tears. She hadn't realized what was going on. Lizzy was bound and determined to make her suffer. This was payback for all the times she was a mean sister, and her punishment was losing Justin.

"Fine. Take him, Lizzy. Laud it over me all you want. And Justin, you can have this fake, stupid bitch. There's a reason Lizzy has never had a boyfriend. After three dates, they all discover who she truly is. A manipulative, controlling, and incredibly cruel psycho who will take everything from you. Your freedom, your personality, and your joy. I may have cheated on you, Justin, but you broke my heart as soon as I gave it to you. You distanced yourself from me and tortured me with coldness. You ruined this. You. Lie to yourself all you want, but it's the truth."

Lizzy laughed, picked up her chair, and sat back down, placing her hand on Justin's leg.

"Typical Judith hysterics. We don't care about you, Judith. Go rant and rave to someone who gives a fuck."

Judith stared at Justin, but he wouldn't meet her gaze. The silence stretched, and Judith waited for one last shred of hope to manifest itself, but none appeared. It was over. Judith turned around, went upstairs, locked the bedroom door, and cried until she could no longer breathe.

The following morning, Martha arrived and loaded up Judith's belongings. Justin was at the gym. Lizzy tried to talk to her, offering a half-hearted apology, but Judith ignored her and went straight to the car. Her guilt vibrated against everything she touched.

She wept for days. Her mom comforted her, but there was no solace. Everything was ruined. Nicolas, whom she loved with a deadly passion, was in jail awaiting extradition. Justin was somewhere aching with her fucking sister. Judith had destroyed every possibility for love.

"Mom, how will I ever want to live again? I lost them both!" She sobbed unrelentingly.

"Honey, I'm so sorry."

"I'm the sorry one. I'm a disappointment to everyone. I couldn't say no to Nicolas. Mom, he can get anything he wants."

"Don't apologize to me. That boy is highly persuasive. If anyone understands, I do. Justin is a fool not to appreciate what you've gone through."

"Do you think Lizzy and Justin will marry?"

"It's doubtful. Honestly, I don't think they are even sleeping together. He has never shown the slightest interest in her."

"I had to leave, Mom. He has ignored me for months. I couldn't take it anymore. When I found Lizzy pouring lies into his head about me and then trying to kiss him, I was done."

"Honey, after everything you've endured in your life, this situation seems unbearably cruel. If there's anything I can do to make it up to you, please let me know."

"Mom, I bet everything on Justin, and it turned out to be the biggest mistake of my life. I was always supposed to choose Nicolas."

"Do you love him?"

"It's not like the hero worship I feel for Justin."

"But you love him."

"With a deadly passion. Nicolas understood my darkness, and he met me there. He helped me through those horrible months with Justin. He was with me every second as I relived my trauma. I wish I had had the strength to board that plane. Why didn't I?"

"Because as much as you love Nicolas, you also realize that he is an emotional wreck. He fed on you like an endless source of ecstasy, with your passion, your trauma and your vitality. That boy really did find his soulmate in you, but I fear that you two are a deadly combination, honey."

"I should have gotten on that plane."

"I disagree. Nicolas is a damaged soul, and he will do anything to survive. I doubt he's received any treatment or medication for his mental illness since he left Utah. He used you like a drug for a year, and without you, I can only imagine what he's been using to cope."

"I wanted to be his drug. I wanted him so bad. I have fucked up my entire life!"

"Sweetheart, life is a long time. Things have a way of working themselves out."

"I loved them both equally in different ways. That's the problem."

"I see how you compare these two men in your heart—your noble hero and your tortured villain. It's more complicated. Your hero is a weak, angry, and emotionally repressed man who doesn't want to be tested too hard. And your villain is a vindictive, broken man without boundaries or self-control. They are both tragically flawed."

"Mom, how do I keep living? I'm so lonely. I don't know what to fill my heart up with now that I've lost everything."

"Life will surprise you, sweetheart. Hang in there."

For days, she sat around the house, listless and depressed. She had no idea what to do with herself. Her mom and Erik were gone, and the house was empty. She stared at her phone every day, trying to think of the right words to win Justin back. Lizzy was still living with him because she hadn't tried to come home. Were they going at it day and night? Did she slip right in and take her place? How could Justin ever be content with Lizzy?

Perhaps it was sibling rivalry, but Judith had always felt competitive with her mom's favorite daughter. Lizzy was plain and didn't attempt to improve her looks in any way, but made up for it by being tall and overly confident. Lizzy was dull and malleable. She kept her opinions to herself and went along with everyone. Whereas Judith was mouthy, told people what she thought and couldn't fake a thing. They were complete opposites.

This mess was her fault. This is what happens when you're indecisive. Nicolas and Justin both loved her, and she hadn't had the strength to cut one of them off. It still made no sense, though. Back in February, before she attempted suicide, Justin swore he would never let her go. Then he turned around and immediately kicked her to the curb! She realized now that Justin was a deeply flawed person. He was insecure, angry, jealous, and unable to cope with his emotions. Justin wasn't a good guy at all. Nicolas was right. She had built Justin up in her head.

She hated losing. Hated it. Lizzy had won. Stolen her fucking boyfriend and she wanted so badly to fight back. Should she sext him? Open a dialogue? Possibly even seduce him back into her arms? She thought of how her therapist had said that she was a sex addict—used sex to deal with her problems to make people love her because she didn't feel value in herself, just like Nicolas. They were two peas in a pod. She cried for the rest of the afternoon, thinking of her soulmate locked up in jail, his life ruined for good, all because of her.

Chapter 46

Justin

Justin stood in the doorway of their empty bedroom and stared at the unmade bed and the crumpled sheets, feeling the isolation like heartburn spreading through his chest. Judith was gone. What the fuck had he done? Why was he such an asshole? He just kept putting it off, day after day, procrastinating on talking to her and working it out. He wanted to race down to Martha's, crawl up to the door on his hands and knees, and beg her forgiveness right this second. How was he to go on living? He thought of the last four months. How Judith pleaded for a second chance, and how he pushed her away. He was a fucked-up piece of shit.

Tonight was his night off. Time to get shitfaced and drown himself in the truth of what an asshole he was. This whole thing with Nicolas had wrecked them from day one, but he let it. His jealousy of that guy drove a wedge between them, and he never gave Judith the time and attention she deserved. On top of that, he allowed shame for his inner caveman to prevent him from developing an honest relationship with her. If he ever got her back, he would come clean about his kink and get her to go along with it.

Since their last fight, he had grown obsessed with a woman's orgasm and discovered how to bring a woman to climax in just about any position. It was crazy that he hadn't learned this before now, and he felt like a jackass. Of course, she loved her hook-up with Nicolas! Like she said, the guy was a God between a woman's legs.

Thankfully, Justin was a quick learner and great at research. Watched a ton of girl-on-girl porn and YouTubed the fuck out of the woman's body. If he had another chance, he knew absolutely that he could compete with Nicolas and give her the best ride of her life. Maybe even get this whole oral sex thing down and blow that fucking Casanova out of her mind for good.

Justin opened the new bottle of Jack Daniel's, took a couple of cans of ginger ale, placed them on the coffee table, and mixed himself a whiskey ginger. He took a long drink, then pulled out his phone, unlocked the screen, and scrolled through Judith's selfie collection until he found one that fit his mood. He pulled out his dick and went to work.

His honey, his perfect honey. Of course, Nicolas wanted her. Every guy wanted her. Why was he such a prick? Why couldn't he handle the pressure of competing with other males? He might have a big dick, but he had a tiny ego. He stopped jerking off and guzzled the rest of his drink, made another, this time with two shots. He needed to get drunk quicker.

Back to work. God, she was so gorgeous. This pic was hot. Her breasts held upright by her arms as she touched herself, her legs wide apart. He remembered how she looked when in the throes of ecstasy. Imagined being up in there, fucking her so hard. Could hear her screams and feel her hands on his ass, urging him to go faster.

He spasmed then let go of his dick, wiped his hand on his jeans. Laid back in the chair and stared at the ceiling. This was hell. He lost his vixen and it was all his fault.

Three more shots, half the bottle gone. This time, he didn't bother with the ginger ale.

What made Nicolas so appealing? Why did she sleep with him in Cabo? They mended their relationship after he shut down their online affair, and things were good. The only answer was that the plans were already in place. Nicolas waited until Justin took off after he created a diversion, stalked her from the beach, then dragged her ass back to his pad. She told him about her problem, saying no to guys, especially if it was saying no to the devil himself.

He thought of his meeting with Nicolas in jail. The guy was such a pretty boy. The kind that both girls and guys panted over like dogs. Thought of their sexting and their deep connection. Clearly, Nicolas was crazy in love with Judith, and it made him hate him even more.

Lying back, feeling helplessly drunk now, Justin heard the door. Fuck. He tucked his dick back into his pants. The sister. God. He had to get rid of Lizzy. Without Judith, there was no reason for her to be here. Maybe she'd think he was sound asleep and leave him the hell alone. He heard a noise in front of him. He opened his eyes, and she was on the floor, down between his legs.

"Hey, cowboy. Let me help you with that."

His jeans were still unzipped, his boxers awry. She reached in, pulled out his dick and began to work it. Drunk and half asleep, he watched, numb. Judith was gone. Did it matter if he let her sister blow him? She didn't know what she was doing, though. Lizzy didn't have Judith's skills. She was awkward, nervous, and seemed not to know whether to give him a hand job, suck him off or what. He felt the urge to push her away and attend to business himself when suddenly, she was on top of him. He stared in disbelief as she slid his dick inside her and heaved up and down.

"Lizzy. No," he protested.

"Sorry. I don't have her skills, but I can ride you, cowboy. Just let me. Okay?"

She took his hands, pushed them off her, and rode him fast. He wasn't wearing a condom. Tried to shove her off before he came, but it was too late.

Lizzy got up and stared down at him, her hand outstretched.

"Wanna come to bed? We can make this last all night."

She gave him a crooked smile. Lizzy didn't have tits, and she was so skinny that he was afraid he might crush her. She was nothing like Judith. Judith was all curves, but underneath those sexy curves was solid muscle from years of rigorous physical exercise. Lizzy looked weak and had poor posture. He doubted she could run a single mile.

Justin was suddenly filled with memories of running shoulder to shoulder with Judith through the night sky, the wind whipping at their backs. Mile after mile. She was so competitive and refused to let him beat her. He loved it. He loved her. Justin felt sick inside. He betrayed Judith by doing this. When Judith moved out, he hadn't cheated on her. It was all based on her jealousy from that one stupid kiss, which he didn't initiate. But now he had legit cheated. He shook his head and pulled his jeans closed.

"Sorry, but hell no. I shouldn't have let you do that."

He glared at her, although it was his fault. Should've pushed her away. What was wrong with him? He was a complete pushover with a woman he despised, but all gung-ho asshole with a woman he was crazy in love for.

"Fine. But I'll be waiting."

He watched her saunter off to his room. Was she sleeping in his bed now? What the hell?

What kind of girl was she? Didn't even try to kiss him. How did she manage to get anything out of fucking him for just one minute?

He thought of how Judith always made sure to have her orgasm. Said she deserved it for everything she did to turn him on, and he was happy to oblige. He'd watch her touch herself until she was nearly there, then she'd ask him to get in there deep, and she'd come writhing against him, climaxing hard, which usually led to him climaxing. It was so hot. Everything she did was hot. He was such a stupid ass for not forgiving her, for just letting her go.

Now, his vicious fantasies all included taking a moment from the violence to grind up inside her and make her climax long and hard. He was obsessed with this now. Hearing her scream in pleasure, and then in pain. And he knew that she'd love it.

Disgusted with himself, Justin grabbed the bottle of whiskey. Fuck the shot glass. He guzzled until his throat burned. All he ever wanted was to figure out how to keep Judith all to himself. He ruined his one chance, and he'd never get over her. Never. Finally, he let the booze take over, and he slid into a snoring, unsettled sleep, dreaming of her taking him to heaven like she always did.

Chapter 47

Lizzy

Lizzy waited six weeks before telling Justin. She made a spaghetti dinner and sat him down, took his hands in hers.

"Justin, I have some news."

"Okay?" He glanced up at her, confused and slightly alarmed.

"I'm pregnant."

"You're what!"

"Remember a few weeks ago? You and me? Well, it must have been that magical time because I'm preggers."

"How can that be? It lasted for only a minute."

"Doesn't take long. You must have some mighty sperm to match the rest of you," she giggled, "I understand you're still fixated on my sister. But we have to make some plans. Okay? I want my baby to know his father."

"His?"

"Oh, it will be a boy," she said with conviction.

"This is unreal. It can't be happening," he protested.

"Well, it is," she assured him and gave him a peck on the cheek.

Part of Lizzy felt terrible. Justin had suffered so much this year. He didn't need the added stress of a baby on top of everything else. But then she thought of how this would bring them together and make her dreams come true with the only man who mattered. It was worth the awkwardness.

"Do you, um, have to keep it?"

She gazed at him, incredulously.

"Justin, let me be honest. I've loved you from the moment I first laid eyes on you. Yes, I'm keeping your baby."

He looked shocked and she wondered why. Lizzy had never hidden her feelings from Justin. She figured everyone on the planet knew she was obsessed with him.

"When is it due?"

"Well, it's only been a few weeks, like next March or April?"

"Are you sure it's mine?" He muttered.

"What? Do you think I'm some tramp like my sister? I'm sorry to disappoint," she said acidly.

"Judith's not a tramp." He glared.

She wanted to argue. Judith had fucked every guy she met since junior high. That definitely constituted a tramp, but she let it go.

"I think if you get comfortable with me, you'll find that I'm exactly what you've always wanted." Lizzy plopped down next to him on the couch. "I'm fun, smart and committed, and I love your house and family. Justin, I think I'm the perfect girl for you."

"I don't see how that's possible."

"Well, it's true. And I want you to commit to giving it a try. Give me a chance. Judith's gone. And when she finds out about the baby, she will never return. You need to let her go."

Justin turned his head away from her, and Lizzy saw a glimmer in his eyes. God, he was really hung up on her. Lizzy had dealt with this her whole miserable life. Seeing all the guys who got their hearts broken by her bitch of a sister. Some of them even hung around afterward with Lizzy, moping for weeks about her. It was sick and pathetic. She didn't understand why. Sure, Judith was pretty, but she was a psycho, impossible to please, had a horrible temper, was way too jealous, and was picky as hell. Why any guy would put up with her was a mystery, and why a guy like Justin would put up with her was incomprehensible.

"Listen, I won't expect you to sleep with me every night. We'll let that aspect of our relationship develop naturally. I'll live here, cook and clean, and we'll get to know each other. Let's see where it takes us. Sound good?"

"I need some time, Lizzy. I can't process this. A kid? Me? It seems impossible."

"It's not, cowboy. And I think you'll make a wonderful dad. Give yourself some credit. I've seen you with your brothers. You're a natural."

He smiled sadly.

"I gotta get ready for work. I guess you can stay for now. But don't expect much. I still love Judith. I doubt I'll ever stop loving her."

"Then why did you basically kick her out? The way you acted during the four months she was here wasn't like a guy who loves his girlfriend. More like a guy who hates her and feels guilty about it. It's okay to hate her. She fucked you over, big time. I couldn't forgive someone for doing what she did."

"Well, there's a lot you don't know."

"What? She sexted him for months, then finally hooked up and fucked him. What's there not to know?"

"I don't wanna talk about it."

"No." She got in his face. "Tell me what you're not saying."

"Judith is a victim in this situation. Nicolas victimized her and abused her."

"Tell yourself that if it makes you feel better, but it's bullshit. Judith wanted him from the moment they met."

"How do you know?"

"Because I know my sister. She can't say no to cock."

Justin flushed angrily.

"Let's get one thing straight. If you live here, you're not gonna talk about Judith like that ever again. Got it? Or you can take your baby and hightail it back to your mom's."

Lizzy was taken aback.

"Oh, sure. Not trying to offend. It's just that I've known her longer than you," she stammered, having gone too far. She was going to have to rein in her sister hatred for now.

"I'm sure you have. But I've known her intimately."

Lizzy smirked and rolled her eyes.

"Whatever, cowboy. Well, are we okay?"

"No, I'm not." He glared at her and closed his eyes in misery.

"Digest this while I go do the dishes. But first." She pulled out her phone and scooted up to him, smiled at the camera, and took a photo. "Let's update our socials and share the good news."

Chapter 48

Justin

Justin sat on the couch in his mom's living room and told her everything. How he had pushed Judith away for months until she finally left. How Lizzy took advantage of him when he was drunk and that she was now pregnant. He cradled his head in his hands, struggling with a splitting headache that had lasted three days. He was never the kind of person to get sick or suffer from any physical ailment, except when he pushed himself too hard at the gym. He didn't know what to do with this pain, both physical and emotional.

"Son, I'm so sorry. Do you love this girl at all?"

"No. Never. She's not Judith."

"Why didn't you forgive your sweetheart, honey? She screwed up, but she loves you, and she begged you to."

"I couldn't stop thinking of her with Nicolas, and it drove me insane. This is more about that fucking criminal getting away with having my girl. I guess I've just punished her."

"Justin, talk to Judith. Try to win her back. Maybe she'll forgive the affair with Lizzy."

"Mom, it was hardly an affair. She practically raped me."

"Are you sure the baby is yours?"

"She says it is."

"Well, son, plenty of girls get pregnant on a hook-up, and then they turn around and find a nice guy who will raise their little bastard. You need to have a paternity test done."

For the first time, he felt a glimmer of hope.

"How do I do that?"

"Tell Lizzy you want it done. Now. You won't take no for an answer."

"God, it would be a modern miracle if it weren't mine."

"I'm not saying it couldn't happen, but it's hard to believe. One time? And as for Judith, I don't feel it's over between you two. First, you have to let this go. What happened with Nicolas was one afternoon. One. He's in jail now. He'll never be a threat again. I told you when I first met Judith that I sensed she was troubled. Then, I discovered last October that it was the case. Girls who have been abused as kids have a tough time saying no to predators. This Nicolas character is a predator. If he had stalked her during your trip to Cabo, she wouldn't have been able to reject him. You have to accept that this is not entirely her fault. If you love her, you will find it in your heart to forgive her."

"It's not just that." Justin flushed. He told his mom everything, but his inner caveman issue felt a touch too intimate to share, and he was uncomfortable forming the words. But here he went. "Ever since I met Judith, I've discovered something about myself that I'm not comfortable with. She awoke some violent passion inside me. Somehow, this wants to manifest itself sexually. With her. I don't want to hurt her, but for some reason, I sort of do."

"I see," she sighed, "my God, you are so much like your father. It's scary."

"What do you mean?"

"Your dad was the same way. He was an aggressive lover. Like a beast. Or maybe even a monster. Acted like a lamb to everyone else. They would never have believed me."

"Oh."

Justin thought back to his memories of when his dad returned from deployment and how the sounds of his parents having sex echoed through the house for hours. Day after day, he heard his mom's screams and dad's grunts. It sounded as though they were in heaven. That was his first introduction to sex. Perhaps those impressions had a more significant impact on him than he realized. It made him so happy to see his mom happy. He never considered that it might be anything other than a lovebird paradise.

"Have you talked to Judith about it?"

"I tried. She said she's fine with it being rough. But I don't wanna be that guy. I wanna be a good guy. So, yeah, I've just pushed her away. It's been hell."

"Honey, let me tell you from experience. She might like it, too. I did. Your dad was a fiend, and I loved every bit of it. We did roll play and rape scenarios, you name it. He tied me up, spanked me, tackled me down, and took me by surprise. It was incredibly romantic, incredibly hot, and a lot of fun. It sounds kinky, and maybe it was. But I would have done anything to keep your father from leaving. When he chose to distance himself for good and forced me to divorce him, he ripped out my heart. Don't do that to Judith. I think some guys are under so much pressure to hold it together that they need to release their stress in some way. It's normal, though. You aren't a freak or a criminal. As long as it's consensual and you aren't putting her in the hospital, there's nothing wrong with it."

Justin stared at his mom, who was turning forty-six in December. Her long blonde hair, streaked with grey, long skirt and baggy t-shirt, prim, reverent, and God fearing. He couldn't imagine it. But just hearing a woman tell him this made him feel one thousand percent better about himself.

"Well, she's gone now, so I've lost my chance to make amends." He glowered at his apartment.

"I wonder if Lizzy stole you just because you were with Judith. I've seen how those girls interact with each other. Lizzy envies Judith. I mean, Judith is gorgeous, but it's more than that. She's authentic. Real. She's her own person. Lizzy is like a ghost trying to be a person. It's sad, really. I'm not sure what their parents did, but it certainly messed those girls up."

"Lizzy's hatred of Judith is off the charts. I should've seen that she was playing me for a fool. Now, it's too late. Why is she so hung up on me? This is awkward and I hate it. I have no interest in her, Mom. I'm not attracted to her, and I don't even like her."

"Well, you need to be honest about this. She has to know her place."

"So, first, I demand this paternity test."

"Absolutely. Then, reach out to Judith. You may discover she is willing to forgive you, and then you can work on forgiving her."

Justin left his mom's house and paused outside, dreading a run-in with that bitch who had taken over his apartment. Lizzy. He straight up hated her. She took advantage of him. Saw he was heartbroken over Judith and connived her way in. He didn't realize what was happening until it was too late. Now, he was tormented by her presence every second, like some horrible movie on repeat. Didn't go straight home after work anymore, spent all his spare time at the gym, in the garage, or hanging out with his mom. He couldn't look at her. Couldn't talk to her. He was a pussy and an asshole. How many guys could claim to be both?

He was now convinced that God was punishing him. This was his penance for being a sick freak, for being an unforgiving asshole. He didn't even try to pray now. That bastard in the sky had forsaken him. Now, he was stuck with a little bastard and a sexual appetite he couldn't satisfy, no matter what he did.

Thought about trying out his kink on Lizzy as a form of punishment she would be happy to endure, but he didn't want to give her the wrong idea. Besides, she was pregnant. Wasn't sure if fucking someone super hard could harm their baby. He was even considering going online and renting a prostitute to appease this appetite for violence. However, he had no idea how to proceed, and he didn't want to risk losing his job.

But his ultimate fantasy was Judith—that vain, hot girl who hit on him so hard. How could God tempt him with this? He was always taught that God didn't give people more than they could handle. That was bullshit.

It wasn't just the sex he missed. Judith was photosynthesis, and without her, he might as well be dead. He took her for granted. That first night after the hospital, when she wasn't ready for sex, why was he so inconsiderate? She had nearly died! Of course, she needed time! It was the jealousy. It warped him completely. Made him hate her and want to see her suffer. He was a monster. Hadn't she already suffered enough?

The night she caught Lizzy kissing him, he should have broken down their bedroom door to explain. Justin was tortured by Nicolas's accusations and by his deplorable behavior towards her. When Nicolas said he broke her heart when he stopped replying to her sexts, Justin nearly felt suicidal. Knew it was his fault that Judith fell into Nicolas's clutches because he pushed her away from the beginning. And after Cabo, he never once tried to understand why she was so sad. His behavior was indefensible. God, would this ever stop hurting?

Back in the apartment, he found Lizzy folding towels and had the strongest urge to grab her by the hair and throw her out of his house. They should've never let her stay. Looking back, he realized how she had been poisoning him against Judith all along.

"Lizzy?"

She stopped folding her towel and looked up.

"What, Justin?"

"I want a paternity test done. As soon as possible."

He folded his arms and looked down at her, feeling his resentment boil at a fever pitch.

"Okay. I'll check into it. Um, there is one issue. I don't have any health insurance. So—"

Fuck. Of course. Goddamn it. There went his savings.

"I'll pay for the paternity test. But I won't pay a cent more until I'm certain it's mine. Got it?"

"That's fair." She nodded. "Give me a DNA sample, and I'll find a company to send it to."

"And I need my bedroom back. You can have the guest room. If the baby isn't mine, you need to move out. I think I've made it clear. I don't want to have a relationship with you."

Lizzy looked close to tears, but he caught a hard gleam in her eye. This woman was determined. God, how could he let this happen? The night Judith caught Lizzy kissing him, he should have stood up for his honey right then and there and kicked her hateful sister out. Taken Judith by the hand, led her to bed and made everything up to her.

"Let's give it time, okay? You aren't giving me a chance."

"I know my own heart. You sabotaged everything between Judith and me and I'm not going to forgive you. I just won't."

Lizzy got up from the floor and threw her hands in the air.

"What will it take to open your eyes? She's not worth you. She's not worth anything! God. It's so fucking hard to deal with men. They are all the same!" she screamed and stalked out of the apartment.

Justin sat on the couch and opened his phone. Judith had changed her Facebook status to single. He wondered if she was dating anyone. It had been two months since she left—the worst, most miserable and emptiest two months of his entire life.

Judith was offline. He wondered what she was doing. The only silver lining in all this was that at least she could never be with Nicolas again. At least he had ruined their love for good. Nicolas was his nemesis, and as long as he got what was coming to him, he could survive. The thought of that criminal getting away with his crimes was unthinkable.

Justin went to his room, undressed, and pulled the blackout curtains closed. If only he could wake up from this nightmare. Lizzy would be gone along with this phantom baby, and Judith would be back lying next to him, where she belonged.

Chapter 49

Nicolas

Six months of jail time, of sucking the guard off for drugs, of getting his ass kicked every time they pulled him out of solitary confinement and tried to return him to the central jail cell. The guard was in love with him now, and Nicolas was able to score heroin and pills. Life was okay when he was high, but when he came down, it was a fate worse than death.

Time had lost all meaning. He was slipping away from reality. All he had was his pain keeping him alive, and he counted his grievances one by one every day. His mother's abuse, Catrina's molesting hands, his father's unfeeling heart, Martha's infidelity, and finally, Belladonna's betrayal.

That was the cherry on top of the sundae. She had betrayed him and chosen the cop over him. She didn't follow her heart and choose her soulmate. Nicolas felt such rage. All his pure, sweet love had crystallized, hardened, and transformed into unbreakable hatred, and he didn't know what to do about it.

Nicolas had no control over this. He lay back as a hand reached in and squeezed his heart until he was transformed by the pain. This scared him. This vindictiveness is what drove him to try to murder Martha, and look how that turned out. He needed to rein in his rage, but he had no idea how.

Maybe he was incapable of love. And what felt like love was just an obsession, like it had been with Martha. But no. He loved Belladonna. She just didn't love him. Not enough. That old, heartbreaking quest to find a woman who would love him, who he could make happy, who would never leave him, echoed through his head until he wanted to tear down all the stars he had prayed to and believe in nothing ever again.

Nicolas no longer saw a way ahead. His life was over. Perhaps when he was sixty years old, he'd see the light of day again. He wanted to end things now. Find something to use as a weapon. He tried to hoard pills to overdose, but he was too greedy and needed to get high every day.

Then, one afternoon, in the throes of a super high, he had an idea. He thought about it until he formulated a plan. That night, he noticed his lover-boy guard giving him the eye, and he sauntered over. He took him to their little hot spot, and after Nicolas had pleasured the fuck out of him, he looked up with bashful eyes and said,

"They are going to send me home soon. You will lose me."

The guard nodded sadly.

"Unless we run away together. Huyamos juntos. Break me out. Sácame. I'll be yours forever."

The guard grinned and shook his head in agreement.

"Mañana."

"Mañana. Sí. Sí!"

Nicolas nodded excitedly, then made out with him for the next ten minutes. Nicolas enjoyed making out with anyone, but this was a way to ensure he would never want to kiss another man again. This guy was gross. Probably had never used a toothbrush in his life.

Back in his cell, doped up and content, he lay back. This might not work out. Even if he got free, he would still have to escape the guard somehow because he sure as hell wasn't moving in with him. But there was the slightest chance at freedom. It wouldn't bring his Belladonna back or heal his heart, but he had to try something. Otherwise, there was no point in living at all.

Early the next morning, the guard pulled him out of his cell and shoved him down the hallway, then took him through a door. In the dim morning light, he led him to a beat-up truck and pushed him into the passenger's seat, shoving his head below the window. They drove for twenty minutes until he pulled up in front of a dilapidated house with the front window boarded up. It was rural, and Nicolas had no idea where he was. Inside, the guard showed him the fridge, stocked only with beer and homemade tamales in Ziplock bags, likely made by his mama. Then he took him to the bedroom and shoved him down on the bed where Nicolas proceeded to thank the guard for his newfound freedom with a spectacular blowjob.

"Me, Marcos."

The guard said afterwards when he sat Nicolas down on the battered couch and handed him a beer. Nicolas looked around the room. The place was filthy, and in the States, it would have been condemned. The air smelled putrid. For a second, he wondered if he had made a colossal mistake. Finally, the guard spoke in broken English.

"Back to work. Be home tonight. I'll keep door locked, okay?"

He kissed Nicolas hard on the mouth and left. The moment the guard shut the door, he began to search. The windows in the bedroom and bathroom were too small to squeeze through. There was no back door. In the dark living room, he decided he needed to pry the wood off of this busted window. Under the kitchen sink, he found a hammer and went to work.

It took forever, and with each bang, he was terrified of someone calling the police. He pried away at the plywood, hammering and kicking until there was a space at the bottom to squeeze through, then he wriggled his skinny body through the opening. He felt a nail dig painfully into his back and splinters pricking his skin. Finally free, he fell squarely into a pile of fresh dog shit. Fuck this goddamn town. He picked himself up and ran like hell.

It took two hours to return to civilization and locate the bus depot. Nicolas hung around the bathroom until he scored a few johns and made enough money for a bus ticket to Tijuana. By noon, he was well on his way to a new life. He was broke. Didn't have a cent to his name, and now he was a wanted fugitive in two countries. But he was free. After six months of brutal ass whippings, forced sexual servitude, and dry periods with no dope resulting in horrifying withdrawals, his fate was now back in his hands.

Once in Tijuana, he made more money for a bus ticket to Mexico City. Three days later, he joined the throng of other sex workers downtown and hit it hard. Within days, he had enough money for a down payment on a dumpy apartment. If only his dad could see him now, barely scraping enough cash together for enough dope and food to get through the day, but he survived somehow.

This was a friendly town. Nicolas started making friends, which was a new experience for him. People liked him and really liked getting high with him. Soon, he was making enough money to score dope for his new buddies as well as himself. He missed Belladonna terribly, but he still felt bitterness and resentment. What she had done to him was unforgivable. Sure, it was only six months in jail, but they were traumatic.

Eventually, though, his curiosity got the better of him. He bought a phone charger and got online. He debated, then finally threw together a fake Facebook account and sent her a friend request. This time, he used the name "Cabo." Figured she'd get the message. She accepted it almost immediately, and he saw a message pop up.

> Nicolas! Is that you! Please talk to me. I miss you so much!

To his shock, he discovered that Belladonna was single and that Justin had hooked up with her sister. So much for her hero. What a jackass. He had to reach out. But first, he had to fix his head fast and overcome his vindictiveness. She was free! Free to choose? Should he message her? He wanted to so badly. But she had broken his heart and left him for dead by getting him sent to jail. It seemed there should be a price to pay for such thoughtlessness.

Nicolas stared at the profile pic of his beautiful girl and tried to decide. Should he say something? Why did he reach out if he didn't want to talk? What was wrong with him? Instead, he closed the app and pocketed his phone. Then he closed his eyes and imagined an alternative reality, where they ran away to Indonesia and lived as soulmates in the life they were meant to have.

This was his problem. He had lived inside his fantasies for so long that he had no idea how to deal with reality. Reality Belladonna was not the same as Fantasy Belladonna, and that realization hurt so bad. Reality Belladonna had betrayed him, and somehow, he had to learn how to live with that. But it was too hard. He had no more room in the part of his brain designated for pain and suffering. It was all filled up. So now, this new pain just traveled over his brain waves, homeless and desperate, crashing into every other part of him, corrupting and collapsing his sanity. He had given Belladonna his whole being, and it wasn't enough.

The overwhelming weight of his quest for love was too much to bear. He had placed all his bets on this beautiful girl, genuinely believing that the universe had finally answered him. As the drugs and fatigue carried him off to sleep, he remembered dancing with her in Cabo, their hearts beating as one, their bodies moving in perfect unison. He had never felt so attuned to another living being as he had with Belladonna. He would never stop loving her, and this brought even more pain. Because he would never be free, no matter how hard he tried.

Nicolas was empty now, devoid of any feeling at all. It was apathy. He didn't care about himself or anyone else. This was both liberating and frightening. He tried so hard to bottle up the rage and discontent his Belladonna had cursed him with. He focused on that perfect afternoon in Cabo San Lucas when he declared his love to her in body and soul. It was incredibly difficult to accept the painful truth that she had chosen Justin. She didn't love him. She was one of a hundred women he had seduced, but she was the only one who mattered. He gave her his heart, and she tried to kill him when she tried to kill herself. How could he let this go?

Eventually, he would. She wasn't with the cop now, which meant she was free. Did he stand a chance with her? Although he was getting sloppy seconds since he clearly wasn't her first choice, was he content with coming in second place? Nicolas decided to live in the moment for now. He had friends, tricks, and tons of dope. Eventually, he'd cave in and reach out to her. But when he did, he had to be prepared. She probably wouldn't like the person he had become due to her betrayal, and there was nothing he could do about that now.

Chapter 50

Judith

The next few months dragged by as she slowly melted into nothing. Two months after she had moved out, Judith found out about the baby in the worst possible way—on Facebook. She stared at the picture of Lizzy and Justin that Lizzy had posted, with Lizzy smiling at the camera, her hand on her still-flat belly, and Justin looking dazed and tired. It ripped her in two. The headline: *Happy couple expecting!*

Is it true?

She texted Justin.

He answered right back.

Yes. I'm so sorry.

She didn't reply and had no words for her sorrow. Now, it was October. Lizzy would be four months along. They'd be going to doctor's appointments together and setting up the guest room as a nursery. She slid on her sneakers for a run, knowing she had to pull it together and survive this, although she had no idea how.

It was dark and chilly as she jogged through the park when she heard her phone ping. She opened her phone and cried out in amazement. It was a message from "Cabo."

Belladonna, I will love you to the end of time. I am haunted by our memories. The only time in my life I ever felt right in the head was when I thought we were together. I was wrecked when you hurt yourself, and I'm so glad you survived, even if it means I lost you for good. Stay safe, and if you ever need to reach out, please don't hesitate. Love forever and always, Nic

Nicolas sent a photo of himself blowing a kiss. His hair was dark again, shaggy and long now, but he was as handsome and sweet-looking as ever.

Judith read his message over and over, as the desire built in her chest and burst forth from her. She stared into those dreamy eyes, remembering how she felt with him in Cabo. Satisfied. Consumed. Her body burned with the memories and the erotic power he had over her. Why had she chased after a rainbow like Justin? She was no heroine, and she didn't belong with the hero. That was the heartbreaking truth.

Judith fired back.

Oh, my God. Nicolas. Where are you?

A week later, she left the airport in Mexico City, took a taxi, and burst into his apartment.

Nicolas—gaunt, anemic, anguished, and dragged through hell, but tragically gorgeous. He twirled her madly, dancing crazily to music throbbing in his head, until they collapsed on his bed.

"I can't believe this is real. I don't deserve to be this happy."

"Neither do I."

She kissed him fiendishly.

"I'm so sorry, Nicolas. Because of me, you went to jail. I have wished I could die a thousand times because of what I did to you."

"Belladonna, why didn't you get on that plane? Why did you bail on me?"

"I was shattered with guilt, trying to be the good girl worthy of Justin."

"So, ultimately, you chose him."

Nicolas sat up, digesting this. Judith caught a hint of anger in his eyes and kissed him.

"Well, I'm here to make up for it now."

"It may be too late." He stroked her face, sadly. "Jail fucked me up. The things I had to do."

"I'm sorry. I didn't realize Justin wasn't worth dying for."

"I can't believe he left you for your sister. What a complete loser."

"I fucked everything up."

"Guess we're meant for each other that way."

"It hurt so bad when I found him with Lizzy. He broke my heart."

"Well, you broke my heart. When you attempted suicide, I almost offed myself in jail. It was so hard to hold on when I thought you were gone forever. I didn't know how I was going to live without you." He couldn't stop kissing her. "All I ever wanted was to find a woman who would love me, who I could make happy, who would never leave me."

"Well, you're stuck with me now. I spent every last cent getting here."

"Does your mom know?"

"Yes, and your dad. I sat down with them before I left. Told them I loved you and was going to live with you. My mom is concerned. But she didn't stand in my way."

"That's generous considering what I did to her."

"I think they plan to visit early next year. On top of that, your dad set up a substantial spending account for me. But really, it's for both of us."

Nicolas nibbled at her neck. He was so frail that Judith wondered if he was ill.

"When your cop visited me in jail, I was sure that was the end of everything. That prick won. He called me a predator. I know I stalked you and drove you crazy all those months. I am a nut case, I'll admit. Nothing has ever made me as obsessed as trying to hook up with you."

"How did you escape?"

"I had to suck off a guard for months to seduce the fuck out of him. By the time he helped me escape, he was so in love with me. Then I ditched him. Not one of my proudest moments."

"You poor guy." Judith kissed him and noticed his eyes were glassy and disoriented.

"We have so much making up to do." He pulled off her t-shirt, pushed her over, and dragged her jeans down over her legs.

"I haven't had an orgasm since our night together in Cabo."

"God, you really are mine. I can't believe what an idiot Justin was to let you go."

"He wouldn't touch me after I got out of the hospital. I waited four months. I begged him constantly and he refused."

He is the stupidest man to have ever lived. Then he throws you over for your sister?"

"He said he wanted to fuck me super hard but didn't wanna hurt me. I told him I could take it rough if that's what he needed, but he wanted to be the good guy."

"What a fucking psycho. That guy can't handle his feelings at all. Geez. I thought I had problems."

"It was so hard to watch Lizzy slowly drag him away. Every day, she was poisoning him. Telling him what a whore I was and how I had cheated on tons of guys. It was hell, Nicolas."

"My God, Belladonna. Do you think you'll ever get over him?"

He already had his mouth on her, and Judith felt her chest pound at the thought of her hero. Could she? She had no idea. So, she didn't answer. Nicolas made her climax so fast that her legs were shaking, her heart was racing, and her body screamed with joy to be reunited with him.

"Was that even a minute? Admit it, I am the better lover, Belladonna. Trust me, you have the right man between your legs."

"You certainly didn't lose your mad skills by going to jail."

"You bring out the best in me. We're broken pieces that fit together perfectly." He kissed her thighs and worked on her until she was moaning, then entered her and pulled her on top of him. "Our bond is so powerful, I believe it will keep us together forever."

"I thought our love was too dangerous to endure."

"It's true. We are volatile, you and me."

"Am I enough for you? I mean, you've been with dozens of women and men, including my mom."

"But I have never felt anything like what I feel for you. Our death match, our crazy getaway, and then all those months of growing closer online culminating in our afternoon in Cabo. I never imagined anyone could exorcise my pain like you have."

"There's one thing, Nicolas."

"What, my sweet?"

"I can't be with a prostitute. I'm way too jealous. I'll end up going around and murdering all your tricks."

Nicolas laughed and threw his arms around her, holding her and thrusting until he groaned with satisfaction.

"I haven't fucked a woman since you and me in Cabo. I'm in heaven right now." She stared at his beautiful face, which she had once beaten bloody. Nicolas swore they traded hearts, but then why hadn't she just gotten on the damn plane? "Sure. We'll figure something out. But, Belladonna, you'll have to satisfy my voracious appetite. And I'm still hurt that you dogged me for that bastard. You'll need to make it up to me somehow."

"I will do anything and be anything you need, Nicolas. I'm all yours."

Chapter 51

Lizzy

Justin asked about the paternity test every day, and Lizzy had no idea what to do. If he discovered it wasn't his kid, he would kick her out in a heartbeat, even with Judith gone chasing after that stupid criminal. He still wouldn't want her. She had begged him to attend the ultrasound with her, and he refused. Said until he was sure it was his kid. he wanted no part of it. Just as she suspected, the baby was a boy. Lizzy told him, hoping that he would light up with joy, but instead he frowned and asked where the fucking paternity test was.

Finally, Lizzy relented. Went online to a fake DNA testing website and ordered a bogus test. It made her feel like shit doing it. But she had no idea what to do. If he gave her a chance, he'd learn to love her. She couldn't give up yet, she just couldn't! The test arrived in her inbox within the hour. Comparing it to other tests she found online, it looked legit. She contacted the customer service number, and it sounded like a real company. This would work. It had to work. But still, she couldn't send it to him. It was an outright lie and also breaking the law. Somehow, she hoped that he would walk into the kitchen one of these days, take one look at her, and fall in love. Then she could throw out the paternity test and start the life she deserved with the man who deserved her.

Morning sickness had knocked her on her ass these past months, so she opted to take a break from school. That meant she stayed at home and was here every second that Justin was. Justin had relented somewhat, probably out of desperate loneliness, and they had sex once more. It wasn't great, and it wasn't in his bed. He looked disappointed after they finished, and she had to initiate everything, but it was better than nothing. Still, it hurt like a dagger in her gut that he didn't want her. And she knew he was jerking off to Judith's selfies. That whore had sent her nude selfies to every human with a dick she'd ever met. Sick and desperate behavior, but it worked. Justin was hung up on the bitch, and she had no idea how to cure him of his love sickness.

Lizzy saved the fake DNA test and went to clean the house. Justin returned from the gym, and they were eating dinner. She had hoped he would spend some time with her tonight, but he had already told her he had plans. Plans for what? Plans to work on his car. Justin had no interest in her. Life with him was hell. Didn't even look at her over dinner, and when she tried to engage in conversation, he was abrupt or ignored her entirely. Justin gave a whole new meaning to passive-aggressive. What was she expecting? She ruined things between him and Judith. It would probably take years for him to forgive her.

"Justin."

"Hmm?"

Staring at his food, moping as usual.

"I guess you heard Judith is living with Nicolas?"

"What?" His head jerked up in shock. Wow. He didn't know. Lizzy was so happy to break this news to him that she felt literally aroused.

"I guess he contacted her, and she bought a plane ticket two seconds later. She was thrilled, according to my mom. She says she should have chosen him from the first."

She watched her poison work its way into his heart, saw his eyes flood with pain, and gloated.

"Where are they?" Justin asked, and he sounded shattered.

"Mexico City. Bet they're going at it like crazy as we speak."

"Lizzy, would you shut the fuck up?"

"I want to free you from this, Justin. Let me help you."

"I don't need your help," he muttered as he stood and threw his plate of stir-fry out.

"Nicolas is a criminal and she prefers him. What does that say about her?"

"I pushed her away. Of course, she's going to end up with him. I wish the justice system worked as it was intended to. If it had, the bastard wouldn't be free now. It makes me boil with rage."

"Me too! I understand how you feel. And thinking of my sister happy when she should be paying for her crimes against you makes me furious."

"What were her crimes? I was the one at fault. She made a mistake, but I committed the crime against my heart and hers. I'll never forgive myself."

Justin picked up his phone and headed outside. Lizzy could tell he was devastated by the news. Probably thought Judith was at home, pining away for him. Well, he should accept the fact that Judith could and would always find a replacement.

She sat around for a while, then went down to the garage to give him a fake apology.

He had his head under the hood. His shirt was off, and she felt consumed by the desire to throw her arms around him and tackle him to the floor. She peeked under the hood.

"Hey, cowboy. I wanted to say I'm sorry. I thought you knew."

"How would I know?" He glared at her.

"Maybe my mom told you?"

"I haven't talked to your mom in a couple of months."

She nodded. "Okay. Still, I'm sorry. I can see it's hard news. It is for me too."

"Why's that?"

"Because my sister doesn't deserve to be happy."

Justin looked at her in amazement.

"You are unreal. I have never met anyone who hates their own flesh and blood as much as you do. Something is wrong with you. By the way, do you have that paternity test yet? I've been waiting for months. You intend to string me along forever?"

"I'm still trying to find a legit company to go through. I'll get there. You can judge me all you want, but you can't imagine what it was like to grow up with her."

"I get it. You felt insignificant next to her. That's gotta suck. But your hatred is off the charts. It makes me feel sick for Judith, who doesn't deserve your cruelty."

"What does she deserve? Forgiveness? She was a mean sister. She treated me horribly every day. Not only that, but she ruined my love life, made my dad hate me, and wrecked my self-esteem. You don't understand who she is, and you never will. You're blinded, like every guy I meet."

"Maybe it's time to grow up and move past it. You are an adult now, right?"

"If I have you, I can grow up. I need someone like you to steady me and make me feel whole," she confessed.

He nodded. Somehow, what she said managed to get through to him.

"Perhaps you're right. I need to let her go. I'll try to. It's going to be hard, though. Thinking of them together rips me up."

"You need to stop thinking about her. I think I can help you." She smiled her crooked smile, placed her hand on his chest, and worked her way down. She was at his belly button, and he hadn't stopped her. "Come on. Close your eyes and pretend I'm her. I don't care."

That was the wrong thing to say. Justin backed up and turned, grabbed a towel and cleaned his hands, then pulled on his t-shirt.

"Not gonna happen," Justin said as he left the garage.

A minute later, she heard him tear out of the driveway. What was it gonna take to catch this man? How the fuck had Judith done it? He was impossible.

Chapter 52

Nicolas

After two weeks of nonstop Belladonna, Nicolas was the happiest man alive. After jail and everything he went through, he was sure he would never feel happy again. But The Secret worked. His self-talk had worked. His long-held prayer to find a woman who would love him, who he could make happy, who would never leave him was finally coming true.

Except there was a problem. He couldn't stop. Right now, he had told her he was taking a walk, but he was actually in an alleyway shooting up. He had a john waiting for him in a parked car around the corner. Told him he'd be right there. What the hell was wrong with him? He promised himself that he'd give it all up—the drugs and the prostitution—if he ever got her back. Here was his chance. So why was he still doing it? And worse, now he was lying to her!

After Nicolas sucked the guy off and was handed a one-hundred-dollar bill, he took it to buy some Benzos. He felt the need to calm down. Lying to Belladonna was causing him severe anxiety, and he knew that soon she'd be able to tell. He had to pull it together. Since she arrived, his addiction had gone into overdrive. Stirring up his hunger for everything. Sex with her, drugs for him. Why did he still need to fuck people for money? It was a thrill, and he loved the thrill. Getting people off was a rush. Controlling their ecstasy and feeling their orgasms got him off emotionally, and he didn't know why.

The next morning, they were having breakfast. Belladonna said,

I need to withdraw some money for food. Would you like to join me for the walk?"

It was awesome having her here. Belladonna was fluent in Spanish, which made life a hundred times easier.

"Sure, sweetheart. Love to."

At the bank, he peered over at the account balance and almost fell over. Ten grand? What the fuck?

"Hey, wanna add me to the account? I mean, you said the money was for both of us, right?"

She thought about it for a second, and he reassured her with his most seductive smile.

"Sure, why not? As long as you promise not to take the money and abandon me for some hot hooker and run off to Fiji."

"Honey, not a chance."

Later that afternoon, the bank card was burning a hole in his pocket. He thought of all the drugs he could buy with that much money, and more so for his new friends. He hadn't invited any of them over because once Belladonna met his friends, she'd know he was using. Wasn't ready to let her in on that just yet.

That night, they lay on the rooftop of their apartment building, staring up at the stars. He watched his beautiful girl, so happy that he could burst with joy. But underneath the joy was pain. Pure, undiluted pain. She didn't choose him. She preferred her cop. And if her cop hadn't thrown her over for her sister, she would have never come here at all. Somehow, that truth wrecked everything. How could she be his soulmate when everything was ruined? His perfect fantasy of how it would be when they were together no longer applied. He had no idea what to believe in now.

"What, my sweet incubus?" She stroked his face as they stared, eye-to-eye.

"It's so hard to let it go. It hurts so bad. You loved him first and chose him over me."

She nodded her head, eyes filling with tears.

"Please forgive me. Please don't do what Justin did to me. I realize I hurt you. I was indecisive, and I couldn't choose. Plus, you have to understand. The night I tried to kill myself, Justin hurt me. He grabbed me by the scruff of my neck and told me that no matter where I went on the planet, he would find me and take me back. He knew I was going to leave him, Nicolas. He would never let me be with you."

"He's the reason I hate cops. Controlling, cruel, manipulative pricks— all of them. How could you ever like him? How could my soulmate be the kind of girl that would even consider a guy like him?"

Belladonna shut her eyes in pain, and he watched in agony. He was causing her this pain, and he felt horrible.

"Justin somehow filled the place in my heart where my dad used to be. It sounds nuts, but his disapproval and coldness reminded me of my dad. It was so hard to earn my dad's love. When I won a competition, he was proud of me and showered me with love and attention, but the rest of the time, I was nothing to him. It messed me up, Nicolas. I'm sorry. Your perfect fantasy is ruined by me."

Nicolas kissed her and pulled her into his arms. He understood. He did. So, why wasn't his understanding enough to mitigate his pain?

"Not ruined. Tainted. I'm just afraid. I'm no longer the guy I was, and I don't think you'll like the guy I've turned into when you finally meet him," Nicolas confessed.

"What do you mean?"

She sat up in alarm.

He couldn't tell her about the drugs. He'd wait on that.

"I'm still doing the sex work. I can't stop and I don't know why."

"Oh." She slumped back down. "Do you like it? Having sex with all these different people?"

"It's not even the sex. It's a rush to control someone else for a few minutes. And when they get their orgasm, I feel like a god. It's pathetic."

"No, I get it. Makes sense."

She nodded, but her eyes were filled with sadness. He was a disappointment. But she had done this to him. Because of her, he was forced to flee to Mexico in the first place! If she hadn't barged in that night, he would have never stabbed her mom. He would have never abducted her and taken her off in the car. He wouldn't be wanted for multiple felonies.

"I'm gonna try harder, okay? I wanted to be upfront. If I'm gone at weird hours, that's why."

"It makes me sad, Nicolas. I want you all to myself. The thought of your dick up inside someone else makes me want to scream in jealous rage."

"I don't often have to fuck anyone, just so you know."

"But thinking of you getting another woman off makes me green with envy."

"I get that. I do. But I'm struggling with my feelings. I feel like everything is fucked up between us now. You wanted your cop more than me, and no matter how hard I try to let it go, it's always there."

She was crying now.

"I'll never be able to make it up to you, will I? I fucked everything up with both of you. I wish I had succeeded with those pills. I can't take the consequences of my stupidity."

He held her in his arms.

"Don't say that. Just because things are all fucked up doesn't mean you don't deserve to live but it may have ruined things between us. Let me try to fix this. Get over my resentment. Hopefully, I can rein it in and we can work past it."

He held her until the urge to get high was so intense that he had to.

"I've got to head out for a bit. I won't be gone long, though, so stay up. I wanna put you in the cuffs and take you to heaven, okay? Let me take a quick walk to clear my head."

He helped her up, and they returned to their apartment.

"Nicolas, the last two weeks have been a lover's paradise. You are my soulmate, and I feel it down to the bone. I love you so much, baby. I hope you can see that."

He stared into her blazing eyes. From the very beginning, his whole body reacted to her eyes. Thoroughly aroused, he considered forgoing the drugs and taking her to bed right now. But the urge—

"I felt it from the moment we first met." He kissed her, then left.

His mind was swirling. He was gonna lose this battle. Half of his heart was evil, black, and corrupted with jealous resentment, and the other half was a passionate, virgin red, filled with love. But the drugs were spreading the corruption, and he was powerless to stop it.

Nicolas went to the ATM, withdrew the maximum amount, and then headed down to the park to find his dealer. He could now afford the best. It was exciting to think of the new levels of high he might achieve. Maybe all he needed was one last high to carry him forward. After that, he could give it all up and work on repairing his heart of its fatal damage.

Chapter 53

Judith

To her horror, things with Nicolas went to shit all at once. A perfect fantasy bubble popped, and Judith was plunged into a nightmare.

Nicolas couldn't quit prostitution, even though they had enough money. He was a sex addict, and it didn't matter how many times a day she fucked him, it was never enough. Judith found herself waiting anxiously for hours or whole nights with no idea where he was. When he saw how much money his dad was sending her, he convinced her to add him to the account and, at once, began spending the money recklessly. Four weeks after she moved in with him, she discovered where the money was going. She woke around three a.m. and, in the bathroom, found him preparing to plunge a needle into his vein.

"Nicolas!"

"What? It's nothing—just a little high. With my dad's dough, I can finally afford the primo and plenty of other goodies. It's amazing."

"What is that?"

"H," he replied defensively.

"Heroin?" she screamed.

"Dope. Smack. Whatever you wanna call it, I mix things up a bit. Mostly with benzos. I need to turn down the volume up here and chill the fuck out." He pointed to his head.

"My God, Nicolas! How long?"

"Shortly after I started fucking people for money, and totally since I went to jail. It helps me cope. I'm not getting any treatment for my mental illness. I gotta do something. You wanna try it with me?"

"Hell no. Why didn't you tell me? Were you getting high in Cabo?"

He looked ashamed.

"I needed something to help me survive without you. I would have never needed the drugs if you hadn't come to the house that night, you know."

She felt the accusation sink in. He blamed her for his misfortunes. For everything.

"I'm sorry you ever met me," she snapped, "clearly, I ruined your life."

Nicolas softened as he tapped the needle on the side of the sink.

"I don't regret meeting you."

"You just need someone to blame all your bad choices on. Coming here was a mistake."

"No! It's not. I'm sorry about this. I didn't want you to find out."

"You were planning on lying to me forever?" she shrieked.

Her stomach sank. Her mom warned her and she was right. Nicolas had spun out of control. This was the worst mistake she had ever made. She couldn't make it work with a drug-addicted prostitute!

"Ah." He looked embarrassed and changed tactics. "Don't give me that look, Belladonna. You're not my fucking dad."

"I'm worried about you. Now I get why you're so skinny and erratic—zoned out. The glassy eyes. The dazed expression. You've been high all this time! Why didn't I realize it sooner? I'm an idiot!"

"You're making a big deal out of nothing."

"Nothing? Nicolas, that shit is dangerous!"

"Trust me, I know what I'm doing." He expertly plunged the needle and tossed it into the sink. His head went back, and she watched a shudder roll through his body. Then, with one hand pushing her toward the bed and the other undoing his jeans as he went, he said, "I'm going on a journey now. What I need from you is one of your amazing blowjobs to send me off into the great deep." He collapsed backwards on the bed, pulled a pill out of his pocket, swallowed it, and then tore open his pants. Tears sprang into her eyes.

"You've changed so much."

"What the fuck, Belladonna?" Nicolas stroked himself, smiling. "Come on, you know you wanna. Torment me, baby. Give me the best happy ending ever. No one can make it last like you do."

Judith got down on her knees, unable to say no. It took forever to get him off. He kept losing his erection, which was nothing like the guy she had that hot affair with back in Cabo. When he climaxed, he didn't even seem to notice and barely ejaculated anything. Was she no longer a good lover? Why wasn't he responsive? Afterward, strung out and staring vacantly at the ceiling, she slumped to the floor and watched him moan, a dizzy smile clinging to his lips. She had lost him months ago. She lay against the wall and cried.

Nicolas went from bad to worse. Access to endless drugs turned him into an insatiable junkie. He made new friends every day and started inviting them over. They all hated her. Called her a stuck-up bitch. Blamed her for ditching their bestie and getting him thrown in jail. They loudly talked shit about her and Nicolas didn't try to defend her. He didn't agree but he was a total pushover.

A few days later, he got in a street fight, was then raped and beaten up. He shrugged it off but spent four days high and only got out of bed to shoot up, piss, and beg her for oral sex. It took longer and longer to get him hard and he no longer came. Worse, he wasn't interested in pleasuring her now. What had happened to her Casanova?

Then he started bringing tricks back to their apartment. She sat on the couch in the living room, paralyzed, as he loudly let a constant stream of guys fuck him. Was he homosexual? He said he was bisexual! She thought he was her soulmate! How had she not seen this side of him? Was this all new behavior or had he deceived her all those months online?

By the time Christmas arrived, he had devolved even further. She was dishing out a box of takeout on two plates for dinner when he walked into the kitchen and smacked her so hard that Pad Thai went everywhere.

"Remember our death match? Wouldn't it be sexy if we re-enacted it? The whole thing. But this time we end it with crazy fucking. I wanna get hard again and I think this will do it." He smacked her again, his eyes blurry and unfocused.

"Nicolas, no. I'm not in the mood. You're stoned off your ass. Quit it." He smacked her once more, and she shoved him back.

"That's my girl."

Nicolas slammed her head into the wall, and she hurled herself at him, shoved him against the sink, forced his head under the faucet and turned on the water. Excited by her attack, he flung his drenched hair back, grabbed her by the waist, charged into the bedroom, and pinned her down on the bed.

"Belladonna, here we go. Let's rewrite history!"

"Nicolas, stop it!"

He forced her and she let him. She watched this beautiful man on top of her, writhing and thrusting, desperately trying to climax, and she felt as if her heart would break.

The following day, she awoke to find her wrists handcuffed to the bed. He was lying next to her, stroking her face.

"Last night was fun. I always wanted to recreate our deathmatch and end it the right way. Finally got me off, which I'm sure you've noticed I've been struggling with recently. I know it's the drugs, but it just means we need to find ways to liven things up a bit. I'm used to getting it up effortlessly, so this is a real struggle for me, being a sex addict and a prostitute. I think I'm gonna keep you in cuffs for the moment. I'm afraid you're gonna leave me."

"Nicolas, you don't need to keep locked up. I'm not leaving."

He thought about this and then nodded in relief.

"I'm a disappointment, I know. To me, too. I don't know what to do about it."

"Let's get you help," she pleaded.

"The problem is, the longer we're together, the harder I find it to get over your betrayal. You say you love me, but you still chose him. I have some ideas on how you can make it up to me, though."

"Please." Tears flowed down her face. "Nicolas, don't do this. I did choose you! Look where I am! You are completely betraying me."

"Betraying you? I'm just having fun. You don't like how big my dick gets when we fight? Impossible. You know, I have a few johns who've asked about you. I'm thinking we should expand our horizons. I could charge a ton, and we could split it. Bet if they see you cuffed to this bed, they'll line up around the block for a go at your pussy. If we're both prostitutes, we can be millionaires down here!"

"Nicolas, what has happened to you? How can you be like this? This isn't the guy I had an affair with back in Cabo. All those months online, you were sweet, sexy and loving! Who are you?"

He sat on the edge of the bed, elbows resting on his knees, hands pointed in prayer.

"You can thank your fucking cop. Jail changed me. Warped me in all sorts of new ways. The whole time I was in there, I nursed my grievances. I'll never be my old self again. And really, I'm good with it. Come on, you need to loosen up."

"It's the drugs. I know it. This isn't who you are."

"I lost myself, Belladonna, when you betrayed me. I can't find myself anymore."

Now he was crying, and she was crying.

"Please, forgive me!"

"My friends are all on my side. They say you fucked me over, and you need to pay. I don't want to hurt you, but I'm hurting so bad. I want to love you, but you never loved me!"

"I do love you! Goddamn it, Nicolas! I made a horrible mistake by not getting on that plane. I never imagined this would happen. I never meant to hurt you."

"You more than hurt me. You destroyed me. There's nothing left. I have to escape every second into drugs now to survive."

"Let me out of these cuffs. Now!" she screamed.

"Whoa. Fine. I'll let you out for a minute. Listen, I have some friends coming over tonight. I'm planning for you to join us. We're gonna load up on Ecstasy then fuck like crazy. It will be awesome, so don't go far."

Nicolas unlocked her cuffs and headed to the bathroom to shoot up. Judith could not comprehend how this had all gone to shit in less than two months. She knew that Nicolas was unstable, but he had morphed into a pathetic addict with absolutely no control right before her eyes. He was happy when she first arrived. They had so many good nights together and it was heaven. What happened? What was it about her that brought out the absolute worst in the men she loved?

Impulsively, Judith grabbed her cell phone and rushed out the door, wearing no shoes, racing downstairs and out to the street. Filled with more sorrow and fear than she had ever felt in her life, Judith unlocked her phone and called her mom.

Chapter 54

Justin

Justin pushed the pasta around on his plate, his eyes fixed on the table. Lizzy was reading a book. She refused to use technology for some phony reason or another. But then, she was also a hypocrite because she loved social media. Justin hated the sight of her. She was starting to show, so it was becoming real. He was gonna be a dad. But part of him seriously wondered if it was even his. She had never given him the paternity test, and he was sick of asking. He felt like she had tricked him and just didn't want him to discover the truth.

Life hadn't gotten easier. He now suffered from a vicious porn habit that was taking over his life. He never really cared much for porn. Preferred the real thing. Trying to satisfy his appetite with videos was the ultimate torture. The build-up sucked, it was all designed for a quickie. Bam-wham, thank you, ma'am. It made him climax too fast when he wanted to drown himself slowly in the sensations—touch, feel, and experience. Her sweat, her delicious juices, her beating heart and trembling body, her vaginal resistance as he forced himself inside her. The fear, lust, ecstasy, and madness. He wanted it all. And he wanted it all with the only woman he couldn't have.

"How's work?" Lizzy asked.

Putting down her Hemingway, deliberately inserting a bookmark. She was as pretentious as hell.

"Fine," he muttered.

How could she not see that he hated her? Was she blind?

"That's good. We have a second ultrasound appointment soon. Excited?"

Why the fuck would he be excited? He wanted to glare a hole through her. What was he supposed to do? Thankfully, she no longer tried to initiate sex. He was content with his hand and Judith's nude pics and needed no interference from her.

"I don't know."

"Listen, I know you've gone through a lot this year. I'm here for you, cowboy. And I'm not going anywhere. You've had your heart broken, and I don't expect you to love me like you loved Judith."

Like I do. Like I do. I still love her. He wanted to say.

"But we need to make this work. You owe me this."

And suddenly, it hit him. Lizzy was manipulating him. Had been doing so for months. Why was he letting her do this?

"Why do I owe you this?"

"Well, you knocked me up."

"I didn't even—"

"Sure, I realize I pushed you. I saw that you were lonely and I thought you'd like it."

"I didn't., he muttered.

Lizzy flushed with embarrassment and looked like she might cry.

"I feel like you haven't given me a chance, Justin."

"I'm sorry. I don't wanna."

"You'd rather live alone, mooning over my stupid sister? She doesn't deserve you! She never did! The night you met us, you should have noticed me, but all you saw were her amazing tits. I knew then that I would have you if it was the last thing I did. Look at me now," she said triumphantly.

"Do you have me, though?"

"Not entirely, but eventually, you'll be so desperate for a fuck that you'll come begging on hands and knees. I'll be all you have left."

Justin doubted that would ever happen. He stared at her hateful, homely face and realized this would never work. He couldn't do it. Couldn't put himself through it another second. He stood.

"Lizzy, I'm sorry. But you need to leave. I can't do this. I can't live with you. Not even for a baby. I'll pay child support if you provide proof of paternity. But I won't live with you."

"Because I hate my sister?" she asked, incredulous.

"Because I don't love you. I will never love you. You practically raped me, which is why you are now pregnant. Just go and leave me in peace."

"But I clean. I cook. Do your laundry. I'm sure she never did any of those things. All she did was make your life hell!"

"Not every day. We had plenty of good times. You don't know everything."

"I do know she cheated on you, and she'd do it again. She doesn't have it in her to be true to anyone."

Justin saw that her jealousy and hatred echoed his own. It was heartbreaking. He didn't realize he was such a monster until he saw this reflection staring back at him.

"Like I said, go. Pack your shit and leave. I need to get back to my own life, and I need you gone to do it. You need to get the fuck out. Now."

"Fine. But this isn't over. Someday, you will be mine, cowboy. Mark my words." Lizzy got up and walked around the table to stand in front of him. "Are you sure you don't wanna take me for one last test drive? See what you're missing out on?"

Lizzy pulled off her t-shirt. Her flat breasts did nothing for him. Justin stared at her dully.

"You can't compete. Sorry. But Judith has my heart. I'll never get it back."

Lizzy smacked him. Tears flowed from her eyes as she shoved her lips to his and kissed him, then left the room. When Lizzy told him that Nicolas had finally contacted Judith, and they were now living together, he thought his heart might wither and die. Now, he imagined them lying in bed together, sharing everything, their limbs entwined. The thought was unbearable.

When he got home in the morning, Martha was there. Justin helped load all of Lizzy's things into the trunk, and Lizzy waited in the front seat without saying goodbye.

In the apartment, Martha took his hand.

"I'm sorry. I can't do this. I love Judith, and I always will."

"I know, Justin. Listen, Lizzy called me last night after you told her to move out. You're not gonna believe this."

"What?"

"Well, this baby might not be yours after all. She had a hookup with a classmate back in May. She's been afraid to find out who the real father is."

"Are you fucking serious?"

Martha nodded her head sadly.

"I'm gonna force her to get this test and let you know for sure, okay?"

"Thank you. What a scheming bitch. Why, Martha?"

"Other than that she's crazy about you? Well, she doesn't know this other boy, and any girl is gonna want to score a daddy for their baby."

Just like his mom warned him, Lizzy was a manipulative monster.

"She fucked everything up between me and Judith."

"I know. This is all so awful."

"Have you talked to Judith lately? Do you know how she's doing?"

"I haven't. I guess things are going okay. Otherwise, she would have called. I was concerned. Nicolas has some severe mental health issues."

"Nicolas looked stoned out of his mind when we met in jail."

"That's alarming. I hope—" Her phone buzzed. "Oh my, it's Judith. Let me answer this. Hello?"

Chapter 55

Judith

"Mom?" Judith tried to control the quavering in her voice.

"Sweetheart? Where are you?"

"Mom, I need help. Please, help me."

"Here, let me put you on speakerphone. Okay, tell us what's going on."

"It's all gone to shit. Nicolas has lost his mind. He shoots up or snorts heroin day and night, pops pills and mixes them with other drugs and alcohol, brings customers home and fucks them in our bed, and wants me to do the same," she cried, "I have no idea what the hell happened to him, Mom. It's gotta be the drugs. He will never forgive me for getting him thrown in jail. Blames me for everything! Is having a huge orgy tonight and I have no place to go. His friends all hate me, and I don't know anyone here. I was an idiot and added Nicolas to the account Erik set up for me. He's spent every last dime on drugs for himself and his friends. Why didn't I see this side of him? How did he deceive me?!"

"Honey, Nicolas is mentally ill and very unstable. If he's using illicit drugs to help him cope, you are in grave danger. You need to get on a plane and come home. Today."

"Mom, I can't. I have no money! Plus, if I leave him, he'll completely unravel. He's codependent and desperate for love, even if he can't love me in return. His friends scare me. They are all deviant criminals. We live in a dump and have been robbed more than once and Nicolas shrugs it off. I think he plans on pimping me out now that we're broke again. He's threatened to keep me cuffed in our bedroom so I can't leave him. I can't believe I let myself be so deceived. Justin was right about Nicolas. He really is a criminal. How did I lose my hero? I hate Lizzy. I fucking hate her for stealing my boyfriend! Mom, I'm a mess!" she cried uncontrollably.

Judith heard murmuring on the line as her mom spoke with someone.

"Judith, we need your address."

"My address? Oh, sure."

"About Justin. Um, there's something you should know."

"Oh shit. Nicolas is coming. Mom, I'm texting my address now. If you don't hear from me again by tonight, please check up on me."

"Judith!"

Judith hit send on her address and screamed as Nicolas grabbed her by the shoulder, took her phone, and disconnected the call.

"Calling Martha?"

His eyes were glazed over, and it was heartbreaking to look at him. He had crashed and burned, leaving nothing but wreckage and ruin. Judith cringed as he dragged her up the stairs to their apartment.

"I don't like you gallivanting off talking shit about me to your family."

He shoved her through the door and pushed her into the bedroom.

"Nicolas, please!" she pleaded, "what the hell has happened to you?"

He stopped and stared down at his hands, and for a moment, she thought she saw a glimmer of remorse. He roughly kissed her, then shoved her back onto the bed, where he grabbed her wrists and cuffed them to the headboard, then sat next to her.

"You don't understand our relationship now, do you?"

"Not this! I thought you loved me. What have I done?"

He held her face in his hand, his expression cold and hard.

"I hate being this way. I can't help it. The evil part of me wants to say, did you think you were going to get away with torturing me for an entire year with your cop, abandoning me in our escape plans, getting me thrown in jail, while annihilating my heart? I bled myself dry for you. I've never loved anyone like I loved you, and you threw me to the wolves. Vindictive is my middle name. So, if I've changed, Belladonna, it's on you."

"I couldn't control any of those things! Justin got you thrown in jail, not me! I do love you, Nicolas. My God, you have no idea what it's like to love two men. Complete opposites that satisfy different parts of me. It's hell!"

"You should have chosen me from the beginning. I'm your soulmate! That cop treated you like shit and I warned you and you still chose him!"

"Nicolas, I know! I see now my mistake. Please, let me make it up to you."

"It's too late," he finally said, "I shouldn't have let you come here. I was afraid I wouldn't be able to control this. I'm sorry, Belladonna. I'm an asshole." He wiped tears out of his eyes and rubbed them on her face. "Here's some of my pain." He leaned over and kissed her sweetly and she moaned. This was her Casanova.

"I swear to God, I will do whatever you ask to make it up to you."

She held his gaze until he looked away, lost in thought.

"It's not enough. Too many months of torturous waiting only to have you completely fuck me over."

He clenched his jaw and turned those dreamy black eyes on her, now as hard as flint.

"So, now you're gonna make me suffer forever?"

"I don't wanna make you suffer. I don't know what I want except to go back to the beginning and do it all differently, but I can't. Why did you choose him? Your choosing Justin is like saying that every person who ever abused me was in the right. That I deserved to suffer. Cause he's one of them."

"Justin isn't one of those people, Nicolas. He's just a jealous guy who doesn't know how to handle his emotions. He's not abusive."

"He is abusive. He's an abuser. I promise you. You don't know him like I do. And just hearing you stick up for him makes my blood boil."

Judith hooked her legs around his waist and pulled her to him.

"Nicolas, can you put him out of your mind? Can we focus on you and me?"

"No. Because now everything is wrecked. I can't even have sex, and I know you're gonna leave me."

"I won't leave you, okay? I can make it hot between us. I have a few tricks." She drew him closer to kiss him. He kissed her, and then a sly look crossed his eyes.

"What about my kink? We could try that. It made me so hot to fantasize about you fucking your cop. My jealousy gets me off and you know it. Since we don't have your cop anymore, I could share you with someone else. I'd come so hard seeing it live."

"Nicolas, I don't wanna fuck some random guy. No."

"Our death rematch last night did something to me."

"Please! Nicolas. I love you! You're ripping my heart out, baby."

He stared straight at her, his eyes brimming with tears.

"Finally, you are starting to feel a tiny bit of what I've felt all this time."

"What happened to the man I fell in love with? That crazy, sweet guy who cared about my feelings. Please, come back to me!"

"That guy wasn't enough to make you get on that plane and abandon your hero cop, so when you tried to kill yourself, you took him with you."

Nicolas rose, eager to leave.

"No!" Judith cried, "don't leave. Let's talk this out!"

"I have to pick up some goodies for my party tonight. This will be your royal debut. Don't worry. Whoever pays the most to fuck you won't be gross. I'm not an animal. And maybe I won't like it. Maybe I will. We'll see. Back soon."

He left their apartment with a slam of the door. Judith screamed until she couldn't breathe. How had she allowed herself to believe Nicolas? How could he love her and yet treat her like this? She lay back in a stupor and waited in misery for him to return

Chapter 56

Nicolas

Nicolas left Belladonna, filled with confusion. She seemed so genuine, as if she truly loved him. He wanted to believe her. This was a nightmare. For nearly two years, he had thought of nothing else day and night but having her in his life and now he was fucking it all up. What was wrong with him? His high was wearing off, and he needed more and more to make it last. Just like he needed more and more to get him off. Was it fucking all these tricks? Was it the drugs? Nicolas felt entirely out of control.

Part of him was happy. He finally had friends for the first time ever. Sure, they only hung out with him for the drugs, but it felt good to have a group since he never had a single friend all through school. Suddenly, they were everywhere! That's why he was throwing the party tonight. His first party ever. He was stressed, though. His friends hated Belladonna. After he told them what happened to him, they all took his side. Nicolas didn't want them to hate her, and he wished he had the balls to stand up to them.

Right now, he just needed to get more stoned. Tons of pain weighed on his chest, as if his whole life were coming to a head, and he couldn't breathe. And now, the worst thing of all, he was struggling to have sex. His poor Belladonna, he was treating her like his whore, making her go down on him constantly. It made him feel like shit. He was the Casanova, and he wanted to pleasure her, but the drugs made him so shaky he couldn't concentrate. Either that or he was so stoned he could barely move. Whatever was wrong with him was getting worse. Fast.

Thinking of her lovely face, drenched in tears, ripped at his heart. He had her cuffed to the bed now, because he was terrified she would leave him. He was so out of control. He had to get himself under control! So what if their love story wasn't perfect? He could work with this. They just needed money. His dad was way too generous, but being a stupid idiot, he had already burned through that nest egg. That's why he suggested prostitution. They could head to wherever they wanted within a few months if she was willing to go for it like he had.

At the same time, he didn't want his honey spreading her legs. What the hell was he going to do? Nicolas had made too many radical changes to his identity. He didn't recognize himself anymore. He lost a ton of weight and he never got enough sleep. He fucked so many people he hardly knew when he was getting off. His body was so overstimulated that he felt nothing. This was miserable. And there she was, like an angel, shedding light on his awful existence. He didn't know whether he hated her or wanted to go down on bended knee and worship her.

Nicolas scored a ton of dope and pills from his dealer and saw a few of his homies chilling on the street corner.

"Coming tonight?" he asked.

"Sure, man! You ready to share your honey?"

Nicolas made the mistake of telling these dudes about his kink and now they were all over that shit. Harassing him day and night for a go at Belladonna. Would she give in? It might get him off, but they weren't the cop, so maybe not. But Belladonna wasn't even down with sex work. Would probably not be cool with this. But he would've never started using drugs if she hadn't driven him crazy with her obsession over that cop. Now the drugs fucked up his hard-ons. He'd try it and see if she'd give in. He really wanted to have an orgasm like he used to.

"Tonight. Be ready!" He promised. Halfheartedly.

He stopped off and invited a couple of hookers, saying there would be plenty of money to be made at his pad. Then, he headed to the park to get high and try not to think about his beautiful girl and all the pain she had caused him.

Chapter 57

Judith

Nicolas returned a few hours later and released her from the cuffs. Tried to make love to her but fell asleep in the middle. Just collapsed on top of her like he'd been shot. She nudged him off of her and onto his side and covered him with the blanket. He never slept or ate. Judith stroked his face in repose and felt a painful, overwhelming love for him. She couldn't leave him. Not now, not ever. He was a mess, though. Jail had broken him, betraying him by choosing Justin had broken him, and now Judith didn't know how to make it up to him. She felt devastated.

Judith crept out of the room into the kitchen and made sandwiches, then returned to bed with the plate. She opened her phone while munching on a sandwich. Lying next to Nicolas, he snuggled against her as she read everything she could about drug addiction and how to deal with a loved one who abuses drugs. It was all unhelpful because it required that the addict choose to get help. Nicolas wasn't going to get help unless forced to.

Judith put her phone down and stroked his naked chest, counting the bones in his rib cage. He was so skinny that it was terrifying. She mentally compared him to Justin and felt a sense of guilt. No guy could compete with Justin when it came to the male physique. Justin was gorgeous. Thinking of her hands on his broad chest and rippling muscles brought back too many painful memories of all the times he had rejected her. And now she was here, and she loved Nicolas with all her heart. She didn't care if he was too skinny.

Late afternoon, Nicolas woke up. Rubbing his eyes, he leaned over and kissed her.

"I fell asleep? While having sex? How embarrassing."

"You needed it. And now, you need this." She handed him a sandwich. "Eat it."

"I'm not hungry." He went to stand but she pulled him back down.

"You aren't leaving this bed until you eat something. You're gonna drop dead from starvation. Do you want that?"

He rolled his eyes, took a bite and his eyes lit up.

"Oh, Belladonna. Delicious. You always remember everything I like. Avocado. Cheese. Tomato. Perfect." He devoured the sandwich then kissed her again. "You're like a mama plus my lover. I love you so much."

"Nicolas, you're like a feral little boy."

Judith felt motherly towards this man, and she loved making sure his needs were met.

"You bring out the feral in me."

He crawled on top of her, tickling her. She giggled and fought, remembering their sexy tickle session in Cabo. She swept Nicolas's long hair from his beautiful face and kissed him again, then asked,

"When are your friends coming over?"

Nicolas sat up and gave her a guilty look.

"Soon. Um, there's one thing."

"What?"

She narrowed her eyes. Was he gonna ask her to get high with him? She didn't want to, but felt compelled to. Judith had told her mom to call if she didn't hear from her again tonight, and she didn't want to get too stoned to answer the phone. She regretted calling her mom. Things were okay with Nicolas. Now, everyone would be worried about her. But should they be? Life with Nicolas was so unstable that she had no idea what was happening from one minute to the next.

"Well, I wanna try my kink tonight. I'm sorry. These guys won't leave me alone about it. I should never have said anything."

"Nicolas, no. I don't wanna."

"Please. Let's try. Other couples do. If you hate it, we'll stop, okay?"

She sighed, "we'll see. If I don't like the look of him, then hell no. I'm not a slut and I don't ever plan to sleep with people for money. What you're asking goes against my nature."

"But it will be hot. Everything with you is hot." He smiled and hopped to his feet. "I'll tidy up the living room and set up the bar. You can hang out in here. But get undressed and be ready. If you go for it, these guys are willing to pay five hundred each."

"There are two of them? No, Nicolas!" she shouted as he shut the door.

Judith took a shower. Soaking wet, she lay on the bed and thought about what to do. What Nicolas was asking was too much. Should she pack up, sneak out the window, and climb down the fire escape? She loved him. Why was he doing this to her? They needed money but she could ask Erik for more. Trying to come to a decision was so stressful that she cried herself into a fitful sleep.

She woke in complete darkness to the sound of laughter, moaning, thumping against the wall and music. Outside the door, Nicolas and his friends were fucking like rabbits, shooting up, popping pills and drinking themselves silly. With any luck, they would forget all about her.

Lying on the bed, the light from her phone illuminating, she scrolled through old pics of her and Justin together. Why was she torn between these two guys? She loved Justin but he was the biggest disappointment of her life. She loved Nicolas but he was quickly eclipsing Justin in the disappointment arena. Why were these guys so messed up? Did she do this to them?

Suddenly, light flooded the room above her. Nicolas stood at the door, naked. Drunk and stoned, it was a miracle he could stand. Two guys shoved their way eagerly past him through the door.

"Belladonna, meet Jackson and Paul. I'm gonna let you choose. I don't care which, and you can have them both if you want. Hopefully, this will do it for me. But you have to be in the cuffs. I hope you don't mind. It will be hot as fuck this way."

"Nicolas, no. I changed my mind."

She cried as he pulled her arms up, and cuffed her to the bed frame.

"We haven't even tried yet." He looked at her, pleading, "Belladonna, you did this to me. Turned me into a raging addict that fucked up my dick. Please give this to me."

"Remember who you are. You said you loved me. Loved me! Where did you go? Please come back to me!"

Nicolas turned and stumbled into the chair next to the bed. He stilled the toppling chair then sprawled in it, hand on his dick. "I'm already lost." His eyes were miserable. Popped another pill in his mouth and guzzled from a half-empty bottle of vodka. Then he lay back, his legs stretched out, his eyes closed. "You did this. Made me so crazy and obsessed with you until you broke my fucking mind which forced me into the drugs."

"I was torn between you and Justin! You can't punish me like this. I'm at the mercy of fate, just like you. Please," she begged, "I met Justin before you. Of course, I tried to make it work! Why can't you see that what you're doing is destroying any chance we have of staying together?"

"I AM trying to make this work. Return to a place where I can feel like you truly love me. Come on. Are you going to choose? Or do you want them both?"

"Nicolas, if it's the drugs that have ruined sex for you, then let's get you help. Look at rehab, maybe?"

The two men looked at each other, then at Nicolas, and laughed heartily.

"I don't need fucking rehab." He flushed with embarrassment. "I just need some live porn."

"Well, you forcing me to do this is rape!" she screamed so loudly that the two men stepped back in alarm.

Nicolas flushed deeply and looked scared, as if realizing it for the first time.

Judith used to think his kink was sweet and was flattered that Nicolas was this obsessed with her. Admittedly, she toyed with him and egged him on, lauding Justin over him and bigging up their sex life, which she now realized was cruel. She remembered how she had indulged his kink in Cabo and made him climax so hard. Should she go along with this? Would it bring him back to her? She stared at the two guys who looked horny and smelled thoroughly disgusting. No way. Not even for her soulmate.

"Nicolas, please. These guys are trashy as fuck. Don't make me do this."

"Did you hear her?" Nicolas looked at the two guys in mock disapproval. "I guess you're both too trashy."

Judith growled and gnashed her teeth as the skinny guy reached over and stroked her ankle. She kicked at him viciously. He laughed, then bared his teeth like he planned to eat her alive.

"Fuck you! Motherfucker. Don't you fucking touch me!"

They were pulling off their belts now, removing their shoes. The skinny guy was unbuttoning his shirt. This was happening. She had trusted Nicolas and thought he loved her, despite his mental instability. She stared at him in disbelief, pleading.

"Please, Nicolas. Remember online? Remember our soulmate connection?"

"What I remember is that you never stopped talking about how much you loved your cop while I begged day and night for you to love me instead. I recall being given the brush-off every time he came around. I remember that you made me play second man, and while it did make me crazy hot for you, it also broke me, and I told you! I warned you about what you were playing at! So don't act like this is a big surprise!"

"I said NO!"

"What can I do about it now? I already told them yes." He looked at her helplessly.

The skinny guy had his shirt unbuttoned, displaying a mural of tattoos on his concave chest, jeans flapping open, dick poking straight out. She fought furiously, trying to knee him in the groin, screaming at the top of her lungs as he crawled on top of her. He shoved her legs apart, pinning them down with his knees. Looked down and fingered her vagina for a minute as he stroked his dick, grinning with glee, then licked his finger.

"Nicolas!" Judith shrieked so hard that her vocal cords felt raw, "please, remember me!"

He stared blankly, his eyes flooding with a tempest of emotion. Took his skull between his hands and shook his head violently. Stressed, realizing he had made a mistake, he now didn't know what to do. Scared of his friends, he didn't want to lose them, but he really didn't want to lose her. Judith could read his mind as it fumbled its way through muddied waters. Nicolas locked eyes with her and shared her pain.

"What the hell? The kink only works in my imagination. Not in real life." She heard him mutter.

"Stop him. Now!"

The skinny guy had paused to roll a condom on his dick, and was now ready. Hooked her legs with his arms, pivoting her hips and positioning himself. She felt his dick prodding its way in as he grunted, but he was drunk and uncoordinated. And then, like sand sifting through an hourglass, he funneled his way in. Once he was up inside her, he groaned loudly.

"Dude. Your honey is so wet and tight. Oh God, Oh fuck!"

He was flushed and delirious as he thrust. She wanted to shut her eyes and escape to another dimension. But no. Fuck this asshole. Judith formed the biggest loogie she could make with her dry mouth and hocked it at his face. He pulled out, looked over at Nicolas in outrage, wiped his cheek, then hauled off and smacked her so hard that her ears rang like Big Ben.

Nicolas jumped up. Judith saw that his dick was limp and felt joyous that this wasn't turning him on. He grabbed the skinny guy's arm back before he could hit her again.

"Not cool, man. She's my soulmate. Fuck this. It ain't doing it for me. My fantasy only works with the cop. IN MY HEAD. What was I thinking?

Get off her. Now! Oh my God, Belladonna. What have I done? I'm so sorry! I—"

Nicolas, suddenly self-aware, shame and regret swimming in his eyes, stared in agony.

The skinny guy shoved his dick up inside her again and went wild. Smacking Nicolas away as he thrust in a frenzied attempt to climax as fast as possible. Her wrists burned from the cuffs as he yanked her viciously, his face leering like a joker's mask. Her ears were still ringing, so when the commotion began echoing in her head, she had no idea it was coming from the living room.

The front door slamming open, cursing as glass shattered. Shrieking, followed by the sound of fists contacting flesh. Running footsteps, driven by fear. Thumping and bumping into walls. The bedroom door burst open, and with it came the most impossible thing on the planet. Her hero filled the doorway.

Justin froze. Stared wide-eyed, mesmerized, as if taking a mental picture of her bouncing breasts and flailing legs. From the side, Nicolas hurled his fist, and the skinny guy collapsed on top of her, his nose spurting with blood. Justin snapped out of his trance and locked eyes with her.

Judith screamed for help.

Chapter 58

Justin

Justin's face was a mask of righteous indignation as he stared around the room in outrage. Took two steps towards the bed, pulled the skinny guy up by his neck, lifted him into the air with one arm, turned, and slammed his head against the door threshold. Once, twice, then he crushed his face against the wall until it sprayed blood and let his shaking body drop. The other half-naked guy looked petrified and Justin barked.

"Lay your ass on the floor and stay there or you're dead!"

Nicolas sauntered forward, pointing in amazement and laughing like a drunken monkey.

"Belladonna, I thought he dumped your ass for your sister!"

Justin moved like the wind. Without hesitation, he punched Nicolas in the mouth so hard that Nicolas flew backward, hitting the wall with a reverberating thud. Justin turned to the skinny guy stumbling towards the door and kicked him in the gut, the groin, and the chest until he fell still. A naked Nicolas reeled to his feet, flung his long hair back, his mouth frothing with blood, and spat out a tooth. Tore off the pointed handcuff key hanging on a chain around his neck, gripped it between his knuckles, and, like a cocky jackass, put up his fists.

"Come on, you fucking cop. One thing jail taught me is to fight dirty!"

Nicolas lunged at Justin, who easily dodged the attack. He lunged again, and threw his fist, clearly stoned off his ass. Justin caught it, shook his head in disbelief, grinned, and drove a fist into his chest, then his jaw, followed by another fist to the nose. Nicolas exploded in a miasma of blood and rage. Justin stepped back, and he heard Judith gasp in astonishment as he kicked Nicolas furiously in the groin with his steel-toed boot. Nicolas grabbed his balls, screaming, and melted in a puddle of agony.

"Hope that breaks your prick for good, you twisted fuck."

Stooping over, he yanked Nicolas up by the hair. His howling soon turned to choking as Justin raised him above his head with one hand and throttled him by the neck. Nicolas kicked his legs frantically, gasping and tearing at Justin's fingers while shuddering from a series of punches to the gut from Justin's free hand. Justin slammed his head repeatedly into the plaster until he was buried in the wall, then ripped him out of the hole and tore the handcuff key from his fingers.

"I would love nothing better than to break every bone in your body for stealing my girl, for being scum. But I'll stop just short of murder."

Justin punched him in the face, again and again, until he was a bloody mass of bruises.

"Justin! Stop!" Judith screamed behind him.

He paused, then hurled Nicolas across the room, where he slammed into the threshold, his forearm snapping as he collapsed to the floor. Nicolas raised his head, groaned in pain, vomited profusely and passed out.

Justin turned, rushed to her side, bent over, and unlocked her cuffs. Judith moaned.

"Why are you here? How?"

He picked her up and held her against his chest, and kissed the welt on her face.

"We've got to make sure this bullshit never happens again."

Justin couldn't believe what he had just witnessed. It was like something out of a Liam Neeson movie. His sweetheart was getting raped while her boyfriend watched. What the fuck? He laid Judith back on the bed, rummaged around until he found her clothes, gathered each foot in his hands, and slid her panties and jeans over her shaking limbs. Went down on his knees in front of her, cupped each breast as he fitted her bra, and reached behind to secure the hooks. Stood and wriggled a t-shirt down over her arms and head. Pulled her to him and kissed her, and still, she couldn't stop crying.

"Missing anything?"

"My passport and phone," she whispered and pointed.

He grabbed them, slid them into his back pocket and pulled out his phone.

"What are you doing?" She slid back to the bed, her arms around his hips, clinging like a toddler.

"Calling the cops so that they can take this animal back to its cage."

"Justin? Don't. Please. Nicolas won't survive prison. Six months in jail have already destroyed him."

"Do you care?"

"I'll never stop loving him. He messed everything up between us, but he's my soulmate and I'll never stop loving him."

Justin shook his head, incredulous. First, he needed to get her back, then he could work on eradicating this bullshit from her mind.

"Anything for you."

Justin pocketed his phone and scooped her up in his arms. Kicked Nicolas's inert form aside in the doorway. She pulled out of his arms and knelt beside Nicolas's body.

"Is he dead?"

She was still crying.

"If only we were so lucky."

She stroked his face and kissed him, and Justin felt his heart thud in anger. How could she care at all about this perverted psycho?

"Come on, baby."

Then he gathered her back into his arms and carried her down the stairs and into the street, and into a taxi, and into a hotel, and into a room, where he laid her on a bed and undressed her as he kissed her head to toe. How had he gotten this lucky? He had believed she was lost to him forever, but thank God, Nicolas was a stupid piece of shit.

"Captain America, you better be planning on doing more than just kissing me."

Judith smiled through her tears and pulled his face to hers. Justin tore off his clothes and, hovering above her like some majestic being, let her hands and mouth praise every inch of his perfect body, basking in the erotic delight of her hero worship. When she pulled him down to enter her, and when he slid inside her, the sensation was pure ecstasy. He grabbed her ass and went berserk. Ten months of no Judith was torture.

With each impassioned thrust, she gained strength until she was replenished. He let her flip him over and ride him with her usual savage lust until he came unbelievably hard, then he let her grind against him through his orgasm, until gasping and moaning with release, she collapsed on top of him.

Instead of rejecting the intensity, he embraced it. He opened himself up and felt her passion overtake him, and he surrendered completely. Unleashed his inner caveman. The rougher he became, the more she screamed with delight. He was unashamed. Finally. Fucking liberation. This was vulnerability. This was love. What was wrong with him all those months? He regretted every second of pushing her away and swore to God that he would never do so again.

They twisted each other back and forth, position after position, climaxing again and then again until they were exhausted and collapsed in a tangle of sweaty, slick limbs. Lost in the afterglow, searching, they found each other. Judith was overwhelmed with emotion. He wiped away tear after tear and whispered.

"Can you forgive me?"

Stroking her face, tracing her eyebrows and lips, psychically begging her to fall headlong into his arms.

"How did you know?"

She brushed her hands across his chest and laid her ear against his heart.

"I was standing there with your mom and I heard the call. Went straight to the airport."

"I was trying to indulge Nicolas's kink, but I changed my mind."

"I can't believe he could be that depraved."

Which was bullshit. Nicolas was deviant scum, and he wouldn't put anything past him, even pimping out his sweet girlfriend.

"He was so stoned. I don't think he understood what was happening. He was trying to pull that guy off me when you arrived."

"Did you tell him you were cool with that?"

"I told him I would try his kink, but after one look at those guys, I was like, hell no."

"But with a different guy, you'd like it?"

"It was only hot with Nicolas, the night of our deathmatch."

"What about with me?"

She bit her lip and smiled coyly but said nothing.

The heavens had opened, and the angels were singing hallelujah. Judith liked it. She liked it! Which meant she would love his inner caveman. After all this shame and repression, Justin was finally about to be set free. He wanted to scream for joy.

"I'm glad I stopped that bullshit. Arrived in the nick of time and saved you like a hero should."

He kissed her again, and she wrapped her arms around his neck.

"I was so shocked when I saw my hero standing in the doorway. But you looked at me like you found the scene fucking hot."

Justin flushed. He had. Seeing Judith being raped was the culmination of nearly two years of torrid fantasies. He wanted to pull that guy off her and take his place so, so, so bad. But he couldn't admit this to her. Not yet.

"I am honored that you gave me the chance to make things right."

"What about Lizzy? What did you tell her?"

Justin grinned and kissed her.

"I kicked her out. Then she confessed to your mom this morning about the baby. She's not even sure it's mine. She's been afraid of having a paternity test done because she initially thought she got pregnant on a hookup. Took one look at me and thought she could score herself an easy-cheesy baby daddy. Guess I have jackass written all over my face."

"Lizzy? I knew she was a bitch, but wow. How cruel!"

"I don't care. We'll do a paternity test and see. If it's mine, I'll pay child support, but that's it. I am so done with her. She's gone, and I'm returning my heart to its proper owner, if you'll have it."

"But I thought you couldn't forgive me."

"Judith, I pushed you into his arms. You have nothing to ask forgiveness for."

Justin couldn't wait to start their new life together. He felt as though God had finally answered him tonight. Showed him how Judith would embrace his kink. His honey needed violent sex, a hero to worship, and someone who made her feel unworthy. That was it. He could eradicate Nicolas by satisfying this trinity of desires. He was as starry-eyed as the night they first met. Even better, he saw their future. The lust between them was as hot as ever, and he still had her mesmerized by his good-guy image. He'd never lose her again.

"Nicolas swore he loved me! I don't know how he could do this."

"Maybe he does love you, but he can't help but destroy what he loves. Look at what he tried to do to your mom."

"He and I are now tied together. I'll never break free. He cursed me the night we met. I can't explain it. I've been under his spell for so long that I don't know myself anymore!"

That fucking spell. It drove him crazy that she couldn't see the manipulation tactics of that psychopath.

"I let this happen. I was off being a jackass while you two forged a bond. Now I have to live with him, taking up some space in your heart." No, he couldn't, and he definitely wouldn't. "As long as you choose me."

He put her hand on his heart. "I swear on my life, I will never push you away again."

"Really?"

"I'm all in, baby. I'm done being a stupid guy. My dad was a stupid guy, and he lost my mom. I swore I would never do that."

"I'll never stop loving him, though. God, I feel like my heart is shattered." She sobbed against him, and Justin desperately tried to think of how to win her back right this second.

"I have been jealous of Nicolas from day one, and that's on me. That night, you met this alpha bird of paradise who looked like a rock star and had sex moves to die for. I felt so inadequate, and I punished you for that."

It was the truth, and it would only make her trust him more and remind her that she had done this to him, making him doubt himself because of her affair with that maniac.

"I don't know how we can make it work, Justin. You've broken me by pushing me away. I'm so insecure now. And then, after Lizzy—"

Insecure is how he needed her. He had to keep her guessing, working for it day and night. Make her feel as desperate for him as he felt for her. Play hot and cold until she screamed for him to tackle her down and let his inner caveman do whatever he wanted. He understood Judith so perfectly. It was a Christmas miracle.

Justin lay back and lifted her to straddle his chest. Compared her to Lizzy and thought of what he would have to settle for. It was time to promise the moon to this woman.

"I confess, I never got comfortable with the way you make me feel. It's so intense, and I don't know why that scared me. Trust me. I'm not scared anymore. After losing you and having to stare at my empty bed for months, I'm ready to commit body and soul."

A cloud came over her face as she wiped her tears away.

"What I want is for you to love me."

"I do love you. I know that I suck at expressing it, but I intend to prove it to you, day and night, from now on."

"How?"

"Oh my dearest, you are coming home with my inner caveman. I am finally setting him free, and he's gonna give you the ride of your life. We are leaving that pathetic, timid, repressed Justin in the dust."

She giggled between kisses.

"How exciting. Will I like him? Your inner caveman?"

"Wait and see."

He wanted to get started on their new relationship right this second. But he restrained himself. As soon as they got home, he would eradicate Nicolas from her mind forever. He was already planning his inner caveman's debut.

"You still want me after breaking your heart? I don't feel worthy now."

Justin studied Judith head to toe—thick, dark wavy hair hanging down over her shoulders, tinted red and gold. Glistening emerald eyes, blazing with passion. A sweet, gorgeous face and full sensual lips. Large boobs and a tiny waist. Long tan legs and a luscious ass. He thought of how she went down on him so perfectly and fucking her tight pussy, and oh God, he was already getting hard again. She worshiped him. He was her hero, and she would never feel worthy of his love again.

"I want you more than ever, if that's even possible. When I saw you cuffed to the bed—what nearly took place—I felt like Captain America, filled with the power to fight evil."

He could feel her body melting around his finger, wrapping tightly as he recited everything she wanted to hear, just like he wanted from day one. All the trauma Nicolas had put her through shoved her straight into his arms. Thank you, Nicolas.

"You certainly have some of his fighting moves. You were impressive."

"I shouldn't have wrecked his dick, but I felt that it was a deserving punishment."

"Do you think I did this to Nicolas? Did I drive him insane?"

"Maybe we both did. He tried so hard to get between us. Tonight, though, it was the drugs talking. He looked baked, fried and served up cold."

Justin was already regretting not killing the little shit. Couldn't believe she still cared about his feelings, even now. That would have to change.

"I will always love Nicolas. He has broken my heart for good." Judith was crying again, and Justin knew it would take everything he had to eradicate that bastard from her heart.

"It seems like we are all breaking each other's hearts these days."

He kissed her and kissed her, then crushed her to his chest. Whatever. By some holy miracle, he had gotten her back, and that's all that mattered.

"Let's go home, sweetheart, and begin the rest of our lives."

Chapter 59

Judith

Returning to the apartment was bizarre. It felt like the place was haunted. Her traumatic memory of finding Lizzy kissing Justin hit her in the face as they pulled up next to the garage. Judith got out, stared at the lawn chairs now covered in snow, and felt desolate. Justin had saved her once again, and his ego was huge. Proving to the world for the second time that he was her hero. It was all back on between them, but it was as though her heart was paper shredded by Nicolas's demise, and she hoped to God he survived Justin's attack.

She was wrecked by her impulsivity. She shouldn't have called her mom. Never dreamed that Justin was standing right there, listening. Should have dealt with Nicolas in her own way and encouraged him to enter rehab. Gone along with Nicolas's kink, because she was convinced that he would've pulled that guy off her of his own free will.

She couldn't stop thinking of Nicolas lying unconscious on the floor. His arm was broken. Justin kicked him in the groin and beat his face in. Would he survive? She hoped he was all right. She turned her head to the window and silently cried. He was gone forever, and her fantasy was destroyed. Her soulmate was dead to her.

How would she go on living? How would they move past all the heartbreak, the Lizzy issue, and the shift in their relationship? Judith had the strongest urge to jump out of the moving vehicle and run like hell. She felt so powerless in her life and hated the feeling. How had she lost control over herself like this?

Justin kicked snow off the steps as he led her up the stairs. The wind was bitter, and the midday sky was dim and gray. Judith felt the cold winter air bite through her t-shirt and feast on her bare arms.

The apartment felt warm and toasty as she plopped on the bed and realized she had no clothes except for the ones she was wearing.

"Justin?"

"What, my love?"

I'm going to need new clothes. I left everything behind."

"It's fine. I'll pay for everything you need, and we'll pick them out together."

"Thanks."

She smiled at him, and he looked at her hungrily. Man, things were going to be as hot as hell between them for a while.

They took a nap and then went shopping in the afternoon. That evening, he had to get back to work. She kissed him goodbye. He left her sitting on the couch, back to her old life. She was already miserable, and it had been less than a day. Again, she closed her eyes, thought of her soulmate broken on the bedroom floor, and ran to the bathroom to throw up.

She wrote Nicolas a long message, telling him she loved him still and always would. She apologized for Justin's attack. Read it, then hit delete. Words meant nothing. She broke his heart when she bailed on him, and by the time she moved in with him, it was too late. He was lost to her for good. She cried until she passed out.

In the morning, she woke before dawn and felt so depressed that she realized she had to get up and go for a run. Peering out the window, she saw that they had a few inches of snow, but not enough to prevent her from getting out of here for a bit. In the yard stretching, she saw Nora shoveling snow off her front porch. She nodded. Nora smiled happily at her. Perhaps she would be forgiven after all.

The exercise was exactly what she needed. It reminded her of when she first moved in with Justin and how she struggled to combat the depression caused by his chronic rejection. Up the stairs and into the kitchen, she was preparing a breakfast smoothie when she heard Justin's car. A few minutes later, he walked in the door and smiled at her.

Justin threw his keys down on the counter and grabbed her as if going to kiss her. Instead, he yanked her by the ponytail and dragged her over to the kitchen table, kicked the chair aside, and shoved her down onto her stomach. Crushing her head with one hand, he tore down her running tights and panties with the other.

"Justin, don't. I'm not in the mood."

"Get ready for the hottest fuck ever, Judith. You're gonna love it."

What the hell? Those were Nicolas's exact words. Justin was reenacting the night she met Nicolas. Why? Why was he doing this? He growled as he wedged her legs apart, frustrated. She heard the tear as he ripped her panties apart, then tugged her running tights down to her ankles and tore them off with her shoes. She snapped her legs together and twisted them around each other. He tried to pry them apart with no success.

"Legs apart. Now."

"Never!"

He lifted her head and slammed it down, then did it again. Nausea swirled through her. She was gonna pass out. Shakily, she spread her legs.

"Do the splits, my gymnastics star. Come on, beauty queen. Show me that award-winning pussy."

"Why are you doing this?" She wailed.

"Judith, meet my inner caveman. Caveman, meet my favorite fuck toy."

"You're a cop! You can't rape me!"

"Shut the fuck up."

He pulled her to the edge of the table, shoving her legs painfully apart. Hand crushing her head, he poked a finger up inside her.

"See how wet you are? I knew you'd love the caveman."

He positioned himself and hit the ground running.

"Justin, stop! You can't do this!"

"Who's gonna stop me, huh? My mom? Your mom? Nicolas?" He laughed. "Baby, you are all mine. You ain't goin' nowhere."

She tried to claw her way up the table, but he dragged her back down and went in harder.

Judith hadn't been raped since she was thirteen. But even then, that creepy old bastard never did anything like this.

"I want this to be as hot for you as it is for me." He whispered in her ear. Repositioning her hips, he gyrated, slow and precise. What the hell? When did Justin discover the G-spot? "It's right there, isn't it?"

She gasped in amazement. His hot breath on the back of her neck. His racing heart, his trembling arms. That familiar tremor of pleasure as it gathered momentum in her pelvis. She moaned and began to shake as he massaged her clitoris while grinding up inside her. Justin hit the bull's eye dead center. The orgasm was like being run over by a car. It dragged her ruthlessly down the road, tearing her to pieces for a full minute. Her hysterics sent him into a frenzy. A realization slammed into her as hard as Justin slammed against her. He wanted to make her love this. Wanted her to enjoy the assault. And to her horror, she did. The violence, the violation, the visceral lust burned its way through her as her body completely betrayed her soul.

"Like that?"

"Fuck, Justin," she moaned, "When did you learn to do that?"

"I've done my homework, like you told me to. It was hotter than anything Nicolas ever did to you, right?"

"It was the hottest." She lied.

Nothing. NOTHING would ever be as hot as that afternoon in Cabo.

"Good. Time for some roleplay, baby. Scream. Beg me to stop."

Obediently, she did.

"Oh my God, Justin. Stop! It hurts so bad. For fuck's sake. Have some mercy!"

Deeper and faster, he thrust until her whole body throbbed with agonizing ecstasy.

He slowed, ponderously.

"Judith, I need more."

"More?"

"I have to do it."

"What?

"I have wanted to for so long."

"What?" she whimpered.

"Fuck you up the ass."

"No, Please, God. Justin, no. I said no. No!"

"You have no idea how many times I have stared at your luscious ass wanting to do this."

"For fuck's sake. No!" she shrieked.

"Fight me. Resist."

Judith wriggled and twisted helplessly. Tried to buck and kick as he laughed. He scooted her down, planted her feet on the floor, positioned her butt at the edge of the table. She had never done this before, nor had she ever wanted to. She felt him probing her tight orifice, terrified of the impending torment. But he took his time, teasing himself with anticipation. Gathering momentum, he shoved past the dry resistance and went in hard.

Penetration. Screaming. Restrained. Writhing. Brutal. Excruciating. Horrible yet satisfying. This was no longer sex. It felt like he was stabbing her to death with his dick. Swiftly, thank God, he dropped his load in an explosion of cursing. Convulsing, he collapsed on top of her. A frenzy of thrusts continued for another minute as he moaned and moaned. Shaking as the adrenaline roiled between them, he pulled out and stood.

"Son of a bitch! That was a million times hotter than any of my fantasies."

He flipped her over, pulled her into his arms with tenderness and affection, and kissed her hard. A kiss of triumph, like they just won a marathon together.

"Oh, I love you, I love you so much! Thank you. Thank you for giving this to me."

Giving this to him? He just raped her!

He laughed. Laughed! Kissing her again and again. Laughing as he licked the tears running down her face. Judith pulled away, trembling head to toe, and stared at him in disbelief.

"Justin, what the actual fuck?"

She gazed ruefully at her brand-new panties now lying in shreds.

"That was so hot, baby. You were perfect."

"Why did you fucking rape me?" she cried.

"What? So, Nicolas can nearly rape you on the dining table, and you love it, but when I do it, you don't?"

"He would never do that!"

I have reimagined that night countless times. Shoving you down to take you from behind. Did I get it right?"

She wiped her eyes. What had she done to her hero? When he said he wanted to let out his inner caveman, she thought he meant cuffs, pleasure and theatrics. Not this!

"Uh, he did take me to the dining table, but I don't know. He wasn't violent."

"What did he do then? You never told me exactly. And now I know why. You were ashamed like I've been because you found it so fucking hot to be violated. But now I wanna recreate the whole thing with you and me down to the finest detail."

His eyes bore into her in that way he did when she could tell he was jealous. His jealousy fueled this obsession. She had warped him. Because he had heard on the phone what transpired between Nicolas and her the night of their deathmatch, she had completely ruined her hero. This was all her fault.

"I told you before. He kissed me all over, but he didn't rape me."

"But you wanted him to."

"I didn't. That's why I surrendered."

"Surrender just means you wanted him to, but you didn't want him to feel like the bad guy. You were giving him permission."

"I disagree. As for right now, you didn't ask or warn me."

"Do I need to?"

"Yes. Obviously." She folded her arms and glared. How could her hero do this? He was a cop. He knew better!

"I don't think so. I think you got off on the rush. And I know I gave you a mind-blowing orgasm. I felt it. On my first try, too. I feel like a fucking Casanova right now."

"Yeah, but it was forced."

"That's what made it so hot, though. Because of your child abuse, you're addicted to thrills. That's what you said, right?"

He looked cocky and self-righteous. Judith felt ashamed for him.

"That is definitely not what I meant. That hurt like hell."

"I hope it did. I want it to. Pleasure and pain, baby. Pleasure and pain."

Justin looked malevolent. His dark eyes seemed almost demonic. Judith felt positively frightened.

"When a couple is into this kink, they discuss it first, then establish what is called a safe word, to stop if things have gone too far."

"Oh," he replied, sounding embarrassed, "well, forgive me. It was my first time."

"Viciously raping a woman?" she snapped.

"I wasn't vicious, Judith. Trust me, what I just did is totally vanilla."

"Compared to what?"

"To about a thousand other kinkier fantasies I jerk off to regularly."

He had been fantasizing about raping her this whole time!

Judith stared and stared at her hero in abject horror. Incapable of accepting what had just happened, who Justin really was.

And worst of all—

How Nicolas had been right along.

Chapter 60

Judith

"In the six months that I've been gone, what has happened to you?"

Justin stared at her, confused.

"I told you months ago that you awoke something in me—my inner caveman. I wasn't comfortable with it at first. Throughout that first year we were together, I fought to keep it under control, which is why I pushed you away. But now I see how I can let this caveman out and still live with myself. And I told you the other night, I was leaving the old Justin behind for good."

"What do you mean?" Judith sat in the dining chair. Her bottom was throbbing in pain. She needed to soak in a tub of hot water.

He leaned over the kitchen island. Hands clasped together reverently. Justin had been raised in a religious home. He looked about ready to say a prayer.

"It's been hard for me. Before I met you, I didn't care all that much about sex. I thought I was a good guy, some prince charming. Girls swooned over me, I guess, but I didn't really notice. They were all the same: sweet, blonde, boring, and lived in my town. I had known most of them since we were kids. But then I met you."

"Okay? How did meeting me change things?" she asked expectantly.

"Haughty, hot, fiery, erotic, aggressive. You're a fucking goddess. But in the beginning, it was hell. I almost kicked you out a few times, cause I couldn't handle what I was turning into. You've wanted me to be more vulnerable. Well, this is me in the raw. Please don't reject me. You have no idea how hard it has been, wanting to be a good guy but having all these urges since I met you. I've nearly gone insane."

"You've been trying to control this since we met?"

"From the first night we messed around in bed. I pushed you away, remember? Because I was overcome with the insatiable urge to get rough."

Judith suddenly felt bad for Justin—this poor, repressed guy.

"Anyhow, I don't feel bad any longer. Cause I know now you like it rough too. Violence gets you off like it does me. We are a perfect fit for each other."

"What makes you think I do?" She looked at him, aghast.

"Well, obviously, your first encounter with Nicolas. But when I rescued you the other night, I could tell you were so excited. You were screaming, but your body told a different story. You were practically begging as that animal raped you. Your nipples were hard, your pussy was dripping wet, your face drenched in ecstasy, moaning, pretending to fight. And I wanted to pull that guy off you and take his place. So bad. In front of Nicolas. With his kink, I'm sure he would've loved it."

She stared at him in disbelief.

"You're fucking delusional."

"I don't think so. I think you've been lying to yourself like I have."

"Those guys were trashy as fuck."

"Maybe not with those guys, but with the right guy. Me, of course."

"Justin, I was terrified. I don't enjoy being raped, and I don't like feeling afraid."

"The fear is what gave you that mild-altering orgasm. And it's not rape in the criminal sense, honey. That implies a lack of desire. I know when you're turned on, and I just seriously got you off. So no, I wouldn't call it breaking-the-law rape."

"Okay? What is it?"

"It's—I don't know—roleplay. Kink. I just wanna play dirty with you. I think, no, I am positive that you loved it. I can read you like a book."

"Justin, I—"

"Please don't deny it," he implored, "you were wet within seconds just now."

"It's because I just got back from my run. Exercise always makes me horny."

"I'll plan accordingly then. But admit it. You loved it, didn't you?"

Did she? Judith thought about it, maybe a bit. She was burning from the pain, and her heart was still pounding in fear. But yeah, that orgasm was insane.

This was coercion. He was coercing her. Justin had already decided for them both, and he knew she was so attracted to him that she'd give him anything he asked for.

"I guess I'm like my dad. My mom told me they were into this kink. She said a lot of couples indulge in this shit together. It's totally normal."

Judith tried to imagine Nora—a sweet, wholesome, quilt-making, stay-at-home mom—playing out a rape scenario and wanted to laugh. Wow. People never ceased to amaze you.

"But Justin. I'm legit scared. You're a big guy. You could easily kill me if you tackled me to the ground. I don't want to end up in the hospital."

"Baby, I'm a cop. One of the first things I learned was how to take someone down without causing serious injury. I know my limits, and I swear to God, I'll never hurt you bad enough to put you in the hospital."

"Well, that's a relief."

"I don't know why I'm like this. Maybe it's just genetic. It's like my whole life, I've been forced to wear this decent, noble, nice-guy mask. But it's so tight that I can't breathe, and I can't speak. Now, I know I still have to wear it in public. But shit. If you can let me be my true self with you, I will make every last one of your dreams come true. I will wine and dine you, make love to you daily, and buy you anything you want. If you let me tackle you down and go at you like the horny beast I truly am, I think you will prefer the real me."

He took her in his arms. Squeezed her and kissed her languorously. She could already see the transformation. Justin—happy. Justin—without restraint. Justin—being vulnerable. It was sweet.

"I have so many fantasies I wanna play out with you. I feel like we are finally getting to know each other. The night we met, and you kissed me in that ditch, it was like I experienced an alien abduction. For the first time in my life, I had a hard-on in public. I remember staring down at your amazing cleavage, your gorgeous face so vain and rebellious, those sassy lips mouthing off to me. I was sucked up into some spaceship where those pervy aliens redesigned my libido in like two seconds. I came back to earth wanting to tear off your gown and take you so hard. You did this to me. Awakened me. Turned my lust violent. That first week I discovered, to my absolute delight, that you were a complete whore. Now you're my whore. Not his. Mine. And I'm never gonna let you go."

Justin stared at her with those soulful, sweet eyes. He looked like an angel as he took her in his warm arms and crushed her to his massive chest once again. Her heart was roaring with adrenaline as he stood back and pulled off his work shirt and pants, letting them drop to the floor. He stepped out of his shoes and pulled off his boxers, stripping naked in the middle of the living room. Judith stared, her heart thumping wildly.

This man was the center of gravity. She didn't stand a chance in hell of resisting him. Mesmerized, like the first night they met when she undressed him with her eyes. His shy, sexy striptease. His lust-inducing hot-and-cold mind games. His alpha-male, porno-hot body. And she had always wanted to be his sex goddess. So what if it was painful? She had lost her soulmate forever. It felt like she deserved to suffer. And if it meant he would finally love her, wasn't it worth it? She relented.

"Okay. If you promise to love me, I guess I'll satisfy your kink. But no more back-door sex. Not today. That sucked."

"I get that. We'll take it slow. I will love you to the end of time for this. Starting now. Come on, sweetheart. I want more."

He flexed his muscles and stroked his cock and grinned as she ogled him. He knew he had her right where he wanted her, at his mercy.

"Let's play a game. We'll call it 'breaking the girl.' Don't worry. Since it's our first time, I'll go easy on you. But when I catch you, and I will catch you, you better fight like hell. I want you to kick my ass, like you did with him."

"What about our safe word?" She asked, trembling with excitement and dread.

"How about—" He thought for a moment, then smiled his iceberg-melting smile. "Hero."

Justin closed his eyes and began to count. She stared at him in utter disbelief. Hero? Justin was pure evil. And this was happening. Her heart was pounding as if she had just been thrust into a horror film. She took off in a whirl of terror.

After a game of hide-and-seek followed by merciless sex games, Justin was passed out. Judith felt sore from being manhandled, and her skin was on fire. When he caught her in the pantry, he smacked her around. She kicked, bit, and scratched like a hell cat, working him into a rabid delirium, and a toxic part of her enjoyed the thrill. But it was connected to her childhood trauma, so she also felt depressed.

He flipped her over his shoulder effortlessly and hauled her off to the bedroom. Gone was the Justin that wanted a milquetoast blow job and vanilla sex. Here to stay was the caveman eager to play out the scenarios he had been fantasizing about since he first met her. Starting with repeated forced fellatio. And he made her swallow again and again, which wasn't very enjoyable when it was being crammed down her throat. While building up to another erection, he declared she had been a bad girl, took her over his knee, and gave her the first spanking of her life, demanding that she beg his forgiveness after each strike. He didn't go easy on her like he promised, and it hurt like hell.

Then, he set her free to find a weapon, any weapon. And when he caught her, if she hadn't used it on him yet, then he would use it on her, whatever it was. Gave her two minutes. She raced around the apartment in a frenzy. She had to get the fuck away from Justin. She couldn't live like this. She couldn't endure this!

What? What? What? Frantically, she dug through her purse and found her pepper-spray, then went to hide in the bathroom.

Two minutes later, he crept in. She was behind the door. She went to jump out and nail him in the eyes, but he anticipated her and slammed the door to the wall. Pinned, he reached around and grabbed the container from her hand. Looked at her in amazement.

"You were gonna pepper-spray me?" He looked incredulous. Then a blackness crept into his eyes. "Were you planning on ditching me?"

She shook her head in terror. He grabbed his keys off the counter and locked the double-cylinder deadbolt on the front door, then grabbed her by the ponytail and propelled her into the bedroom. He placed his keys on top of the ceiling fan blade above the bed.

"You try to steal those and get away, you'll wake me up. And if you ever try to leave me again, you will live to regret it."

He forced her down on her stomach and crawled on top of her. Held her head down.

"This is gonna burn, baby. But it was your choice."

"Justin, no. Please, I'm sorry."

"I'm a cop, so we gotta play by the rules. It is, after all, a game about breaking the girl."

"Hero! Hero!" she screamed.

He ignored her.

Starting at her neck, he sprayed. Across her shoulder blades, down her spine, along her side boobs, setting her on fire. Her skin felt blazing hot. She screamed in discomfort, trying to rub it away helplessly. Justin flipped her on her back and held her hands above her head.

"Good choice. This is pretty sexy. Keep on screaming. And fight me. Don't go willingly."

Judith growled and thrashed, clawing tooth and nail. Gnashing her teeth, she almost caught him by the ear and he smacked her. Eyes locked with each other as they fought—him for dominance, her for dignity. He pried her legs apart with a satisfied smirk.

"I hope this hurts so good."

The heat from the pepper-spray made her burning skin sweat bullets. Bodies slick as he forced her flexible limbs painfully up over her shoulders. Hands pinning her ankles, he grunted, shoved up inside her, then drilled his way to hell. She bit her lip in agony and refused to scream, which only egged him on. She pinched and scratched his back and shoulders until he was nearly demented. Skin sliding on skin, he rode her viciously like a bull stampede during San Fermin. Victory bells burst free as he climaxed, the cacophony immediately collapsing him into a dead sleep.

Shaking head to toe, she pushed him off her and went to find her phone. Researched what to do when your skin has been pepper-sprayed. Then took a long, cool shower, softly sponging her inflamed back with a mild soap. Dressed and cleaned, the burning had subsided somewhat, but she was still trembling.

Judith sat on the couch, eyeing the ceiling fan. Even if she got out, then what? Call her mom and move back in with Lizzy? She had no one. Nicolas was dead, for all she knew. It was miles from town, and Nora wouldn't help her if she had gone along with this kinky shit with her own husband.

Judith closed her eyes in misery. It was unbelievable. Justin was a sadist who looked like the sweetest hero ever to exist. This is why he was so closed off all those months and never shared anything with her. He was ashamed of the real him. Underneath that good-guy facade he was an angry, aggressive, domineering, savage, misogynist with a rape kink.

Her love for Justin was now forever tainted by a trauma bond. And yet, she felt emotionally closer to him than ever before. His vulnerability was a poisonous aphrodisiac that she feared she would grow addicted to. She had wanted so badly to be his ultimate sex fantasy. Be careful what you wish for. Her fallen hero was complex, twisted, and utterly terrifying. He would give her anything to feed his carnal appetite now, and she realized that this meant he would never let her go.

As her mind turned back to Nicolas, her heart hemorrhaged in agony. Remembering their hook-up in Cabo reduced her to racking sobs that aggravated her burning skin. Tender, sensual, passionate, filled with affection and raw desire. Nicolas both loved her and hungered for her, and he told her so again and again as he worshiped her with his body. She didn't feel defiled by his touch, and he was never cruel. She could climax at the very thought of his lips on her skin and once again wished she were lying there with him in the doorway.

Judith had lost her soulmate. He self-destructed, and then Justin finished him off. How would she ever survive the fallout of their ruined relationship?

Torn apart by this ill-fated love triangle, Judith tried to make sense of her feelings. She was as confused as she'd been from the start.

Justin gave her security and warmth, but his heart was cold, and from now on, his affections would be brutal. No matter what he claimed, he didn't love her, and she feared he would never love her.

Nicolas gave her love, and his heart was warm but without security, and life with him proved impossible due to his addiction to sex and drugs. She thought she could be his rock and roll, but he couldn't forgive her, and in the end, he rejected her love.

She would never be loved by either man who possessed her heart. Crushed by this painful realization, Judith buried her head into the back of the couch and cried until she had nothing left to feel.

The Third Year

Chapter 61

Nicolas

That fucking cop. Took away his Belladonna, and now he would never have her again. Rescued her in the worst way possible, too, by wrecking his body and destroying his livelihood.

His broken arm healed, but it took weeks. Worse was what happened to his dick. He suffered a ruptured testicle from Justin's attack that went untreated. His scrotum was bruised and swollen. He developed a fever and experienced such pain that even drugs couldn't mitigate it. When he started pissing blood, he went to the hospital. They had to do surgery, and he nearly lost one of his testicles, which was beyond traumatic.

Now his dick was damaged. His boners didn't last, and they didn't get that hard, but he deserved it after what he did to Belladonna.

For weeks, Nicolas struggled to turn tricks, lost his apartment, and found himself homeless, begging for enough cash to get a cap of heroin each day. He lost more weight and would lie on a park bench staring up at the sky, starving, throbbing with misery, thinking of her, trembling with self-loathing, hot tears leaking down the sides of his face.

During those months in jail, he had undergone a resurgence of his vindictive nature. He knew it wasn't Belladonna's fault. It was all because of that cop, even her suicide attempt. But he couldn't share his suffering with him, so he had to make do with her. The day she showed up at his apartment, he almost wanted to warn her and rebuff her, terrified of what his psychotic heart would demand of him.

Nicolas spun out of control so fast. Just a dumb junkie with no restraint. He went nuts with all the new goodies he could now afford and let everything fly off the handle. He finally had some friends for the first time in his life, but they were all assholes using him for the drugs. And like his dad, he was a pushover.

Belladonna wasn't into his kink, and looking back, it was a dick move to force her. Seeing the other guy on top of her wasn't at all hot, and he felt a distinct urge to murder him. He should never have let it happen. Why did he let that happen? Why did he let those guys push him around? Why didn't he protect her? Nicholas had no idea what was wrong with him. He had been a self-destructive deviant for so long that change felt impossible.

The truth was that the cop did love her. When he burst through that door and kicked everyone's ass, Nicolas realized he was the better guy. Even if he was a manipulative, coldhearted asshole, at least he would never pimp her out. This thought was torture because that cop was scum and had no idea how to love Belladonna. What did that make him? He would hate him and envy Justin forever, but he won.

Nicolas wanted to be Belladonna's hero, but when he had the chance, he blew it and couldn't understand why. Maybe he couldn't handle relationships. Perhaps his obsession with her had ruined whatever chance they had to begin with.

Finally, he was back to turning tricks, but he found it unbearable to be with a woman. Belladonna tormented his every waking thought. He lost her, the only girl who ever understood him or loved him. He read through their months of texts like they were the Bible. Watched her sex videos and thought about her constantly, embracing the pain like an early Christian martyr. By some miracle, he won the heart of his soulmate, then immediately fucked it up. Because she had chosen the cop? Of course she would! The guy owned her. She didn't have a say. Why was he so insecure and riddled with jealousy? His obsession with getting some love had ruined his ability to live. It was tragic. All he ever wanted was for someone to love him, but when Belladonna loved him, he chose to hurt and humiliate her. He really was the devil.

Nicolas followed her on Facebook, watching her life progress with the good guy while he spiraled further and further down. She never posted anything now. Only Justin shared photos of them. Belladonna looked unhappy in every picture, her eyes glazed and gazing past the camera, and he wondered why. He wanted her to be happy, even if it wasn't with him.

He only fucked guys now, and his loins endlessly ached to pleasure the only girl he ever loved. Wondered if he could ever be with a woman again. He felt eternally committed to Belladonna. She had his heart entirely. He was an asshole that ruined things between them, but he would love her forever.

The last time he stood in front of a mirror, he no longer looked like a prince. He lost a couple of teeth, had new scars on his face from street fights, his skin looked like shit, and he had track marks everywhere. Gone were his gorgeous physique and eye-cocaine looks. He looked older than his old man. Wrecked from birth. Made Catrina's whore at four years old. He should never have been born.

Five months after he lost Belladonna, Nicolas called his dad and begged for help. He was done with his life, having come so close to death too many times. Sick of sucking guys off and starving day and night. Sick of living on the streets. Sick of trying to escape his pain. He realized he hadn't wanted to live for years. He was constantly trying to find a new way to kill himself. He would never get Belladonna back, so gone was his quest for love. What he needed now was hope.

Nicolas vaguely remembered them finding him in the park, packing him into a car, and riding him far away—lights, sounds, nurses, a gurney.

And silence.

Chapter 62

Lizzy

The day after Justin kicked her out, he ran to Mexico and rescued Judith. Lizzy was in such misery that she confessed to her mom about the hook-up with Patrick. She didn't tell her that she was certain, but still, there was room for doubt. It was hell. She lost her chance with Justin. In the following weeks, she lay around watching her belly grow with the child of a man she barely knew and despised and desperately thought about what to do.

Reflecting on her life, Lizzy realized she had never felt loved by a single man, especially not by her father. Of course, she would chase after a guy who would never consider her. And still, it was wrong. Wrong for Judith to have him. She was a whore, and she didn't deserve a guy like Justin. Less than a week before she went into labor, Lizzy finally got the nerve to send Justin the fake paternity test. It would take a lot of commitment to live this lie. She would have to fake it every second of every day, but it was either that or raise the kid on her own with no father and a slim chance of ever having a father. The more Lizzy learned about men, the less she liked them.

She sent the PDF to Justin with a text.

> Here's your proof. I'll text you when I go into delivery. I want you there with me.

She imagined them together, sitting at the dining table, holding hands in misery. She giggled at the thought of Judith crying. Stupid bitch. It wasn't over yet. She was going to get that guy, if it took the rest of her life.

After a day, he sent a one-word reply.

> Okay.

That was it. She didn't fucking care if he was miserable. Justin was on her blacklist now as well for throwing her over and taking her slut sister back. She was going to make their lives a living hell from now on. Eventually, Judith would cave in and hand him over on bended knee.

She showed up at their house the next day and the day after that. Ignored Judith, who looked like she wanted to murder her. Lizzy felt thrilled with delight. She was privately shocked that they didn't even question the paternity test. Just showed how stupid Justin was. He deserved to be taken advantage of, and she intended to rake him through the coals.

The delivery was a disappointment. Justin sat out in the lobby and refused to be in the delivery room when the baby was born. She was induced, and labor took only a few hours. After she gave birth and the baby was cleaned up, he came in. He looked at the infant coldly, then left. If she still had a heart, it would have been broken by his disregard, but Lizzy had long since left her feelings behind in a box, along with hundreds of miserable memories of having her heart broken. She didn't want love. She wanted power and prestige, and Justin was the man to give it to her.

Being a mother sucked. She could no longer take off whenever she wanted. Her mom was off gallivanting across the globe with Erik. Justin worked all night and then slept during the day. Judith wouldn't touch the baby with a ten-foot pole. So, it was all on Lizzy's shoulders. She hated everybody, but mostly herself, for losing her chance with Justin. Now, every effort was so much harder. Every contrived moment alone with him was torture because all he wanted was Judith. She made sure to disrupt their time together as often as possible. Siphoned every dime she could from Justin's bank account, lying about all sorts of things she needed for the baby, and watched him squirm with anger.

Lizzy was not cut out to be a mother. The baby screamed endlessly. She hated breastfeeding. Although it was nice to have tits for a change, the constant burden of feeding the little monster was hell. She lay in bed thinking of them together and thought of all sorts of horrible ways to kill them. Considered setting the garage on fire or sabotaging Justin's car. Anything. But who would watch the baby? It's not like she could cart the screaming brat around while she was off conducting her homicidal plans.

True to Justin's word, he gave her money, but that was it. He didn't hold the baby or even look at it. He didn't want either of them. She was always in the way. And for this treatment, she devised further and further ways to torment them. Judith didn't speak with her when she crashed their house, except for when she told her to get lost. The hatred between them reached a new level, and Lizzy gloated over the unhappiness she caused as a result of her lie. If she couldn't have him, she was gonna make damn sure that Judith regretted every second of being with him.

When the baby was six months old, Lizzy suddenly grew tired and fell into a deep depression. All of her efforts proved fruitless. He would never leave Judith. She should've had an abortion. Her plan failed. She stopped bugging them as much and lay around with her crying son until her mom finally pulled her out of bed and started sending her to a counselor for postpartum depression. Some of it helped. She still hated Judith and schemed a way to steal Justin, but she was able to function better after confiding to her counselor what she had done.

Her counselor was horrified and advised her to come clean. But that was never gonna happen. As long as there was the slightest chance Justin would hook up with her, she would keep the lie going. Besides, lots of kids were adopted. Did it matter if he wasn't the biological father? Justin was the father that she would have chosen. That's all that really mattered.

Lizzy tried a few more times to seduce Justin, and her efforts were met with total failure. In the end, she threw in the towel and took the scraps she was given. A few snatches of alone time each week with the man of her dreams. Trying with all her might to erase Judith from the apartment and pretend that it was just Justin, her, and George, the way fate had intended.

Chapter 63

Judith

In the months following her reunion with Justin, Judith fell into a state of profound numbness, during which she stopped caring about anything. She lost Nicolas, so she might as well be dead. Then, while mourning her soulmate, Justin saved her and reversed their roles. No longer a sex goddess, she was now his sex slave.

Overnight, Justin morphed into an ardent, vicious lover and took the time each day to make sure he was satisfied. The price was high. The pain was exquisite. And she willingly gave him everything he wanted. His hunger was unquenchable now, as he bled her dry and devoured her, bit by bit.

She always believed it was Nicolas who would consume her with his clingy codependency. No. It was her hero. It was weird. Nicolas put her in the cuffs, pleasured the hell out of her, and got off to pretend screaming, while Justin loved bondage, inflicting pain, and making her scream for real.

Justin reminded her daily of how he had saved her in a way that made for legends, but she felt more like he rescued her in order to sacrifice her to an angry God. Judith recited how grateful she was for him, as it had now become an essential part of their foreplay. Pleading for forgiveness, confessing to him that she was unworthy, got him so aroused.

She didn't understand why she did it when it made her feel sad and dirty, and she could never admit it to anyone. Nicolas was dead right when he warned her that Justin was abusive. Her hero cop was abusive, and it thrilled him to teach her his sick and twisted love language.

Life had become one of extremes. On the one hand, Justin was now open and vulnerable. Freely affectionate, he showered her with compliments and love. Passionate kisses, flirty texts filled with sexy emojis, and plenty of self-made porn—in eternal competition with Nicolas.

Justin went down on her regularly, and yeah, he had definitely done his homework. He was nowhere near as good as Nicolas and never would be, but he sure as hell tried. He had an eagle eye and watched constantly for signs of her daydreaming, determined to eradicate Nicolas from her mind forever. And he was as obsessed with her orgasms as he was with his own.

He treated her like a princess. Bribed her with beautiful clothes, expensive jewelry, and tons of erotic lingerie. Overnight, he turned into a charismatic extrovert. Took her out to frequent house parties with his church friends where they drank and played games. The men drooled over her and lavished Justin with accolades for his hot fiancée, and the women fawned in open but companionable jealousy.

Justin whisked her off on royal cabin adventures and a road trip to California in his hot rod, and showed her off like a gold star on his uniform wherever they went, just like Nicolas said he would. Posted endless pics of them on social media. Forced her to work out and run in marathons with him, and shared online every single fun thing they did together.

Bragged that he now had triple the number of friends, all due to her. He was uninhibited, chatty, and a joy to be around. A keeper of the peace who took care of his family and professed to her daily his adoration. In so many ways, her hot cop had become her ideal hero. But on the other hand—

Justin was also a sadist with an insatiable rape kink and there was no line he was too afraid to cross. He convinced himself she loved it, that when she begged for mercy, it was just part of their roleplay. That when she screamed out their safe word, "Hero," she really wanted him to keep hurting her. That when she cried, *No!*, she always, always meant, *Yes!*

Although he crushed her spirit with his alpha-male aggression, she found him hotter than ever. His hot-and-cold mind games made her act desperate and trashy, and his sex scenarios got her horny as fuck. The erotic violence fed a toxic masochism she never knew existed inside of her. Justin sauntered around like a porn king, and she groveled on all fours. That old fear she had before they met, that she might end up with a guy looking only for a free whore had come true. He reminded her repeatedly that she had awakened his inner caveman, and satisfying him was now her responsibility.

Still, her heart wasn't in it. If it were, then why did she think of Nicolas constantly? Spend whole days lost in the reverie of their perfect rendezvous in Cabo. In his bed, in his arms. Their sexy competition. The pleasure, the joy. The hopeless desire to spend forever with him. Why did she pull off to the side of the road while on her runs to sob uncontrollably because she felt so miserable? Why did she no longer dream about her future? She was stuck, frozen, and she had no one to turn to.

Silently, she ached for Nicolas. Feared that wherever he ended up, it was indeed a place where he could prostitute himself for drugs and satisfy his deviant appetites until he dropped dead. So when she learned that Nicolas had finally called his dad and entered rehab, she cried for joy—she hadn't felt so happy in months. The universe had answered her prayer.

She checked her messages every day, sending him cosmic messages to reach out. To remember her. To save her. Someday, she knew he would. And she'd hold on until then. All she had were her memories of Nicolas before he fell apart. It was the only light in her darkness and the only love left in her heart.

The terrible news hit three months after Justin rescued her. Judith was making dinner when Justin came in. His face looked haunted and so very sad. He handed her his phone. The paternity test was in a PDF, and it stated that Justin was the father. She slumped to the table in shock, and he bent down in front of her.

"This means nothing, okay? I already told her I'll pay her child support, but that's it."

But Judith knew Lizzy wouldn't be content with just money, and she was right. Lizzy was at the house mid-afternoon the next day, demanding cash and making plans. She didn't leave until Justin went to work. Didn't have two words to say to Judith. Justin stared at her in agony, trapped behind Lizzy's demanding presence, and they both knew that their new life would now be hell.

When the baby arrived, Lizzy insisted that Justin be present for the birth. Judith didn't bother going to the hospital. Worse, Lizzy took a billion pictures and posted them all online as if they were a happily married couple.

The baby didn't look anything like Justin, but no one seemed to notice, apart from Judith. Part of her believed this was all a trick, but she had no proof. Lizzy told everyone it arrived early, but the baby was huge. Despondent, Judith struggled to adapt to her new life, but it only worsened.

By the summer, Lizzy was sleeping over. Even though Justin worked a graveyard shift, she acted as if she owned the house and moved in a ton of baby items, taking up residence in the guest bedroom. She ignored Judith and cooked dinner, did the laundry, and went grocery shopping without consent. Judith had no idea what to do, and neither did Justin. The whole situation made Justin furious, and Judith had to endure the fallout of his stress behind closed doors.

This went on and on, wearing Judith down. Lizzy was trying to replace her, and she desperately wished that she would. If only there were a way to escape this fucked-up situation she had brought upon herself. But Justin would never let her go. She was his perfect girl now, precisely what he had always wanted. Broken in like an old pair of shoes, and there was no way in hell he was going to give her up after all that blood, sweat, and tears.

And so Judith languished in loneliness, pining away for Nicolas day after day, thinking only of him, wishing to God she had run away with him before he fell apart. While wearing a paper-thin mask of contentment for Justin, she sank deeper and deeper into a fugue state until all she wanted was a way out of her life. Away from this miserable existence, out in the sticks. Away from a man whose passion filled her with pain and made her feel wretched. Away from that stupid-sister-crazy-psycho baby mama.

Chapter 64

Justin

After Justin rescued his sweetheart, he decided to take out a loan to get their custom dream home started, something he hadn't wanted to do, hoping to pay for it as he went, but he realized they needed to start building their future now. He threw himself into establishing an intimate relationship with Judith, restoring their love with exquisite care.

She joined him in the shop, handed him tools, and listened as he taught her how engines worked. During breaks on the saggy old couch, they took to the sky like a couple of lovebirds. Justin showered her with compliments and asked how she was feeling morning, noon, and night. Justin returned to the gym, and Judith joined him. Together, they trained to run a 5K in the spring. He restored a car for her and encouraged her to go to college.

He was good with God again. God had sent Judith into his life to liberate him from the miserable, uptight farm boy he had been for so long, because he had some mercy after all. He prayed daily and felt worthy again. Realized that all of the supposed evil inside him was just a myriad of harmless sex games. They didn't mention kink in the bible, so he was off the hook. It was fine, and Judith loved it, so he would still get into heaven.

Their lovemaking took on epic proportions. Justin tried everything, and Judith was game for it all—the rougher, the better. He thought he was a good guy, and although she loved his image, what she truly wanted in the bedroom was his inner caveman. It was a rush to know he had her completely under his control, just as he had always wanted.

Justin still played his hot-and-cold mind games. All it took was a few days of the cold treatment, and his sex-addict sweetheart would spread her legs out of sheer desperation. He knew exactly how to push her buttons, exactly how to give her endless orgasms, and exactly how to make her scream to her heart's content. He embraced a life fueled by wanton lust and looked back at the stuffy guy lacking in self-confidence that she had first met with shame and embarrassment. He was the Casanova now.

He reminded her constantly of what he had sacrificed by forgiving her, and she gave him everything, satisfying his kink perfectly. All he ever wanted was to replace Nicolas, and now he was the one instigating the death match and taking her by force. They acted out every single one of his fantasies, and their orgasms detonated like atomic bombs. Nothing would ever satisfy him again like their violent trysts. Judith let him harvest a lifetime of rage and resentment, distilling it into pure ecstasy.

Justin became addicted to devising hotter and hotter scenarios. His favorite role play included Dirty Cop, where he'd pretend to arrest her, feel her up for weapons, at which point he'd give her a hot orgasm. Shove her down between his legs and cuff her to the steering wheel. Indulge her kink by masturbating inches from her face until she was begging to blow him, then force her to suck him off as he held a gun to her head. Or Run, Girl, Run, where he'd chase her down into the ditch during one of their late-night runs, shove her face down into the dirt, and fuck her as hard as possible, right there. It was raw and filthy—an exquisite blend of pleasure and pain.

Sometimes, he had to straight-up bribe her. After jerking her out of a dead sleep and dragging her down to his garage to play Sex on the Sawhorse for the first time, she was so traumatized that he was forced to treat her to a spa day to ease the pain, as well as buy her a lovely diamond bracelet. His kink was vile, and he knew that. So he convinced her this was all just for fun, nothing serious. She had consented to indulge his inner caveman as long as he proved that he loved her. And love her he did, more so each day.

The best part? He could never break her. Judith fought like hell every single time. Occasionally even kicked the shit out of him when he was tired. Her terror was genuine, her screams were piercing. And her haughty, proud demeanor that had made him so crazy for her from the start never faded. She was tough and resilient, so he got to break the girl over and over again. Judith was his sexual soulmate. His. So, fuck you, Nicolas. He would never give her up for any amount of anything. Life with Judith was now a dream come true.

And then the news came. When he first heard he was the father of Lizzy's child, he felt as if the garage roof had caved in on him. He couldn't move, and he couldn't breathe. However, nothing could have prepared him for the awful months that followed. Having to visit the hospital for the delivery was traumatic because he didn't love this woman and was bullied by her. He stared at the newborn and felt nothing, which made him feel like a criminal.

The months that followed were a living hell. He couldn't play out his sex games with the same reckless abandon as he used to. Watched his savings deplete as he gave Lizzy more and more money. He lost sleep and developed a mortal hatred for his baby mama. Didn't want her to touch him or even come near him.

The situation with Lizzy only grew worse. She became the owner of the house, and neither Justin nor Judith could stop her. She was relentless. Justin soon realized that Judith was distancing herself from him, and he grew scared. Did she think he wanted to replace her with Lizzy? Never.

Then, one afternoon, when Judith was meeting with a college counselor to sign up for college classes, Lizzy climbed into bed naked and tried to initiate sex. He shoved her off him.

"I thought I was clear last year, Lizzy. This isn't gonna happen."

"What? You don't want me now that I've had your baby?"

He pulled his tired ass out of bed and got dressed.

"Are you trying to drive me out of my own house? Whatever you think is between us doesn't exist. So please, have some decency and go get dressed."

She got up and turned to him.

"Justin, you are mine. You just don't know it yet."

Then she left his room. Her naked body did nothing for him. He couldn't believe that she and Judith were sisters. Lizzy left the house shortly after, and when Judith got home, he went at her in a frenzy and called in to work sick so that they could celebrate their hiatus from Judith's psycho sister.

In the afterglow, Justin said,

"It looks like both you and I have an obsessed psycho stalker. You have Nicolas, and I have Lizzy."

"I can't believe she climbed into bed naked. How creepy. Was she planning to rape you?"

"That's just about how we had sex the first time, so yeah."

Judith was quiet, and he knew why. Anytime he brought up Nicolas, she grew silent.

"You still think of him, don't you?"

"Nicolas has a hold on me, and he always will. He told me that night in the car that he had cast a love spell on me, and I feel like he did."

"My love will eventually break his curse."

Judith didn't reply, and Justin hoped to God that didn't mean she still cared for the scumbag. He tried so hard to make her happy, but he could tell she wasn't happy. He hoped that it was just the Lizzy problem bringing her down, and everything he gave her from his heart and soul was now enough. It bothered him that she shrank from his touch, pretended to be asleep when he got home from work, and shared nothing with him. This sucked, but like a true-blue whore, she never could say no sex.

Justin made it his second full-time job to spoil his sweetheart. He locked her inside when he went to work, rarely let her out of his sight when he was home, bought her anything she wanted, and replaced Nicolas between her legs. Next item on the list was to put the ring on her finger.

He sensed that Nicolas still stalked them on Facebook, and every time Justin posted a new pic of him and Judith, gloriously happy, doing everything as a couple, including building their dream home together, he felt malicious glee, imagining his anguish and misery. He fantasized about their wedding. Their honeymoon, all the gorgeous photos he'd post, twisting the knife into that junkie whore from two thousand miles away. Or maybe he'd be a fool and take his honey to Vegas and do the deed all in one weekend. Whatever it took to make Lizzy realize she didn't stand a chance in hell.

Chapter 65

Nicolas

Nicolas was amazed. Somehow, he was healing. The constant urge to fuck someone had left him when he treated the drug addiction, and surprisingly, the therapy worked. Martha was right all along. He just needed some professional help. After sixty days in rehab, his dad was picking him up today, and he felt drained of all life. Nicolas had ruined his chance with Belladonna and would never get over it. He would never get her back, and he didn't know how he would go on living now.

His dad pulled up to the curb. Martha was with him. Nicolas vaguely remembered them picking him up off a street bench and taking him to a hospital. Saint Martha was turning his dad into a saint as well.

They drove through an unfamiliar city until they stopped in front of some high-end condos, led Nicolas up a flight of steps, unlocked a door, and ushered him inside. The condo was furnished. Nicolas felt his face burn. This was too much. He didn't deserve this.

His dad sat on the couch, and Martha took the opposite chair.

"First. We're delighted to see that you successfully completed the rehab program. Martha says it's one of the best in the country."

"Where am I?"

"Chicago."

"How am I in Chicago?"

"I chartered a plane and took you here myself. Martha chose the rehab center."

"How am I back in the States and not arrested?" Nicolas asked incredulously.

"There's a warrant out for your arrest in Utah, but I've consulted a lawyer. First, Martha, in her statement to the police, just about covered your ass on all counts. You owe your freedom to her. So, you are off the hook for her abduction, her attempted drowning, and the knife attack, which was declared an accident by all three witnesses. Second, your abduction of Judith is what's on your warrant. She told the police that your fighting and explosive sexual encounter was consensual, much to Justin's frustration. These ladies want to help you, son. Our lawyer says that if Judith won't press charges against you for taking off with her in the car, the prosecutor might drop the whole case. Of course, the police still intend to interview you, but your lawyer will be there every step of the way."

"All this time, I didn't even need to run away?" Nicolas asked, aghast at his stupidity.

"Maybe not. Currently, we hope to have all charges dropped, and Judith is totally on board. No matter what you've done to her, she still cares about you. Of course, Justin isn't thrilled, and his statement tells another story of the events that night, so we'll see what happens. You will need to return to Utah and deal with the warrant at some point. So, get ready to be questioned by the police and to go before a judge. We'll work through everything with the lawyer. For now, we thought it might be worthwhile to change your legal name."

"Change my name? How?"

Erik looked at Martha, and she nodded in response.

"We took care of that for you."

Erik pulled a piece of paper from a folder and handed it to Nicolas. He looked at it, and tears filled his eyes. It was his birth certificate. Under father, it no longer said "unknown." Instead, it read Erik Michael Stanley. And Nicolas's new legal name was Nicolas Michael Stanley.

"I should have done this years ago. I should have fought for you and stood up for you, and I didn't. Please forgive me, son."

Nicolas turned to his dad, threw his arms around him, and burst into tears.

"But I'm such a worthless piece of shit. Look what I did to Martha! Not to mention what I did to Belladonna! I don't deserve redemption."

"Let us be the judge of that, dear boy." Martha leaned over and kissed him. "Part of this whole package." She gestured to the room. "Is the requirement that you continue therapy weekly for at least one year. I have appointments set up with a psychiatrist who is a friend of mine, as well as two different counselors. One to treat your sex and drug addictions, and one for child abuse. Additionally, you must maintain contact with your sponsor and stay clean. You need to commit to this, Nicolas."

Nicolas shook his head eagerly.

"You were right from the beginning, Martha. I'm so sorry I didn't listen to you."

"There's more." His dad leaned forward and put his hands together. "I want you to come work for me. We'll take it slow and show you the ropes. Martha and I believe you have the potential to be successful in sales. We have new leads pouring in daily, and I struggle to keep up with them all. I haven't been pleased with any of the talent I've hired, either. I'm willing to give you a chance. You won't have to worry about the construction end. I've got guys for that. Mainly, I oversee the generating of new business and, of course, the design of new builds. But I need someone to help with sales. It's all been a bit much to do on my own for some time. I need someone I can trust who will abide by my business model. I want to train you, Nicolas, in hopes that you will take over for me someday."

Nicolas looked at him, speechless.

"You want me to come and work for you?" He stood and paced the room.

"I do. And this wasn't Martha's idea. It's mine. I've been thinking about it since you moved in with me, and I should've asked from day one. I don't know why I didn't. Nicolas, I judged you and threw you away, but I swear on my life, I did not get you institutionalized. Once you were in the system, it was out of my hands. To my shame, I didn't fight for you. I assumed what the cops said was true. I wasn't aware of your mom's illness, but I have since had the case against your mother investigated, and it is clear she was poisoning you for years. It's a lot worse than I thought. You were in the early stages of liver failure at fourteen years old because of her. Even if you had tried to kill her, it would have been, in my opinion, self-defense. I know we have a significant hurdle to overcome, but I'm willing to try. Please say you'll join my team."

Nicolas was flabbergasted. He thought of his exodus to Mexico, his prostitution, his descent into drugs, and how he fucked it all up with Belladonna. To think it might have all been avoided was too much. Besides, his dad actually loved him?

"Look at me now. I'm emaciated, I have track marks, and I'm missing teeth. I look like a homeless bum! Not to mention, Justin broke my dick! I can't sell high-end, off-the-grid housing to the rich."

Martha stood and pulled him into a motherly hug.

"Nicolas, the track marks will heal, and you will gain weight. You are beautiful, and your confidence will return as you undergo therapy. As for your lovely smile, we have already thought of that. We'll have some restoration work done and have a plastic surgeon repair the scars on your face. Every bad deed can be undone."

"And no son of mine is gonna live with a broken dick. We'll have a specialist look into that as well. We have the money. It's just a matter of time and patience. I know he beat you up badly. Judith told us everything. When we heard what happened, we tried to track you down, but you had already disappeared. Thank God you reached out."

Nicolas was crying again. This was too much. He didn't deserve this. He deserved to die. Especially after what he did to his soulmate. Why the fuck had he lost his mind like that? In all these months and in rehab, he still didn't have any answers.

"I'm so sorry about Belladonna," he sobbed into Martha's hair, "she was my soulmate, and I ruined it. I was so eaten up with vindictiveness and drugs that I had no control. And my friends were influencing me, telling me constantly how she fucked me over and deserved to pay. I don't know how I became so evil, but I'll never forgive myself."

"Sweet boy, I understand. Life pushed you over the edge, but multiple factors contributed to your situation. I'm so happy you are open to change. This is what I wanted for you from the first night you abducted me."

"I hope she's happy with her cop and lives a good life."

Nicolas saw Martha and his dad share a knowing look, and he wondered what it meant.

"Son, get dressed, and let's take you out to eat. I'll show you where our office is located. You have clothes in your closet and food in the fridge, and, yeah, I even splurged on a car."

Erik pulled out the keys for the condo and car and placed them on the table.

As Nicolas showered and dressed, his mind was swirling. This was like the Prodigal Son story in the Bible. He had no idea his dad liked him, much less loved him. How could he ever feel worthy of this second chance? He realized that was the catch—the thing that would push him to go on living. He would strive to be worthy of this second chance every day from now on. Reach out and apologize to Belladonna. And somehow, he would learn to live with himself again.

Filled with the first flutter of excitement he had experienced since reuniting with Belladonna, he left the condo with his father and soon-to-be stepmother. For the first time in his life, Nicolas felt as if he were part of a loving family.

In the months that followed, life began to improve. Nicolas, as it turned out, was a chip off the old block and exceeded expectations. He proved he had business acumen and sales skills. Erik was grateful and relieved to discover that his son might have the makings of his successor. Nicolas finally found a purpose for all that charisma.

Nowadays, when he stalked Belladonna online, he no longer boiled with hatred at her happiness without him. He believed that she held a memory of him, the good him who loved her and wanted to whisk her away with him forever. This gave him hope that she still thought of him that way, instead of as the monster he had become at the end.

Nicolas knew he would never love anyone like Belladonna, and no matter how hard he tried, he could find no peace. His soul was lost without her, somewhere aching. He wanted to talk to her so badly, but shame prevented him from reaching out—that, and the fact that she looked gloriously happy with Justin.

He longed for her and felt incomplete, but at least he could make it through the day without getting stoned. He looked forward to waking up each morning and felt gratitude for being alive after trying to destroy himself for so long.

His face and body healed with the help of a few surgeries, and he returned to the gorgeous guy he once was, but this time, he didn't care. He didn't need his good looks because he no longer needed validation. And that was true freedom.

One night, on the first anniversary of their last day together, he did it. Nicolas opened his laptop, clicked on her name and typed the words.

> Belladonna,
>
> Please don't reply. I lost you for good, and you made the right choice. Your hero saved you. He's the better man, and I know you're happy now. Even though it breaks my heart to see it. Just let me say this. I wish every day that it was I who had met you first, won your heart, and made your dreams come true. I know with my whole being that we were destined for each other. You were the girl for me and I was the guy for you—in another reality where I wasn't such a mess. I hope in our next lifetime, we can make things right. Forgive me if you can for the monster I became in our few short weeks together, but know that I do and will always love the girl who ripped off my disguise and forced me to face my demons. Good luck with your life.
>
> Yours forever,
>
> Nic

About the Author

Tanya Madsen has a BA in English and a passion for emotional drama. When she's not working her day job as a technical writer, she writes novels, plays computer games, cuddles with her fur babies, or relaxes in the mountains. She lives in Northern Utah with her husband and four grown children.

http://www.tanyamadsen.com

www.ingramcontent.com/pod-product-compliance
Lightning Source LLC
Chambersburg PA
CBHW030915300726

48970CB00001B/167